Keith Miles was born a ███████████████████████ on to read history at Oxf██ ✔ **KT-176-991** some years before becoming a ███ ████ ████ ███ has written plays for television, radio and the stage and has contributed to many series and serials. He has also published several novels and short stories and is currently at work on a new book. Keith Miles lives in Warwickshire with his wife and two children.

David Butler is a popular writer for the stage and television whose many successes include EDWARD VII, DISRAELI AND LILLIE.

£1.50

Keith Miles

# We'll Meet Again

A novel by Keith Miles based on the London Weekend
Television series created by David Butler

Futura
Macdonald & Co
London & Sydney

A Futura Book

First published in Great Britain in 1982 by
Futura Publications, a Division of
Macdonald & Co (Publishers) Ltd
London & Sydney

This novelisation copyright © David Butler and
Keith Miles 1982

ISBN 0 7088 2146 4

Filmset, printed and bound in Great Britain by
Hazell Watson & Viney Ltd, Aylesbury, Bucks

Futura Publications
A Division of Macdonald & Co (Publishers) Ltd
Holywell House
Worship Street
London EC2A 2EN

# CHAPTER ONE

Market Wetherby had endured three and a half years of war and it had come through the experience surprisingly well. There were surface changes, of course, as in every other town in East Anglia, but the place remained in essence very much what it had always been. Iron railings might have disappeared from houses, air raid shelters might have sprouted up in gardens, signposts might have been uprooted or blacked out, and official posters might have turned a stroll down the High Street into a parade of warnings and pleas and restrictions and advice, but Market Wetherby was strangely unaltered by it all. In a time of crisis, it had been true to itself.

Jack Blair, landlord of The Plough, often reflected upon this fact. He was proud of his home town. He marvelled at the spirit that had been shown, at the quiet determination to carry on as if nothing had happened, at the way that old values and rhythms had somehow survived. Whenever the subject came up in the Lounge Bar – and it did, quite regularly – Jack would smile, rest his arms on the counter, and say that it would take more than Hitler and the Third Reich to upset the people of Market Wetherby. The town had strength of character.

He was given further proof of this when, one bright morning in an otherwise dull March, he came out of the front door of his pub with a pair of stepladders and a bucket. The scene that confronted him was as old as the town itself. It was market day and the stalls were being set up in the square as they had been every Wednesday for hundreds of years. Wartime shortages limited the range of goods on sale and petrol rationing meant that no motor vehicles were available, but the stallholders had nevertheless turned up in force. Jack Blair was heartened by what he saw. He mounted the stepladders, rested his bucket of water on the top, pulled a wash leather from his pocket and then gazed around the square once more with affection.

A horse whinnied as it was unharnessed from its cart and rewarded with a nosebag; a dog yelped as a well-aimed kick discouraged it from trying to poach one of the dead rabbits that were hanging so invitingly from metal hooks; an old woman at the china stall hissed her annoyance when the teapot she had carefully unwrapped parted company with its handle; a distinctive tang was carried on the wind as a makeshift slab was set up and covered with mackerel and salt cod.

Jack Blair dipped his wash leather in the water and squeezed it out. He felt happy, reassured, at home. It seemed as if nothing could disturb the measured pace of life.

Then the jeep arrived. It came out of nowhere and juddered to a halt on the edge of the square. Engine revving impatiently beneath the great American star on its bonnet, the vehicle looked alien and menacing. It began to inch slowly forward across the cobbles.

The whole atmosphere had suddenly changed. Docile inhabitants of a sleepy country town had now become watchful, defensive and, in some cases, openly hostile. All eyes were on the two uniformed figures in the jeep, which finally stopped in the middle of the square. The newcomers got out and looked around. It was left to the driver, a short, dark, flashy character with a ready smile, to break the silence.

'Hi!' he said, waving an arm to include everyone in the greeting. He exchanged an uneasy glance with his companion, a tall and rather lean young man, then took a few steps towards a cluster of people near a handcart. Raising his voice and widening his smile, he asked a question that had no trace of irony about it. 'Say! Anyone here speak English?'

The silence continued. Even Jack Blair, normally the most friendly and talkative man, chose to say nothing. Like everyone else in the square, he had been startled by the intrusion and was not at all sure what to make of the two visitors.

After looking hopefully around the faces on all sides of him, the driver gave an expressive shrug of his shoulders and went back to the jeep. He and his companion got in and the vehicle was soon in motion again. As it came to a narrow gap between two stalls, the driver made a slight error of judgement and clipped the edge of one, causing its entire display to cascade to the ground.

'Hey!' protested the angry stallholder.

'Somebody speaks English,' noted the driver.

The stallholder had now found his voice and let out a stream of abuse at the departing Americans, but they had already turned down a sidestreet and were safely out of earshot. Everyone was talking now, grumbling, arguing, questioning, sympathizing with the injured party, making vain threats on his behalf.

'Bloody Yanks!' muttered Albert Mundy, who had watched the whole episode from outside his grocery shop.

A big, fleshy man in his fifties, Albert had a round face that looked cheerful in repose but which was all too often hardened into sourness. As another jeep swung into the High Street, followed by a third, then by a couple of heavy lorries, the frown deepened and Albert took it back into his shop. As well as being a grocer, he was a sub-postmaster which meant that one half of his premises was a mass of posters and advertisements. It also meant that there was a lot of preparation each morning before opening time and his wife, Vera, was already there busying herself behind the counter.

Vera Mundy, still in her late thirties, was an easy, pleasant woman with fair hair and bright, alert eyes. Married in her teens, she still retained much of the youthful prettiness which had attracted Albert to her, though her natural high spirits had been dampened over the years by his more dour temperament. She had a softness of manner and genuine interest in people that had made her popular

7

with the customers. There were those who felt sorry for her, tied to a husband who was so much sterner and older than she was.

'Did you see that?' demanded Albert, jerking a thumb towards the open door of the shop. 'Damn Yanks!' He went to the window and peered out at the convoy of vehicles that was now picking its way through the market. 'I remember them in France more than twenty years ago. Full of their big ideas. Telling us how to win the war. *Us*, that'd been sweating it out in the trenches since 1914. Yanks! There's not one of them can stand to attention or salute his superior officer properly. No discipline, see. No smartness, no spit and polish. They don't look like soldiers, they don't act like soldiers.'

'Not supposed to be, are they?' said Vera, trying to look through the window over his shoulder.

'What?'

'They're not supposed to be soldiers. United States *Air* Force. That's what it said in the paper.'

'United States Army Air Force, to be exact,' he replied, moving away from the window. 'They were known as the US Army Air Corps until a couple of years ago. Not that it matters. Army, air force, navy. Yanks are all tarred with the same brush.'

He was behind the counter now, checking through a pile of delivery invoices. Careful not to let him see her, Vera stole a glance into the square. Americans still had glamour for her.

'And only one thing on their minds,' he continued, turning to run his eye over the shelves at the rear of the shop.

'He's coming here,' said Vera, unable to stifle the excitement in her voice. She took a step back and stared at the doorway, a hand moving involuntarily to her hair.

'I wouldn't give you tuppence for any of them,' sneered Albert, warming to his theme and not hearing his wife. 'Any man fool enough to let his womenfolk get mixed up with those—'

8

'Cigars,' drawled a voice behind him.

'*Cigars*?' Albert wheeled around in amazement and saw the chunky figure of Master Sergeant Joe McGraw.

'Sure. I'm fresh out. Havanas . . . Coronas . . . Panatellas. You know, cigars.'

'I haven't seen a cigar since 1940,' said Albert, savagely. 'Don't you know there's a war on?'


After leaving the town square, the first jeep had driven down a sidestreet that had given it a kind of potted introduction to English architecture as it moved past medieval stone, Tudor half-timbering, Stuart solidity, Georgian elegance, Victorian Gothic and Edwardian compromise, all jumbled amiably together in a way that fascinated the two Americans. Then they had found something else to fascinate them. Coming around a corner they had seen two of the town's most attractive young ladies walking towards them. In the gentlest possible way, the jeep had mounted the pavement and more or less pinned Rosie Blair and Letty Mundy to the wall.

The grinning Americans were on their feet, stretching forward over the windscreen.

'You chicks wanna ride?' asked Sergeant Mario Bottone.

There was giggling and indecision and token resistance, but it was not long before the jeep was heading out of Market Wetherby with four people aboard. Rosie, who was now sitting beside Mario as he drove happily along, was the younger daughter of Jack Blair and, like her sister, caused more than the occasional problem for her father. She was a vivacious, laughing, full-cheeked girl with dark hair that was worn shoulder-length. Mario had taken an instant liking to her. He flashed her a smile.

'I'm Mario. That guy in the back seat with your friend is Harvey.' He lowered his voice to give a joking warning. 'Lieutenant.'

'And what are your names?' wondered Lieutenant Harvey Wallis.

He leaned closer to Letty who became quite coy. An attractive, impulsive girl, she looked and sounded older than her seventeen years. Though she had been keen to accept the ride in the jeep, she was now a little shocked by her own boldness as well as being worried by the thought that her father might find out about it.

'Go on, Letty. Tell them,' advised her friend.

'That's a nice name,' said Harvey. 'Letty.'

'Rosie!' she snapped, as if she had been betrayed. 'You shouldn't have told them. I mean – we don't even *know* them.'

'You do now, honey,' said Harvey, using his easy charm and soft Connecticut accent to try to make the girls relax.

'Well, hiya, Letty!' Mario called out. 'Hiya, Rosie!'

Letty was feeling a bit less shy and nervous now. 'I work at The Roxy,' she volunteered. 'Usherette.'

'A movie theatre?' asked Harvey.

'No, it's our cinema.'

'Okay. Seven o'clock. The Roxy. We'll come looking for you.'

The speed and confidence with which Harvey had made the arrangement took Letty's breath away. Mario was equally direct.

'And where do we find you, Rosie?'

'Oh,' she murmured, less ready to commit herself. 'Daytimes I work up at Dereham House for the Major.' She made Mario wait for a few moments. 'Evenings – most evenings – I work for my Dad. At the pub.'

'A real English pub?' He was thrilled.

'The Plough.'

'You'll be there tonight?'

'I might be . . .'

'Listen, honey. I got the body and you got the style. Do we have a deal?'

Rosie continued to be unsure even though Mario was persistence itself. The jeep had travelled a fair distance by now and the novelty of the ride was wearing off for her. Also, she had a prior engagement.

'Thanks for the ride, Mario, but I've got to get out.'

'No hurry. We got all night.'

'What do you take me for?' The men laughed. 'Anyway, I'm supposed to be up at Dereham House. To get the Major's tea.'

'So what is he – some kinda cripple?' asked Mario.

'No.'

'Okay, let him get his own tea,' suggested Harvey.

But Rosie was determined. 'Are you going to stop this thing or not?' she demanded.

'What ya think, Harvey?'

'You'll meet us in the pub tonight, Rosie?' pressed Harvey.

'I might . . .'

'Might!' he cried with mock despair. 'And you, Letty?'

'I can't!' she wailed. 'I'm on duty.'

Harvey put a comforting arm round her shoulder and she smiled across at him. Her coyness was quite forgotten. They had come round in a circle and were now heading back towards the town. Rosie could see that she was not going to be allowed out of the jeep until she had made some sort of promise.

'What about it, Rosie?' urged Mario.

'All right,' she conceded. 'But you must let us out now.'

'Rosie, don't be such a spoilsport,' said Letty, nestling into Harvey's shoulder. 'This is fun.'

'Your father wouldn't call it fun, Letty.'

'We're not doing any harm,' retorted her friend, but the mention of Albert Mundy had made her sit up.

'This will do fine, thanks, driver,' said Rosie.

Reluctantly, Mario brought the jeep to a halt then bent over to Rosie to collect a parting kiss. She eluded him expertly and hopped out on to the roadside with a teasing laugh. Letty followed her and then turned to plant a kiss on Mario's cheek.

'There!' she said, triumphantly.

'Okay, baby. You win – I'm all yours.'

And at that precise moment, Sergeant Mario Bottone decided that he was glad to be in England, after all.

As Helen Dereham drove through flat Suffolk farmland, the fields on either side of the road were quite deserted. Her Austin Seven, bumbling along at its usual modest pace, had passed no other vehicles on the journey and had seen no signs of life. Some people might have found the stillness eerie and disconcerting but Helen drew an odd kind of strength from it. She loved the bareness of the landscape at this time of the year, the feeling of being quite alone under an open sky. Now approaching forty, Helen was a handsome, intelligent and unaffected woman who was renowned at work for her cool efficiency and respected in the area generally as the gracious wife of Major Ronald Dereham. It was only when she was out on her own in the emptiness of the countryside that she remembered she had a romantic side to her nature as well.

Ahead of her in the distance she caught a first glimpse of Market Wetherby as the spire of the Parish Church of St Stephen came into view, pointing towards heaven with its characteristic certainty. Then something appeared above the spire. It was coming closer and closer with every second. Helen saw, then heard, then literally felt the presence of the huge American bomber as it thundered over her at no more than a thousand feet. It was a B-17, one of the Flying Fortresses which had been assigned to the new Air Base nearby. Descending towards her out of the sky like a giant condor, it suddenly made her feel very vulnerable.

Helen brought her full attention back to the road ahead only just in time. Around a bend, and totally without warning, came a jeep and two big trucks, all heading straight at her, on her side of the road. Panic made her pull hard on the driving wheel and send her car veering over to the right, but the jeep had now swung to its own left as well and the two vehicles were still on a collision course.

There was more desperate turning of wheels and the tortured screech of brakes. The jeep ended up in a ditch, the first truck lurched off the road then blundered headlong into a tree, and the Austin Seven found itself miraculously unharmed. Helen switched off the ignition, tugged on the handbrake, then leapt out of her car and ran across to the truck. It had stopped at a crazy angle and its driver was now slumped ominously over the wheel, blood trickling from cuts on his face.

'Excuse me!' shouted Helen, tapping on the window of the cab. Inside the driver rallied enough to turn a glazed eye in her direction. 'You were driving on the wrong side of the road!' She looked round at the dozen or more GIs who had rushed up to see what was happening. 'Come on, then. I shall need some help to get him out.'

Five minutes later, while the bulk of the Americans were trying to manhandle the jeep out of the ditch, Helen was attending to the wounded driver on a grassy slope, gently removing his boot as two of his colleagues supported him. Another jeep came speeding up the road and snarled to a halt beside the Austin Seven. A big, well-built man jumped out and strode over to them. His tone was peremptory.

'What the hell's happening here?'

'Do you mind not yelling like that?' Helen did not bother to look up.

'We had an accident, sir . . .'

'I can see that, sergeant,' snapped Major Jim Kiley.

'This man has a fractured right tibia,' announced Helen.

'He has, huh?' Jim nodded at Helen. 'Who's this?'

'And severe bruising to the lower rib,' she continued, calmly. 'He needs medical attention.' Helen stood up and faced him now. 'If I might make a suggestion . . .'

'No use taking him to the base,' said Jim to the sergeant. 'Dispensary can't cope. Take my jeep, get him to Combat Wing Hospital.'

'If you don't mind him travelling in my car . . .'

'Kind of you, ma'am, but I don't think he'd fit,' replied Jim.

'No disrespect, ma'am,' said the sergeant, doing his best to hide a smile, 'but is this here a real car?'

'Certainly,' she said. 'And if it's treated properly, it works perfectly well. It's also economical with petrol, which we think rather important.' She turned back to Jim. 'He could be seen straight away at the EMS – Emergency Medical Service Hospital. That way.'

'Well . . .' Jim rubbed his chin.

'I'm a doctor there. Helen Dereham.'

'Major Jim Kiley, ma'am.'

'How d'you do, Major?'

'Hi. And thanks,' he said, shaking the hand that had been extended towards him.

'If you follow me, I'll show you the way . . .'

While Helen went back to her car, Jim told the sergeant that he would take the injured man to the hospital himself. The sergeant passed on the message in a loud bark.

'Okay, you guys. You heard the Major. Let's get these trucks moving again. We ain't got all night.'

'No, but I'll bet the Major has,' said an unidentified voice.

When he had seen his passenger helped carefully into the jeep, Jim sauntered over to Helen who was sitting in her car. The news that she was a doctor had introduced a greater politeness into his voice but there was still something about him that made her bristle.

'When you're ready . . .'

'I'm ready now, Major. And may I say that I hope the American Air Force flies better than it drives!'

Before he could reply the car had pulled smartly away.

An hour or so later Jim and Helen were coming out of the Cottage Hospital together, having got to know each other a little better. He had been impressed at the way she had taken control, filing the details of the accident, organizing X-rays of the fracture, making sure that the patient was properly looked after. For her part, she had been surprised at the real concern he had shown about his man and at his interest in the facilities of the small hospital. Helen had also noticed how many nurses had smiled in admiration at him.

Yet there was still a kind of unresolved tension between them. They were both aware of it.

'Just let me know as soon as he's fit to travel,' Jim was saying, 'and we'll do the rest. Oh, and thanks for all your help.' He paused, then spoke more quietly. 'Mrs Dereham?'

'Yes?'

'Back there on that corkscrew of a road, when you nearly hit our lead truck . . .'

'When your truck nearly hit me!' she corrected.

'I think an apology's in order.'

'Oh?' She was bristling again.

'My boys were tired. They'd crossed the highway some place back there middle of nowhere, missed the route, re-crossed it, got the whole convoy screwed up. By the time they found the route again, they were driving on the right side of the road.'

'The wrong side.'

'Well, *our* side.'

'Major Kiley, if you're asking me to apologize . . .'

'No,' he said, seriously. 'I'm the one who's doing the apologizing.'

Helen was disarmed for a moment. She told him that there was no need for an apology and then offered her hand again. He shook it firmly, holding on to it a fraction too long and saying what a pleasure it had been to meet her. Helen was about to move away but thought better of it.

'If nobody else has done so, Major, may I welcome you – all of you, that is – to Market Wetherby? To England?' She felt strangely embarrassed by what she was saying. 'After three and a half years, you may find some of us a little war-weary . . . a little shabby . . .' She looked self-consciously down at the coat she was wearing, then found a brisk smile. 'And we are glad to see you.'

She walked off quickly towards her car.


There was peak activity at the new Air Base. Convoys of vehicles and equipment were arriving at regular intervals and ground crews were working at full stretch to cope with the B-17s that were landing in quick succession. Like the scores of other American airfields in Britain, this one – home of the USAAF 525th Bomb Group – was a sprawl of hastily-erected buildings at the far end of the one main runway. The Base had a control tower, quartermaster's stores, armoury, repair workshops, barracks and messes for air crews and ground crews, offices, a guard-house, fuel tanks and, inevitably, hangars.

When Jim Kiley reached the control tower, he found it humming with activity and nodded his approval. He found Master Sergeant Joe McGraw talking to a warrant officer and motioned him to come out on to the balcony. Jim leaned on the rail and watched two B-17s land one after the other, both leaving burn marks on the concrete. Overhead, several more planes were stacking in the sky, waiting for clearance to come in.

'They'll be coming in all day and all night, Mac,' he said, quietly. 'From all points of the compass. After crossing the North Atlantic, taking in Goose Bay, Labrador, Reykjavik, Greenland and Prestwick up there in Scotland, they'll be dog tired, not thinking straight. They'll need all the help you can give them. The radio room and emergency crews will stay on maximum alert until our last ship has made it here to the Base. That's all.'

'You're worried, sir?' asked McGraw.

'You're damn right, I'm worried. Every B-17 in the Group. Four squadrons. Fifty of the most advanced, sophisticated and expensive bombers the world has ever seen. And who's flying them?' McGraw knew better than to answer. 'A bunch of High School kids!'

McGraw nodded in agreement. He was a hard-nosed veteran who had been in the Air Corps longer than he could remember and who knew all there was to know about his job. Effectively in charge of the B-17s' technical back-up on the ground, McGraw was a vital part of the establishment and Jim relied heavily on him. The noise and the smell of an airfield made McGraw feel at ease, but he knew that a large number of the men on the Base, ground staff as well as air crew, were young and highly inexperienced. This only increased the weight of the responsibility that he and Jim had to shoulder.

They watched in silence as another B-17 began to circle the airfield before making its descent. Instead of lining up to land on the runway, however, it headed straight for the control tower and roared over it with only a few feet to spare.

The men on the control tower had automatically ducked.

'Mac!' yelled Jim.

'Sir?'

'I want to see that fool pilot in my office.'

By the time that McGraw had found his jeep and driven out across the concrete, the B-17 had landed on the runway then taxied to its hard-standing, using its outer engines to manoeuvre. When the engines were finally shut down and the four great propellers were still, McGraw got out of his vehicle to direct the ground crew as they put chocks under the massive rubber wheels and prepared to help the airmen out of the plane.

On the nose of the B-17 was the name that McGraw knew would be there – 'Ginger Rogers' – accompanied by a large coloured picture that showed off the famous legs to suitable advantage. Only Captain Red Burwash would have had either the devilment or the ability to fly at the control tower in that way.

'Hiya, Mac!'

It was Red himself, a big, brash, jovial man in his late twenties, waving from the nose window. McGraw was pleased to see the grinning face with its large, golden moustache and its rather florid complexion. In Red

17

Burwash, for all his faults, they would have at least one first-rate pilot on the Base.

'You made it, Captain,' called McGraw.

'Lieutenant Krotnik in yet? Before us?'

'No, sir. "Ginger Rogers" beat him to it.'

Delight spread over Red's face and he disappeared from the window. The crew were now getting out and treading on English soil for the first time. They looked excited but fatigued, and very, very young.

When Red finally emerged, he was given the message from Major Jim Kiley. He went over to the office straight away and was soon standing to attention in front of the desk as Jim paced angrily up and down.

'Flying that low over the roof of the control tower! You damn near decapitated five senior officers, including me! I ought to throw the book at you!'

'You wanna dock my pay, sir?'

'If regulations permitted, it'd be more than your goddam pay I'd dock!'

'Yes, sir.'

'Enlighten me,' said Jim, glowering at the erect figure in front of him. 'What the hell did you do it for, Red?'

'A bet, sir.'

'A *what*?'

'With Herman . . . that's Lieutenant Krotnick, sir. He took off from Prestwick eight minutes before us. I bet him ten dollars I'd make it to Base before him. I did, so . . .' He paused and swallowed hard. 'So I celebrated.'

'Well let me tell you that your "celebration" damn near cost this Bomb Group one brand new B-17. And that's without trying to kill yourself – which'd be no loss – plus your crew of three and six sergeants.'

Jim was too roused and appalled to say anything else for a minute. He waited for Red to speak, tapping a foot in irritation.

'They all had bets on, too, sir,' Red admitted at last. 'I'm sorry about the . . . er, "celebration", sir. But I figure in this life you either come first or you're nothing.'

Jim fingered his short, dark moustache and then leaned in very close to the other man.

'Captain, in this Group you either do it by the book or you're grounded for the next hundred years.'

'Sir.'

'Which means you're confined to quarters.'

'But—'

'And you don't get off this Base until I've worked out what the hell I'm going to say to the Colonel about you. Now, beat it!'

Red came out of the office feeling as if he had just flown through intense flack. Welcome to England.


The afternoon sun had brought them out to play tennis on the lawn at the back of Dereham House, a fine building that dated back to the late Georgian period. Since they wanted only exercise and amusement, they were content simply to keep the ball in play. Even so, they worked up sufficient thirst to be grateful to Rosie when she brought out cool drinks for them. They were still sipping their squash when Helen came home. She gave her husband a token kiss and smiled at her daughter.

'Who won?' she asked.

'It wasn't a proper game,' said Pat.

'If it had been, I wouldn't have stood a chance,' added her father. 'Pat would have beaten me hollow.'

Even now, at his most casual, Major Ronald Dereham somehow managed to look neat, rather military and unmistakably English. He turned to his wife and remembered something.

'Oh, you had a 'phone call, darling . . .'

'Did I?'

'Some American. One of the new lot from the Base.'

'Americans!' said Pat, scornfully.

'What was the name, Ronnie?'

'Kiley, I think. Yes, Major Jim Kiley. He's the Air Executive. Second in Command.'

'I see.' Helen was quietly impressed. 'Any message?'

'He just wanted to thank you for something or other. Seemed like a good sort, I must say.'

'Americans are all very well, in their place,' announced Pat. Two terms at Cambridge had made her more forthright about her prejudices. 'Mother thinks the same as I do, I'm sure. Americans should be kept at arm's length.'

'Oh dear!' said Ronnie, smiling. 'I've asked him over for drinks on Saturday evening.'

Helen Dereham came very close to blushing.

# CHAPTER TWO

Only a day after the Americans had arrived, Vera Mundy found herself wishing that their airfield was much further away. The town was directly in the flight path of the B-17s and the noise which their four 1,200 hp Wright Cyclone engines could generate at low altitudes was deafening. It also made it difficult for Vera to communicate with the other members of her family.

'Albert!' Her yell was no match for the plane that was climbing over Market Wetherby. *'Albert!'*

She was in the room at the back of the shop, working at the end that doubled as both kitchen and dining room. Stirring soup with one hand and frying rissoles with the other, she decided to abandon both tasks for a moment to cover her ears as another B-17 roared overhead. When the worst of the noise was fading, she lowered her hands and went through the curtained archway that led to the shop. Albert was totting up figures on a piece of paper.

'Don't you want any dinner?'

'Didn't hear you, Vera.'

'I'll dish it up.'

'Be with you in a minute,' promised her husband, returning to his calculations.

When Vera went back through the curtains she found Letty already there, sitting at the table rather demurely. Four places had been set. One of the plates had a crack in it.

'Dinnertime and never anybody here to eat it,' complained Vera, back at the stove.

'I'm here,' said Albert, coming in. 'Where's his lordship?'

He sat at the head of the table without even glancing at Letty. Vera began to serve the soup direct from the pan.

'Over the hall. Practising.'

'Practising, Vera!' He sounded disgusted.

'You won't let him have a piano here so where else can Peter go except the hall?'

'Give him a piano and he'd drive all my customers out of the shop. *And* he'd drive me potty. *And* he'd never get himself a proper job. Piano! No thank you!'

Both Vera and Letty had heard this outburst so often that they knew it off by heart. Albert Mundy was a man who liked to strengthen his decisions by repeating them time and again. Yet another B-17 went over the town, causing Albert to look balefully up at the ceiling, then he grabbed the bread knife and cut himself a jagged hunk from the loaf on the table. He pointed upwards with the bread knife.

'Twentieth, this morning. To my certain knowledge. All very well within reason. Allies, that is. But nobody asked them to come over here and deafen us.' He attacked his soup with a spoon and slurped it noisily. Peter Mundy slipped in and took his seat at the table in time to hear another familiar theme of his father's. 'Who needs the Yanks, anyway? Get yourself into a scrap, up to you to get yourself out of it. Without dragging others in.'

'It isn't like that, Dad,' said Peter, reasonably.

'Isn't it?'

'Even Wellington couldn't beat Napoleon on his own.'

'Couldn't he?'

'Not without Blücher.'

'Blücher! Blücher! A blooming Jerry!' snorted Albert. 'Comes in at the last moment when it's all over and claims all the credit.'

'Anybody else for bread?' asked Vera, trying to stop the argument early on.

'Just like the Yanks,' continued Albert, spooning more soup into his mouth. 'The Duke didn't need blooming Blücher – and we don't need these fancy flipping Romeos!'

'Yes, we do, Dad.'

'You calling me a liar!'

'No. 'Course he isn't, Albert.'

'S'all right, Vera,' he said with a gesture that told her to be quiet. 'Mr Cleverdick here, who's learned it all at school from books, but doesn't really know anything—'

'Dad, all I'm saying is that if you're going to fight – which I don't believe you should—'

'Ha! What we'd like to know is what you *do* believe in!'

'But if you do,' said Peter, clinging to his point, 'then you need all the friends you can get.'

'You call them *friends*!'

Vera could see the danger signs. She jumped up and started to clear away the soup plates, hoping to distract attention once more. But Albert was not to be deflected.

'Trouble with our military expert here,' he said, retrieving his plate from his wife's grasp, 'is that he hasn't got a clue what he's talking about. Fighting, my son, is one man's guts and nerves and . . . and *esprit de corps* against another's. And no blooming chance of talking your way out of it!'

'I don't understand a word anybody's talking about,' said Letty, baffled.

'And nor should you, my duck. War is man's work. Not for softies like your brother!'

Vera was now moving around the table, serving rissoles and wet cabbage on to clean plates, and urging Albert to finish his soup. She seemed to spend most mealtimes acting as a buffer between her husband and son. Peter and Letty were twins and the physical resemblance was obvious, but their temperaments were very different. Vera often wished that Peter was more like his sister, less ready to challenge and argue.

Having chewed and swallowed a mouthful of bread, Albert was ready to express more resentment.

'Had one of our new "friends" in the shop yesterday, didn't we, Vera? Asking for cigars!'

'The ones I saw . . .' began Letty.

'What about them?' asked her father, sharply.

23

'They looked nice. Like . . . like film stars. Clark Gable and Tyrone Power and—'

'Looked. *Looked!*'

'Yes, Dad.'

'Letty, my duck. I'll only say this once . . .'

'What?' She was beginning to be frightened now.

'Where those fancy Romeos are concerned, you make sure that it's only "look". Understand?'

Letty had a rush of guilt as she thought of the lift she had accepted the previous day. Her father would explode if he knew about that. She fixed her eyes on the rissoles.

'Yes, Dad.'


Rosie Blair examined her face carefully in the mirror as she put on the lipstick. She was wearing slightly more make-up than usual but nothing like as much as she had worn the night before, when she had been expecting Mario Bottone and Harvey Wallis to come looking for her at The Plough. Vi Blair had been so shocked by her sister's dramatic use of mascara, eyebrow pencil, lipstick and rouge – not to mention a plunging neckline that had revealed a roguish if smudged beauty spot on the left breast – that she had called Rosie a tart. And there had been an additional blow. Because their leave had been cancelled at the Air Base, the Americans were not able to come into the town. Rosie had rushed out of the Lounge Bar in tears.

This evening would be different. She was certain of that. There had been something about Mario that had convinced her he would turn up at the earliest opportunity. Rosie was right. As she was applying the last dab of face powder, she heard the sound of heavy trucks pulling up in the road outside. She ran to peep between the drawn blackout curtains and she saw a dozen or more GIs jumping eagerly down on to the pavement. She raced back to the mirror for a final scrutiny, then headed for the stairs.

When she reached the Lounge Bar it seemed full of

American uniforms and loud voices. The GIs were laughing, boisterous but good-humoured and they had crowded around the bar to get their first drink in an English pub. Mario Bottone was sitting on the counter, trying to calm the men down and take orders. Jack Blair, rather stunned by the sudden entry of the newcomers, simply watched in astonishment.

'Okay, okay, okay, okay!' shouted Mario. 'Cut it out, you bums!'

'What ya mean?' yelled Sergeant Hymie Stutz, the shortest man in the room but one of the most ebullient. 'I wanna drink!'

'I know what you want, Hymie! So shut it!'

'Watch it, Bottone,' warned the other.

'Listen, you guys!' ordered Mario, compelling attention by his sheer flamboyance. 'For the benefit of all you bums who don't know no better, this here's a quaint old English pub. And it was here centuries before Lincoln freed the slaves. And before . . . before all that history stuff. Now, what they don't like in quaint old English pubs is guys like you guys busting in and acting like know-nothing bums! So cut it out!' With his colleagues now subdued a little, Mario did a swift roll-call, looking from face to face. 'Okay, who we got here? Wilbur . . . Harold . . . Alvah . . . Julius . . . Irvin . . . Arizona . . . Elmer . . . Gene . . . Arnie . . . Ezekiel . . . Howard . . . Buzz . . . and Coogan!'

'What about me?' protested Hymie.

'What about you!' Mario swung round to face Jack. 'That's fourteen. Plus me, fifteen.' He pulled out a wad of notes from his pocket. 'Scotch on the rocks for fifteen, then we'll see how we go. Okay?'

'I'm sorry, sir,' said Jack.

'Huh?'

'I've got bitter, that's about all.'

'Bitter?' Hymie had never heard of it.

'Draught bitter beer, sir.'

'No scotch?' asked Mario, horrified.

'I'm afraid not, sir. And I'd be obliged if you'd come

down from there, please.' Mario hopped off the counter. 'Thank you.'

'Jeez, fellers. No scotch. Let's see how we make out some place else.'

'Good evening, gentlemen . . .'

Rosie had now come up behind the bar where they could all see her. Their decision to leave was rescinded at once.

'Me? I've always liked this English bitter,' said Sergeant Elmer Jones, who had the good fortune to be standing closest to Rosie.

'Me, too!' agreed Hymie.

'What would you like, sir?' she purred at Elmer, bringing a wistful smile to his chubby, open face. 'A pint or a half?'

'I'll take a gallon, ma'am.'

Fat, clumsy and easy-going, Elmer Jones was usually something of a figure of fun among the GIs but they all envied him now as Rosie reached for a glass tankard and flashed her teeth at him.

'Hiya, Rosie,' called Mario, sitting on the bar-top again and showing everyone that he knew her name, 'I promised I'd come, didn't I?' He addressed the men. 'Okay, I'll tell you what you're gonna drink. You're gonna drink—'

'Draught bitter, sir,' interrupted Jack. 'When you get down from there again. We do have chairs, you know. At no extra charge.'

'Okay, okay. Make it fifteen glasses of draught bitter. Fifteen half-pints of bitter.' Mario pointed at Rosie. 'And *she* gets to fill the glasses.'

The general murmur of approval made Rosie glow with pleasure and she was soon happily serving the appreciative customers. At the other end of the bar, her sister, Vi, was watching her with real concern. She knew Rosie's weaknesses all too well.

It was an old, untidy building in a street off the town square and it had not been designed as a cinema at all, but when it had been converted into The Roxy and it had

26

introduced the glories of Hollywood to the local people, it had become one of the most popular places in Market Wetherby.

'Come on, this is it,' said an excited Harvey Wallis, leading a group of GIs towards the cinema.

'Kinda small, ain't it, Harv?' complained a voice.

Another man glanced at the stills in the glass frame and found John Wayne staring back at him with a rifle over his shoulder. 'Hey, I seen this movie six times already,' he said.

'Who cares about the movie?' asked Harvey, then joined the scramble through the main door.

When they had bought their tickets, they went through into the auditorium where the film was already in progress in front of an attentive local audience. Laughing, joking and bumping into each other in the dark, the GIs made such a commotion that a chorus of hissed requests for silence came from the patrons. Harvey was not deterred.

'Letty? Where are you, Letty?'

There was another barrage of comment from the darkness. On the screen, horses were galloping across a plain. Harvey raised his voice above the sound of gunfire and called again. A torch emerged from the blackness behind him. Harvey grabbed it and turned its beam on to the face of the usherette who had been holding it.

'Aren't you Letty?'

'What if I am?' she giggled.

'Fellers, this is Letty and she kisses like Lana Turner.'

And with Letty's help, he proved it there and then.


Vi Blair ran the back of her arm across her brow to wipe off some of the perspiration. Even on a cold morning, toiling in a field for an hour was warm work. She gripped the hoe and started again, quite unaware of the fact that she and her companion, another Land Army girl, were being watched from the road by a soldier in British Army uniform. Tom Cutts, an eager, fresh-faced but rather nervous young man had cycled out to this part of the Dereham estate in the hope of seeing Vi Blair. It took him a long time to pluck up enough courage to speak to her.

'That you, Vi?'

She looked up, collected a knowing grin from her friend, Sheila, then walked slowly across to the fence.

'Up and about early, aren't you, Tom?' she said.

'On leave, en I?'

'Go on! You lads are always on leave. All beer and skittles, the army.'

'Saw you, didn't I?' he said, trying to sound casual. 'At The Plough.'

'Daresay. We get all sorts in.'

'Don't reckon you saw me, Vi. Or you'd have said "hullo", eh?'

'Of course,' she replied, knowing that it was a lie. She had pretended not to see Tom at the pub in order to avoid the very situation she now found herself in. 'Bet you're having a fine old time on leave. No worries – except where the next drink comes from.'

'That's it, Vi!' There was a pause. 'No, it isn't . . .'

'Oh?'

'I was really looking forward to it, coming home and that. But the town is dead. Nothing happening.'

Seeing what was coming, Vi told him that she had to get back to her job. 'Get me the sack, you will, Tom Cutts,' she said.

'Vi, come out with me, will you?' he pleaded.

She thought about it for a long time, shrugged, shook her head. There was an element of desperation as he repeated his invitation.

'So long, Tom,' she said and went back to the field.

Tom waited for some time but she did not even look in his direction. He picked up his bicycle and rode off dejectedly.

Vi felt sorry for him but she was not going to get trapped into spending an evening with him out of pity. She liked Tom well enough and had always had a cheery word for him, but that was as far as it went. There was another reason why she felt sorry for him and for those like him. The competition was too strong for them. After only one evening in the presence of a crowd of GIs, she could see that Tom and his pals would always come off second best. Compared with the smart, well-groomed Americans, the British soldiers looked almost slovenly. The GIs had more money, better food and far greater confidence. More important, they were well-mannered and completely at ease in the company of women. And beside the halting Suffolk dialect of men like Tom Cutts, the various American accents sounded bewitching.

As Vi thought about the previous evening, she had a vision of Rosie serving drinks, flirting shamelessly and lapping up the flattery from the GIs. At the time she had felt worried for her sister, foreseeing the possible dangers. Rosie had never known her mother and it was a role that Vi had had to take on to some extent, since there were limits to what a father can do on his own. It had made her very protective towards Rosie and not a little bossy at times. But she had not only been motivated by a maternal concern for her sister in that Lounge Bar. Something else had been at work and she now realized what it had been. Jealousy.

A droning noise brought her out of her reverie though she did not at first know what it was. She saw that Sheila had moved off and left her quite alone in the field. Vi got down to her job.

High above her, moving in a swift, menacing circle and glinting in the early morning sunlight, was a German fighter, the feared Messerschmitt Bf 110, flying inland on a solo raid to cause as much damage as possible, searching for the airfield but more than ready to destroy at random. As its two Daimler-Benz engines gave it maximum thrust, it dipped its nose and screamed down out of the sky like a thunderbolt. Its first target was a young British soldier who was pushing his bicycle up a steep gradient. Tom Cutts hardly had time to turn and see the tell-tale shape when a hail of tracer bullets ripped into him and threw him backwards into a ditch.

Half a mile away, Vi Blair had heard the firing and looked up to see the plane soaring up again. The pilot had tasted blood and was after a second victim now. As he banked and swooped, Vi knew that she was the new target and it made her shake with fear. Throwing down her hoe, she began to race madly across the open field, vainly searching for cover as the ME 110 stalked her.

It came in fast with its machine guns blazing, the shells biting deep into the soil behind the running figure. It was only a matter of seconds before Vi was torn to pieces by the bullets – that was what she felt. Then the miracle happened. An American jeep which had been coming up the road suddenly swung through a hedge and charged towards her in the middle of the field. When it had got between her and the oncoming plane, it braked violently and its driver jumped out, grabbing Vi and pulling her to the ground. A last angry burst of gunfire sprayed across the ground as the fighter reached the bottom of its descent and levelled off. It now went low and hard over the trees to the north-west and found its main target. Explosions and alarm signals could be heard coming from the new Air Base and great columns of black smoke began to rise up in the distance.

Vi Blair had been knocked breathless by the fall and fear kept her eyes tightly closed. When she finally opened them she saw the face of Master Sergeant Chuck Ericson only a few inches away. He smiled at her.

'I guess I owe you an apology, ma'am,' said Colonel Rufus Krasnowici, pulling on a thick cigar. 'An apology to you and all the folks around here for the noise my B-17s are making all day and every day.'

'You mean, your Flying Fortresses, Colonel.'

'Correct, Mrs Dereham. I'm keeping them in the air from first light till sundown, familiarizing my crews with

your RAF emergency and communications routines . . .
Air Sea Rescue. Location of your ack-ack and barrage
balloon sites . . .'

'Colonel—' she began.

'But after all our previous training under a clear
Californian sky, I will say your English weather's proving
a mite troublesome.'

'Should you be telling me all this?' asked Helen.

'I can't see why not, ma'am!'

'My husband never tells me a thing,' she confessed.

'That reminds me, where is Major Dereham?' he wondered, looking around. 'I don't see him.'

'He was called away to take a telephone call. Look, do
let me help you to another drink . . .'

'Thank you, ma'am. Wonderful party, by the way.
Much obliged to be invited along.'

Rufus was quite sincere. Now just fifty and as tough and
craggy as all the other Base Commanders, he knew the
importance of trying to include some leisure in a tight and
demanding schedule. His first few days in the area had
been hectic, not least because he had chosen to land his
B-17 on the runway only minutes before the ME 110 had
begun its 'scalded cat' raid. For Rufus it had been, literally,
a baptism of fire. The Air Base had been taken completely
unawares and the amount of havoc that a single German
fighter had been able to create in a matter of seconds had
been astonishing. The new Commander had seen a bomb
dump exploded, the Dispensary destroyed, a lorry blown
up, some ground staff killed or wounded, and a few of his
precious B-17s laced with enemy bullets. He had also seen
the Air Base in a state of near-panic as the vast majority
of its men had their first, brief, terrifying experience of a
combat situation.

An evening in the restful atmosphere of Dereham House
was just what Rufus had needed. He glanced across the
crowded sitting room and saw Jim Kiley coming in with
Pat. He grinned. Jim needed to relax as well.

'That's it, Major Kiley,' Pat was saying. 'Now you've seen everything.'

'And I couldn't have asked for a more delightful guide. Thanks, Pat. You've got a great house here.'

'We think so.'

Pat Dereham had forgotten all her prejudices against Americans now. Without even trying, Major Jim Kiley had made a big impression on her and she had followed him round for most of the evening. He was polite, charming, cultured and well-informed about the country to which he had come. The obvious dedication he had to his job had struck her at once though authority seemed to sit very easily on him. What Pat had still not been able to find out was why such a handsome and supremely eligible man had never married.

'Major . . .'

'Hmm? . . . Oh, sorry. I was just looking to see how the Colonel was making out.' Jim had in fact been staring over at Helen, an elegant figure in her evening dress, regretting that he had not been able to speak to her properly. Her eyes had caught his but Pat had interrupted the moment. 'Maybe I should circulate. Do my duty . . .'

'I was telling you about Daddy,' she continued, not wanting to let him get away. 'How he got his DSO.'

'Ah yes.'

'And in 1940 he was very nearly captured by the Jerries in Norway. Got out by the skin of his teeth. What else? . . . Let me think. Oh yes. At the end of that year he was — what's the expression? — "mopping up" the Italians in Cyrenaica with General Wavell. And since then he's spent most of his time in North Africa. I suppose he's been quite busy, really. Not that he'd ever tell you. Daddy is so modest and stiff upper lip and fearfully British.'

'I'm beginning to realize that,' said Jim.

At that moment Ronnie came back into the room looking as immaculate and imperturbable as ever. He saw Jim standing with Pat.

'Is my daughter taking care of you, Major?'

32

'Thank you, yes. I couldn't be in better hands.'

'Major Kiley's promised to show me over the Base,' said Pat, beaming.

'Don't let her make a nuisance of herself,' warned Ronnie.

'Believe me, I won't,' said Jim, smiling at her. 'But you've been holding out on me, sir.'

'Me?'

'I've been hearing the truth at last. You told me that you were a farmer.'

'I am.'

'Uh-huh. How was the farming in Norway? And North Africa, eh, *Major*?'

'Ah . . .'

'I've found you out.'

'Did you know they built your confounded airfield on my best land?' he said, a twinkle in his eye. 'Still, you must excuse me. Trying to find my wife.'

'She's over there, Major Dereham,' volunteered Jim, turning instinctively to where Helen was. 'With the Colonel.'

'Oh thanks. Now don't let Pat bully you . . .'

Ronnie left them and made his way through the clusters of people to the far side of the room. He had taken an instant liking to Jim and had been amused by the impact that the American had had upon his daughter. So much for her claim that they should all be kept strictly at arm's length.

As soon as she saw the expression on her husband's face, Helen knew that he had something important to tell her. She detached herself from Rufus and moved over to the curtains with Ronnie. It was not difficult to guess who had just telephoned him.

'Bertie?'

'Yes, darling.'

'When?'

'Midnight tomorrow.'

'Oh no!' she protested.

33

''Fraid so.'

'Just when we were getting used to having you about the house again.' Helen pulled herself together. 'Sorry. I'm being a fool. I know that you have to go.'

'We've all got different wars to fight. These chaps in their way. You, and Pat, in yours.'

'She's behaving rather oddly this evening.'

'Can't blame her, Helen. Not when the place is crawling with exotic air force types.' He glanced around at the dozen or so American uniforms. 'They seem a decent enough bunch, for all their noise and cigar smoke. But I've no doubt they prefer something a little more flamboyant than anything we care for.'

Helen did not answer. Her attention had been momentarily distracted by the sight of Jim, happy and relaxed, making her daughter laugh with some remark. Helen turned back to Ronnie.

'Bertie. Did he give you any idea?'

'You know better than that, darling.'

'Sorry,' she said, accepting the reproach.

'Let's just say that it's somewhere over the water.' His voice became more intimate. 'I think it's time we booted this lot out.'

Helen gazed fondly at him and forgot everyone else in the room. It was at times when he was about to leave her that she learned how much she loved her husband.


Master Sergeant Chuck Ericson, tall, rangy and impassive, sat on his bunk and brought a gleam to his shoes with a soft duster. Chuck was flight engineer in Red Burwash's crew and he was an essential feature of the 'Ginger Rogers'. No other crew member of the B-17 had such a wide and detailed knowledge of the mechanism and functions of the bomber, and certainly none carried that knowledge as lightly as Chuck did. He was experienced, respected and popular with the others. He was a young man with great strength of purpose.

'Gee, I'm bushed!' sighed Elmer Jones, coming in and flopping down heavily on his bunk.

He was followed in by two more members of the 'Ginger Rogers' crew, Mario Bottone, radio operator, and nineteen-year-old Danny Coogan, waist gunner like Elmer himself.

'My radio's burnt up so much juice, I still got static coming out of my ears!' Mario complained. 'Chuck, you been through all this training crap. How was it in 91st Group?'

'Worse.'

'That guy, Kiley – he's working us to death. Like we was knuckle-headed mules.'

'He has to, Mario,' said Chuck, tying up the laces on his shoes. 'Word is that this outfit's got to be combat-ready by the 15th.'

'Meanwhile, all leave is cancelled till further notice,' said Coogan, as if it were a monstrous injustice.

'Yeah,' added Elmer, supine on the bunk, 'that Kiley's got us all locked up good and proper. What does he think we are – monks!'

Chuck was now on his feet, brushing his uniform tunic with care. Mario drew the attention of the others to this then leaned over towards Chuck.

'You heard what the man said. "No six-hour passes will be issued for any purpose." That means you, bud.'

'So what?' Chuck was unworried.

'You're not gonna . . . ?' asked Elmer, wide-eyed.

'You're outa your skull!' yelled Mario. He paused, realizing where his colleague was going. 'Didn't you hear what Red was telling us about these English ice-maidens?'

'No.'

'They're poison!' Mario grinned at the others. 'What did she promise you, huh?'

'Who?' Chuck had tensed.

'The ice-maiden. The one in the quaint old English pub. Rosie's big sister.'

'Button your lip, Mario.'

'Aw, come on, Chuck. She musta said something. You went over to the pub last week.'

'She wasn't there.'

'Natch! She saw you coming!' Mario's laughter was short-lived because he was lifted from the ground by his tie. 'Hey, Chuck! Okay, okay, okay, okay!'

'So button it!'

'*Okay!*' Mario was in pain.

'Something else, knuckle-head,' said Chuck, still holding him tight. 'One morning when you're sitting up there in your radio room, fifteen thousand feet over Berlin, no place to hide, FWs coming at you all round the clock, cannon shells exploding under your ass – then you'll wish that the Exec had worked us to death some more. Got it!'

'Yeah, Chuck. I got it.'

Chuck let go, nodded to him in an abrupt gesture of farewell and went out of the room. Elmer and Coogan both looked across at Mario, who was loosening his tie.

'If he don't make it, Major James Kiley will tear his ears off and send them to his mother!'

A few minutes later, Chuck was lying in the long grass waiting for a jeep to pass with two white-helmeted MPs in it. When the coast was clear, he rose silently, went over to the perimeter fence, climbed it with the ease of an athlete then ran off into the gloom beyond.

# CHAPTER THREE

The Lounge Bar that evening was crowded with local civilians and both Jack Blair and his younger daughter were kept busy at the beer pumps. Rosie was not happy with life at all.

'It's not fair, Dad,' she said over the hubbub.

'What's that, love?'

'No leave . . . no fun . . . no girlfriends. Mrs Dereham says they're all confined to the Air Base. Until they get back from their first raid.'

'And that'll be a day to remember,' sighed Jack.

He served another customer then caught sight of the slim figure in uniform who had just entered.

'Give Vi a shout will you, love?' he said casually.

'But she's tired out from work, Dad.'

'*Now*, please . . .'

There was enough firmness in this to send her scurrying off to the back room, calling her sister's name loudly. Chuck Ericson had now made his way to the bar and was being eyed speculatively by Jack.

'I said I'd come back, Mr Blair.'

'Yes.'

'Did you give your daughter my message?'

'Yes.' Jack's tone was deliberately non-committal.

'Well?'

'She read it.'

'That all?'

Disappointed not to meet Vi then when he had called the first time, Chuck had scribbled a note for her: 'Do I have to wait for another German raider?'

'She told me to give you this,' said Jack, filling a glass with draught bitter and setting it down on the bar. 'For saving her life.'

It was not all that Vi had told him. Her gratitude towards Chuck had been over-clouded by the news of what had happened to Tom Cutts that same morning. Vi had blamed herself for sending him off as she had done, believing that she had indirectly caused his death. Because of the guilt she felt about Tom, her father was not at all sure that she would be keen to meet Chuck again so soon.

'Mr Blair, I *must* see her again.'

'Must?' He glanced down at the drink.

'And thanks,' said Chuck, sipping it.

'I reckon you're entitled to see Vi. *If* she wants to see *you*.'

He turned to look along the bar and Chuck followed his gaze. Vi was standing in the doorway to the back room. Rosie was beside her, gaping at the GI, realizing that he had come for her sister. Vi stood there for a long time as if trying to make up her mind then, seeming to ignore her visitor altogether, she walked past her father, told him that she would be half an hour and went out at the other end of the bar. Jack was amused by the bewilderment on the face of the American. He whispered something into Chuck's ear.

Vi Blair was in the alley at the side of the pub, leaning against a brick wall, a coat around her shoulders to protect her against the chill night air. She heard the door open and shut.

'Chuck?'

'Yeah.'

He pulled a small torch from his pocket and shone it in her face rather tentatively. She could feel that he was nervous.

'You came round before, Dad said. Why?'

'I wanted to see you again.'

'You're the only American in Market Wetherby tonight. You're not supposed to be here, are you?'

He shrugged, then ran his tongue over his lips.

'Violet . . .'

'Yes?'

There was another pause and he was clearly annoyed by his own embarrassment. 'Jeez! I knew just what I wanted to say . . . back up there on the Base. Now . . . I can't say it.'

'Try,' she encouraged.

'After that plane came over . . .'

'I would have been shot, if it hadn't been for you.'

'No, no. I didn't mean that.'

'I'll never forget it,' she promised.

'Listen,' he asked. 'There was a moment . . . before I drove you across to that place—'

'Dereham House?'

'There was a moment . . . I remember it so clear.' His hand had stopped shaking now and the beam of the torch was steady. 'Don't you?'

'Yes,' she confessed.

'And afterwards I felt just empty. Leaving you there.'

'I was all right, Chuck. Just some mud to wash off.'

'Toughest thing I ever did . . .'

'Oy!' yelled a man's voice from the end of the alley.

'Getting back into that jeep. Driving off.'

'Put that light out!' ordered the voice.

Chuck heard it this time and the torch was switched off. He and Vi were now more or less in complete darkness.

'I knew then . . . more than anything else in the world . . . I wanted to see you again.'


When she had waved her husband off at Market Wetherby railway station, Helen Dereham had been assailed by all the usual fears. She did not know when, or indeed if, Ronnie would come back. The thought had kept her standing on the platform in the drizzle long after the last coach had vanished into the tunnel further down the line. Since that evening Helen had sought to relieve her anxieties by losing herself in her work and her other commitments.

'Darling, if the hospital rings for me . . . I'm out for an hour or two. All right?'

'What?' Pat was on the sofa in the sitting room, not listening.

'And tell Rosie as well, please,' said Helen, adjusting her hat in the mirror above the mantelpiece. There was no sound from her daughter, who was staring blankly at a letter in her hand. Helen turned to face her. 'I was in your room earlier, Pat.'

'Oh?'

'Looking for you . . . Books everywhere, clothes thrown all over the place. You haven't packed a thing.'

'No.'

'But, darling—'

'Cambridge can wait,' interrupted Pat, sharply. 'I'll go up again after the war. If they'll have me.'

'You know how your father feels about it. He'll be terribly disappointed.' She perched on the arm of the sofa. 'Why, Pat?'

'Because . . . because I'm going to join the ATS!'

They both knew that this was a lie. Helen spoke softly and asked if that was the only reason.

'Isn't it enough? Everybody else is getting on with the war and doing their bit. Daddy. You. Why shouldn't I?'

'Because it's such a waste, darling!'

'I mean, even the Americans . . .'

Her voice tailed off and she looked down at the letter in her hand. Helen now understood why her daughter was in such a depressed mood. Evidently, Major Jim Kiley had written to her to refuse the invitation to lunch that Pat had sent him on impulse. Helen tried to be as tactful as possible.

'The war will come to an end, sooner or later. And the Americans will go home again. And we'll be left to pick up the pieces.' She saw Pat grow tense. 'Your father was saying that, in all the rush and tumble . . . it's easy to lose sight of the things that matter.'

'Did he mean me or you?' asked Pat, bluntly.

'All of us. We have to keep the balance.' Helen now

spoke with a surge of passion. 'Pat, a wrong choice now . . . a wrong decision will affect your whole life!'

'I'm sorry, Mummy. I've made up my mind?'

Helen was fearful. 'About . . .?' she murmured.

'Cambridge, of course.'

'Oh.'

'As to anything else . . . I don't know. Jim . . .' It was Helen's turn to tense and her daughter noted it. 'Jim Kiley was saying at our party that we all have to live from day to day. Because for some of us, there won't *be* another day.' She examined the letter again. 'The trouble with decisions . . . choices . . . you don't know until afterwards if they're wrong or not.'

'Until it's too late.'

Helen could see that further discussion would be pointless and in any case she had an appointment to keep. She therefore took her leave and set off to walk to the village hall, a journey that was long enough to give her time to think in detail about the conversation she had just had. What disturbed her most was the fact that her daughter's refusal to return to university was so clearly linked to her infatuation with Major Jim Kiley. Particularly since Helen's own feelings about Jim were so mixed. She still could not understand what had prompted her to ring him up and apologize for her daughter's temerity in sending him an invitation. In the event, Jim had explained that his duties would make it impossible for him to accept but Helen knew just how angry and betrayed Pat would feel – and with justification – if she ever found out about that telephone call.

By the time that she had reached the village hall, Helen had persuaded herself that it was all for the best that Jim was absorbed in his duties, that she was not really attracted to him and that she was going to put him completely from her mind. Then she saw the notice pinned up on the door and realized that she was about to chair a meeting of a committee whose function was to decide on an official

41

welcome for the Americans. The irony of it all made her wince.

Within minutes of the start of the meeting, Helen had begun to regret that she had suggested that Albert Mundy should be a member of the committee.

'I don't see why we have to do anything for the Yanks,' he was saying, tapping the trestle table in front of him with his finger.

'That's absurd!' announced Phyllis Lambourn.

'Why?' he challenged.

'We can't just ignore them.'

'I can!'

'Oh!' she exclaimed in sheer exasperation.

Phyllis Lambourn was a big, dark-haired, handsome woman in her early forties, capable if pushy, and affable in a patronizing way. She was an effective member of a number of local committees, but was not enjoying sitting on this one with Albert Mundy. Though he was a self-styled Tory, she refused to believe that she had anything in common with him and always referred to him as 'that dreadful tradesman'.

Along with Helen, Jack Blair, Albert Mundy and a few others, Phyllis was stationed at the draughtier end of the village hall on a folding chair. She would have preferred to have held the meeting at Dereham Hall, except that that would have brought out the more obsequious side of the dreadful tradesman.

'I can ignore them,' Albert went on, 'and so can everybody else if they've a mind. The King, and Mr Churchill, and gentlemen like Major Dereham will still be here when them interlopers have packed their traps and gone. And good riddance, I say!'

'Mr Mundy,' said Helen, pleasantly, 'I spoke to my husband on the telephone less than an hour ago. Naturally, he had other things on his mind, but he did say that he hoped our arrangements for welcoming the Americans would be a success. They have come all this way, thousands of miles, leaving everything behind them – their own country, their families and farms and jobs, to fight here in England.'

'Like 'em or not,' Jack Blair added, 'they're our allies.'

'Foreigners!' snorted Albert.

'Mr Mundy, they're fighting for us,' argued Phyllis.

'And you can put your shirt on it – some of 'em'll die for us!' said Jack with feeling.

Helen had observed that neither Jack nor Albert looked at each other at any point. Enemies for many years, they sat well apart and addressed all their remarks to the chair. It was Albert's turn again and his finger got busy on the table.

'Begging your pardon, Mrs Dereham, you being the Major's wife and that, but I've faced the Hun, too. Same as the Major. Cold steel to cold steel. I've met Frenchies, Wops, Dutchies, Diggers and fellers the colour of boot polish. And you can take it from me that one Englishman's worth three Jerries, half a dozen frogs and as many of them blooming Americans as you like!'

'Rubbish!' Jack protested.

At that moment a B-17 flew past over the town and the smooth but insistent drone made them all pause and look up. When the noise had subsided, Helen put her case.

'My own feeling is that we are considering ideas for a welcome from too narrow a viewpoint. Something we have lost sight of is how young most of these Americans are – barely in their twenties. What I ask is this: If I were thousands of miles from home, in a foreign country, how would I like those foreigners to welcome *me*?'


Colonel Rufus Krasnowici stood at the window of his Air Executive's office and watched another plane getting ready for take-off. Jim Kiley, still in flying gear, had just come in and was mad as hell.

'I don't get it, Rufus!'

'You know the kind of thing: "The citizens of Market

Wetherby welcome the men of the United States Army Air Force . . . our gallant allies . . ." etcetera, etcetera.'

'Fine! Let them hold their welcome ceremony and keep out of our way!'

'Ease up, Jim,' advised Rufus, turning to him. 'My boys have got to relax some time.' He cleared his throat, knowing that Jim would not like the next bit. 'Anyhow, I promised Mrs Dereham I'd go along with anything she has in mind. Within reason.'

'*She* phoned?' Jim was startled.

'She's a helluva fine woman. While our own hospital's out of commission and damn little chance of replacement stuff coming through yet, I don't want any personal antagonism fouling up relations with the local EMS hospital. That clear, Jim?'

'Yes,' he grunted.

'There's nobody admires American womanhood more than me. But, by God, there's something special about these blue-blooded English women. Look, get to know her better.'

'But—'

'That's an order, Jim.'

'I know Mrs Ronald Dereham well enough already. *And* her daughter.'

'Oh?'

'And I wish I didn't!'

The smile evaporated from Rufus's face.


Whatever reservations some individuals might have had, the general response to the news that a Dance was to be held at the village hall was an enthusiastic one. Most people in Market Wetherby took their lead from Helen Dereham and agreed that it was their duty to provide some sort of official welcome for the American servicemen. It was the women of the town, young and old alike, who looked forward to the occasion most. Phyllis Lambourn, estranged from her husband for some time now, practised

44

the steps of a slow foxtrot to a borrowed record of Joe Loss and his orchestra. Vera Mundy plucked her eyebrows and tried to rid her best dress of the stink of moth balls. Letty Mundy, concealing her excitement from a watchful father, dreamed about seeing a certain lieutenant again. Rosie Blair experimented with a variety of hairstyles. Pat Dereham came out of her gloom. And girls from the neighbouring villages decided that they were residents of Market Wetherby as well.

But it was at the Air Base itself that the news had had the greatest impact. Men who were bored, strained, fatigued, on edge, and about to undergo the terrors of their first bombing mission were now told that they could have a whole evening at a Dance to let off steam. It was like a stay of execution. When the time came for the convoy of trucks and jeeps to set off for the town, every vehicle was packed with laughing, joking, jostling, boasting GIs.

Captain Red Burwash, chewing on a cigar of almost Churchillian dimensions, sat in the back of a truck with the crew of the 'Ginger Rogers'. Elmer Jones, trying vainly to hold in his stomach, was being teased because his tunic was now too tight for him. Mario Bottone was running a comb through his hair yet again and talking about his plans for the first woman on whom he could lay his hands. Danny Coogan was giggling happily. Harvey Wallis, navigator on the 'Ginger Rogers', kept on about the best usherette in Britain. Only Chuck Ericson remained silent.

'This girl of yours, Chuck,' said his captain. 'Introduce me.'

'I'll introduce you, sure. But she's not my girl.'

'Hey, Skip,' Mario interrupted. 'Thought you had no time for these English dames.'

'One of them gets me into a corner, Mario, I'll shoot my way out!'

'This uniform just doesn't fit!' wailed Elmer.

'The uniform is perfect,' said Mario. 'It's *you* that doesn't fit, Elmer!'

The convoy arrived in the town square and the men

moved eagerly towards the village hall, which had been cleaned and hung with flags and trimmings especially for the occasion. Chairs had been placed around the walls so that the central area was clear for dancing and trestle tables at the far end were covered in a selection of refreshments. When the visitors had all come in and been met by the first nervous welcome from the local people, the hall was quite full.

After an awkward pause, during which nobody quite knew what to do or say, the curtains parted with a swish to reveal a small stage on which a trio of musicians was seated beneath a banner that read: 'Market Wetherby Welcomes The 525th Bomb Group Of The USAAF'. A roll on the drums silenced the people in the hall and then Helen Dereham, looking more relaxed than she felt, stepped out of the wings with Colonel Rufus Krasnowici. Though the microphone refused to behave itself, Helen made a short, gracious and much-admired speech. As the applause for her was fading, Rufus stepped forward to thank her and the town for the warm welcome.

When he had finished and left the stage with Helen, the band struck up – Peter Mundy at the piano – and proceedings were officially under way. Rufus claimed the privilege of the first dance with Helen and the couple circled the floor to a rather jerky arrangement of 'Always'. Others quickly found partners and the limitations of the band were soon overlooked in the general euphoria.

Jim Kiley watched Helen closely and thought how poised and dignified she looked as she moved around the hall. Anxious to avoid her, he now discovered how pleased he was to see her again. He was far less pleased to see her daughter.

'I got your cruel letter, Major Kiley,' she said, coming up.

'Cruel?'

'You turned my invitation down flat.'

'No, I didn't.'

'Is that the truth?' she pouted.

'The Air Force turned it down. I had no choice. As I explained when I wrote, all leave was cancelled.'

'That wasn't just an excuse?'

'Of course not, Pat.'

Jim now found that he was dancing with her and he was by no means happy about it, especially when he began to feel a few sly amorous squeezes. Pat was at her most attractive and elegant in a long silk dress but there was an urgency about her that rang alarm bells somewhere inside him.

'So you would have come . . . if you could?' she pressed.

'For you, Patricia . . . anything!'

'You're laughing at me.'

'No, I'm not.'

'I forgive you,' she whispered, brushing her cheek against his. 'Provided you dance every dance with me . . . and no one else.'

The band grappled with the last few bars of their opening number and then brought the dance to a close. While the couples clapped in appreciation, Rufus led his partner across to where Jim and Pat were standing.

'Thank you, Mrs Dereham. But if you'll excuse me, I'll get back to the Base.'

'Must you, Colonel?'

'Against my personal wish, ma'am, believe me. But Jim here will keep an eye on things. Make sure my boys don't overstep the mark.'

'Why don't you stay and let *me* go back?' Jim offered.

'I know what I want,' Rufus insisted. 'I want you, Jim, to stay here with all these nice people and *enjoy* yourself.'

'But—'

'No arguments.' There was a sparkle in his eye as he turned to Helen. 'I'd take it kindly, ma'am, if you'd see that he really does enjoy himself.'

'Of course, Colonel.'

'I'll find your driver, sir,' Jim suggested, still seeking an escape from the situation.

'I can find my own, dammit! What's the matter with you, man? Forgotten to ask a lady for a dance?'

Rufus saluted Helen and moved briskly off towards the exit. The band were now tackling a quickstep. Though neither of them had really wished it, Jim and Helen were soon dancing together, stiffly and mechanically. She spoke first.

'You think all this a waste of time, don't you?'

'It's a break in concentration. Just when I'd got the men all keyed up for a combat mission. Time to relax is *afterwards*.'

'Is it?'

'Mrs Dereham, I'm sending up air crews full of greenhorns against German aces who've already had three years' experience of fighting RAF bombers. I've still got hillbilly sergeant gunners who've got it stuck in their fool heads that the sky over Europe is just another turkeyshoot! First morning they get up there, they won't even know what's hit them.'

Beneath his abrasiveness, Helen sensed a genuine fear for his men. She looked around at some of the GIs dancing close.

'They're so young,' she said.

'They're the best age for the job.'

'Do you blame me, Major? For the . . . break in concentration?'

'I don't *blame* you, no. But it is a break and I hope they don't have to pay for it. Up there.'

They danced on in silence for a few moments as she tried to nerve herself up to make a kind of apology.

'Major Kiley . . . I think perhaps I've misjudged you.'

'Oh, I doubt it,' he replied with amusement.

'What my husband has to do is very different from you, of course . . . but the burden of responsibility is the same.'

'I guess so.'

'Ordering men into battle to face the enemy. Knowing for sure that they won't all come back . . .'

'As for your husband and me . . .' He looked deep into

48

her eyes before he continued. 'It isn't only the job that's different. I bet all the gold in Fort Knox to a bent nickel he handles it different, too.'

Helen thought about this, then nodded. He smiled. She recalled something else.

'One of his RSMs once told me that when things were at their very worst, Ronnie was always kindest and most considerate towards his men.'

'Whereas you figure me a cold, callous, hard-nosed son of a b—' He checked himself. 'Son of a gun.'

'That is the impression you give, Major. But I haven't seen you when things are at their worst.'

'You won't have long to wait, Mrs Dereham. And I'm sorry you don't like my style.'

'Whether I like it or not doesn't matter, surely?'

He searched her eyes again and said nothing more until the end of the dance. The music stopped and they parted.

When the band struck up for the third time, Chuck Ericson made yet another vain tour of the hall in search of Vi Blair. He decided to ask Rosie where she was but she was fully occupied in choosing a dancing partner out of Mario Bottone, Elmer Jones and the diminutive Hymie Stutz. She astounded all three contenders by going off with Danny Coogan. Mario found some compensation.

'At least she picked a sergeant from the "Ginger Rogers". If she'd gone for Hymie, the dwarf of the 525th, who couldn't get into our crew in a million years . . .'

'Watch it, Bottone!' yelled Hymie, his moustache twitching.

'Look at Harvey,' said Elmer, staring with envy as the navigator cruised around the dance floor with Letty Mundy held tight in his arms. 'Some guys get all the luck!'

'Say, what happened to that broad of yours, Chuck?' asked Mario.

'Who cares?' replied Chuck, feigning disinterest.

The music stopped once more and he wandered morosely across the hall as the couples broke up. Then, at the very moment that he had given up all hope, Vi Blair came into the hall through the main door. She was panting slightly as if she had been running and her face was flushed. A number of hopeful GIs converged on her and asked for a dance but she pushed through them and made straight for Chuck. His heart missed a beat.

'I was afraid you wouldn't come.'

'I nearly didn't, Chuck.'

'You didn't want to see me?'

'It isn't that . . .'

Peter Mundy announced 'The Anniversary Waltz' and then sat back down at his piano to play the first few bars. Chuck and Vi soon found themselves standing in the middle of the dance floor with other couples moving all round them. Vi managed to blurt out the truth.

'In a way, I suppose . . . what it is . . . I'm frightened.'

'Of me?'

'No.'

'Then . . .?'

'Somebody I used to know . . . He was killed. Not long ago.'

Chuck was beginning to understand. He slipped an arm gently around her and took her right hand in his.

'Let's just dance . . .'


Crammed into their jeep and all wearing full flying gear, the ten members of the crew of the 'Ginger Rogers' were driven out to their plane. Dawn was rising slowly over the airfield and the rural stillness was shattered as the first engine of a distant B-17 sputtered, coughed and then burst into a roar. The noise had been amplified almost unbearably by the time that Captain Red Burwash and his copilot had clambered into the cockpit, settled into their leather seats and checked the array of dials, levers, cranks, compasses, light switches and control yokes in front of them. For all his cheery bravado earlier, Red now felt dry and hollow inside. The strong aroma of metal, fresh paint and gasoline did not help. It reminded him of the newness of the plane and of the inexperience of his crew.

In the snug, glass-windowed nose compartment that he shared with the bombardier, Harvey Wallis checked his navigational instruments and tried to stop his hands from trembling. Mario Bottone, glad that he was tucked away alone in the middle of the bomber, tested his radio equipment and hoped he was not going to be sick again. Chuck Ericson was in the top turret, counting the other B-17s as they took off from the runway; knowing that he would be the key man in any emergency aboard the plane. Elmer Jones and Danny Coogan were getting their first feel of their guns in the waist section, backing into each other nervously in the narrow space. Elmer was perspiring almost as much as the man in the ball turret beneath the fuselage. The rear gunner, however, was shivering with cold. He began to say his prayers.

This was the worst time, just before take-off, the real test of nerves and character. Every member of the crew was suffering in his own way, and it was the same in all the other planes.

Red Burwash was given clearance, the engines were switched on and the 'Ginger Rogers' was soon contributing to the great, angry symphony of sound. It taxied to the runway, pointed its nose due east and then followed in the wake of its colleagues.

As the squadrons of B-17s passed over Market Wetherby in the first light of a fine morning, Helen Dereham stood at the window of her bedroom and looked up at them. She heard the door open behind her and someone came to stand at her shoulder.

'Well, Pat, it's started . . . And God alone knows when it's going to stop.'

# CHAPTER FOUR

April had brought warmer temperatures and clearer skies to Market Wetherby and it had given the grass a darker shade of green. Dairy cows had been turned out into the pastures for the first time that year and arable farmers had been able to carry on with the important rituals of ploughing and sowing. Sunshine had not only helped the town itself to lose some of its wartime drabness and display its many attractive features, it had also lifted the spirits of the inhabitants. Gossip in the shops started to have more humour in it.

But there was another side to it all. April provided bombers' weather and the United States Army Air Force was able to continue with its policy of daylight raids into Germany. Cows, sheep and other livestock now began to be disturbed by the organized pandemonium in the skies and Land Army girls began to see the huge shadows of B-17s flying across the furrows where they worked.

More missions brought more casualties back to the Emergency Medical Service Hospital and Helen Dereham had to work overtime.

'How'm I doing, Doc?'

Helen looked up in surprise from the chart she had been studying at the end of the bed. She had thought that Danny Coogan was still unconscious.

'Am I gonna make it?' he asked, his voice faint and hoarse.

'Of course, sergeant,' she assured him.

'You wouldn't kid a fella?'

Helen went round to the side of the bed and looked down at Coogan. He had been one of the casualties in that first bombing mission which had taken the 'Ginger Rogers' to Bremen and back. Badly shot up by tracer bullets from a Focke-Wulf, he was now swathed in bandages from the head to the lower part of his chest. She believed in trying to be honest with her patients.

'If you'd asked me a few days ago, I might have had to think about it – but not now. You're on the mend.'

'Sure don't feel like it.'

'Are you in pain?'

'Don't feel a thing. Just thirsty.'

Helen nodded to the pretty, fair-haired nurse who was standing by the door. Ann Weston came across, filled a glass with water from the carafe on the bedside table and helped Coogan to sip it.

'You were lucky, Sergeant,' Helen told him. 'We had to take a pound and a half of lead out of you.'

'Thanks,' said Coogan to the nurse.

Helen could see that he was tiring again and she bent over him. 'Don't try to talk. Just rest. In a week or so, you should be on your way to one of your own Air Force's hospitals.'

'I sure hope not, Doc.'

'Why not?'

'No nice nurses with pretty legs . . .'

The effort of turning his head to look at Ann had tired him even more and his eyes began to shut. Helen let him drift off to sleep again and then went out into the corridor with the nurse.

'Keep an eye on him. The next twenty-four hours could be critical.'

Ann nodded and glanced back with concern at the ward they had left. Some of their patients from the Air Base had already died in the hospital. She hoped that Sergeant Danny Coogan was going to pull through somehow.

Helen went into another ward and did her rounds then was given a message that she had a visitor waiting for her in her office. When she got there, Jim Kiley was studying the books on the shelf. He was in a serious mood.

'So what's the score?'

'I'm sorry about Captain Mason. There was nothing we could do.'

'Yeah. The miracle was he got back at all.'

'Our facilities are very limited, I'm afraid, Major. When all is said and done, this is still only a cottage hospital.'

'It does a great job of work,' he insisted. 'Sergeant Coogan?'

'I doubt if he'll be fit to fly for a long time. If ever.'

'As bad as that?'

'He's lucky to be alive.'

'Yeah. I guess.'

'Your men are having a bad time, Major . . .'

'We're right on the ball!' he retorted, his professional pride throwing him straight on the defensive. 'Strategic bombing in daylight hours while the RAF keeps up the nightime raids. We're really showing the Luftwaffe what . . .' He paused, gave her a tired smile. 'No point trying to kid you.'

'I shouldn't have said anything,' she apologized. 'I was asking you to breach security.'

'Security? What use is that when you see our boys carried in here on stretchers each time we send them off on a mission? Yes, Mrs Dereham, we're having a bad time. A mauling. My men have got plenty of guts and ability – but they're short on experience. And up there, experience is everything. We've a lot of catching up to do yet.'

'You'll do it.'

'Thanks.'

Jim was grateful for the compliment. It came at a time when he needed it most because he was feeling very sensitive about his job. His Commanding Officer had prevented him from flying on any of the missions – though taking part in the Bremen raid himself – and Jim had been restless and frustrated ever since. His training procedures could only teach the men so much and he longed to be up there with them, part of the formation, helping, advising, using his expertise where it would be of most value.

'Was there anything else, Major Kiley?'

'Yes,' he said, putting his professional cares aside for a moment. 'Are you on duty all evening?'

'No, I'm going off soon.'

'Well – uh – could I offer you a drink or something?'

'That's very kind of you,' she said, briskly, 'but I'm expected at home shortly. My daughter is going back to Cambridge tomorrow.'

'Yes, of course . . . By the way, I'm sorry about . . .'

'A young girl's passing infatuation, Major. It's kinder to forget it.'

'I'd be only too happy to. I didn't encourage it, you know.'

'Yes, I know.'

There was an awkwardness between them for a minute and then he gave a small token salute and made his farewells. It was only after he had left that Helen noticed her hands were clenched tight.


'So I am out of the window and down the fire escape in my shirt tails. And she's throwing my pants and coat after me, and I can hear her saying: "Go on – shoo! Out of here, you nasty cat!" . . .'

Mario Bottone had many stories about the unexpected return of husbands and this one got the usual raucous laughter from his companions. One person in the Lounge Bar that night, however, did not enjoy the tale. Picking up his glass, the young British soldier sauntered over to the bar and put it down in front of Jack Blair.

'Fill it up, Charlie?' asked the landlord.

'No thanks, Jack. I'll look in again later on – when the smell's cleared a bit.'

Since the remark was aimed directly at him, Mario stiffened then got ready to throw a punch. Red Burwash grabbed his arm and restrained him while the soldier walked out through the door.

'You heard that! You heard that, Skip!'

'Take it easy, Mario.'

55

'Lousy Limeys! We come over to fight their war for them – you'd think they'd be grateful!'

'Look, knock it off will you!' ordered Red.

'Sure, sure . . .'

Mario sipped his beer but was still ruffled. Like the rest of the crew of the 'Ginger Rogers', the radio operator had flown back from his fourth mission earlier that day and it had been a harrowing experience. Red knew that it had left his men taut and in need of relaxation, which was why he had come along to The Plough with them. Some of them had a low flashpoint in situations like the one that had just arisen and Red wanted to be on hand to keep them out of trouble.

Red bought another round of drinks and then glanced around his men, noting the difference that four bombing missions had made to their faces. All of them seemed years older. Mario was still as cocky and incorrigible as ever but there were dark hollows forming under his eyes. Elmer Jones was still the butt of the crew's humour though there was now a hint of pathos about him as well. Chuck Ericson was still an excellent flight engineer but had become intense and jumpy. Harvey Wallis was still the most assured of them, yet he had quietened and became rather secretive.

'Here's to Danny!' Red lifted his glass.

'Danny Coogan!' said the others.

Harvey emptied his glass in record speed, clapped Red on the shoulder in gratitude and told them all he had somewhere to go. He had left the bar before they could begin to speculate where he had gone. Harvey did tend to keep things to himself these days.

Chuck Ericson looked after him with envy, knowing that Harvey was going to The Roxy. He himself had planned to take Vi Blair to the cinema as well but she had rocked him by announcing that she had already arranged to go with a friend.

Rosie Blair now came into the bar with a tray of glasses and she was immediately the centre of attention. She

56

giggled at the wolf whistles and rolled her eyes provokingly when someone told her she was a second Hedy Lamarr.

'Hey, Rosie, you going to the movies?' asked Mario.

'Don't know. Depends on Dad.'

'How about it, Mr Blair? Can your daughter come out tonight?'

'Well, Vi's gone out so I've no one to help me,' said Jack. He chuckled as Rosie's face clouded. 'But I daresay I can manage.'

'Thanks, Dad.'

'Yeah, thanks . . . Uh, just give us a nod when you're ready, Rosie.'

'Oh, I'm spoken for,' she said, pert and mocking.

'Spoken for!' Elmer Jones sounded like a barrage balloon that had just been punctured.

'Who's the guy?' demanded Mario, aggressively.

'You'll see,' she promised and put the tray down before going further along the bar to serve a customer.

'Jeez, Mario!' The barrage balloon was completely deflated now.

'Yeah, yeah! I heard, Elmer!'

They began to mutter angrily to themselves, casting a rueful glance from time to time at Rosie. Red Burwash, older and wiser, had watched it all with wry amusement. He put a consoling hand on the shoulder of each man and included the morose Chuck in his comment.

'Dames! They'll get you down every time, fellers. I did tell you, but you wouldn't listen.'

'Dames!' echoed Mario, bitterly.

'We still going to the movies, Mario?' asked Elmer.

'Maybe . . .'

'How about you, Chuck?'

'Why not?' he said, wearily.

'We oughta make tracks or we'll miss the second feature.'

'Hold on there, Elmer,' said Mario. 'Something I want to find out first. Sit tight, baby.'

Mario did not have to wait long. A few minutes later, some members of Herman Krotnik's crew came noisily into the bar, looking for a few beers to help them unwind. Krotnik and Red Burwash were arch-rivals and there was a watchful antagonism between their respective crews. In the case of Mario Bottone this antagonism usually settled on one particular member of the rival crew.

'Well, look what the cat brought in!' he sneered. 'Hiya, Stutzie!'

'What ya call me?' challenged Hymie Stutz.

'Stutzie Tootsie. That's your name, ain't it?'

'You watch your lip, Bottone!'

'Can't you take a joke?' asked Elmer.

'And you, Fatso!'

'You looking for something!' retorted Elmer, stung by the jibe.

'What if I was?' Hymie was quite fearless.

'You want to be careful, Stutzie,' warned Mario.

He had taken a step nearer Hymie now and bunched his fists ready for the fight that seemed inevitable now. A big, hefty, square-jawed man took his place beside his sergeant.

'Or what?' drawled Captain Herman Krotnik. Mario and Elmer were now having second thoughts about a fight. 'Or *what*?' repeated Krotnik with greater edge.

'They were trying to rile me, Captain,' said Hymie.

'I'd say they'd done a pretty good job,' observed Red, drily.

There was a brief moment when it looked as if there were going to be a free-for-all between the two crews and then Krotnik defused the situation by clapping Hymie on the back and grinning broadly.

'He's like your boys, Red. Full of pepper.'

Krotnik turned to the bar to buy a round of drinks for his men and the danger was over. Then came the shock for Mario and Elmer. As Rosie Blair came tripping along to serve the newcomers, she saw Hymie standing there and waved happily to him.

'Won't be long, Hymie! Dad says I can come.'

'No hurry, baby,' he said, nonchalantly.

There was a long and incredulous silence.

'Hymie Stutz!' gasped Elmer.

'I just don't believe it!' Mario was reeling.

Hymie basked in the astonishment and struck a debonair pose. It was left to Red Burwash to have the final word on the incident.

'Dames! You guys will never learn!'


Helen Dereham was lying back in an armchair when her daughter came into the sitting room with the coffee on a tray. It was an effort for Helen to sit up and she had to stifle a yawn as she did so.

'Thank you, darling,' she said, taking the cup from Pat.

'You look exhausted, Mummy.'

'We've about half the staff we could do with.'

'It's not just the Hospital,' her daughter pointed out, sitting on the sofa, 'it's all the other things you do. Have you ever stopped to count the number of committees you belong to?'

'Everybody's needed these days.'

'That's what I keep telling you,' said Pat with a smile.

'Yes, I know, darling,' Helen went on, quickly, 'but, as your father says, the most useful thing you can do is to go back to university and finish your degree.'

'I will.'

'Then, if the war's still on – which Heaven forbid! – you can find some kind of work that's right for you.'

Pat considered this, then nodded. 'Everybody seems to be doing something to help. The whole country. Even down here in Sleepy Hollow. I mean, who'd ever have thought of Market Wetherby with a bomber base?'

'Quite.'

They sipped their coffee and then looked up at the mantelpiece as the clock chimed. It was ten o'clock on a warm spring evening and they were both aware that it was the last nightcap they would be able to share for several weeks.

'I'm surprised that Daddy didn't ring again.'

'Are you?'

'Before they sailed off to wherever it is. He didn't exactly give much away, did he?'

'Your father might have invented the phrase,' said Helen, fondly.

'Phrase?'

'Careless Talk Costs Lives.'

'Yes! You know, I think Daddy should have gone into the Silent Service, not the army.'

They laughed easily and Helen felt a companionship that had not been there for some time. She knew that Pat had had her problems and that she was trying to cope with them in her own way, but so much had been left unsaid between them. Helen began to wonder how her daughter now felt about Jim Kiley. She sat back and introduced the name very casually.

'By the way, Major Kiley called in at the Hospital this evening.'

'Oh?' Pat sounded equally casual.

'He seems devoted to his men.'

'Is that so surprising?'

'Not really, I suppose.'

'If you're saying am I still pining for him, the answer is "no". I must have embarrassed you all horribly. I've been reading too much romantic poetry lately – Knights of the Round Table, Young Lochinvar . . .'

'Major Kiley is hardly Young Lochinvar!'

They laughed again and Helen felt a sense of relief.


Chuck Ericson walked arm in arm with Vi Blair over the small bridge and heard the ripple of water in the darkness. His despair had been short-lived. Having left The Plough and made his way disconsolately to the cinema, he had been startled to meet Vi and another girl in the foyer. Instead of being rejected in favour of another young man, Chuck was now invited to join the two girls and he had sat between them during the film, holding hands with Vi.

Now that the other girl had gone home, they had come for a stroll to the part of the river that was most popular with courting couples. Rustling in the bushes told them that they were not the first ones there but they did not mind this. They turned to face each other, stood nervously for a moment, and then kissed away all their doubts and fears and wrong assumptions.

The intervals had been fairly regular. It had been almost nine when Albert Mundy, still wearing his dark ARP uniform and his habitual scowl of disapproval, first sounded off about his daughter. At ten he had begun to ask where and with whom she was that evening. An hour later he was getting agitated because she had not yet returned home, and at midnight the real explosion came.

'I'm waiting no longer, Vera! Look at the time!'

'Stay here, Albert. Please.'

'If she has gone to that blooming cafe like you say, I want her out of there. Unsavoury, that place. The Yanks go there – and I will not have Letty messing about with that lot. They're not fit company for her.'

'Peter's there as well,' she argued. 'He'll bring her home.'

'Yes, and he shouldn't be out at this hour either!'

'Young people are entitled to a bit of fun, dear,' said Vera, at last finishing the ironing.

'Fun!' he yelled, rising to his feet and hurling his newspaper down into the chair. 'Those two think of nothing else *but* fun! There's him only interested in playing the piano in a jazz band and her spending all her time dressing up and acting like a tart!'

'Albert!'

'It's true, woman. You saw the way she was dolled up tonight. All that paint on her face. Almost as bad as that Rosie Blair.' A grim satisfaction came into his voice. 'Yes, *he's* got two right little madames to worry about. Rosie and Vi. Even chance which one of them gets up the spout first.'

His jaw tightened. 'But it's not going to happen to my daughter!'

'Shouldn't you be making your blackout rounds?' she asked, trying to deflect him.

'Not till I know where she is, Vera.'

'I told you. The cafe.'

'I'll get round there right away!'

'Don't go making a scene, Albert,' she said, intercepting him at the door. 'Think what people would say . . . look, I'll put the kettle on for a cuppa. If she's not back when we've had that . . . But I'm sure she will be.'

Vera patted her husband's shoulder as if trying to calm a frightened animal. She was anxious that her husband did not go out in search of Letty because she had a good idea with whom her daughter might be. As she thought now of the way that Letty had danced with Harvey Wallis all night at the village hall, she was eternally grateful that Albert had not been there to see it.

'Listen!'

'What?'

'Listen, woman. In the garden. Voices.'

Albert's hearing had been acute. At the bottom of the small garden, his daughter had just detached herself guiltily from the arms of Harvey Wallis because her brother had arrived at the back gate.

'Who's that? Who's there?' Peter had asked.

'It's me,' she had said, stepping into the light, her peak-shouldered, narrow waisted coat still open.

'Oh . . . hello.' Peter was embarrassed.

'Hi,' mumbled Harvey. 'You get on in, kid.'

'Better not let Dad catch you,' Peter warned his sister.

'We'll go in together,' she decided.

'Hey, baby, give a guy a break!'

'I have to go in, Harvey. Honest.'

'Two more minutes, that's all I ask.'

Torn between her feelings for him and her fear of her father, Letty told her brother to wait for her and she stepped back into the shadows with Harvey. His hands

62

went under her coat again and the kisses were hungrier than ever. The warning came too late.

'Letty! Quick!' whispered Peter.

But Albert Mundy had already stepped out of the back door, now wearing his white helmet with the letters ARP on the front. He switched on the large torch in his hand and immediately caught Letty and Harvey in its beam.

'Harvey!' she hissed in terror.

He released her, stepped back then hurried off into the darkness. Albert's fury had been aroused now and he lurched forward.

'What's this? What's going on?' He swung his torch from Letty and stopped in surprise when it picked up Peter, mouth agape. The beam flicked back to the trembling Letty. 'Who was that?'

'I don't know,' she stammered.

'Don't know!'

'I . . . I was coming home and he just . . . stepped out and grabbed me.'

'What!' Albert went quickly out into the lane and shone the torch in all directions. There was no sign of anybody. He remembered Peter. 'And where were you?'

'I'd just got back, Dad.'

'Right. Inside – both of you.'

They hurried indoors with Albert at their heels. Vera was alarmed by the sudden entry and asked what the trouble was. Peter, caught up in the lie and very uncomfortable about it, nevertheless went along with it for his sister's sake.

'Someone grabbed Letty.'

'Who was it?'

'That's what I'm trying to find out,' said her husband, taking charge. 'Well?'

'I don't know,' Letty replied.

'Now listen, my girl. I want to know what was going on out there. Everything! Everything, mind.'

Vera helped her daughter to a seat and crouched beside her holding her hand. Years of having to deceive her father had made Letty Mundy fairly adept at lying, even in the most difficult situations.

'I was just coming home . . .'

'Alone?' asked her father.

'Yes. Peter was somewhere behind me. I got to the gate . . .'

Vera nodded, encouraging her daughter to go on. Letty had decided on her story now and almost believed it herself.

'I was just opening it when this feller came up. He was laughing.'

'It was one of them!' Albert snarled. 'I saw his uniform.'

'Well, he just caught me . . . and kissed me.'

'Was that all?' said her mother.

'Yes. Then Dad came out with his torch and the feller ran off.'

'Thank heavens it was nothing worse!'

'Nothing worse, Vera! Nothing *worse*! Our daughter jumped on and pawed about at our own back door!'

'Well, there was no real harm done, Albert,' she said, lamely.

'And what if Peter hadn't arrived when he did? What if I hadn't gone out there?' Albert was working himself up into a rage now. 'I don't think you realize what we're talking about here!'

'Dad, he didn't really hurt me or anything.'

'That's beside the point, girl. I said it all along – animals! They're animals, those people! Well, this one is not going to get away with it, I can tell you. I'll make him pay for what happened out there! You just see if I don't.'

Suddenly Letty Mundy was very scared indeed.

# CHAPTER FIVE

Security at the Air Base was tight. A high perimeter fence, topped off with thick barbed wire and patrolled day and night by MPs and Alsatians sealed off the area. The main entrance boasted a pair of formidable iron-mesh gates and when these were open there was still a long, brightly painted swing-arm barrier across the road. It bore the command 'Stop' and the MP on sentry duty was there to make sure that everyone did just that. Behind the barrier was the gatehouse itself, manned by an MP sergeant who had achieved his rank by virtue of his physique, his undoubted authority and his intricate knowledge of every one of the hundreds of rules and regulations to which the GIs were subject. The easiest way to get into the Base was, unquestionably, to fly in.

From where Sally Bilton was standing, it looked impregnable, hopeless. A pale, attractive if slightly unkempt woman, Sally was in her late twenties but seemed older and wearier. She braced herself. Though she was nervous about speaking to the guard, she had come a long way with the child in the pushchair and did not want to squander the effort by giving up at the last moment. As she approached the barrier, she could see a sergeant MP outside the gatehouse, talking to a shorter but equally solid individual who wore the stripes of a master sergeant on his sleeve.

'I'd like to talk to someone in authority, please,' she said.

'You gotta pass, ma'am?' asked the sentry.

'Well, no . . .'

'What's up? What's the problem?' asked the sergeant MP, coming forward. He put a finger to his helmet. 'Can I help you, lady?'

'I want to see someone, that's all. Whoever's in charge.'

'Of the gatehouse, the Base or the Air Force.'

'Well, here,' she said, responding to his gruff humour with a faint smile. 'I heard you're taking on civilian workers and I wondered if I could get a job. Part-time or anything.'

'You'd have to see the Quartermaster.'

'Could I . . . speak to him for just a minute, please?'

'You'll need an appointment,' said the MP sergeant, pleasantly. 'Sorry, lady. You'll have to write in first, and you'll have to be checked out.'

Master Sergeant Joe McGraw, taciturn and impassive, stood by the gatehouse and watched. Sally's disappointment was evident and he was interested in the way that she tried to hide it.

'I see. Well, thank you,' she said.

At that moment Helen Dereham's car came down the road and caused the boy in the pushchair to point and gurgle. Sally moved aside as the vehicle pulled up at the barrier.

'I'd like to see the Commanding Officer, please,' Helen called through the open window.

'What is this? Visitors' Day?' asked the sergeant MP. 'Do you have an appointment, ma'am?'

'No.'

'I've just been telling this other lady. Without an appointment, no can do.'

Helen got out of the car and walked up to him. She was poised and determined and her voice had a crispness to it.

'Sergeant – would you kindly let Colonel Krasnowici know that Mrs Dereham – Dr Dereham – is here?'

'Certainly, ma'am. Right away.'

Impressed by her manner, the MP sergeant saluted, went into the gatehouse and picked up the telephone. As Helen waited her eye fell first on McGraw and then Sally.

'Hello. You're Mrs Bilton, aren't you?'

'Yes, ma'am,' said Sally, respectfully.

'And this is – don't tell me – William, isn't it?'

'Fancy you remembering!'

'Well, I did deliver him! You have a girl as well, don't you? How are they both?'

'Oh, they're fine. Quite a handful.'

Helen noticed the involuntary frown on her face. She glanced back at McGraw, then at the gatehouse, then at Sally again. 'Is something the matter?' she asked.

'Oh, no. Just . . . well, trying to get by on my husband's army allowance . . . it's difficult. I was hoping I might find some work here in the laundry or something.'

'And you can't?'

'Might be a chance. But it's going to take some time.'

'I see. Well, I hope it works out.'

'Thank you, Mrs Dereham . . . Come on, Billy . . .'

Sally swung the pushchair around and began to walk slowly back up the road. McGraw's eyes did not leave her for a second. The MP sergeant, meanwhile, came quickly out of the gatehouse and gave Helen a smarter salute than before.

'They say you're to go right on in, ma'am.'

'Thank you, Sergeant.'

She got back in her car, waited until the swing-arm had been moved and then drove through into the Air Base. When she reached the small administrative block an amiable young man in uniform was waiting to show her into Jim Kiley's office.

'Come on in, Mrs Dereham, and take a seat.'

'This is not a social call, Major,' she warned. 'I was expecting to see the Colonel, to be honest.'

'Rufus has gone to a conference at Divisional Head-quarters. I'm holding the fort. Can I help?'

The fact that she had come at all told him it was serious. He wondered why she hesitated so long.

'There's no delicate way to put it,' she said at last. 'A girl in the town was assaulted last night.'

'Assaulted?'

'Coming home from the cinema.'

67

'Poor kid . . .' Realization made him tense. 'One of our fellows?'

'I'm afraid so, Major.'

Jim digested the information slowly, pulling at his moustache and staring out of the window. A thought occurred to him.

'Was she actually –?'

'No. It happened just outside her house. Her father was coming out to look for her and her brother was on his way home. They frightened the man off.'

'How is she now?'

'Still very shaken.'

'Understandable . . . Er, have they been to the police?'

'Well, no. I talked to her father and advised against it. You and the Colonel, all of us, know how important it is to keep everything friendly between your Base and our people, and this –'

'Could throw one big spanner in the works.'

'Quite. I told him that you'd have some way of dealing with it yourselves.'

'We certainly do.' Jim took out his pen and reached for a notepad. 'I'm grateful, Mrs Dereham. And glad the father had the sense to come to you first.'

'I am chairman of the Goodwill Committee.'

'Amongst your other accomplishments,' he said, then became businesslike. 'Now – who was the man?'

'She doesn't know. She walked home alone.'

'And he was waiting and jumped her?'

'I assume so.'

'Well, could they describe him? Anything distinctive?'

'All they could make out was the uniform . . . oh, and she thought that he was drunk.'

'Very likely . . . Any badges of rank? Was he a GI, a non-com?'

'Major, it was very sudden and almost pitch dark at the time. Letty Mundy was the girl. Her father is a difficult man, I'm afraid. Of all the people in Market Wetherby, Mr Mundy is the one least likely to approach this calmly.'

'You mean, he resents us?'

'Yes. None of us wants him stirring up trouble. But in the circumstances, he would find many to support him.'

'Including you, Mrs Dereham?' Jim immediately wished that he had not made the remark. Helen stiffened and shot him a glance. 'I take that back. My point was . . . well, you naturally feel protective towards the girl. And we have over two thousand men on this Base.'

'It should be simple to find out which of them had passes last night and eliminate the ones with alibis.'

'Yes, but the others would all have to be investigated and interrogated as well. Now you talk about resentment. I am equally concerned about preventing it on our side.'

'You would rather let this slide?' she challenged.

'Like you, I want it settled quickly and with the least fuss. But we have to get it in proportion.' He sat on the edge of the desk and smiled. 'After all, what actually took place? A girl was kissed unexpectedly by an American serviceman who'd probably had a drink too many.'

'It was only the merest chance that it wasn't a great deal worse, Major Kiley!' she said, her anger growing.

'That's a supposition. Now, I'm not trying to minimize what happened. But like you, we would not want this to be seen as too important.'

'It *is* important. You said I was protective towards Letty. Aren't you being just as protective towards your men?'

'That's part of my job.'

'There are other considerations.'

'If the man can be found, he'll be punished.'

Helen got to her feet, afraid that she was going to lose her temper entirely. When the conversation had started, she had found Kiley helpful and receptive. She now decided that he was not going to cooperate at all, and asked him sarcastically when they might expect to hear the result of his investigation.

'Hard to say. After all, we are here to fight a war, primarily.'

69

Seeing her bite back a rejoinder, Jim was suddenly concerned that she might have misunderstood him. He crossed to open the door for her. Helen ignored the gesture, and swept past him.

'Goodbye, Major.'

'I'm genuinely grateful to you for giving us the chance to handle this. I hope you understand our position.'

'Oh, yes,' she said, levelly, 'I think you've made it very clear.'

When Helen Dereham drove out of the Base, she was annoyed and mystified. Jim Kiley had managed to make her angrier during their brief meeting than she had ever felt with a man before.

The lie which Letty Mundy had invented on the spur of the moment turned out to have far-reaching consequences. Customers at the shop soon heard the story from the vengeful father or the anxious mother, and the whispers reached all over the town. Reactions varied. Some, like Phyllis Lambourn, believed that a girl out at midnight on her own was inviting trouble. Others, like Rosie Blair, pleasurably scandalized, simply wanted to know the intimate details of what had happened. Others again, like Vi Blair, wondered why the tall lieutenant who had left The Roxy with Letty on his arm had not seen her safely home. But the majority reacted with fear and resentment. More than one mother stopped her daughter from going out in the evenings and more than one embittered local at The Plough began to talk about reprisals against the man concerned.

In defiance of Helen's advice, Albert Mundy reported the matter to the police and announced that he wished to press charges against the offender. Sergeant Wilson, the slow-moving, avuncular but sage old policeman, tried to calm Albert down, conscious of how relatively untroubled the relations between the town and the Air Base had been so far. While sympathetic towards Letty, he did not feel that the incident was a prosecution matter and pointed out how embarrassing it could be for her and for her family if she had to go into court. If the man responsible denied her story and claimed that she had in fact led him on, it would be a case of his word against hers. Letty might then have to be cross-examined about her moral background and, however blameless that might be, question marks might well hang over it afterwards in the minds of the local people. All things considered, Wilson said, it was best to leave the whole thing to the military authorities. They would punish the man their way.

Balked, hurt, outraged and still smouldering, Albert Mundy was now even more damning in his comments about the Americans. Mealtimes with him were a strain for Vera and a positive test of endurance for Peter, who was conscience-stricken about his own part in it all. Letty Mundy herself suddenly began to know the true meaning of panic.

Lieutenant Harvey Wallis sat in the nose-compartment of the 'Ginger Rogers' and tried to concentrate on the job in hand. The B-17, now returning from a mission, was passing over the British coastline but thick cloud was making the navigator's task a tricky one. Harvey's table was fixed at the rear of the roomy compartment, against the left side, and from his swivel-chair he was able to look out through the plexiglass windows at the propeller of number two engine as it whirred manically. Directly above the windows were two vital instruments suspended from the fuselage formers. Nearest the rear bulkhead was the gyro magnetic compass and to its right was the radio compass. Harvey had consulted both constantly but he still did not feel confident that he knew exactly where they were.

Red Burwash spoke to him on the intercom.

'Where the hell are we, Harvey?'

'I don't know, Skip.'

'Whaddya mean, you don't know!'

'We been flying round in circles so long.'

'Ball turret – can you see anything down there,' Red asked.

'Nothing but cottonwool, Skip,' said a voice into his headphones.

'You want I should call the Base and get a fix?' suggested Mario in the radio compartment.

'We're under orders not to use WT or RT.'

Red glanced round as Harvey came up into the cockpit to crouch beside him. The navigator looked tired and anxious.

'Without radio, we'll need a visual fix.'

'I'm going down,' decided Red.

'But, Skip, in this cloud the whole formation could be just below us.'

'You gotta better idea?'

The 'Ginger Rogers' dropped its nose and began to lose height steadily through the heavy banks of cloud. When the visibility improved it levelled off and its crew had a view of a distant patchwork of fields and farmsteads. Back in the waist section, Elmer Jones was impressed.

'Pretty, ain't it!'

'But where in tarnation are we?'

'We must be *somewhere* near the field,' promised Harvey, still crouching beside him. He peered through the plexiglass. 'Yeah – look! The river! And there's the railroad! That's it, Skip!'

'So where's the airfield?'

'Right there! Where the river starts to loop!'

'Great!' Red Burwash was as relieved as his navigator. 'Well, better take this ship down. Looks as if we're last man in. When we get back, Harvey, keep your flak vest on. You'll need it, if I know Kiley.'

Harvey winced and lowered himself back into the nose compartment where the bombardier gave him a tired smile. The 'Ginger Rogers' had been on a long, dangerous and exhausting flight and each member of the crew was anxious to be back on the ground.

72

Red Burwash chose his line and brought the plane down on to the runway with a gentle bump. As the inner engines cut out and the B-17 taxied to a standstill, he looked out in surprise.

'Somebody's grabbed our hard-stand. Mario – get me the Tower!'

'Okay, Skip,' said Mario, flicking a switch.

'B-17, identify yourself,' said a voice from the control tower.

'Uh – 6I – 30942, Captain Burwash. Some joker's taken our hard-stand!'

'What's your Group, Captain?'

'Aw, come on! 525th, Market Wetherby.'

'Congratulations,' said the voice. 'That was a perfect landing. But this is the 91st Bomb Group at Hardwick.'

Red Burwash gulped and stared through the window again. The planes all around him were B-24s. He closed his eyes and shuddered as he imagined what would be said back at Market Wetherby when it was known he had landed at a Liberator Base.


McGraw knelt down and looked into the pond. Minnows were darting about and the water seemed alive with larger fish who cruised around aimlessly in the shallows near the bank. Laughter caused the American to stand up and peer over the bushes that obscured his view of the far side of the pond. A girl, no more than four or five, was playing a little game on her own, throwing leaves into the pond, watching them swirl away and then running to keep up with them. She was a thin, pale but energetic child and McGraw thought that there was something vaguely familiar about her.

It was only a matter of minutes before her game brought her running around the hedge towards him. She stopped, more in surprise then fear.

'Hello,' she said, smiling. 'Are you a Yank?'

'Yeah,' he nodded, glancing down at his uniform. 'Guess so.'

'Any gum, chum?'

'Do you like gum?'

'Don't know. Never had any. I only said it because . . . that's what we say to Yanks.'

'I have some chocolate.'

McGraw took a small Hershey bar from the pocket of his tunic and offered it to her. The girl reached forward and took it but jumped back quickly when McGraw tried to pat her curly head.

'What do you say?' he asked.

'Thank you, mister.'

He looked up and saw Sally Bilton coming towards them from the other side of the pond, holding the hand of her son who was toddling busily along. She came up to McGraw.

'I saw you at the camp, didn't I?' she asked.

'Yeah.' His thumb jerked towards the girl. 'This one yours, too?'

'Yes. Betty. Did she ask for that chocolate?'

Betty looked quickly to McGraw, fearing that the gift would be taken from her if he told the truth, but he announced that he had given her the chocolate and she was freed from the stern gaze of her mother. McGraw, expressionless and laconic as ever, waited a few moments before speaking again.

'Your husband's in the army, that right?'

'Tank Corps . . . North Africa.'

'Rough. You out for a walk?'

'We live quite near. A little cottage. Back there . . .'

He nodded then bent over to ruffle Betty's hair. This time she did not step back and rewarded him with a wink that told him he had won a new friend.

'You share that with your brother, you hear?'

McGraw tipped his cap politely to Sally and then set off in the direction of the Air Base. Behind him he left two children whose mouths were already coated in chocolate

74

and a mother who had started to ask herself once more who the strange man was.


When Colonel Rufus Krasnowici was roused, his eyes blazed, his cheeks reddened and the words came out of his mouth like the rattle of machine gun fire.

'Dammit, Jim, they'll be laughing from here to Alconbury!'

'I know, Rufus.'

'Bringing down their Fortress in the middle of a Liberator Base! Were they blind as well as stupid! Not only did they get separated from their squadron, but from the whole damn formation!'

'I did make that point. Don't worry.'

'And Red Burwash of all people! If one of our best pilots can make a mistake like that, what will some of the others do! I hope you tore him into little pieces, Jim.'

'I did. And roasted them over a small fire.'

'That fool navigator, too.'

'Lieutenant Wallis got his share,' promised Jim.

'An error of that magnitude over Germany and we'd have one Fortress less on the Base. Keep them out of my sight, the whole damn crew of the "Ginger Rogers"! Just keep them out!'

Jim Kiley took his leave and went straight to his office. He opened the door, crossed quickly to a cabinet, took out a glass and a bottle of whisky then poured himself a stiff measure. It was only when he was downing it that he noticed Helen Dereham.

'They said . . . I could wait,' she apologized.

'Ah.' He emptied the glass, then held up the bottle to her by way of an offer. When she shook her head, he put it away. 'Well . . . hi.'

They were both tentative and watchful, neither ready to take the initiative, both remembering the uneasiness of their last meeting.

'I understand that you called at the Hospital,' she said.

'Dropped in on Coogan. Had some good news for him.'

'That young man could use some good news.'

'The Bremen mission, our first. Coogan shot down two FWs and an ME 110. The FWs have now been confirmed by RAF Reconnaissance, and the ME is a probable.'

'I see.'

'I don't think you do, Mrs Dereham. Means a lot to a gunner to notch up victims. Coogan was thrilled.' He fiddled with the glass. 'Colonel's recommended him for a medal as well. Nearly in tears when I told him.'

Helen did not reply. She had seen Sergeant Danny Coogan when he was brought into the operating theatre. In the context of his appalling injuries, the talk about his 'victims' seemed rather grotesque. She changed the subject.

'I'd hoped for a word with you, Major, but you'd left.'

'We do run to telephones, you know.'

'They have their limitations. People can hang up on you.'

Jim accepted the rebuke. The day after her last visit, Harvey Wallis had come to him and told him the truth about the alleged assault on Letty Mundy. After bawling his man out, Jim had rung Helen with the curt message that the offender had been found and was being dealt with by his superiors. Before Helen had been able to press for details the telephone had been put down at the other end. A letter from Rufus to Albert Mundy had confirmed the situation. Like Helen, Albert had been incensed that no details were given and had been wounded by the feeling of being palmed off.

'Letty Mundy came to see me.'

'Who? . . . Oh, the girl.'

'She made a clean breast of it. Your man was quite innocent.'

'She'd have saved all of us a lot of trouble if she'd said that at the start. I gather she lives in fear of her father.'

'Mortal terror.' Her voice softened. 'Why didn't you say anything? Lieutenant Wallis obviously told you the truth.'

'No actual harm had been done. And that poor kid would only have gotten more stick from Mr Mundy.'

'Very noble of you in a way, Major.'

'Noble?'

'You must have realized that by not letting out the facts, you would be accused of covering up for your men.'

'We may not be fine English gentlemen, Mrs Dereham, but we like to think our hearts are in the right place.'

'That makes me feel even worse.'

'Hey, you've no call to bring yourself down. Okay, you were taken in by that story about a drunken assault. So were lots of other people.'

'But I –'

'Please!'

'Confession is good for the soul, Major.' She took a deep breath. 'When I left here last time, I was certain that you wouldn't exactly strain yourself to find the man in question. So I went straight to the police. As it happened, Albert Mundy had done the same thing but that doesn't matter. I misjudged you enough to report the matter officially. I even talked about resigning from the Goodwill Committee. I'm at least partly to blame for the suspicions and unpleasantness.'

'There'd have been unpleasantness, in any case,' he replied. 'We've come late into a war you've been fighting for three years. Our boys are a little too brash, a little too different – and they don't take no from your girls too easily.'

'No . . .'

'It'll blow over, Mrs Dereham. Let's just hope it'll help to create a little more tolerance between us all, a little more understanding for the future.'

Helen was grateful for his attempt to make her feel better but it had exactly the opposite effect. It had taken some effort to come to him and apologize and it had left her subdued. There was no sign now of the antagonism she had expressed towards him earlier.

'I think you'll find most of our people very willing to make up for their narrow-mindedness.'

He thought about this then walked across to her. It was the first time she had not been cold and formal whilst they were alone together. He tried to take advantage of the fact.

'I'm sure the two of us could do a lot.'

'How?'

'What would be better than if you drove into town with me and had a drink?'

'I'm sorry, Major,' she said, the coldness flooding back. 'For many reasons, which I need not go into, that is out of the question. I'd better leave before I outstay my welcome.'

'You couldn't do that,' he said, quietly.

'Oh, I assure you, I could. Good day.'

She had gone through the door before he could say another word. Jim Kiley cursed himself inwardly for trying to rush things yet again. His attention was then caught by the poster on the wall that showed John Bull and Uncle Sam shaking hands across a blue Atlantic. The caption was: 'Hands Across The Sea'.

He glared at it for a moment and went back to the whisky bottle.

# CHAPTER SIX

It was well past midnight and the rain was scouring the airfield. The repair crew was working by the glare of some jerry lights they had rigged up, trying to fasten a patch over a gaping hole on the port wing. A makeshift canvas canopy gave them some protection but they were still soaked to the skin. On the nose of the 'Ginger Rogers', proudly daubed beneath its logo, were the five bombs that showed its tally of missions. Beneath these the swastika bore witness to the GAF fighter that had been shot down. Master Sergeant Joe McGraw, the tireless line chief who was supervising the operations, was more concerned about the other reminders of combat. On its last mission the 'Ginger Rogers' had sustained extensive damage and it was far more difficult to put that right than to paint a bomb on the nose of the plane.

'How'd she come through, Mac?' asked Red Burwash, the collar of his jacket turned up against the rain.

'There was a hole in that wing you could see daylight through – if there was any daylight! Her left stabilizer was shot to blazes. That was a lucky landing, Captain.'

'Lucky, hell! It was damned good flying. No 2 engine's still over-speeding. I had to come home on three.'

'You could get to Berlin and back on two,' McGraw said.

'I just don't want to have to keep proving it.'

McGraw came dangerously close to smiling. He could see that Red was trying to hold himself erect and steady, and smelt a faint whiff of alcohol. Evidently, Red had celebrated his safe return in the usual way. It was a long walk back to the buildings and McGraw eased up slightly.

'You want one of my boys should run you back to your quarters, Captain?'

'Don't you think, I'll make it, Mac?' grinned the other.

'Oh, sure but—'

'I'll be okay. Just take care of my baby.'

Red moved in closer to the 'Ginger Rogers' and patted her affectionately. He then touched his cap to McGraw and wandered off unsteadily into the rain. McGraw watched him go. He was as deeply and emotionally involved with the B-17s as any of the flyers, including Red Burwash, but he was not as extrovert and demonstrative as they were. McGraw showed his love of the planes in the obsessive care he took of them and it was this that made him wheel round on his men now.

'C'mon, you bums! Get this crate patched up! We ain't got all night!'

It was well past three o'clock before he finally got to bed, but he was up next morning at his usual hour. One of his first duties was to report to Jim Kiley's office. Rufus was also there.

'Grand total of six,' announced McGraw.

'I thought we only lost five,' Jim said.

'Lazy L — the one that spun off the runway — her back's broken, Major.'

'A write-off?' asked Rufus.

'The best we can do is turn her into a Hangar Queen — use bits of her for spares. We sure as hell need 'em, Colonel. I been hollering for replacements, spare parts and—'

'We all have, McGraw. Everything meant for us was diverted to North Africa. So we're reduced to thirty-three operational planes — the basic Group strength — with no spares!'

'We might patch up another couple, if there was time. But all the others need modifications and overhaul.'

'Yeah.' Rufus pondered, then dismissed McGraw. 'And keep up the good work. We're counting on you.'

'Yes, sir, Colonel. Thank you,' He saluted and went smartly out into the corridor.

'That's it, then,' sighed Rufus, turning to Jim. 'The

weather's scrubbed all operations for the next four days. There'll be no flying except for instruction of trainee aircrew. That time's for McGraw and his boys to get those planes in shape.'

Jim nodded, silent and preoccupied. Rufus recalled a suggestion that had been put to him by more than one of his staff.

'Might be chance to give the men some leave. Most of them haven't been off the Base for nearly three weeks now. Should be no harm in letting them go into town. What d'you think, Jim?'

'As long as it's not a stampede.'

'That unpleasantness we had a while back. All cleared up now, is it?' asked Rufus.

'Most of it. Some diehards'll go on distrusting us, of course.'

'Like Mrs Dereham?'

'I guess,' said Jim, ruefully.

Rufus was more observant than Jim had imagined.


Mario Bottone crept alongside the hut and then peered cautiously around the corner. His head jerked back as a sergeant came riding up to the hut on a bicycle, dismounted, parked it near some other bicycles and then went in through the main door. Mario peeped around the corner again. Seeing that the coast was clear, he came swiftly around to the front of the building, passed one bicycle back to a pair of eager, chubby, waiting hands and then grabbed another one for himself. He and Elmer Jones were soon pedalling happily through the main gate in the morning sunshine. It was their first escape from the Base for some time and they were both determined to make the most of it.

Neither man was very expert in the saddle and Elmer, in particular, had some perilous moments along the way. Both were grateful that there were no hills to test them and they were still in high spirits when they reached

Market Wetherby. Disappointment set in when they found that The Plough was not yet open. They stood in the square and complained for a few minutes, then wheeled their bicycles off in search of some alternative attraction. It was called the Empire Cafe.

The place was in a sidestreet and it had begun life as a fish and chip shop. Wartime restrictions on the supply of fish had persuaded the owners to convert the premises to a cafe, but the most uncritical patrons could not say that the conversion had been entirely a success. At the far end were the frying vats, gleaming when they were first installed but now dulled by time and neglect. In front of the vats was the counter which had a small confectionery section at one side and a glass display for buns and sandwiches at the other. Choice was severely limited. A sinister-looking tea urn only added to the general impression of scruffiness and scarcity.

Down one wall were four or five tables with chairs and down the other, built to give an illusion of privacy, were five chest-high wooden booths. Then, of course, there was the smell.

Mario Bottone grimaced but Elmer Jones beamed.

'It's like a kind of drug store – soda fountain.'

'What a dump!'

'I like it, Mario.'

They sat down at a rickety table, apparently the only customers. Elsie Foster, the plump, pleasant, middle-aged waitress, came waddling towards them in her brown dress with its cream bib and apron. Her head inclined towards them as she spoke and they could see the cream frill was secured by hairpins.

'Yes? What would you like?'

'Can we get a drink of some sort?' asked Mario.

'Tea, coffee, milk or lemonade?'

'Any beer?'

'Oh, no. We're not licensed, you see.'

'Then it's gotta be two coffees,' said Mario, resigned.

'I'll have a banana split,' decided Elmer.

'Sorry,' Elsie replied, quite baffled by the request. 'We don't have any bananas.'

'I'll just take the icecream, then. Strawberry, chocolate, whatever you've got. Just mix it up.'

'We don't have *any* icecream. Not of any sort. Not for the duration.'

'Duration?' It was Elmer's turn to be puzzled.

'Of the war.'

'Just get us the coffees,' suggested Mario.

As Elsie went off towards the counter, two people stepped out of the booth at the far end. The young man stopped to pay the waitress but the girl began to walk towards the door. Mario brightened as he recognized her.

'Hey! Letty! Hi there, baby!'

'Hello, Mario . . . Elmer.'

'Ain't this a coincidence!' exclaimed Mario, slapping the top of the table with a hand. I was just looking for you. Here I am with a pass – and nobody to make it at. So I asked myself, who's the cutest gal in town? And the answer came up – Letty!'

She was flattered enough by this to giggle. Peter now joined them and nodded to the two Americans.

'You remember my brother, Peter,' she said.

'Oh sure. The big bandleader,' cackled Mario.

'Hi, kid.' said Elmer.

'So it's okay, Letty? We have a date?'

'A date – with you, Mario?'

'Sure. We'll go take a walk, or do whatever else passes for amusement in this metropolis.'

'But I already have a date,' she explained, embarrassed to have to speak about it in front of Peter. 'I'm meeting Harv . . . I'm meeting somebody else later on.'

'Yeah, okay. I'll be around . . .'

Mario tried to shrug off the rejection but when Letty went out with Peter, the charms of the Empire Cafe disappeared for him and he announced that they were leaving. At that moment, Elsie arrived with two coffees and a plate which bore a single dry tea biscuit. Elmer was moved.

'Hey, look, Mario! It's a cookie!'

When they finally came out of the cafe, they mooched around for a while and then began to cycle slowly back towards the Air Base. They had found Market Wetherby at its quietest and were both feeling distinctly let down by the lack of excitement. Then they saw her.

'Get a load of that!' Mario said with a whistle.

Pat Dereham was climbing over a wooden gate, revealing a pair of long, shapely, silk stockinged legs as her skirt rode up. While the men were seeing a great deal of her, she did not even notice them. Her mind was still on the battle she was having with her mother over her decision to give up her studies at Cambridge. Helen had been shaken when her daughter had arrived home the previous night and Pat knew that her father would be equally hurt by her decision.

'Hi!' called Mario.

'Oh,' she said, seeing them leaning on the handlebars of their bicycles and grinning at her. 'Good afternoon . . . Are you out for a ride?'

'Just cruising around and admiring the scenery,' explained Mario, glancing at her legs again. 'I'm Mario. Mario Bottone. One of the Brooklyn Bottones. This here's my buddy, Elmer.'

'Pleased to meet you,' said Elmer, goggling.

'How do you do?' she replied. 'My name's Pat.'

'I don't believe it! Pat! That's my favourite name!'

'Hey, I didn't know that, Mario,' grunted Elmer.

'I'm sure I've seen you somewhere before,' continued Mario, ignoring his companion. 'I never forget a . . . face.'

'Perhaps it was at the Welcome Dance.'

'That's it, honey! The Dance!' Encouraged by her smile, he pushed his bicycle a little closer. 'You work here?'

'Not officially. I may help out on the land for a while.'

'It's a swell place, Pat! I'd be tickled to show you the sights!'

'I know this part of the world quite well, actually. I live here.'

'Oh.' Mario's expression changed. 'Then I guess you've already met some of the guys from the Base?'

'One or two.'

'Yeah? Who were they?'

'Colonel Krasnowici and Major Kiley. They came out to the house for drinks.' She could not understand why Mario backed away and Elmer opened his mouth in horror. 'You probably know them.'

'The Colonel and Major . . . oh yeah. Wonderful human beings,' said Mario, back in the saddle now. 'I hope you'll excuse us, lady. We gotta move. Duty calls. Come on, Elmer.'

'Bye now,' said Elmer, touching his cap to her.

They cycled back to the Air Base as quickly as they could, only to find the owners of their respective bicycles waiting for them with some straight questions. The trip into Market Wetherby had been a failed mission in every sense.


McGraw heard the scream and acted instantly. He had been walking past the pond where Betty was playing with her stick, poking it into the water and jiggling it about to create ripples. Evidently, the girl had slipped and fallen in. McGraw had hauled her out in a matter of seconds. Though it was shallow near the bank and only her feet had got really wet, Betty was whimpering and shaking. He took a packet of chewing gum from his pocket, peeled the silver paper off one stick of it and then popped it gently into her mouth. The crying stopped at once and she began to get over the shock of the splash into the water. Sally Bilton could now be heard in the distance, calling her daughter's name. There was enough anxiety in her voice to make McGraw pick up the girl and strike off in her direction. After calming her mother, McGraw told Betty to go into the cottage and take off her wet shoes. The girl scampered off happily.

'She'd never do that for me,' confessed Sally as her daughter vanished into the cottage.

They walked back slowly together and had reached the front gate before he spoke again. His voice was flat and non-committal.

'I'm sorry you didn't get that job at the Base.'

'They said they'd taken on everyone they needed. I wanted laundry work or something, but they send it out to . . . civilian contractors.'

'I know . . . Your husband's in tanks, that right?'

'Yes.'

'Enlisted man?'

'He's a corporal,' she replied, not understanding.

'Must be tough on your own with two kids.'

'We have Stan's – my husband – we have his mother staying here.'

'That make it easier?'

'Twice as hard!' she confessed with a rather desperate laugh. 'Anyway, thanks again, Mr . . .'

'McGraw.'

'Would you like to come in?'

'No, thanks. I have to get back. Take care now.' He walked away and then stopped. 'This summer, you teach her how to swim.'

Sally Bilton watched him go, more puzzled then ever.


Vera Mundy was coming to the end of a long, hot, tiring afternoon in the shop and looking forward to closing time. Albert had slipped out and Letty, supposedly there to assist her, had been too abstracted to be of much use, so Vera had taken the full weight of the work alone. She served the two garrulous women with their groceries and then turned wearily to the last customer in the shop, a thin, sharp-faced, nattily-dressed man in his early thirties.

Vera could not see his face under the snap-brim hat but she noticed the rather garish tie and the flashy tiepin.

'Yes, sir?'

'I'll have two dozen eggs, six pounds of sugar and as much jam as you can spare,' said the glib Cockney voice, adding, as Vera stared at him in amazement, 'And a big kiss!'

'Sid!' She had simply not recognized him at first.

'Large as life, Vera, me old love.' He winked at Letty as she came up behind the counter to stare at him. 'Husband in?'

'No,' said Vera, still trying to accommodate the surprise. 'Albert's at a Civil Defence meeting. He takes it all very serious . . . But what brings you down here?'

'Where else would I come, if not to my own sister? It's what families are for, innit?'

A shadow of anxiety passed across Vera's mind as she thought of some of the possible reasons that had brought Sid Davis to Market Wetherby. He seemed to read her mind at once.

'Nothing like that, Vera. I been bombed out. Nowhere to go. Thought, p'raps, you'd put me up for a week or two.'

'You weren't hurt, were you, Sid?'

'Only a scratch or two,' he lied, playing on the sympathy he had always been able to find in his sister. 'So, is it on? Can I stay?'

'Well, if it was only up to me . . .' The problem brought a frown to her face. 'You'd have to speak to Albert.'

'Natch. I'll wait.' He winked at Letty again.

'Don't you know who this is?' asked Vera, putting an arm around her daughter's shoulders. 'It's Letty. Letty, this is your Uncle Sid.'

'Pleased to meet you,' she said, shyly.

'Letty? Little Letty? But the last time I saw her was . . . ten, eleven years ago. You've changed, darling. Well, well, well . . .'

'She's nearly eighteen now, Sid.'

'And pretty as a picture,' he said, rolling his eyes at his niece with avuncular lechery. 'Bet she's good for business. Yes, and I'm sure she's having a rare old time with all these Yanks!'

'Oh, Letty's not interested,' said Vera, though the colour that had come to her daughter's cheeks suggested otherwise. 'Anyway, we shall be shutting up soon. Letty, why don't you take your Uncle Sid through to the back room? I'll be through myself directly . . .'

An hour later, settled into Albert Mundy's chair by the fireplace, Sid was making his sister and his niece shake with laughter as he boasted about a few of the experiences that had coloured his recent existence. His cheeky wit and his plausibility made Vera forget some of his past faults and she was almost persuaded that she was glad to see him again. Letty, still young and willing to believe the idea of living and working in London possessed a glamour that had always attracted her, was thrilled simply to hear her uncle's easy references to famous parts of the capital. Sid actually managed to make her take her mind off Harvey for a while.

Peter Mundy, when he came home from school, was less ready to be taken in by the newcomer. Aware of this, Sid tried again and again to ingratiate himself with the boy but somehow could not manage it. He began to get irritated.

'I can't get over you still being a schoolkid, Peter.'

'I leave this year.'

'And what, then? Army, is it?'

'Maybe . . .'

'It's a wonderful life, Peter.'

'I see you didn't join up,' observed his nephew, tartly.

'Not for want of trying, mate,' retorted Sid, his face a study in disappointment. 'I was dying to do my bit. Had medical after medical, but they just wouldn't take me. I've got these feet – fallen arches. Big blow. Still haven't got over it.'

'And what do you do instead?' asked Peter.

'This and that,' replied Sid, evasively. He turned away from Peter and gazed down at Letty's legs until she grew embarrassed and tugged down her skirt. 'Forgive me staring, love, but I couldn't help noticing that you paint your legs.'

'A lot of us do, Sid,' said Vera, defensively. 'You can't get stockings these days.'

'Not down here, maybe . . .'

He reached for one of his cases which were standing beside the chair. Taking care not to let any of them see inside, he opened it and pulled out a pair of nylons, tossing them to Letty with a seedy benevolence. As her jaw fell and she examined the gift, Sid produced another pair and handed them to Vera.

'For special occasions. The latest thing from the United States. Nylons!'

Both women were so overjoyed that they let out shrieks of joy and thanked him profusely. Albert Mundy, who walked in on all the excitement, wanted to know what was going on.

'It's Sid,' explained Vera. 'My brother, Sid.'

'I'm not a fool, Vera. What's he doing here?'

Sid reacted to his brother-in-law's aggressive, unwelcoming, who's-been-sitting-in-my-chair tone by weakening his own voice and rubbing his right thigh. 'You'll excuse me not getting up, Albert,' he said, 'but it's my leg.'

'What's wrong with it?'

'Bit stiff, that's all. But getting stronger. I can at least walk on it properly now.'

'You injured it?' asked Albert, only half-believing it all.

'We wasn't expecting the air raid, you see. I didn't make it to the shelter.'

'Sid was bombed out,' Vera added, quickly. 'He lost everything. I said we . . . we could put him up for a while.'

'Here?' Albert was appalled. 'For how long?'

'Only for a week or so. Just till I get over it. Of course, if it's not convenient . . .'

He hauled himself to his feet and limped a step towards

Albert, who was very much aware of being watched by all the other members of the family. Grudgingly and totally against his own wishes, Albert said that Sid could stay a week. Vera thanked her husband with a kiss, then told Sid that he would have to share a room with Peter.

'Anywhere, Vera. You know me – I'll fit in. And don't worry, Albert, old son. I won't be no trouble to you . . .'


The formation was flying overhead once again and the combined noise of the engines was deafening. Pat Dereham seemed undisturbed by it as she stood in the middle of the lawn and gazed up. Helen came out, her hands over her ears and waited until the multiple roar had subsided. Pat told her that the B-17s had been taking part in a series of training flights designed to teach the pilots how to stay in a tight and well-defended formation.

'You seem to know a lot about it, darling.'

'I don't, but Rosie does. She hears all the gossip from the Air Base. Rosie says the men complain like made about how hard they're being pushed. They come into the pub and have a few drinks then cry on her shoulder about Major Kiley.'

'Major Kiley?' The name could still unsettle her.

'They all think he's a slave-driver, apparently. Rosie says—'

'And what else have you done today, Pat?' interrupted her mother, anxious to divert the conversation. 'Apart from listening to Rosie, that is.'

'Nothing, I suppose. Been bored out of my mind.'

'Poor darling!' sympathized Helen. 'Though it's your own fault. If you'd stayed at Cambridge . . .'

'*Please.* We've been over all that.'

'All right,' sighed her mother.

They strolled across the lawn to the flowerbeds. Pat was talking about joining the WAAFS but there was clearly something else on her mind. Eventually, she worked back around to it.

'Although they hate him, they all say he's a brilliant pilot. Jim Kiley, I mean. He actually takes the lead plane himself and teaches them up there, where it matters. He was at the front of that formation that went past earlier on.'

Helen Dereham began to understand the reason why her daughter had come back to Market Wetherby.

# CHAPTER SEVEN

Chuck Ericson lay on his bunk and pretended to read a paperback novel. Mario Bottone and Elmer Jones, spruce and jaunty in their best uniforms, took it in turns with the clothes brush and did all they could to persuade Chuck to join them for an evening on the town. Inwardly, their flight engineer was desperate to go in the hope of spending some time with Vi Blair again, but something was holding him back like a steel hand. He told the others that he was in no mood for company and returned to his book.

The door opened and Hymie Stutz came in to confront them.

'You guys on pass?'

'What's it to you, Stutzie?' asked Mario.

'If you go to that pub, you leave Rosie alone. You hear?'

'Get lost, midget!' sneered Mario.

'Yeah – beat it!' said Elmer.

'I'm warning you, Bottone – you, too, Jones. She's my girl. If either of you so much as lay a finger on Rosie . . .'

But Hymie was addressing thin air. The two friends had pushed past him and left. He stamped his foot in exasperation and then strutted out himself.

Chuck now got up off his bunk, flung his book down and opened his locker. He took out his uniform and held it at arm's length, trying to summon up the will-power to put it on. But it was in vain. He hooked the uniform back on its rail and then threw himself once more on his bunk, closing his eyes tightly as if in pain.

Mario and Elmer, meanwhile determined to make this outing more successful than their last, sat in the back of a truck with all the other men on six-hour passes and reviewed the possibilities. When the truck dropped them off in the town square, the two men headed straight for the

Empire Cafe. Mario found what he was looking for and waved a hand familiarly.

'Hi, Doll!'

'Hello . . .'

Letty Mundy was sitting in one of the booths with her brother and her uncle. As the two Americans squeezed in beside her, she performed the introductions.

'This is Mario and Elmer – my Uncle Sid.'

'Sid Davis. Glad to know you, boys,' he said, assessing them quickly.

'How do you do, sir?' said Elmer.

'Yeah, hi,' added Mario, more interested in talking to Letty. 'Well, is this it, baby? Is tonight our night?' He took her hesitation as a sign of encouragement and leaned in close. 'Okay, I know you gotta work at the movie house first, but what do you say? Shall I pick you up after the show?'

Before she could reply, Harvey Wallis came into the cafe and strolled over to the booth. Letty's face brightened and she stood up involuntarily, causing Mario to move back.

'Hi, troops,' said Harvey, pleasantly.

'Lieutenant,' muttered Mario, nodding.

'What you doing here?' asked Elmer, innocently.

'Time we went, I reckon,' said Harvey.

Before the astonished faces of the two Americans, Letty got up from her seat, edged past the others and then went out of the cafe holding hands with Harvey. Sid was pleased that he had been right in his assumptions about his niece's private life.

'That the boyfriend?'

'Looks like it,' grunted Mario.

'Fancy her yourself, do you?' asked Sid, grinning.

Peter Mundy was starting to feel more and more uncomfortable.

'There is no truth in the rumours,' said Mario, recovering his good humour. 'We are just good friends.'

'Well, I must be off,' said Peter over the laughter.

'Where to?' Sid wondered.

93

'Band practice at the Hall.'

'Can I come with you?' asked Elmer. He saw Peter's surprise. 'I play a bit myself. I'd like to sit in. If it's okay?'

'I suppose so . . .'

'See you at The Plough later on, Mario,' said Elmer and went out of the cafe with the young pianist.

Mario Bottone sighed. The evening, which had looked so rich and promising when they were in the back of the truck, had got off to a rather depressing start. Sid could sense his disappointment.

'You've been deserted, old son. Did my niece stand you up?'

'Not really.'

'Be wasting your time there, anyway. She's a good girl. And too young for it.' He indicated the coffee which Letty had left behind her. 'She hasn't touched her drink.'

'Don't blame her.'

'You have it, Mario. Go on.'

Mario sipped the coffee and pulled a face. Sid then took a hipflask out and unscrewed the top. He poured some of the contents into Mario's cup and then into his own.

'Here, I wouldn't waste this on the others. If we was in London now, Mario, I could introduce you to some friends of mine and there'd be some real action.'

'I bet,' said Mario. 'From London, are you, then? Thought you didn't look like a local guy.'

'Oh, I came from round here, originally. But it's a bit tame for me – know what I mean? I moved down to the Big Smoke as soon as I reached the age of discretion. That's where it all happens!'

'Yeah!' Mario recognized a kindred spirit.

'You know, I think we're going to get along just fine, Mario.' He lifted his cup. 'Cheers, mate!'

They toasted each other amiably, neither yet realizing how important their chance meeting at the Empire Cafe had been.

*

In the first few weeks that Letty Mundy had worked at The Roxy as an usherette she had had to be reprimanded by the manager more than once for not concentrating on her job. Letty had been so entranced by what was happening on the screen she stood in the middle of the aisle staring up at it when she should have been showing patrons to their seats. Since Harvey Wallis had come into her life, however, she was not so easily diverted by the lush escapism of the current film. It seemed to her that her handsome lieutenant had just stepped off a Hollywood set himself and that she was now involved in a real-life romance with one of her favourite stars. If she was reprimanded now, it was for day-dreaming in the darkness at the rear of the stalls.

After leaving the cafe and working her evening shift at the cinema that night, Letty had rushed out to find Harvey waiting for her and had flung herself into his arms. They had walked down by the river again and found a secluded spot among the bushes. They had lost all track of time.

When Harvey had eventually brought her back home and given her a last, lingering kiss, they had both under-stood just how deeply involved they were. Letty was almost shining with pleasure as she tripped in through the back door. Albert Mundy took the smile off her face at once.

'What time of night do you call this?' he demanded, furious that she had disobeyed his order to come straight back from the cinema when it closed.

'I didn't know it was so late, Dad.'

'Well, you're back now, dear,' said Vera, conciliatory as always. 'Better go to bed now.'

'Not till she tells us where's she's been.'

'Back to the cafe . . .'

'You're lying, my girl. Your uncle was there all night and he didn't see you.' He advanced on her, his temper rising even higher. 'You were with one of them, weren't you?'

'We only went for a walk,' she confessed.

'A . . . a walk!' Albert seemed on the point of spontaneous combustion. 'After you were attacked by one of them! Didn't that teach you what they were like?'

Letty had still not told her father the truth about the supposed assault. She was now beginning to wish she had not admitted that she had been for a walk. Her mother looked alarmed, torn between defending her daughter and discovering the truth.

'Were you *alone* with him?'

'Well . . .'

'I'm sure you weren't, Letty,' said Vera, hinting gently.

'No! No, there were four or five of us.'

'Who else was there?' pressed Albert.

'Rosie . . . Rosie Blair. And Vi, her sister, Vi. I met them. They said – come along. To the bridge and back.'

Letty had seized on the names of the two girls that her father would be unable to check upon because of his feud with Jack Blair. A glance across at Vera told her that she had her mother on her side. Vera touched her husband's arm.

'If it was all just a bit of fun, Albert . . .'

'Fun! Fun! Mixing with the likes of them after what I've said! I ought to take my belt to you, my girl!'

'No!' protested Vera.

'It's not fair, it's not fair,' cried Letty, breaking down and letting the tears flow.

'You keep away from those damn Blair tarts, do you hear? Or I'll do more than give you a leathering. They're corrupt, those girls! That father of theirs lets them run wild. If you so much as speak to either of them again . . .'

Letty's crying had taken on a note of hysteria and she was trembling all over. Vera was beside her, trying to comfort her and Albert could see that his words were having no effect. With a final, terrible warning, he sent his daughter off to bed. But he had very little sleep that night.

Early next morning, still in her nightdress, Letty was standing at the back door of the house and searching the sky with her eyes and her ears. Peter, in pyjamas and dressing gown, came up behind her, surprised to find her up.

'What are you doing, Letty?'

'They'll be taking off about now . . .'

'Come back inside,' he advised.

'It's not a training flight today. It's a mission. But not a dangerous one. They call it a milk run.' She was trying to reassure herself. 'It's a place they've been to before so they know what to expect. No real danger. They drop their bombs as if they're delivering the milk. Then come back safely.'

'If Dad catches you out here . . .'

Letty nodded and followed him back into the house, starting to shiver. She knelt down at the gas fire and lit it with a match. Peter opened the curtains and raised the blackout blinds. Then he came and sat over by his sister.

'Heard him shouting at you last night. Was it bad?'

'Horrible.'

'Uncle Sid just laughed. Honestly, I could have kicked him! He can't leave soon enough for me.' He checked to see that they could not be overheard. 'It was Harvey, wasn't it?'

'Yes.'

'Well, don't ever admit it to Dad. You know him. The sight of an American uniform is like a red rag to a bull for him.'

'I hate him!' she said.

'He means it all for the best, Letty. He's just trying to protect you . . . Fancy a cuppa?'

'Please.'

Peter found the kettle and filled it under the cold tap. It was soon warming over the central ring of the gas stove. He turned back to Letty in time to see her holding her stomach and wobbling slightly as if having an attack of vertigo.

'Are you all right?'

'Fine,' she said, recovering. 'I just felt funny for a moment.'

'It was standing at the back door like that. You'll catch your death of cold.' They sat down opposite each other. 'You'll have to watch it from now on, Letty. He'll have his eye on you.'

'He won't stop me seeing Harvey.'

'It's going to be difficult,' he pointed out, gently.

'He won't stop me! Nor you! Nobody will!'

'I'm only trying to help,' he said, 'which is what I've done so far, isn't it? I mean, I'll cover as much as I can. But Dad is very suspicious. He sees wrong in everything . . . Letty, it can't be *that* important.'

'It is to me.'

'But you've been out with half a dozen of them.'

'This one is special. I love him.' Defiance hardened her face. 'And he loves me!'

'I've . . . I've never been in love,' he mumbled, embarrassed. 'I don't know what it's like. But I do know it's something special – and you have to be really sure.'

'I am sure, Peter.'

'But how?'

'I'm . . . going to have his baby.'

Letty was almost as shocked as her brother now that she had actually put it into words. For a moment she did not even hear the mounting rumble as the planes began to fly overhead.


The 'Ginger Rogers' left the English coastline behind and flew out across a dark and choppy sea. Its crew were tense but confident and even had a moment to think about other things. Mario Bottone was remembering the long and profitable chat with Sid Davis which had made the trip into Market Wetherby so worthwhile. Elmer Jones was still overjoyed at the thought that Rosie Blair had finally agreed to go out with him and there was the added bonus that it would be a body-blow for the possessive Hymie

Stutz. High up in the top turret, Chuck Ericson recalled the good wishes that had been sent back to him from Vi Blair and wished that he had taken the opportunity to see her the previous evening. Harvey Wallis, having checked his guns as soon as they were over the water, now reviewed the decision that he had taken with the advice of his captain. It was a mistake to allow himself to get too emotionally entangled with Letty and he accepted that he had to end the relationship. He would explain it to her when he got back.

Red Burwash warned his crew to put on their oxygen masks because he was taking the 'Ginger Rogers' up to a higher altitude. Unlike Red and his co-pilot, the others had no heating in their compartments and they had zipped themselves into their heavy, cumbersome leather and sheepwool flying jackets. The thick gloves that they wore made it difficult to operate the delicate machinery before them, but at 17,000 feet – their present altitude – the temperature was twenty degrees below zero and so the gloves were essential. They all knew that if they were hit by shrapnel at this height, the blood that spurted out of them would freeze the instant it reached the cold air.

The 'Ginger Rogers' was at the heart of a formation that kept tight and true. Major Jim Kiley had told them time and again that their survival depended on their proximity to the B-17s all around them. The stragglers became the main targets for enemy fighters, and they were now heeding that warning. The planes and their full bomb-loads were still over the sea when the P 47s arrived on time at the rendezvous to provide fighter cover to the target and back.

From his position in the nose compartment, Harvey Wallis could see the coastline of Belgium ahead and far below. The command would soon come for the formation to climb higher, out of range of the flak fields which reached 17,000 feet. Weather conditions were perfect for the bombers and there was no heavy cloud to stop them flying at their optimum height of 23,000 feet. Harvey knew that many of the German fighters that would try to intercept them were at their best at a lower altitude and the floor stipulation of the B-17s was thus another significant safety factor. It was still daylight bombing with all the dangers that that policy implied, but the Americans had learned from experience and certain risks had been lessened. As the 'Ginger Rogers' soared over enemy-occupied territory, therefore, Harvey Wallis felt secure, untroubled and in control of his particular duties.

It was just another milk run.


Sally Bilton's cottage was a small, neat but unattractive Victorian building of light-coloured brick. The line in the front garden was pegged with washing and a child's tricycle stood on the path. McGraw overcame some last-minute doubts and knocked on the front door. It was opened by Sally herself, hair tousled, old dress covered by an apron, face looking harassed after a row with her mother-in-law about the latter's fondness for too much sugar in her tea.

'Hi, Mrs Bilton. Could I have a word?'

'Oh. Yes. Come in.'

McGraw stepped into the narrow hall and followed her into the living room which was small but tidy. Sally's mother-in-law, a lazy, nosy, feckless widow in her late fifties, was at the table finishing off the remains of a frugal lunch. Ruby Bilton was not at all pleased when an American serviceman walked in and she shot an accusing glance at her daughter-in-law.

'Good day, ma'am,' said McGraw.

'This is my mother-in-law, Mrs Bilton . . . Sergeant McGraw.'

'Master Sergeant,' he corrected.

'Oh yes?' Ruby was watching him like a hawk.

Nervous and embarrassed, Sally now picked up her son who was toddling around her legs. McGraw greeted him and asked where his sister was. He could sense that Ruby was reacting unfavourably to his obvious friendship with

Sally and her children so he came straight to the point of his visit.

'That job at the Base. I had an idea. All the laundry's sent out to a contractor.'

'Yes.'

'Well, it takes ten days or so to come back. Now, my boys on ground crew, they get their fatigues in one heck of a state – mud, grease, oil, the lot. We need someone to take care of 'em, more on the spot, kind of.'

'You mean, you want me to do it?' asked Sally, surprised.

'That's the idea.'

'How many things would there be?'

'Thirty, maybe forty sets of fatigues – once or twice a week.' He glanced around dubiously. 'Could you handle that here?'

'Oh, yes. We have a boiler out the scullery and – it would be all right, wouldn't it, Ma?'

'You'd be paying for it?' said Ruby, still suspicious.

'Well, sure. Whatever's the going rate. Look, you'd probably like to think about it.'

'Oh, no,' replied Sally, anxious to accept the offer. 'I'm used to greasy overalls.'

'My son, Stan – her husband – is a motor mechanic.'

McGraw nodded and took in the photograph on the mantelpiece of the man in khaki battledress. He guessed that Stan Bilton was in his early thirties.

'I . . . I don't know how I'd get the soap and stuff I need,' said Sally, worried by the problem.

'No sweat. We can get it from the Base. Whatever you want.'

'Wonderful . . . When do I start?'

'I'll send a coupla guys over tomorrow, if that's okay.' He saw the gratitude in her face. 'And don't thank me – you'll be doing us a favour.'

There was an awkward silence and then she offered him a cup of tea. Mindful of all the work he would have when the bombers returned, McGraw told her that he had to go. He said goodbye to the watchful Ruby, ruffled the boy's hair playfully and then went out into the hall. Sally went with him and saw him out. She was thrilled at the offer. She was finding it a real struggle to feed four mouths on what she had of her husband's pay. Money from some laundry work would be a godsend to her and she was not at all concerned about the effort involved. She came back into the living room with the sort of smile she thought she had forgotten how to wear.

'Isn't it marvellous, Ma!'

'Have to wait and see, won't we? I know one thing — you'll have your work cut out.'

Sally Bilton could see that she could expect no help from Ruby. Somehow it did not seem to matter.

They had been standing on the control tower for a long time, scanning the skies with binoculars and checking their watches. When the distant drone of the returning aircraft was first heard, they fell silent. A captain came out with the news that the formation was returning intact. Although the bombers had met stronger resistance than they had anticipated around the target area, all bomb-loads had been dropped according to plan and the full complement of B-17s was coming home safe and sound. Whoops of joy greeted this news and Rufus, aware of where much of the credit should go, immediately praised Jim Kiley. His rigorous training methods were starting to pay dividends in every way.

McGraw had his crews standing by as the planes began to land and taxi to their hard-stands. Some had taken a lot of punishment and there was plenty of repair work ahead, but none of the aircraft had any problems coming in safely. Rufus and Jim watched each one, proud, reassured and extremely relieved. Then the 'Ginger Rogers' started its approach to the runway, dropping a lurid red flare as it did so. Jim Kiley saw the warning.

'Wounded!'

'Meat wagon!' yelled Rufus, and an ambulance began rolling within seconds. 'Let's get over there, Jim.'

As soon as the 'Ginger Rogers' touched down, they could see the damage to the nose compartment and the fuselage. Fire trucks and two ambulances were standing by as the plane finally shut down its engines and stood there wounded and bleeding. The jeep arrived just as Red Burwash was lowering himself onto the tarmac. He was exhausted.

'You all right?' asked Rufus.

'Yeah.'

'What happened?' said Jim, assessing the damage.

'A Focke-Wulf tailed us most of the way back, out of range. Just as we reached Dungeness, he made a run at us – right through the formation.'

'You got him?'

'He got Eddie, my bombardier.'

'Anyone else?' asked Jim.

'Lieutenant Wallis, the navigator . . . he's in bad shape. And one of our waist gunners.'

Medics were starting to bring the wounded men out of the plane. Both Mario and Elmer went to help the men lowering the flexible stretcher into which Harvey was strapped. Blood covered his chest and he was wincing with agony as they set him down on the concrete. Red Burwash and Jim Kiley crouched down beside him. Red began muttering to himself.

'Crazy son-of-a-bitch . . . talking about this dame all the way there. He was gonna break it off – he wasn't gonna break it off! He just couldn't make up his mind.'

'You'll be all right, son,' promised Rufus.

Harvey opened his eyes then made an effort to speak.

'He wants a cigarette,' said Jim.

Mario lit one up at once and passed it to Red, who held it out in turn to the prostrate man.

'Thanks, Red . . .' whispered Harvey.

As his lips shaped to take the cigarette, his body suddenly went limp, his head fell sideways. Red Burwash stared down at the dead man for a long time before saying anything.

'Crazy son-of-a-bitch . . .'


Sid Davis was telling his usual tales of business successes in London and Vera was letting herself be quite impressed. Peter, however, was not hearing a word of it. His mind was still fully occupied by the news that his sister had given him early that morning. He had been so confused that he had sought advice from the one person he could trust in the town – Jack Blair – and he had been given what he thought was sound advice. Unfortunately, Letty had not been interested in that advice when it was passed on to her. So while Sid boasted away and Vera listened, Peter was in a torment of worry.

'Here she is, then!' said Sid.

Letty had made great efforts to look her best. Harvey would be back soon, and it was the least she could do. She had washed her hair and put it up, then taken extra care with her make-up. Sid was impressed enough to whistle.

The telephone rang from the shop and Letty looked up eagerly. It *had* to be for her. Peter went to answer it and called for Sid. Letty's face dropped. While Sid was on the telephone, Peter came back into the room and gave his sister an apologetic shrug. Vera caught the signal and looked ahead at what would follow if Letty's evening went according to plan.

'You can't go out, Letty. Not after what your father said last night. It's madness. He'll go berserk when he finds out – and I'll get the worst of it, not you!' She was irritated further by Letty's silence. 'You don't care, do you!'

'I'm going out,' said Letty, quietly, 'and I'm going to see . . . who I'm going to see, and *nobody* is going to stop me.'

Vera found herself pulled both ways at once yet again. Before she could decide what to say, Sid came in with a troubled expression.

'It was Mario.'

'Mario?' repeated Letty.

'I was supposed to meet him at the pub. Can't come. Spot of bad luck. Two of their chaps got killed today.' Sid hesitated but Letty had heard the name before it was spoken. Her heart tightened and denial screamed inside her head. 'Just when they thought they was home. The bombardier and – and that Harvey feller. You know.'

Sid's casual announcement of the news only strengthened the impact. Letty began to sway, then stare straight ahead, then look up hopelessly towards the sky. Then she rushed out into the garden. Vera made to follow her but Peter stopped her gently with an arm.

Outside, looking upwards again as the drizzle began to fall on her face, Letty Mundy mourned the death of Harvey Wallis and her mouth opened in a long, despairing, silent cry.

# CHAPTER EIGHT

Rosie Blair's face could not keep secrets. When she answered the door at Dereham House and saw him standing there in uniform, her mouth gaped, her eyebrows soared and her cheeks ripened to the colour of tomatoes. She invited him into the hall then scurried into the sitting room. Helen was still at the desk with a pen in her hand.

'It's 'im, M'm,' Rosie whispered.

'Who?'

'The one I was telling you about. That drives all the boys at the Base so hard. The one they can't stand. Major Kiley.'

'Here?' Helen was surprised. 'Well, you'd better show him in.'

Rosie went out and Helen immediately got to her feet to smooth down her dress and glance at herself in the mirror. She had had time to compose her features before Jim Kiley came in.

'Good day, Mrs Dereham.'

'Major,' she replied.

'I hope you'll forgive me for dropping in like this, without telephoning first.'

'I was just writing to my husband,' she said, then wondered why she had told him.

'Oh, yes. How is Major Dereham?'

'He's fine, thank you.'

'That was quite a show they put up in Tunisia. Important victory.'

'Yes.'

'And your daughter – Pat?'

'Also very well, thank you.'

Jim was ill at ease and not helped by the direct, questioning look she was giving him. He shifted his feet.

'Is there something I can do for you?' she asked.

'Both the Colonel and I feel very badly about not having thanked you properly for your hospitality, and for not having made any attempt to repay it.'

'I told you that wasn't necessary, Major.'

'Nevertheless, we have been remiss. We have also neglected the Goodwill Committee.'

'That was formed largely to welcome your men to Market Wetherby. It is now more or less discontinued.'

'Exactly.'

Jim was looking and feeling more uncomfortable than ever. It had not been his idea to contact Helen and he was only there now because Rufus had insisted. His discomfort was greatly increased by the ambivalent feelings he had towards Helen herself. He was grateful when she invited him to sit down.

'I'll level with you, Mrs Dereham. We are facing a situation of friction between our Base and your community.'

'I don't think it's all one-sided.'

'I'll be the first to admit that. You can't expect the arrival of thousands of foreign soldiers and airmen – what amounts to an invasion force, in fact – not to cause an upheaval. But there are ways to lessen the tension. We want everything to go as smoothly as possible while we're here.'

'Naturally. So do we.'

'Now, most of the time, everything's fine. But there are areas, social areas, where there is friction. Only a few incidents yet, but they are on the increase.'

'So I understand, Major. But how can I help?'

'You have a lot of influence, Mrs Dereham. People round here all seem to look up to you. We would like your co-operation, and that of your committee, to find ways to defuse the situation before it gets out of hand.'

'We're happy to do what we can,' she said, evenly. 'Yet I should point out that the officer your Colonel delegated to liaise with us did not even bother to attend our meetings.'

'I'll make sure you get someone else.'

'If he could also inform us of any specific cases of complaint your men have at their treatment or reception locally, it would be of value.'

'We'll discuss the whole thing fully and let's hope that between us we can come up with some constructive suggestions.' He was on his feet again. 'Well, that's about it, I guess. Thanks for seeing me, Mrs Dereham . . .'

'Not at all.'

'That just about covers all I came for,' he said, starting to move towards the door. Then he stopped and muttered to himself. 'Hell, no, that's not all I came for.' He swung round to face her. 'It's a while since we talked, and I keep thinking we kind of got off on the wrong footing.'

'I'm sorry. I don't follow you.'

'You and me. We – well, to some extent, we have to work together and see each other because of the hospital and so on. Can't we be a bit easier on ourselves? I mean – isn't it about time we buried the hatchet?'

'I wasn't aware of any . . . unpleasantness between us, Major.'

She stiffened automatically when he smiled at her. It was her only defence when her feelings were so uncertain.

'No, not exactly,' he continued, the smile broadening. 'But when we first met, I thought, here's someone I could get to like. And I had the impression that maybe you thought the same about me.' He paused for a reply that did not come. 'What I'm saying is that we haven't had a chance to get to know each other. Whenever we've met, it's formal or in a hurry or in passing.'

'I still don't follow you.'

'I'm asking you to have dinner with me – a drink at least. Somewhere we can just be ourselves.'

'I'm afraid that wouldn't be possible,' she said, rather too primly.

'You mean, not at the moment?'

'I mean, not ever. It's out of the question – although, of course, I am perfectly willing to work with you whenever the occasion arises. I fail to see, in any case, how relations between us could affect the matters we have been discussing.'

'You're right, of course,' he agreed, uncomfortable again. 'They don't come into it, do they?'

He thanked her and was shown to the door. Helen watched him drive away and then heard Pat coming downstairs rather hastily. She was patently disappointed.

'Why didn't you call me?' she asked.

'The Major was only here on business.'

'You should have let me know.'

'It never occurred to me, Pat,' she said, leading the way back into the sitting room. 'I thought you'd got over all that.'

'Well, I have,' replied Pat with a laugh. 'I had a silly crush for a couple of days. Nothing more.'

'Thank heavens!'

'Still, I do like him. It's a pity to miss him.'

'Well, I'm sorry, Pat. I think it's most unlikely that he'll be back.'

Helen sat down at the desk again and picked up her pen. She had only written a few words on the flimsy paper when she began to be nudged by guilt about the way she had dealt with Jim Kiley.

Pat had moved to the window but his car was out of sight.


The arrangement with Sally Bilton was working out extremely well. Grimy fatigues were washed, ironed and returned in half the time that it took the civilian contractors who handled the bulk of the laundry for the Base. McGraw was pleased with the results though his face never showed it. One bonus of his visits was that he brought chocolate and candy for the children and seemed to be developing a real friendship with them. Ruby Bilton resented this bitterly, though it did not stop her from helping herself to her share of the children's gifts and from cadging cigarettes from the obliging McGraw. Though she did nothing whatsoever to help with the washing, Ruby nevertheless reserved the right to criticize the way that her daughter-in-law went about it and to urge her to ask for a higher wage. She also kept hinting darkly to Sally that the helpful and amenable McGraw must have ulterior motives. Taking her text from Albert Mundy, the older woman believed that all the Americans were after only one thing, directly or indirectly, and that McGraw would show his hand eventually. Sally took no notice.

'Letty, you'll have to pull yourself together,' said Peter, gently. 'You'll have to think what you're going to do.'

'I can only think about one thing. He's dead . . . Harvey's dead.'

Letty Mundy was hunched up in front of the fire, her face pale and drawn, her large eyes still moist with tears, her hair tousled, her lipstick smudged, her arms wrapped tightly around her. Her whole being was paralysed with grief. Each time that her brother had tried to talk to her about the future, she had either not heard him or she had burst into such a flood of tears that Peter had backed off. He was very conscious that certain decisions could not be put off indefinitely.

'Now don't start crying again. We have to talk.'

'I don't want to.'

'I'm trying to help you!' he pleaded. 'There's the baby to consider. It doesn't show now but in another month or so . . . well, you won't be able to hide it. Then what?'

She shrugged in despair. Peter, a schoolboy forced into a role that most adults would find difficult, advised her that she ought to tell their parents. It was a case of choosing the right moment.

'No!' she said, shocked at the idea.

'Letty—'

'I'd run away first! That's what I'd do.'

'Listen!' he counselled, a hand on her arm. 'What you do is to tell Mum. She won't like it but she'll stand by you. Then you let her tell Dad.'

'He'd kill me!'

'No, he'd shout and yell, maybe. It'd be hell for a time, but he'd accept it. He'd have to.'

'If only Harvey was still alive. Harvey would've faced up to them, told them we'd have got married. Then it would've been all right.'

'You don't know that for sure, Letty,' he pointed out.

The truth of this stunned her for a moment, then she began to cry hysterically again, her fists clenched and her body shaking violently. Peter made some clumsy and ineffective attempts to calm her but had to give up. When the hysteria had passed and the crying had become a series of pitiful sobs, their parents came in from the shop. Albert, in his habitual beige overall with its pencils in the top pocket, was complaining about the shortages that hampered their trade. Vera, in a flowered wrap-around pinafore, was upset because they had been unable to oblige a customer with ingredients for a child's birthday cake. Their conversation had got them to the middle of the room before they noticed Letty.

'Not snivelling again, is she?' said Albert. 'What now?'

'You know, Dad,' said Peter.

'Not blubbering over that damn Yank still! Okay, so he was killed — but there's lots of our boys been killed, too. I've never seen Letty shed so much as a single tear for them!'

Letty got to her feet and ran out quickly, ignoring her father's yell for her to come back. Vera managed to placate her husband a little, but he was still irritable. When Peter said that he was going over to piano practice, his father delivered another attack on his son's hobby and told him that he had to deliver some groceries before he could go to the hall. Protest was squashed viciously and Peter went out, cowed.

It had not been important for the groceries to be delivered that day and Vera said so.

'Do the lad good,' Albert replied. 'Got to learn there's more to life than books and bloody music. High time he learned to pull his weight round here!'

'He's your son, Albert,' she reminded him.

'Don't I know it! Worked my fingers to the bone for both him and Letty, and what do I get for it? Nothing but aggravation. No appreciation. Nothing.'

Vera Mundy had the wisdom not to answer.


The B-17s were flying in tight formation under a bank of thick cloud when the attack came. Fighters from the defence corridor bases in Holland, France and Germany arrived in force to engage the bombers and the whole sky became a clamorous battlefield. Bullets chattered, shells exploded, rockets screamed and smoke poured from a dozen wounds as gunners on both sides claimed their first victims. The speed at which it was all happening was bewildering and it was impossible to assess which side was coming off best. One thing only was certain: the theory that a formation of B-17s was well-nigh impregnable had been dramatically disproved.

When the film came to an end and the spool continued to spin around noisily, nobody in Jim Kiley's office spoke immediately. The jerky, grainy quality of the combat sequence had somehow added to its stark brutality.

'There it is, then,' said Jim, as the blinds were raised to let in the daylight. 'Actual combat film taken by the Photographic Unit during last Tuesday's raid on Düsseldorf.'

'You're going to show that to aircrew?' asked Captain Lester Carson in a voice full of misgivings.

'The pilots and the bombardiers have seen it already,' Jim explained. 'I want everyone to see it, especially incoming personnel.'

'Surely, we're not in the business of scaring them silly before they've had any experience?'

'No, Lester. But we are in the business of preparing them for what to expect.'

'Jim's right,' agreed Rufus. He pointed at the projector. 'That's the closest they'll get to the real thing until they're actually in the middle of it. I want groundcrew to see it, too.'

'Why, sir?' asked Lester.

'There's a lot of resentment, natural enough, I guess, for the guys who're up night after night patching up the ships that the "fancy flyboys" throw around in the air. Do them good to see just what an easy time the "flyboys" have up there.'

Jim Kiley nodded, then picked up the telephone as it started to ring. He talked into it quietly as Rufus continued to press home his point to Lester. When he put the telephone down again, Jim was smiling. The others noticed and their conversation ceased. Jim became aware that they were both watching him.

'Sorry about that. It was Mrs Dereham . . . she's invited me to dinner on Saturday.'

Colonel Rufus Krasnowici had a special look for occasions like this.


It was still early evening but the Empire Cafe was fairly full. Vi Blair had been sitting alone at a table when Pat Dereham had arrived, and although Vi had been in a despondent mood she had managed a smile of welcome and allowed Pat to join her. The two girls sat and talked while a group of British soldiers further down the cafe tried to attract their attention with a whistle and a few, as they thought, bold shafts of wit. Both Pat and Vi studiously ignored them and the men, who were members of a local Ack-Ack Unit, started to complain loudly that the girls of Market Wetherby had no time for them now that the Americans had come to the area.

Seated in one of the booths, Sid Davis looked around to see what the noise was all about but an aggressive stare from one of the men, a sergeant, made him turn back to Letty Mundy. It had taken a present of some new make-up to entice her there and get her out of the house at last, and Sid was proud of this achievement. Though not understanding the full nature of her involvement with Harvey Wallis, he could see that she was in need of comfort, diversion and a lot of cheering up. He had told her more about the glamour of London life and a smile had actually played around her lips when he had suggested that she might go there with him. Letty then remembered her father and knew that he would not allow it, but she thanked her uncle for the invitation, quite unaware of its darker undertones. For all his faults, Sid, with his easy, spivvy patter, had done what Peter had so far failed to do. He had made Letty think about something else.

Her spirits were not revived for long. Mario Bottone and Elmer Jones came into the cafe. When they drifted over to the booth and sat down beside her, Letty felt it all over again. Harvey was dead and all his promises had died with him.

The sight of American uniforms had stirred up the bitterness around one table and the British soldiers were expressing that bitterness audibly. They had even more cause for resentment when a third American entered and went over to join the very two girls who had ignored them so completely.

'Hello, Vi . . .'

'Oh. Hello.'

Chuck Ericson waited until it was clear that she was not going to invite him to sit down. He pulled out a chair and lowered himself into it, his eyes never leaving her. Vi Blair, self-conscious that she was still in her Land Army uniform, brushed back her long, curly blonde hair and mumbled an introduction.

'This is Chuck, Chuck Ericson – Pat Dereham.'

'Hello,' said Pat, receiving a nod in exchange and starting to feel very much in the way.

'Long time no see, Vi,' he said.

'Yes.' Her emotions were in a turmoil. Having spent so long hoping to see him, she was not at all sure that it was what she wanted now. 'I hear you've been busy.'

'Yeah, they keep us at it. The Major doesn't believe in letting us sit around too much.'

'Major Kiley?' asked Pat, at once interested.

'Yeah.' He stared across at Vi again. 'Elmer told me . . . told me you'd been asking.'

'I just wondered how you were,' she said, trying to sound offhand.

'Oh – so so. It's not so easy to get a pass these days. But I got one today. And I was thinking, maybe we could do something.'

'I'm busy – helping Dad out at the pub.'

'How about now?' he suggested. 'We could walk home or something.'

'No, I'm sorry. Pat and I have to go.'

'Well, it's all right,' said Pat, quite at a loss to understand the situation. 'I don't mind if—'

'We must leave now,' interrupted Vi.

There was more than a hint of desperation in her voice. Pat thought it best to go along with what she wanted. They said goodbye to the disappointed Chuck and left the cafe. Even in the street outside, Vi Blair still had the look of a hunted animal, and as she hurried off towards The Plough, she did not seem to notice that Pat Dereham was walking beside her.

Chuck, meanwhile, looked down at the coffee cup that Vi had abandoned and fingered the rim gently. Deeply hurt by her attitude, he nevertheless felt that it was no more then he deserved. For reasons which he still did not grasp properly himself, he had avoided seeing her and she had clearly been wounded. His fear now was that he would never get the chance to explain to her what had really happened to keep him away.

His musing was disturbed by a familiar, rasping voice and he glanced across to the booth opposite.

'Yeah, he was a good scout,' Mario was saying.

'The best!' agreed Elmer, sadly. 'Harvey was just great!'

'He thought a lot about you, Letty,' said Mario. 'In fact—'

'I think I'll have to go, Uncle Sid,' she said, afraid that she would burst into tears again if they kept talking about Harvey in this way. 'Please.'

'It's early yet,' Sid argued.

'I'm sorry. I really must go.'

Sid was annoyed by her request, having already made a prior arrangement with Mario that would keep them both at the Empire Cafe for a while longer yet. Elmer saw Sid's reluctance and offered to walk Letty home himself. He was on his way to pick up Rosie for their evening out so could escort Letty at the same time.

Anxious to get away now that the memories of Harvey had begun to flood back again, Letty thanked Elmer and rose to leave with him. From where the British soldiers were sitting, it appeared that the sexy usherette from The Roxy was being taken off by one of the Americans and they resented it. As Elmer walked past them, one of the men stuck out a leg and tripped him. Elmer went sprawling, much to the amusement of the soldiers.

'Enjoy your trip?' asked the sergeant, grinning.

'What was that for?'

'You want to watch where you're going, fat boy,' warned a corporal.

'Come on, you guys! You did that on purpose!'

'Want to make something of it?'

The sergeant was on his feet now, and dangerous. Having been made to look a fool, Elmer felt he could not back down in front of Letty. The British soldiers rose behind their sergeant, realizing that there was no standing down. In the terrible silence that followed, Chuck Ericson sauntered over and stood between the two men.

'What's going on, guys?' he asked.

'He tripped me, Chuck!'

'Probably couldn't help it. Some people are just too goddam big for their boots.'

There was a fearless, muscular quality about Chuck that made him a very different proposition to the roly-poly Elmer. The sergeant was not ready to take him on as well, and Chuck knew it. With a look of cool defiance, he dared the other men to do differently. Then he went out with Elmer and the terrified Letty. The danger had passed.

'Blimey! That was close!' said Sid Davis.

'Pity!' sighed Mario, who had been watching in case he was needed. 'I could use a little action.'

'Not when I'm around, please!' added Sid, anxious to keep clear of any trouble. A fight at the cafe would have brought the police and everyone present would have had to be questioned. Sid Davis had his own reasons for wanting to avoid any contact with the police. He bent over towards Mario and raised a pair of quizzical eyebrows. 'Well?' he asked, hopefully.

'I can get the stuff, Sid.'

'I knew you could! When?'

'Not so fast, old buddy. There's two things I gotta know. First, what's my cut of this here deal?'

'You can trust me, Mario. We're partners. Fifty-fifty.'

'Second, I don't want to be caught by the MPs with a load of hot merchandise. When I have it, I gotta dump it quick.'

'Don't worry. I got the perfect outlet.'

'It'd better be!'

'It is, so leave it to me. In a week or two, we'll both be rolling in it. Mario, mate – we're in business!'

They shook hands on it.

# CHAPTER NINE

It was the first time that McGraw had accepted her invitation to join them for an evening meal and the atmosphere, though polite, had been a little strained. Sally Bilton had wanted to show her gratitude for the way that he had found her some work and she had made great efforts with the food. Her mother-in-law, by contrast, was against the whole idea. She resented the chatterbox affection that her grand-daughter, Betty, had for the American, and sat there grimly in her polka dot dress and old cardigan watching sourly as McGraw tucked into his meat and potato pie, apple tart, cake and scones. Billy's only contribution was to fall asleep in his cot and snore gently.

'That was terrific, Mrs Bilton,' said McGraw, looking down at his empty plate. 'Really elegant.'

'Thank you. Will you have that last piece of apple tart?'

McGraw did not take a lot of persuading and earned a glare of envy from Ruby as he began to eat the tart that she had mentally reserved for herself. Betty, her mouth edged with jam, beamed up at the guest.

'What's your real name?' she asked.

'McGraw.'

'No. No, your *real* name.'

'Oh. It's Joseph. Joe.'

'Joe . . .' said Betty, savouring the name.

'GI Joe,' added Sally.

'Yeah. Most of my friends call me Mac.'

He addressed himself to the apple pie under Ruby's stern gaze. Betty experimented with his name a few more times then turned to Sally.

'I don't want Joe to go away.'

'No fear of that, honey,' he promised. 'Looks like we'll be around for a good long time.'

'But Grandma said you were leaving – and the sooner the better.'

Caught off her guard for a moment, Ruby was trapped, but she denied the accusation with indignation. She claimed that she had only been repeating what she had heard others in the town say about the Americans.

'Guess we were bound to upset a lot of folk,' said McGraw. 'We shot our mouths off when we first came. When people see our guys kidding around – letting off steam when they're off duty – and they think of their own servicemen, like your husband, for instance . . . The British have had it pretty rough for the last three years, while we seem to be having a fairly easy ride.'

'That's no reason to want you out of the country,' said Sally, angrily. 'Anyone who's met your boys, like I have, knows they're decent and nice – and just as brave as ours.'

'Mighty fine of you to say so, Mrs Bilton.'

'It's only the truth.'

Sally saw that Betty had finally finished eating and told the girl that it was time for her bath. Ruby was asked to take the girl off and, for all her muttered protests, she did so, first cadging a cigarette from McGraw's full packet of Lucky Strikes. Sally was still feeling hurt on his behalf.

'Those people who resent you . . . I'll tell them. I'll tell them how kind you've been to me and the children.'

'Nothing kind about me, Mrs . . .' He looked across at her. 'There's too many Mrs Biltons around here.'

'Why don't you call me Sally?'

The smile began around his eyes and travelled slowly to his mouth, transforming the whole of his face. She had never seen him beam like that and it embarrassed her slightly. She began to clear away the things on the table. He thanked her once again for the meal.

'It was nothing special.'

'It was real, Sally, that's what it was. Made on a real stove, in a real kitchen.'

'Yes, it must be awful to be away from home,' she said. 'But at least you can look forward to going back one day.'

'There's nothing to go back to. I don't have a home, not since I was a kid. Only the Army, then the Air Corps.'

'Don't you have . . . anyone waiting for you?'

'Nope.' He could see her concern. 'Hey, there's nothing to be sorry about. That's how I always wanted it.'

'I just thought . . . well, you're so good with children.'

'Don't let my boys hear you saying that, Sally. I'd have to bust half their heads open to get any respect.' He finished the last spoonful of apple tart then handed the plate to her. 'Thanks. Last coupla months I been too busy to think much about eating. Grab a hamburger or a sandwich, and get back to the job. Keeping those crates flying.' She came back to the table and sat down. 'What's your husband like, Sally?' he said, quietly.

'Stan? Just ordinary – you know. Kind, nice. He's a good mechanic. Starting to do quite well till the war came along. We were going to save up, get a better house and that.'

'What's wrong with this? It's no fancy duplex but it's got everything you could want. He's a lucky guy to have it to come back to. And the kids . . . And you.'

It was one of the nicest compliments that anyone had ever paid to Sally Bilton and she did not know how to cope with it. She was about to stammer her thanks when Betty came scampering in, virtually naked, to collect her wooden duck from the cot. She held it up to McGraw.

'Donald always comes with me in the bath.'

'Lucky feller!'

'Is Uncle Joe staying the night, Mummy?'

'Of course not! I mean . . .' The child's innocent question had brought a glow to Sally's cheeks.

'No, honey, I have to get back to the Base,' explained McGraw with a chuckle.

'Anyway,' whispered Betty to him, 'I'm glad you're not going away.'

'Tell you a secret, honey. So am I.'

Inwardly, an even more confused Sally Bilton echoed the statement.

When she saw the guests who had been assembled for the dinner party, Pat Dereham was certain that the evening would be a disaster. Her mother had invited Major Riggs-Danby, Indian Army, retired, a caricature military man with all the classic English prejudices; Sir Arthur Maylie, one of the local landowners, a dull-eyed, crusty, unprepossessing man of middle years, and his wife, a long, silent glacier of a woman; Mrs Troughton, an elderly lady with a querulous manner and a distinctive county voice; the Rector of the Sub-diocese, Mr Powell, a strange, thin, ineffective man with a weak handshake; and Phyllis Lambourn, looking at her most predatory in a dark dress and glinting earrings.

'They're a ghastly bunch!' Pat protested.

'The best I could do at short notice, darling.'

'What's the Major going to think?'

Before Helen could remind her that it had been Pat's idea to hold the dinner party, there was a loud knock at the door. Though her first instinct was to run and open it, Pat had already decided that she must change her tactics with regard to Jim, and so she drifted off into the sitting room, leaving her mother to welcome the last guest.

Until she opened the front door, Helen Dereham had not realized how much she had wanted to see him again. He looked relaxed and almost debonair in his best uniform and the arrogance to which she had objected earlier had disappeared entirely from his gaze and his manner. While she glanced at the gifts that he was carrying, trying her best to remain businesslike, his eyes roved admiringly over the smooth, rounded shoulders that had been revealed by her extremely un-businesslike low-cut dress. She asked him to step into the hall and he presented her with the first gift.

'Chocolates!'

'An old American custom.'

The gift was astonishing in a country which had started severely to ration sweets and chocolate the previous July, and the second gift, a bottle of whisky, was equally unexpected. Helen began to say that she could not possibly accept the presents but he brushed her remarks aside and put both items on the hall table. As she led the way to the sitting room, he thanked her for the opportunity to get to know her better, clearly assuming that he was the only guest. When he was met by the searching eyes of the others and by the welcoming smile of Pat, his face fell slightly but he recovered gallantly and suffered introductions to them all, even managing a compliment for the gushing Phyllis whom he had met before.

Like her daughter, Helen began to fear that the dinner party was going to prove a big mistake. Jim had so little in common with the other guests – and some of them were more than willing to let him know it. She suddenly couldn't bear him being the victim of their snobbery.

'Would you care for a glass of sherry, Major?'

'Thanks, Mrs Dereham.'

Two hours later she saw that her fears had been groundless. The combination of good food, sweet wine and a warm evening had done wonders for her guests and, as they sat over coffee, there was laughter and badinage and a general feeling of goodwill. What intrigued Helen most was the fact that a new Jim Kiley had started to emerge. In place of the curt, authoritative, single-minded and self-opinionated Air Executive whom she thought she knew, she was meeting an extremely well-educated man from a wealthy Boston family, who had distinguished himself, as far as her guests were concerned, in all the right fields.

Jim won Colonel Riggs-Danby over when he announced that he had played polo in Simla and knew that part of the world well. He astounded both Phyllis and Pat by admitting that he had sailed his yacht in the Americas Cup a number of times. And he so impressed Sir Arthur and Lady Maylie with his charm and his seriousness about his job, that they invited him to visit their house. Pat, of course, was totally enraptured, try as hard as she could to conceal the fact. Mrs Troughton appraised the star guest and decided that she was not, herself, beyond the range of his battery of charms, and Jim completed his conquest of the guests by offering Mr Powell a Havana and getting an eager acceptance.

It had been a most successful dinner party.

'Well, I guess I ought to go now.'

'So soon?' asked Pat, reluctant to let him.

'I have a briefing for tomorrow.'

'For what?'

'I'm afraid I can't tell you, Pat. After all, you could be a dangerous Nazi spy.'

The others laughed politely and they expressed their own disappointment that he had to leave. Jim thanked them and went out into the hall with Helen.

'You never told me that you were at Princeton,' she said.

He grinned, opened the front door and strolled across to his jeep. Helen followed, glad that she could not be seen from the sitting room whose curtains were drawn.

'Nice try, Helen,' he said.

'I don't follow . . .'

'Oh come on. You wanted to freeze me off. You're too warm a person yourself, basically, to do it on your own. So you got a bunch of friends you thought I wouldn't hit it off with. Only your plan backfired. They turned out to be more fun than you expected.'

'You charmed them, you mean.'

'See? That's a confession. It was a pretty mean trick.'

'Yes, it was.'

Helen was admitting it to herself as much as to him. The plan had been nowhere near as calculated as he seemed to think and failed, in any case, the moment she welcomed him. When she took him in to meet her guests, she had realized, suddenly, that she had made a dreadful mistake. She simply did not know what she had really wanted.

'There's only one way I'll forgive you, Helen.'

'Is there?'

'Yeah. Come out with me.'

'I told you!' she protested, at once pleased and exasperated.

'Tell me again.'

'I have a husband.'

'Sure. I met him. He wouldn't want you to sit and mope in your ivory tower like the Lady of Shalott.'

'Look, even if I wanted to,' she said, reasonably, 'it's just not possible. I'm too well known locally.'

'There must be something people wouldn't object to. How about a walk? Hey, what was that place the Rector was talking about over dinner – Blesham Abbey?'

'It's an old ruin. Very pretty.'

'Okay, then. I've been here for months in Constable country and I've seen none of the sights. I'm culturally starved. You can take me to see the Abbey. Tomorrow.'

'But I'm on duty at the hospital.'

'Till what time?'

'Three.'

'Fine. I'll pick you up then.'

Before Helen could answer, his jeep was pulling away down the drive.


Jack Blair polished a glass with his tea cloth and looked uneasily around the Lounge Bar. It had very nearly been the scene of serious trouble and he had to accept that one of his daughters had been indirectly responsible for what had happened. Both the girls had been adversely affected in their different ways by the arrival of the Americans, and their father had been unable to do anything about it. Vi Blair, older, more sensible, less impetuous, had developed an interest in one particular GI and been hurt as a result, but it was her sister, Rosie, who had become the real problem. She seemed to flirt compulsively with the men and held out promises which she had no intention of keeping. Elmer Jones was a case in point. He had been given the impression by the vivacious barmaid that she would go out with him the next time that he was on leave, and he had prepared himself for this event with great thoroughness. Yet when he had arrived at The Plough earlier and spoken to her, Rosie had pole-axed him by saying that she had made no definite commitment with him.

What had made Elmer's plight worse, and Jack Blair's control over his premises a little shakier, was the fact that Hymie Stutz had been on hand to advance his own claims. He and Elmer were soon arguing violently about which of them was going to take Rosie out. Then a few British soldiers, the ones who had been at the Empire Cafe, joined in the argument, insisting that it was time Rosie shared her favours among the local lads. The situation had reached flashpoint and even Jack Blair's intervention had not been enough. Charlie, the British sergeant, had actually been about to throw a punch at the landlord himself when a couple of MPs, always on the alert for trouble in the town, came rushing in.

The situation had calmed at once, but it had left Jack Blair wondering what might happen next time. Rosie came up to him and told him that she was going off to the cinema. Her father tensed, wondering with whom she had finally elected to go, fearing that it might provoke more comment and hostility. But Rosie Blair ignored British and American servicemen alike and walked out of the Lounge Bar with her sister.


The chance for which Sid Davis had been waiting arrived the next morning. As he came into the living room, tousled, yawning, unshaven, still in his dressing gown, he saw Albert, already dressed, reading one of the Sunday papers. Sid asked where his sister was.

'Gone to church. With Letty.'

'Is young Peter with them?'

'He plays the organ once a month there. We take our civic responsibilities very seriously in this family.'

'Notice you're not with them, Albert.'

'I was out till very late with my Civil Defence duties,' said Albert, irritably. 'The vicar understands.'

'I bet. Fancy a cuppa?'

'Breakfast was over two hours ago, Sid. There was tea available then, if you'd wanted it.' He put his paper aside and stood up. 'And while we're about it, how many weeks is it now since you asked if you could stay just for a week?'

'Time flies when you've been made welcome,' said the other, ingratiatingly. 'But my leg's much better now, so it shouldn't be long before I'm strong enough to be off. Soon as I hear from a friend who's trying to fix me up with a new flat.'

'You go on about London so much, I'm surprised you can bear to be away.'

'Yeah,' Sid agreed, grinning.

'Letty tells me you offered to take her there . . .'

There was veiled suspicion behind the question and Sid tried to allay it by saying that he had offered to take the whole family to London to repay them for their hospitality. Albert made it quite clear that he would never allow Letty to go off anywhere on her own.

' 'Course not, Albert. Not that you'd need to worry. Letty's a good girl. You've brought her up properly.' Seeing that his brother-in-law was slightly mollified by the remark, Sid worked around to the subject he really wanted to discuss. 'Yes, should be off in a day or two. Got my business to take care of.'

'Business?' snorted Albert.

'Matter of fact – funny enough – it's more or less in the same line as you.'

'What d'you mean?'

'Foodstuffs and that. In a small way, of course. I'm a sort of 'andler, a middleman.'

'For what?'

'Like I said. Restaurants, 'otels and such like, they don't

want to keep stock too long, even in these days. They pass it on to small retailers, make a bit of profit on the side.'

Though trying not to take any of it seriously, Albert was nevertheless intrigued. 'What sort of stuff?' he asked.

'Mostly canned goods. Peaches, meat loaf, dried milk – that sort of thing.'

'But that's illegal!'

'Legal – illegal – so what? It's an old custom. Oh, the Ministry of Food might clamp down on it one day, but till then nobody bothers.'

There was a long, thoughtful pause and Sid knew his plan was starting to work.

'How d'you get hold of it?' said Albert.

'Got my regular suppliers. They tell me they want to get rid of something. Might only be a few tins, then again it might be whole boxes of stuff. I do all right – and some of the shops I deal with, they make quite a bit as well.'

'You've been here all this time and you've never mentioned it before!' complained Albert.

'I never imagined you'd be interested,' replied Sid, surprise written all over his face.

'The biggest headache a shopkeeper has nowadays is how to keep up supplies.'

'Yes, mate, but strictly speaking, this is not – well, it's not stuff you'd put on the shelf. More a case of under the counter. There's no points or ration books involved. 'Course – that means you can charge a bit more.'

Albert Mundy sat down again and picked up his paper. He read it for no more than a minute, then put it down again as he considered what he had heard. Sid Davis smiled. He had his brother-in-law hooked.


Dereham House was basking in the late afternoon sunshine when they arrived back. They had had a surprisingly enjoyable time together and were both exhilarated by it. Neither of them had really paid much attention to the Abbey that they had visited.

'Well, here we are,' she said, coming into the hall.

'And here we stay.'

'No, Jim.' Her manner was pleasant but firm.

'Just one drink.'

'Look, I told you. We must stop this now.'

'When can I see you again?' he pressed.

'You can't.'

'I'll keep on asking, Helen.'

'I think I'd be surprised if you didn't.'

They laughed. Though they were very conscious of the dangers, each of them was keen to see the other again. They were happy and relaxed for the first time together. It was a revelation.

The mood was shattered in an instant.

'Mummy . . .',

Pat Dereham had been standing in the doorway of the dining room and they winced at the thought that she must have overheard them. She looked pale, wounded and sullen. She told Helen that she had been trying to get in touch with her.

'I was at the hospital, darling,' lied her mother.

'I rang there. They said you left early.'

'I took your mother for a walk,' admitted Jim.

Pat did not even look at him. She stared at her mother until Helen realized that it could be only one thing.

'You had a call from Uncle Tommy . . . from the War Office.'

'Oh, no . . .'

'It's Daddy. There was a tank battle. He was badly wounded.'

'How badly?'

'They don't know. He's being taken to the Base Hospital at Tunis – then they should be able to tell.'

Helen, lost and stricken, turned to face Jim.

'I'm sorry,' he said, quietly. 'I'd better be going. I hope it's not as bad as you think.'

He looked at Pat but she was still ignoring him completely. The news about her father had been made unbearably worse by the knowledge of where her mother had been. Jim left quickly.

Helen, still overcome with remorse and anxiety, tried to speak to her daughter but the words would not come. She went instead to the telephone and began to dial a number.

Sally Bilton was standing beside the river, gazing absently into the water, her whole body drooping under the weight of her sorrow. McGraw, who had heard the news at The Plough, had come straight over to find her. He got close enough for her to be aware of his presence but he did not know what to say. The tank battle which had wounded Ronnie Dereham had cost Stan Bilton his life. His widow was still in a state of profound shock. McGraw took her hand gently in his and simply stayed there, offering an unspoken sympathy. Sally gave a stifled sob and began to shake. Leaning against him, she let the tears flow at last.

Betty Grable was about to say something important when the trouble started. Letty, trying to watch the film from the back of the aisle, was suddenly grabbed by the young British soldier in the seat next to her. When she tried to pull herself free, he tugged her harder and forced her to bend down beside him.

'What's the hurry, Letty?'

'No, don't! You're hurting me, Ron!'

'Then stop fighting me. I only want a cuddle.'

'Ron, *please*!' she protested, squirming as he tried to grope her.

'Hey, you! Leave her alone!' warned an American voice.

'Keep out of this, Yank,' warned the soldier.

But Chuck Ericson was already on his feet, gripping the man who was holding Letty and forcing him to release her. Letty was screaming now and the whole cinema reacted. Other British soldiers came storming up the aisle and the many Americans were rising from their seats as well. Mario and Elmer, who had been sitting on the outside of Vi and Rosie Blair respectively, went to see what the noise was about.

Chuck's first punch floored a British private and acted as a signal. The battle cries went up at once.

'Bloody Yanks!'

'Limeys!'

The fighting which began at the rear of the auditorium soon spread throughout the cinema. Fists flew, boots swung, heads butted and teeth closed on flesh as the violence that had been threatening to erupt for some days now turned The Roxy into a writhing, grappling, screeching mass of bodies. Mario made his way to Chuck, giving and taking blows as he did so. Elmer tried to calm the terrified Rosie and Vi. Betty Grable, sublimely unaware of the riot, went into her best dance number.

'Get the girls, Mario!' ordered Chuck.

He did not need to be told twice. He fought his way back to Elmer, grabbed the British soldier who was now trying to punch his friend in the stomach and lifted him over the row of seats in front. Chuck followed him, recognized Vi, took her arm and led the way towards the emergency exit. Elmer went after him with Rosie, a protective arm around her shoulders.

'Letty! We must get Letty,' cried Vi.

'Leave her to me,' said Mario.

She was crouched on the carpet in the aisle when he got to her, fighting all around her in the darkness. As Mario bent down to help her up, he saw the fist of a British corporal swing towards him, took the blow on his shoulder and then replied by kneeing the man in the groin. The sergeant, however, did manage to land a punch on Mario's face and it sent him reeling. As his adversary moved in for the kill, Mario recovered quickly, took Letty's torch from the floor and hit the oncoming soldier straight in the mouth. As the first gouts of blood reached the man's uniform, Mario took hold of Letty again and pulled her unceremoniously towards the exit.

He had a fleeting glimpse of Betty Grable's legs before he pushed his way through the door and out into the night. The others were waiting and they all adjourned gratefully to the pub.

Jack Blair was dismayed to hear the story of the riot but he knew that it had been virtually inevitable. It had shaken up Rosie but it had had a different consequence for Vi. This was not the first time that Chuck Ericson had arrived in time to save her.

Letty, still trembling like a leaf, wanted to get home. She had not dared to imagine what her father would make of it all.

'I'll take you home, Letty,' volunteered Mario. 'Might as well finish the job.'

And before the surprised faces of the others, she took his arm trustingly and went out into the street.

# CHAPTER TEN

She was discussing a case with the consultant physician when the message came that she had a visitor. Helen excused herself and went down the corridor to her office. Jim was standing outside the door. He saluted her courteously, exchanged a few polite words of greeting and then followed her into her office. Once inside, his manner became more familiar.

'You're looking well, Helen.'

'Thank you.'

'There's a lot of things I could say. That was the most harmless. And one of the truest.' He won a brief smile from her. 'That's better.'

'I'm sorry, Jim. You caught me at a bad time. The consultant is here.'

'I wanted to ask how your husband is.'

'He's still in hospital in Tunis.'

'How bad is it?'

'The tank he was in took a direct hit. They got him out but his back – there was some damage to his spine.'

'Jesus . . .'

'It's a matter of rest and recuperation. They're flying him home.'

'I see.'

Jim was unsure how to take the news and Helen gave him no help. Her face was quite impassive. There was a knock on the door and a nursing sister interrupted them.

'Dr Heywood was asking if you had the notes on Mrs Bevan.'

'Yes, of course,' said Helen, giving her the clipboard that she had been holding. 'I'll be along in a moment.'

As soon as the woman had left, Jim took a step closer to Helen and asked her what time she finished work.

'Not till seven.'

'I'll come back.'

'But I have to go straight home.'

'I'll see you home, then,' he persisted.

'Pat's there. She'll be waiting.'

'Is she still clocking you in and out?'

'More or less.'

'Look, Helen, when are you going to tell that daughter of yours to grow up!' he said with controlled anger. 'Maybe I ought to talk to her myself.'

'I don't think that would help, Jim,' she sighed. 'I told you it would be difficult for us to keep meeting. It's . . . As you would say – it's not on.'

Helen opened the door and went back to her work.


Whenever the skies that June were clear enough over Europe, the B-17s from the Market Wetherby Air Base were flying on combat missions and taking part in the systematic bombardment of selected targets in Germany. Casualties from these outings were still high and the ambulances were always busy when the planes limped back to the airfield. Experienced crews often tormented new arrivals with gruesome tales of spectacular deaths 20,000 feet over enemy territory and rookies about to fly on their first mission were asked with callous jokiness about their next of kin. But the veterans knew in their hearts that for them, as much as for the newcomers, each mission could so easily be the final one. They had also learned that the most important person to have as an invisible eleventh member of the crew was Lady Luck.

Elmer Jones never forgot this. Superstitious by nature, he had developed a whole series of rituals to bring him and his colleagues good fortune.

When the 'Ginger Rogers' had returned from a mission late one afternoon, therefore, Elmer was at the door as usual, counting off the members of the crew as they emerged, like a child chanting a nursery rhyme. The others teased him about it but nobody tried to stop him. From Captain Red Burwash down to the most junior man on board, each one had his own individual way of appealing for luck.

The crew went off to be de-briefed and then made for their quarters. No passes had been issued for that evening and so the men had to make their own fun at the Base, playing cards, drinking, arguing, listening to Glenn Miller records on an old gramophone. Elmer, lying on his bunk, was amazed to see Mario Bottone putting on his best uniform, clearly intent on leaving the Base illegally. Taking his cue from the radio operator, Chuck Ericson also began to get ready for an evening in the town. Both men had commitments that could not wait until the next pass was issued. Elmer, feeling that they had used up their ration of luck for the day when they were over Germany with an escort of three enemy fighters, warned against it.

'You guys are crazy! If the MPs catch you, you'll be in the slammer before you can blink.'

'First, they gotta catch us,' said Mario.

In just over an hour, while Elmer was still back at the Base fearing the worst, the two men were walking into The Plough. Jack Blair was both surprised and alarmed to see them. His pub was out of bounds to Americans for the next week as a result of the riot at the cinema, and he did not wish to risk an extension of that ban by being caught serving the men now.

'Dad!' implored Vi, who had been touched that Chuck had gone to such pains to see her again.

'Have a heart, Jack!' added Sid Davis, who had been waiting there in the hope that Mario would show up.

'All right. Half an hour,' conceded Jack. 'Then out you go, the pair of you – the back way!'

Chuck thanked him and then found a quiet corner to talk to Vi. All the doubts that he had had about their friendship had vanished now and he wanted to be with her all the time. The feelings were mutual. Vi was more animated than she had been for a long time and she sat with him and planned and dreamed and hoped. Whatever else the fight at The Roxy may have done, it had brought two people very close together.

Mario had moved with Sid to an even quieter corner to discuss the success of their business venture. The first few consignments of goods had already been spirited out of the Base and the storeroom at the rear of Albert Mundy's shop was filling with boxes stencilled with the initials U.S.A.A.F. Sid, the middle man, was pleased with the progress so far but less pleased when Mario demanded payment there and then. Under the table, pound notes and dollar bills changed hands. Mario stuffed them into his pockets and thought about the future.

'We're gonna clean up on this!'

'Only if we box clever,' warned Sid. 'Now, listen, pal. If we're seen a lot together, people are going to ask why. Before they make the connection, we got to provide one. And Letty's it.'

'Letty?'

'I don't care if you fancy her or not, Mario. You got to make out you do. Which gives you a reason to call at the shop to see her Uncle Sid from time to time. Got it?'

'Sure. But supposing Letty won't play along?'

'Oh, you should have no trouble there. Especially, if you give her a good time at the dance.'

'Dance?'

'Didn't I tell you? We're going to branch out a little. You and me's going to organize a dance. On the Fourth of July.'

'Independence Day!'

'Let me get you another beer and tell you all about it . . .'


McGraw had brought a carrier bag full of groceries for the family and he had given her a whole packet of cigarettes, but Ruby Bilton did not show any gratitude. As soon as he went out of the room, she clicked her tongue and scowled.

135

'Disgustin'!'

'What is?' asked Sally.

'Letting him put her to bed like that.'

'Betty's very fond of him, Ma.'

' 'Course she is. Only 'cos he stuffs her with sweets and chocolate. That's all she sees in him.'

'You don't do so badly, either,' retorted Sally, watching the older woman light one of the cigarettes she had just been given.

'Buying his way in. An excuse to keep coming round.'

'Joe doesn't need an excuse. He's been a good friend to us. And he's very fond of the children.'

'Children! We all know why he keeps coming here.'

'Why?'

'Sniffin' around. You should hear what people are saying, my girl. They're not blind, you know.'

'And you listen to talk like *that*!' demanded Sally, anger getting her to her feet. 'What do you tell them? Well?'

'I . . .'

'Well?' pressed her daughter-in-law.

'I tell them there's nothing to it,' lied Ruby. 'I say that you do the washing for them and he's fond of little Betty and Billy.'

'And that the children are always here when he calls. And *you're* always here!'

'You can't stop people thinking things,' replied Ruby.

'He's a decent man, Ma. One of the most decent I've ever met. But some people can't help making everything seem dirty.'

'I suppose,' began Ruby, slyly, 'they'd understand it better if we got more out of it.'

'What d'you mean?'

'They're rolling in it up at that camp. Food, drink, fags. The life of Riley. While we have to go without.'

Sally was so disgusted with what her mother-in-law was suggesting that she turned away from her. McGraw came downstairs. He seemed to be totally unaware of the tension between the two women, and talked easily about putting

Betty to bed and sending her to sleep with a story. Sally offered him another cup of tea but he refused.

'There's some left in the pot,' she said.

'No, I have to get back, Sally. I've a long night ahead of me.'

'They work you too hard.'

'Tell that to the Air Force . . . Well, goodnight, Mrs Bilton.'

'Goodnight, Sergeant,' said Ruby sweetly.

'Be seeing you, Sally.'

She started forward to show him out and then checked herself, conscious of what Ruby had been saying a little earlier. McGraw waved her back.

'It's okay. I know the way out,' he said and left the room.

'He should do – by this time!' added Ruby.

Sally swung round on her mother-in-law but Ruby was not at all perturbed. She inhaled deeply and then blew a small cloud of American tobacco smoke into the air.


The Independence Day Dance gave Jim Kiley and Helen Dereham the perfect opportunity to meet. She was relaxing in the sitting room when he arrived, listening to one of her favourite records.

'I shouldn't have told you that Pat was going out to the dance. I might have known you'd take it as an invitation.'

'Wasn't it, Helen?'

'Come in and sit down.'

'Lead the way . . .'

They sat opposite each other and Jim noticed how preoccupied she looked. She read the question in his eyes.

'I'm sorry. I'm not very good company tonight.'

'You don't have to make bright, hostessy talk. I can't think of anything I'd like better than just to sit here with you and listen to Brahms.' He smiled at her surprise. 'Symphony Number 3. Last movement . . . Smoke?'

'No thanks.'

'Mind if I do?'

'Go ahead.'

'Something on your mind?' he asked, lighting the cigarette.

'Ronnie is coming back tomorrow.'

'I shouldn't have come barging in, then.'

'No, I didn't mean it like that, Jim. I've only just heard. I thought I ought to tell you.'

Jim nodded, thought about it for a moment and then stubbed out his cigarette in the ashtray. 'Yeah. That's my cue to shove off.'

'Please, don't!' she said quickly. 'Now you're here, I'll make some coffee. Real coffee at that. Our local shop seems to have found a secret supply. I won't be a minute. Sit tight . . .'

Brahms had finished revolving on the turntable by the time she came back with a tray. Jim had been staring at the framed photograph of Ronnie Dereham and was beginning to understand just how awkward the situation was.

They talked neutrally for a while and then Helen mentioned the recent spate of casualties that had passed through the hospital.

'They're so young, Jim. How can you keep doing it to them?'

'There's no other way. Sure they're young, but they're fit. If they weren't, they'd never get through their twenty-five missions.'

'It's just so cruel to ask anyone to go through that so often. Is it possible?'

'Very possible. I did mine last year. Which is half the problem. Since I've been through, I practically have to get an order signed by General Ira C. Eaker himself before I can take off.'

'You fly missions?' she asked, alarmed.

'Not as many as I'd like. Rufus kept me grounded at first but I persuaded him at last.'

'I didn't know . . .'

They drank their coffee in silence for a while then started

to chat about the dance. Remembering the incident at The Roxy, she said she hoped that there would be no trouble. Jim assured her that they had plenty of MPs in attendance who would keep things well under control. Though he had no inclination at all to go along himself, he was all for the dance.

'Since it's the Fourth of July, we let them go ahead. And why the hell shouldn't they have a few laughs, hold a girl for a while? Pretend that's what's real. Forget the whole stinking war.'

Disenchantment set in as soon as they stepped into the hall. After paying the five shillings entrance fee they were confronted by a few couples circling warily to 'I'll Be With You In Apple Blossom Time' as played by Peter Mundy and his makeshift band. The decorations were perfunctory and unimaginative, with no real attempt to suggest that it was Independence Day beyond the hanging of the Stars and Stripes above the heads of the musicians. Red Burwash surveyed the scene and was less than impressed. His question to Herman Krotnik was heavy with scorn and tinged with disbelief.

'*This* is Independence Day Gala Night?'

'One of your guys set it up, Red,' Herman said.

'Bottone won't be one of my guys much longer if he's loused this up! I'll strap him to a goddam propeller on the next mission!'

'Hey, look! They got booze.'

The men drew minimal comfort from the sight of a hatch at the far end, through which beer and stout were being sold, and they sauntered off towards it. On the way they heard other voices making other threats about what was going to be done to Mario Bottone. So far, however, there was no sign of the co-organizer.

Within half an hour, the hall was fairly full. Red Burwash had come to celebrate the Fourth of July. Herman Krotnik was there because his crew had teased him into it, betting him that he would not dare to shift his bulk around the dance floor with a woman in his arms. Elmer Jones, like Hymie Stutz, was there to be with Rosie and disappointment was waiting for one of them. Chuck Ericson was there to share the joy of a whole evening with Vi Blair. Letty Mundy, talked into going by her uncle, was trying to banish the memories of Harvey Wallis. Vera Mundy was there to keep an eye on her and to enjoy a dance herself. Ruby Bilton, in common with a gaggle of older women, had paid her five shillings simply to drink stout and watch. McGraw was there in the spirit of enquiry. Phyllis Lambourn was there to see if the occasion was any better than the dances which the Goodwill Committee had laid on, as well as to strike up a closer acquaintance with some of the American officers. Pat Dereham was enticed along in the hope of seeing Jim Kiley.

Expectations were being dashed all around the hall, and although Peter Mundy and the band were working their way relentlessly through their repertoire – now extended to include 'Deep In The Heart Of Texas' and 'My Devotion' – they were not generating any real excitement. Even when they played melodies from the American hit parade, the music remained quintessentially English. As an event, the Independence Day Gala Night was proving to be something less than a success.

'Hey, Mario!'

'Come here, you bum!'

'Give us our dough back!'

'We've had better nights in a morgue!'

When Mario Bottone finally showed up, he was greeted with gibes and complaints from all sides. He seemed unconcerned by the abuse as he made his way to the stage where the band, in a last desperate effort to connect with the spirit of the occasion, were forcing their way to the closing bars of 'Manhattan Serenade'.

Sid Davis had also slipped into the hall, pleased at the sell-out of tickets and even more delighted at the consignment of goods from the Post Exchange at the Base, which he and Mario had just been unloading at the rear of Albert's shop. Sid sensed the general disapproval but knew that his partner had a plan to redeem the evening for all those present. He joined in the clapping as the band fell silent. Mario now stepped up to the microphone and ignored the catcalls.

'Ladies and gentlemen!' he called. 'Guys and gals! Now, listen – listen! This is an Anglo-American evening in honour of Independence Day, okay?'

'What's the pitch?' asked a sceptical voice from the crowd.

'We're all grateful to Peter Mundy and the boys . . .'

'Yeah – for stopping!'

'That was the Anglo bit,' said Mario. 'Now for the American.'

'What you gonna do?' shouted Hymie. 'Whistle "Dixie"?'

'Better than that. Ladies and gentlemen, let me introduce Corporal Hank Duseli . . . Pfc Moe Rosen . . . Sergeant Harry Kickshaw . . . and Private Lee Schwartz.'

Four men began to make their way towards the platform, the last named carrying a small bell-shaped box under his arm. The band – all three of them – vacated their places and the Americans took over. Without waiting to see if his companions were ready, Corporal Duseli sat at the piano and began playing loud, upbeat boogie music that brought a great cheer of recognition from all the GIs in the hall. Pfc Rosen joined in with the drums and Sergeant Kickshaw supplied a steady buzz of rhythm on the double bass. When Private Schwartz took out a cornet and added its strident melody line, applause broke out and couples rushed to the floor, dancing now with real abandon.

From that point on, the real celebration began. For two of those present, it was considerably more.

'You mean it? You really *mean* it?'

'Yes.'

'I can't believe it! I've spent days thinking up ways I could talk you into it and . . .'

Vi Blair kissed him then put her head on his chest. They were standing against the wall outside the back of the hall and Chuck Ericson had found the words to propose to her.

'It was all settled weeks ago,' said Vi. 'I knew you were going to ask me and I knew that I'd say yes.'

'Oh, God, I love you!'

'I love you,' she said and kissed him again.

'We'll have to tell your father, Vi.'

'He'll probably say we should wait.'

'I don't want to wait!'

'Neither do I . . . Will you have to get permission?'

'Yeah, it has to go through channels. I have to ask the CO.'

'Will that be difficult?' she asked, sensing his unease.

'They don't like us to get married – but they can't stop it if you're determined. And boy, am I determined! Let's go back in. I can't wait to tell the guys.'

'No, Chuck. Don't tell anyone yet,' she said.

'Okay. My next day off, we get a ring, right? That's when we tell them. Come on . . .'

They slipped back into the hall in time to hear Elmer Jones coming to the end of his solo rendering of 'St Louis Blues' on the harmonica. The applause was deafening and Rosie Blair was leading it. She had had no idea that he was such a talented musician and forgot all about the rival claims of Hymie Stutz as she rushed up to congratulate him.

Before the American quartet could continue with their next number, some new arrivals brought a note of tension to the proceedings. The British soldiers, who had been involved in the riot at the cinema, pushed their way to the middle of the floor where Mario, Elmer and Chuck were now standing. Charlie, the sergeant, his face still bearing the scar that an usherette's torch had given him, acted as spokesman. Everyone feared another fight and the MPs began to close in, but the soldiers had come with an apology. They and the GIs were on the same side and they would never win a war together if they kept taking a crack at each other. Charlie offered his hand.

Relief gave way to laughter and there were handshakes all round. At Market Wetherby, if nowhere else, Independence Day had been marked by a step towards Anglo-American unity. But even at the height of this new burst of exhilaration, unanswered questions hung in the air like the remnants of the tattered bunting. Ruby Bilton was asking herself why McGraw had sneaked out from the hall so early on. Phyllis Lambourn, flushed with pleasure after all the dances she had had, was asking why Pat's features were still clouded. Red Burwash was looking around the members of his crew and asking how many of them, himself included, would be alive to celebrate another Fourth of July.

The question that was dominating Letty Mundy's mind was of a different order. Dancing cheek to cheek with the attentive Mario and feeling happy for the first time in weeks, she allowed herself to ask if she might have found the solution to her problems after all.

'The only doll I wanna be with is you.'

'Do you mean it, Mario?'

'Would I say it, if I didn't mean it?'

The last waltz suddenly seemed to be the answer to her prayers.


Pat Dereham arrived home with her features still shadowed by disappointment. When she went into the sitting room, that disappointment gave way to a more violent emotion. As she stared down at the occasional table, she saw two empty coffee cups and an ashtray full of cigarette butts. She now knew for certain why Jim Kiley had not been at the dance.

# CHAPTER ELEVEN

The United States 8th Bomber Command had persisted with its policy of daylight raids in spite of daunting losses and stern criticism from certain British quarters. Each American officer knew off by heart the words of the Casablanca directive, issued in January of that year and ordering 'the progressive destruction and dislocation of the German military, industrial and economic system and the undermining of the morale of the German people to a point where their capacity for armed resistance is fatally weakened'. That directive had become the basis for a game of deception, as the US Bomber Command used one ploy after another, some successful, some disastrous, all highly dangerous, to carry it out. The B-17s and B-24s had a thousand miles of coastline to choose from when plotting their courses, and the Luftwaffe was thus forced to disperse and thereby weaken its units over a wide front. Each new mission was another stage in the game, the latest throw of the dice, a deadly battle of wits between Allied bomber formations and German fighter controllers, a weird mixture of skill, planning, nerve, uncertain weather and luck.

Nobody was more aware of this than Colonel Rufus Krasnowici at the Market Wetherby Air Base. As he jabbed a finger at the map on Jim Kiley's office wall, he knew that he was pointing at the graveyard of his men and his planes.

'So that's it?' asked Jim Kiley.

'Yeah. The RAF's concentrating on Hamburg. We'll get either Hanover or Warnemunde – the Heinkel factory.'

'They're way beyond fighter support,' said Lester Carson.

'And both ringed with more Anti-Aircraft batteries than a hound dog has fleas,' added Rufus.

'We're on the alert for tomorrow?'

'If the weather holds, Jim. What does Cloudy Joe say?'

'Set fair over the next seven or eight days, sir,' said Lester.

'So we'll get maybe three, four smacks at them. This is the Big One for us.' Rufus looked down at his left arm which was in a sling. 'And I have to go fall off that damn silly bicycle!'

'I'll try to lead them the way I know you would, Rufe. Sorry you won't be able to come with us.'

'Crocodile tears, Jim. You've been waiting for a chance like this ever since you got here.'

' "Father," he said, "I cannot tell a lie." '

All three of them laughed and then Jim Kiley took a closer look at the map. Hanover or Warnemunde. It would be no milk run this time. He and his squadrons would be attacking the most well-defended targets so far. Rufus had been right. The Big One.


Albert Mundy, wearing his overall and his frown, came into the back room and stopped short. Seated at the table with Letty, Peter and Sid, and being served tea by Vera, was a grinning American serviceman who had clearly made himself at home.

'I didn't think I was gonna have the pleasure of meeting you, Mr Mundy,' said Mario.

'This is Mario, Dad.' Letty tried to conceal her anxiety.

'Mario Bottone,' said Sid. 'My pal.'

'Bottone? What kind of a name is that?'

'Italian. My folks were from Naples. But I was born in the good old US of A.'

'We're just having a cup of tea, Albert,' said his wife.

'Will you join us?' offered Sid.

'No, I've . . . I've got customers waiting.'

Ordinarily, Albert would have exploded at the sight of a GI in his living room but Mario was evidently Sid's contact at the Air Base and so could not be offended. The deliveries to date had been prompt and at a reasonable price, enabling Albert to make a tidy profit when he sold the goods to selected customers. But there were disadvantages to the arrangements, as he was finding out.

When Albert went back into the shop, Mario announced that it was time to go. Letty was keen to see him to the door but Sid told her that he wanted to walk part of the way with Mario so that they could have a chat. Peter watched the two men leave.

Later on, he had the chance of a quiet word with his sister.

'You really like him, don't you? Mario?'

'Of course.'

'What do you think . . . well, what's going to happen?'

'I don't know,' replied Letty, who had hardly let herself dare think about it in any depth. 'What's your opinion?'

'I just hope they don't get into trouble. Land Dad in it.'

'Who?' she asked, quite baffled.

'Mario and Uncle Sid.'

'What do you mean, Peter?'

'Well, you've got eyes in your head, surely. You must know why Mario keeps hanging around.'

'Because of me. I always knew that if I just waited, everything would turn out all right.'

Peter stared at her in amazement. It had obviously never occurred to her that Mario might have another reason for keeping in touch with the Mundy household.


Helen Dereham stood on the platform at the railway station. She was not looking forward to her husband's return. Shocked by the news that he had been wounded in action, her one immediate thought had been to try to get to him. Yet now that he was actually on his way back, she found herself almost dreading the reunion. As she saw the train steaming towards her in the distance, she made a special effort to conquer her misgivings and to give the man, whom she knew she still loved, the welcome that he needed.

The engine panted along the track beside the platform before coming to a noisy, hissing, dripping halt. Doors opened to let a few passengers off and a handful of others on. Helen could see no sign of Ronnie and she was tempted for a fleeting moment to believe that he had not come. Then she saw a door of one of the First Class compartments open to let a nurse step out. The woman turned to take out a folding wheelchair, opened it, then held it while two soldiers helped out the injured Ronnie Dereham. He looked pale, thin and wasted and his eyes had the watchful look of a cripple. The nurse had lifted his legs on to the support bar of the wheelchair before covering them with a blanket. Ronnie gazed around with vacant eagerness until he saw Helen.

'Hello, my . . . my darling,' he said.

'Welcome home,' she replied, forcing a smile when she wanted to burst into tears.

It was almost impossible to lift him into her car and he kept apologizing for his disability, but she knew that he would have hated it had she been waiting for him with an ambulance. Conversation on the drive back was uneasy. When he was back in his own sitting room, he explained exactly what was wrong with him. His daughter, too, had to fight back the tears.

'Is it *that* bad?'

'I'm afraid so, Pat. The base of my spine was crushed . . . I've lost control of my legs, all feeling from the hips down.'

'But you'll get better . . .'

'We have to face facts,' said her mother. 'It's permanent.'

'It's better to spell it out,' added Ronnie, 'and not raise any false hopes. But don't worry. I won't always look and feel like a drowned kitten. As for our games of tennis . . .' He broke off as a spasm of pain made him close his eyes for a second. 'Do forgive me. I'm still not a hundred per cent.'

There was a knock on the door and Rosie came in, her

expression a mixture of pity and ghoulish fascination. She had a message for Helen.

'Oh, Major Kiley phoned.'

'What did he want?' Helen knew that Pat was watching her carefully.

'To ask if Major Dereham was back – and how he was.'

'Thank you, Rosie.'

'Night . . .' said the girl and, after one more stare at the man in the wheelchair, she went out again.

Ronnie was touched. He had clearly paid no attention at all to the glances that had passed between Helen and Pat. There was a vulnerability about him which made his daughter move impulsively towards him. She knelt beside his chair.

'Oh, Daddy, I'm so glad you're back . . .'

She leaned her head against his knees and he began to smooth her hair gently. In time Helen was able to meet his smile.


The Big One started early the following morning. When the green signal flare went up from the control tower, the first of the B-17s massed for take-off rolled forward down the runway with Jim Kiley at the controls. To his left was the co-pilot, Lieutenant Hansen, a young, able officer who found Jim's presence reassuring.

'Red Leader commencing take-off,' said Jim into dozens of ears, but his next words were for Hansen. 'A little more juice.'

As the leader plane accelerated to achieve lift-off, the next B-17 was revving its engines at the far end of the runway. Aircraft took off at thirty second intervals from airfields all over East Anglia, and the sky was soon alive with Fortresses and Liberators. The 'Ginger Rogers' was not the only bomber that got lost for a while in the cloud and when it flipped through turbulence, Red Burwash realized that another B-17 had been there only seconds before. Eventually, he made contact with his formation and took up position.

The target area was Warnemunde, which meant that the crews would have to endure their cramped conditions for up to eight hours and more. It would call for a high tolerance of discomfort and an ability to resist the terrible assaults of claustrophobia. It would test the crews and the machines of the 525th Bomb Group more thoroughly than anything they had experienced.

Jim Kiley was relieved to be leading a combat mission once again. Like most B-17 pilots, he had tremendous faith in the plane, which was at once a rugged fighting weapon and a masterpiece of delicate engineering. It was stable, reliable and totally predictable, with ailerons and elevators that were unusually responsive for a four-engined craft and made the wheel easy to handle even at high altitudes. Formation flying was also helped by the gate-like throttle levers which made power changes so effortless.

As they flew at 10,000 feet across the dark expanse of water, Jim issued a stream of advice to the rest of the B-17s.

'Keep it tight there. Keep it tight. You new crews – don't panic or try to dodge when we hit trouble. You'll leave yourself wide open if you break formation. Tail gunners, keep watch for twin-engined ME-210s sneaking up your vapour trails to blast you. Any ship gets blown out of the sky, another's got to fill the hole in the formation at once. Short bursts, you gunners. That ammunition's got to take us all the way there and back. Now keep it tight. Fly like we're on display at a Presidential review . . .'

Enemy radar had picked up the bombers while they were still massing over the British coast and Luftwaffe pilots were airborne as soon as they were crossing Holland. The escort of P47s engaged with the German fighters, but damage was inflicted on the Fortresses in the first combat and Jim's jaw hardened as he saw one of them so pulverized that it dropped like a stone from the sky. On his command, the hole was immediately blocked by another plane and the formation surged onwards.

The Messerschmitts and Focke-Wulfs that harassed them could only fly for about ninety minutes on internal fuel and eventually had to return to base for more. This gave the formations a breathing space as they muscled their way across the German frontier but their support planes were only short-range fighters as well, and they, too, were peeling off to head back to their airfields. As the bombers roared on, they knew that they were on their own. The next battle with German interceptors would be much more hazardous.

'The Luftwaffe's out there again,' warned Jim. 'I can feel it.'

'I got 'em! I got 'em!' yelled his tail gunner over the intercom.

'Don't shout! What do you see?'

'Tail gunner to pilot. Six FWs at four o'clock, climbing.'

'Mark them.'

'Four FWs at nine o'clock, level,' said another voice into Jim's ear.

'Keep your eyes peeled!' he ordered the other planes. 'High Squadron, Low Squadron. They're heading in . . . This is it!'

The FWs chose their moment and then screamed into the attack. Elmer Jones, waist gunner in the 'Ginger Rogers', fired in short bursts as one of the fighters rocketed past. A favourite technique of the German pilots was to pierce the formation from beneath, soar high above it and then descend out of the sun. Jim had warned his men but it was a difficult manoeuvre to counter. Another B-17 lost its purchase and went into a spin. Elmer, well-placed to catch a glimpse of the tragedy, only counted four parachutes emerging from the stricken aircraft. When the next FW came within range, he treated it to a much fiercer burst of his fifty-calibre machine gun.

Jim Kiley and his men fought a running battle across Germany until they reached Warnemunde. Heavy flak became the main problem now and the sky was like a gigantic firework display, all colour and explosion and sudden death. Though his plane was buffeted by near-misses, Jim held his course.

'Navigator to pilot. We're at our AP, on target.'

'Bomb-bay doors open . . .'

'Forget the flak,' ordered Jim. 'Make it good now!'

'I'm on it!'

The first lethal cargo of bombs streamed out into the cold air and screamed down towards the target area. Other planes released their loads and Warnemunde was carpeted in smoke and destruction. The formations flew on, tightened, then altered their course for home.

They were back over Holland before the next attack came and more than one B-17 was flying on only three engines.

'Right waist to pilot. FW squadrons at seven o'clock, coming to nine o'clock level.'

'Fighter high!' warned another voice. 'Here he comes!'

The Focke-Wulf sent down a hail of bullets, spintering the plexiglass. Lieutenant Hansen arched and fell sideways. As he flew on, Jim Kiley felt the blood seep through his combat dress. And he wondered just how many more of his men were going to die.


McGraw wanted to get back to the Base well before the B-17s came in. Sally asked him if he could come back later but he told her it was out of the question. As they talked quietly by the sink, Ruby Bilton, grim-faced and irascible, sat in her chair by the fireplace and glowered at them. Betty had been drawing a picture.

'Uncle Joe! Uncle Joe! See what I've drawn!'

'He's not your uncle!' snapped her grandmother. 'Stop calling him that.'

'I don't mind, Mrs Bilton,' said McGraw.

'But I do,' she retorted. 'He's not anything to do with you, Betty. Remember that.'

Sally was stunned rather than annoyed. Whatever was decided, it was not going to be argued out in front of the little girl. She sent Betty off to her room. Reluctantly, she left, handing her drawing to McGraw.

'What's got into you, Ma?'

'It's time somebody said it.'

'Said what?'

'I've had just about as much as I can stand.'

'Do you mind explaining that?' Sally had her hands on her hips, the defiance rising in her.

'Everyone pointing, everyone talking about us. Because of you and – It's not right!'

'That people talk?' asked McGraw.

'Carrying on under the same roof as the children. I won't have it in my house!'

'But it's not your house,' Sally reminded her. 'It's mine. And what I do or don't do in it is *my* concern.'

'Like me to go, Sally?' said McGraw.

'You know I don't, Joe,' she replied, making no attempt to hide the affection in her voice. 'This house, everything in it . . . it's yours as much as mine. You can do what you like.'

'You're shameless!' muttered Ruby.

'I'd be careful what you say, Mrs Bilton,' warned McGraw, stepping towards her.

'Are you threatening me?'

'No. Just advising you to mind your own business.'

'Do you know who you're talking to?' she gasped.

'I surely do. The most disagreeable, selfish, mean-spirited old woman I've ever met. How the kids could have a grandmother like you, and how Sally's stood you for six years, I can't imagine. But I know one thing – she's suffered more in that time than you could make up to her in a lifetime of repentance.'

'Get him. . . out of here!' spluttered the old woman.

'I'm not the one who's going,' he announced. 'You are. So, beat it. You've got your own home to go to and you're not wanted here. So get moving. And *now*. If you haven't packed your bags and cleared out in ten minutes, I'll carry you out and dump you in the road.'

'And I'll help,' added Sally.

Ruby goggled at them for a moment then opened her mouth to abuse her daughter-in-law, but McGraw took another step forward and she got the message that they were serious about her departure plans. She scuttled out, grumbling noisily.

'I think she's going,' said McGraw with a smile.

Sally looked up at him with gratitude and awe.


All over Market Wetherby, people had been waiting by their telephones for news about the bombing mission. When the formations passed over the town in the early morning haze, everyone had known where they were going and what sort of dangers they would encounter. Vi Blair was in an agony of apprehension for Chuck Ericson, and she cried with relief when he rang her from the Base to tell her that he had returned safely. Letty Mundy, tormented by the thought that Mario might be torn from her in the same way that Harvey had been, spent the whole day in a brooding silence and could not be coaxed out of it until she heard that Mario had come back.

Among the many others who had worried about friends or sweethearts was Helen Dereham. After hearing that Jim had rung the house, she contacted the Base next morning to be told in confidence by Rufus that he was leading the formations over Germany. She steeled herself to concentrate on her work and her mind had gone blank for an instant when a telephone call alerted the hospital to the fact that the casualties from the mission were high. But Jim, miraculously, had not been among them. She almost ran to him when she saw him waiting outside her office.

'Jim . . . you're safe!'

'Just about.'

'I didn't know. I couldn't ask anyone about you . . .'

'I'm fine. How's Hansen?'

'I helped with the operation. He may lose the sight in one eye. But he should pull through.'

'We've kept you pretty busy, I'm afraid. You've been working non-stop in that operating theatre. Do you know what time it is?'

'I've lost track of time,' she said, wearily.

'Four in the morning.'

'As late as that? Then what are you doing here?'

'What d'you think? Come on, Doc. We'd better get you home.'

He took her by the arm and led her through the main door. The cool night air refreshed them and they paused in the middle of the forecourt to breathe it in. Stars twinkled above them in a clear sky.

'My jeep's over there.'

Helen desperately wanted to go with him but she knew that it was impossible. 'Thanks, Jim. I have my own car,' she said.

There was a long pause and then she found herself in his arms, responding to his kiss with a passion that she had denied for too long. When the kiss ended, they both knew that it had committed them irrevocably. It was something that neither of them had intended. But neither of them had been able to resist.

'Goodnight,' she whispered, shaken.

She hurried to her car and drove off without looking around again. He stood there, watching, until she was completely out of sight.

# CHAPTER TWELVE

Another day, another mission, another terrible price to pay. The surviving crews returned to their quarters and tried not to think about the latest batch of missing faces. They were too tired to sleep and simply lay on their bunks or lounged against walls, morose, subdued, emotionally drained. Like the others who had come back from a long day in the sky, the crew of the 'Ginger Rogers' suffered from the delayed shock of combat. Chuck Ericson was trying to write a letter to Vi but his pen would not move. Elmer Jones, flat on his back, was playing his harmonica but its notes only reinforced the mood of sadness and dejection. Mario Bottone was leaning against the window frame and staring out through the glass, but he saw nothing. One of the other gunner sergeants blew meaningless smoke rings into the air. Nobody had anything to say.

The door opened and Hymie Stutz came in. His usual aggressive manner had disappeared and he stood there with his head lowered. Eventually, Mario spoke.

'What d'ya want, Hymie?'

'Buzz . . . our left waist gunner. You know . . . ?'

Elmer stopped playing and Chuck put down his letter. The gunner sergeant stubbed out his cigarette. For once, Hymie seemed lost for words.

'Well?' asked Chuck.

'Doing great, they said. Be up and about in no time. Half an hour ago, Krotnik says, he . . . haemorrhaged . . . Blood everywhere . . . And before anybody could . . . Buzz just kicked off.'

They were all looking at him now, a hurt, crumpled little figure trying to cope with the loss of yet another friend.

Mario went over to him and spoke as gently as he could. 'Hymie . . . Beat it, huh?'

'He still owes me a dollar forty. But I just seen the guys come round with . . . ya know, with the bag. They cleared out Buzz's locker. And now there ain't nothing left.'

He looked despairingly around each of the faces and then went slowly out.

Chuck Ericson picked up his letter again. Elmer Jones started to play his harmonica. Mario Bottone gazed vacantly through the window once more. And a new cigarette sent smoke rings into the air.

'What would you do, Helen? To begin with, I hadn't heard from him, or about him, for six months! Then completely out of the blue, he phones! His destroyer's got a walloping hole in it, and he'll be on leave in London while it's being patched up.'

'Oh . . .'

Helen was not really listening to Phyllis Lambourn. She was watching Ronnie out in the garden, sitting in his wheelchair and trying to serve tennis balls at a galvanized metal dustbin lid that had been hung from a tree.

'What on earth is one supposed to say to one's "ex" of all people?'

'I don't know,' murmured Helen, then the sight of Ronnie prompted a question. 'Is he all right . . . not wounded?'

'I didn't ask. He sounded chirpy enough. Will I go up to town and meet him at The Dorchester? For a drink.'

'A drink?'

'And anything else that occurs to him,' said Phyllis with a well-bred giggle. 'Well, we all have to make sacrifices in wartime, don't we?'

'Yes, we do,' agreed Helen, still gazing at her husband.

'Anyway, darling, as you've got all those onerous duties of yours to perform in London, why don't we go up together?'

'It's a thought . . .'

It was not one that appealed to Helen but she had to give some token consideration to the notion in order to get rid of Phyllis. She followed her guest out through the front door and waved her off, then went back in to get ready for work. By the time that she had changed and gone into the sitting room again, Ronnie was already there, sorting through some gramophone records. Tired from his exertions in the garden, he had come indoors for a peaceful hour with his pipe and some music. She kissed him, put the record of his choice on the turntable, then set off for the car.

Ronnie lit his pipe and puffed at it thoughtfully as he settled back in his chair. The opening chords of Bruch's Violin Concerto in G Minor filled him at once with a curious feeling of nostalgia. His mind went back over the years of his marriage to Helen and he reviewed the wonderful times they had shared together. When the first movement ended and the reflective yet sensuous Adagio began, the power of his memories made him gaze longingly at the photograph of his wife that stood on the table beside the fireplace. She was wearing a long, then fashionable dress and looked so young and striking.

On impulse, Ronnie lifted himself up by taking the weight of his body on his hands, reached for the mantelpiece and tried to use it for support, inching his way towards the photograph. When he got within reach of the table, he lost his balance and fell to the floor, knocking the table over with a crash.

He was still trying to untangle his limp, useless legs when Pat rushed in.

'Daddy!' she said, helping him back into the wheelchair with some difficulty. 'What on earth happened? Are you all right?'

'Nothing to worry about, darling.'

'But—'

'No harm done . . . I think.'

'Where were you going?'

'Over there,' he explained, pointing to the table. Pat set it right again and then picked up the photograph. The glass in the silver frame was cracked. 'My favourite picture of your mother. Clumsy fool that I am! I've ruined it!'

'Where is she?' asked Pat in a tone that implied her mother was partly responsible for the accident. 'If Mummy had been here—'

'Your mother is where she's needed most. At work.'

'At work,' muttered Pat.

'She wore that dress the night we heard Heifetz . . . at the Queen's Hall. We seemed to have time to listen to music in those days.' He sighed as the record came to an end. 'Now she has to be at the hospital seven days a week. And when they do give her a break, like tomorrow, she has to rush off to London.'

'Why does it always have to be *her*? Why not somebody else?'

'Because somebody else is not half as good at getting things for the hospital out of those stingy people at the Ministry.'

'She ought to spend more time here with you, Daddy.'

'Oh, don't worry about me, Pat. I may look like a knocked-out old tank, but I'm not going to rust away for ever.'

She returned his smile then looked down ruefully at the picture of her mother.


The Lounge Bar at The Plough was crowded with GIs but the place was unnaturally quiet. Most of the chatter came from the few locals present and the only laughter was from a grey-haired woman on her fourth bottle of stout. Conversation between the Americans was brief and muted, and there was a sense of exhaustion about them all. Even Chuck Ericson, normally so boisterous and talkative, simply wanted to sit at a table with Elmer and Mario, saying nothing. Vi Blair could not understand his attitude towards her.

158

'I can't get a word out of him, Dad.'

'Don't try, love. These lads had the stuffing fair knocked out of them last week. And their pride's hurt, too, I shouldn't wonder. Give Chuck time.'

'Doesn't he love me any more?' she asked, deeply hurt. 'If he thinks that . . . that he's made a mistake about me, why doesn't he say so.' Her acute distress had taken all the colour from her face. 'We're *engaged*, Dad!'

'I haven't forgotten, Vi. Any more than Chuck has.'

'He can hardly bring himself to say "hello".'

'Lad's got two things on his mind,' explained Jack Blair. 'One of 'em's you.'

At that moment the door opened and Red Burwash came in with Herman Krotnik. They pushed their way to the bar, anxious to buy a last drink before closing time. Their buoyant manner was thrown into relief by the subdued atmosphere. When they had ordered two pints of beer, Red looked around the bar with disapproval.

'What gives, Herman?' he asked.

'I don't like it, Red.'

'Nor do I,' replied Red, slapping the bar-top with his hand so that he attracted the attention of the others.

'Look,' began Jack Blair, as he pulled the pints, 'most of us here in Market Wetherby . . . we knew the boys . . . the ones who didn't come back. And we'd all like you to know how sorry we are.'

'We're sorry, too,' Red answered, loud enough for all to hear. 'Coupla days ago, we were drinking with them . . . eating with them . . . shooting craps with them. But being sorry for them won't get us in the air to fly another mission! Right, Herman?'

'Right!'

'They were great guys – all of them. But their work's done. We're still alive and we still got work to do. Stick with the living, Jack! It's not the dead who need your sympathy!'

It took a little time for these sentiments to be appreciated by the others but then the chatter slowly picked up and the

GIs seemed to have been freed from their earlier somnolence. Conversations now regained some of their old sparkle and animation.

Vi Blair wanted her father to explain something. 'Well, Dad?' she asked. 'One of them's me, you said . . .'

'Ah. Yes. There's you, Vi. And there's this war he's got on his hands. He's being pulled in different directions.'

'I suppose so . . .'

'So just bide your time, eh? I wouldn't make things harder for Chuck than they are already.'

Vi nodded and looked across at Chuck. He was still hunched over his beer but he was at least talking to his companions now.

Red Burwash had swallowed half a pint of beer and heard something that made him grin broadly.

'Are you sure, Herman?'

'Sure I'm sure. Got it out of that old woman, Lester Carson. After I'd twisted his arm.'

'No missions for two weeks!'

'Two weeks stand-down for the whole 8th Bomber Command.'

'Wowee!'

'And anybody says the 8th don't deserve it,' challenged Herman, glaring around the room, 'I'll knock his teeth down his throat.'

'Two weeks!' repeated Red.

'I'm gonna get good and drunk every day.'

'And nights?'

'Nights, too.'

Red Burwash came to a decision, finished his drink in one mighty gulp, slammed his glass down and then crossed to the table where the three members of his crew were sitting.

'Listen to me, you guys! Tomorrow, you poor saps have got leave coming to you. And I'm taking you up to London. Okay?'

'Why London?' asked Elmer.

'What's the deal there?' said Mario.

'I'll be on the first truck out of the gate. So don't you miss it, or I'll have your hides for shoe leather!'

'Thanks, Skip,' said Chuck, 'but I—'

'Don't thank me! I mean to show you guys that there's another world out there. Some of you got too fixated on this one-horse town.'

The remark was intended for Chuck, whose engagement to Vi had not pleased his captain at all. Red made his way back to Herman Krotnik.

'London's full of slick chicks. One day, maybe Chuck'll thank me for saving him.'

'And one day, maybe he'll bust you in the kisser,' said Herman, who was more perceptive than might be supposed.

'Time, gentlemen! Time, gentlemen, please!'

Jack Blair called the signal for customers to empty the last drop in their glasses and get to their feet. Chuck Ericson, however, remained seated. Without even looking in her direction, he knew that Vi Blair was hovering behind the bar.

'Come on, Chuck,' urged Elmer.

'Out, Fatso!' ordered Mario.

'Uh?'

'Out, out, out!' yelled his friend, pushing him forward.

The place was emptying fast. Vi went over to stand by Chuck and waited for him to speak first.

'Vi . . . You heard what the Skipper said . . . I can't not go.'

'I was hoping we . . . I was looking forward to the day in the country that we promised ourselves. Just us.'

'Listen,' he said, trying to explain. 'All you get to see in here is a crowd of maniacs horsing around. But up there . . . we're one crew. I'm part of them . . . they're part of me. Just one of us screws up and we're dead. No second chance.'

'I know it's been a rough week for you . . .'

'It's been hell, Vi,' he admitted, standing to hold her hands. 'I . . . I *can't* not go to London.'

She fought against her disappointment and nodded, then she kissed him gently on the lips. Jack Blair included Chuck in his shout to the stragglers.

'Time, gentlemen . . . please!'


Helen Dereham cycled along the country road and felt grateful for the cooling breeze. She was travelling between two different worlds and she knew that she could not belong to them both. Behind her was the world of her family – Ronnie, Pat, Dereham House, social position, middle class respectability; ahead of her was an uncertain world of danger, glamour, emotional complication, a world that could explode into nothingness on the next mission to Germany. Her duty told her that she must stand by her husband, but her heart was suggesting that she might commit herself further to Jim Kiley. Either way she was going to hurt someone deeply and not come out of it unscathed herself.

As she came round a bend and had to cope with a slight gradient, her mind went back again to a conversation that she had had the previous night with Ronnie. He had been waiting up for her when she had got back and he had given her such a warm welcome. When she offered to make her trip to London an excursion for the day, he had insisted that she stay the night, see a show perhaps, at all events give herself the treat that she deserved after all her strenuous work at the hospital. Then, as she had offered to help him upstairs, he had announced that it would be so much easier if he slept downstairs. Helen knew that he had done it to save her the trouble of struggling up two flights with him, but it was an odd sensation, nevertheless, sleeping under the same roof as him yet in a different room.

Ronnie had been so ready to encourage her to enjoy herself a bit and to have a break from Dereham House and its responsibilities. Unwittingly, he had made possible a closer relationship with Jim. It was this consideration that helped her to make up her mind.

She turned down a rough track that led to the woods and then pulled over to the jeep that was parked behind some bushes. Jim gave her a grin but she was still nervous about being seen and recognized, glancing furtively around her. He found a combat jacket in the back of the jeep and put it around her shoulders, sticking his hat on her head.

'Okay?' he said, leaning in to kiss her.

'No, please don't,' she replied, pulling away. 'Jim, I can't see you again. Not like this. We're bound to meet . . . at the hospital . . . in the town . . . but, Oh God! You know what I mean.'

'Yes.'

'You do understand?'

'I understand very well. You love me—'

'No!' she said, not daring to think about it.

'As you must know, I love you. What I don't understand is how you can pretend it's not true.'

'Do you think because I . . . because I can't get you out of my head that I don't still love my husband? Do you?'

Instead of answering her, he pulled her close and kissed her full on the mouth. She did not resist and the embrace was long and intense. Then Helen broke away and picked up her bicycle again.

'You can't go . . . not like this.'

'Goodbye, Jim.'

'At least let's talk about it.'

'There's no point.'

'There's every point, Helen,' he argued, still astonished by her decision. 'Today. We'll talk some time later today.'

'I'm going to London.'

'For good?' he asked, the idea paining him.

'Just overnight. On official business. There's still a war to be fought, you know. And perhaps . . .'

'Go on.'

'And perhaps a few hours away from here might help me to come to my senses.' She handed back the hat and the combat jacket. 'Forgive me,' she said. 'It was all my fault.'

163

She began to cycle back towards the safer of the two worlds.

If Albert Mundy had been the sort of man to savour the ironies of life, he might have drawn some wry amusement from the situation. Instead, it had only intensified his bitterness. What his children had done to him, he believed, was in both cases a deliberate insult. Because he hated Americans, Letty had befriended one of them and he was powerless to object since he was indirectly in partnership with the man. Because he had a long-standing dislike of Jack Blair, his son, Peter, now having left school, had actually gone to work at the pub. Albert had been betrayed by them both and nothing that his wife could say would persuade him otherwise.

'Fancy a noggin, Albert?' asked his brother-in-law.

'Some of us have work to do!'

'So do I, mate. Me and Mario's having a little business discussion over at The Plough . . . Oh, any message for Peter?'

'No!'

'I'll just give your kindest regards to Jack Blair . . .'

Sid Davis set off jauntily across the town square. He represented yet another of the ironic tricks that had been played on Albert. The brother-in-law who was resented and distrusted had made himself indispensable to the running of the shop. Instead of being able to throw him out, Albert had been forced to let him stay.

Letty, Peter, Sid. A conspiracy. He began to wonder if his wife was going to stab him in the back as well. He went into the shop and was reassured to see her serving a customer at the Post Office section. With all her faults, Vera would not let him down.

Sid, meanwhile, indifferent to his host's worries, was sipping his first drink and complaining that Mario was late for his appointment. Half an hour passed and the complaints became louder. Jack Blair called in Peter from the cellar where he had been stacking the crates of empty bottles.

'Seen Mr Bottone?' asked Jack.

'No.'

'He's messing me about,' said Sid. 'I got things to do. People to see.'

'Shall I tell him you were after him, Uncle Sid?'

'It's not just me, Peter. There's Letty. He's neglecting her.'

'Letty?' asked her brother, concerned.

'You'd see for yourself the state she's in if you was still at home, son. Breaks my heart, seeing how she feels about Mario. You can't tell a girl like her she's got eyes like deep pools one day, then not bother seeing her for a week. I mean, it's not blinking fair!'

Right on cue, Mario himself came rushing into the bar. He looked as if he had been running and was still panting a little.

'Sid, I got three minutes before the posse catches up with me.'

'No time for me to buy you a drink, then,' said the other, putting his wallet away at once.

'Come on, come on – what's the deal?'

'The deal, my old son, is the biggest thing I ever dreamed up. Er . . . let's step over there where no ears can hear.' Sid led him to a quiet corner and then continued. 'We made a packet out of that Gala Dance. Right?'

'When I finally got my share out of you.'

'What d'you say to us making that kind of profit every week? How? Let Sid tell you. Those mates of yours up at the Base. What they got their tongues hanging out for? I mean, what's their number one priority? Money? Medals? Getting the first boat home?'

'Dames,' said Mario, flatly.

'Right first time. Dames. Now it so happens that my close friend and London business associate, Benny, counts among his personal friends the classiest, sexiest, most '"patriotic" girls in town. The like of which you've never clapped your peepers on.'

'So, you reckon we can—'

'Yes, Mario. It's going to be our pleasure to arrange for these dames to meet your mates. For which privilege they'll pay through the nose – and you and me'll be quids in.' He paused, but was disappointed by the lack of enthusiasm. 'Well, don't fall over yourself!'

'First, I gotta see the dames.'

'Mario, I'm the middle man. Take my word for it.'

'I get to see the dames first – or no deal.' Mario checked his watch. 'Time to go.'

'Okay, I'll fix it up. Benny ain't going to like it, but if you insist . . . Now, how soon can you get a pass to come up the Smoke?'

'Up the what?'

'The Smoke. The nation's capital. London!'

'Oh, sure. The Smoke. Tonight . . . when else.'

Sid Davis was so delighted that he bought Mario a drink after all. This deal would be the most profitable yet.


It was a modest but comfortable hotel near Russell Square and it was very busy when they arrived. Most of the guests who were coming in and out were servicemen of assorted nationalities and Phyllis Lambourn picked out a Polish airman, a Free French Major and two blond Norwegian sailors as the most personable of the Allies on show. Unfortunately, they all had a woman with them, except the Major, who had collected a matching pair. Helen Dereham put her identity card back in her bag and came over from the reception desk.

'Packed out. Thank heaven I booked.'

'The bar's closed,' said Phyllis.

'I think I'll go straight to my room.'

'And ages before Dicky gets here,' hinted the other.

'I'm right at the top and there's no lift. But why don't you come up for a moment, Phyllis?'

They climbed the stairs to a small, musty attic room with a sloping ceiling and rather austere furniture. A large jug of water stood in a bowl. Both were cracked and neither was needed. There was a tiny bathroom through the low door in one wall.

Phyllis kicked off her shoes and sat on the bed. 'What a perfectly beastly room, Helen!' she said.

'I shan't be in here long enough to notice.'

'I suppose when this was a large, family house, the slavey had this room – poor little cow!'

'By the time I get back from my meeting, I'll be too tired to care,' said Helen, unpacking her overnight bag.

'My God! You don't know how lucky you are!' Phyllis announced suddenly.

'Lucky?'

'Busy as a bee with your patriotic duties – and your hospital – and your family. I've got nothing. Nobody.'

'There's your husband.'

'Ex-husband. And let's not pretend that Dicky really wants to see me. He's probably been stood up by his latest girl and hauled me in to fill the gap. I know it – yet like a fool I still come running!'

'Nothing's easy these days, Phyllis. For any of us.'

'This evening I've got a chance – about a hundred to one, all right – but a chance of picking up the pieces of my life and sticking them together. If I don't make a muck of it, or . . .'

'Or?'

'Or Dicky doesn't come to the conclusion that he was right, after all, about our divorce . . .' She looked at Helen sadly, her defences down for once. Then she thought about her friend's situation. 'Whereas you and the charming, amusing, ever-loving Ronnie . . . well, you know exactly where you are with him, don't you?'

'Yes,' said Helen, quietly.

'Your whole life a straight road from the cradle to the grave. No mistakes, no failures, no complications. Lucky!'

Without even trying to, she had touched on a raw nerve.

Helen, cool and normally so restrained, responded with a rare burst of anger.

'Oh, for God's sake, Phyllis, you're being utterly ridiculous! Why can't you stop thinking about yourself, and just be grateful and glad – if only for one evening – that Dicky *does* want to see you? He may simply want female company, your company, and the chance to forget mines and torpedoes and living in wet clothes day and night! Only you can know whether you want your husband back, but you don't have to impress him – or seduce him. Just be yourself, and don't try so bloody hard and maybe he'll come back to you. If that's what you really want.'

Phyllis gazed at her in astonishment, wondering what had provoked the outburst. There was a deal of truth in what had been said but it did not make her like Helen any the better for it.

Jim Kiley hurled his bag into the back of the jeep and climbed in behind the wheel. He was going to London to join Rufus at a conference with General Ira C. Eaker himself presiding. It was a top-level number, and he would get his opportunity to ask a question that had been troubling him for some time now. In the previous week, the 8th Bomber Command had made its most intensive and sustained effort so far. On the Saturday, over three hundred B-17s had attacked Heroya, Trondheim and Bergen. The 525th Bomb Group – led by Jim himself – had been given its first assignment on the Sunday when Kiel and Warnemünde had been the targets. On Monday, Jim and his planes had been back there again, this time over Hamburg and Hanover, one part of an all-out bombardment of the area.

Wednesday had seen the deepest penetration into Germany so far when an armada of planes from the 525th and other bomb groups had flown their cargoes all the way to Oschersleben. The overall devastation caused by these missions had been so impressive that some people were calling it Blitz Week. It was a name that Jim Kiley detested. His overriding concern was not for the statistics of bombs dropped or targets hit but for the details of Bomber Command's losses.

What those who boasted about a Blitz Week were forgetting was the fact that it had swallowed up around ninety crews — some nine hundred young men either killed, wounded or captured — and put over a hundred B-17s out of action. A normal combat loss of five per cent was acceptable. When it reached a staggering twenty-five and more, it became, in Jim's view, totally unacceptable. The question which he intended to put to General Eaker was this: how many more Blitz Weeks would there be before he found that he had no bomb groups left?

Jim remembered the other reason that was taking him to London. The jeep shot away and was soon flashing through the main gate.


That evening saw Pat Dereham and her father in the sitting room, discussing a subject that had been bound to come up sooner or later. Ronnie was trying to be reasonable yet firm, but he was making little headway against his daughter's determination.

'I just want to stay here, Daddy.'

'For my sake?' he asked.

'Partly.'

'Oh, Pat! That won't do. You've got your own life to lead. You'll regret Cambridge in the end. The war won't last for ever and—'

'Only partly. The other thing that brought me home . . . oh, Mummy knows what I mean!'

'Don't I get let in on the secret, darling?'

'It's sort of complicated,' she admitted, wishing that the topic had not arisen. 'Between Mummy and me, I mean.'

'I see,' he said, rather lost.

'I know she's having a dreadful time at present, what

with the hospital, and all those extra jobs everyone makes her do, and . . .'

'And me,' he supplied.

'No, Daddy! Not you!'

He stirred the coffee that she had made for him and pondered. He could sense her discomfort and tried to find its cause.

'I wonder, does all this . . . preamble, have anything to do with—?'

'A man. Yes.' Having confessed this, Pat became more agitated than ever. 'Don't you see, Daddy? She's being horrid – and silly – and unfair! And – oh, hell!'

'Unfair? To you?'

'To us all!'

Pat realized that she had said more than she had intended but it was too late to call back the words now. Ronnie sipped his coffee, his expression giving nothing away at all.

# CHAPTER THIRTEEN

Although she was tired from the long meeting, Helen Dereham decided to walk back to her hotel so that she could see something of London. The city looked grey and sad in the early evening sunshine. There were less buses and fewer taxis and almost no children to be seen. Window displays had a half-hearted quality about them as clothes shops sought to promote utility garments, bookshops offered War Economy editions and food stores sold their limited supplies subject to rationing. The Luftwaffe had left its mark everywhere and Helen lost count of the number of damaged or bombed-out buildings. More distressing was the sight of a large gaping hole in an otherwise complete row of premises, a hideous disfigurement like an eye gouged out of its socket. Posters abounded. The tone was imperative. People whom she passed, especially the servicemen, had a kind of forced gaiety about them, a determination to keep smiling that had nothing to do with genuine happiness.

Helen was glad when she reached the hotel. Visits to London in the old days had been wonderful occasions, but now she was feeling faintly depressed. She collected her key from the clerk and then turned to see someone waiting for her by the door to the bar. It was Jim Kiley. Her immediate impulse was to get away and she made for the stairs. Jim got there first.

'You can't walk out on me twice in one day.' He had hold of her arm and she could not escape without a scene. 'My friend, the barman, says he's got vodka. Real Russian vodka.'

She came to a decision, went into the bar and found a seat. He joined her and ordered two glasses. It cost three shillings and sixpence. She diluted her drink with water.

'How did you find me?' she asked.

'Phoned your secretary at the hospital. And don't bawl her out,' he said as her anger showed. 'She had no reason not to tell me . . . Drink up. Then we'll find some place to eat.'

'No.'

'Helen . . .'

'You can't have forgotten what I said.'

'Don't you like vodka?'

'What?' She looked down at her glass. 'I've never tasted it before.'

'You won't taste it now with all that water you added. Come on. Can't insult our Russian allies. Here's to us!' He raised his glass to her and, reluctantly, she lifted hers and sipped it. 'Well?'

'Jim, this is silly. I must go.'

'Don't, please. I need cheering up. I've just left Rufus. Boy, what a meeting we had with the top brass! Still can't get my way with Rufus, though. Any other CO takes it as normal his Exec. flies combat missions. But not Rufe. He won't let me go again. Thinks it's too dangerous.'

'I'm glad,' she said, looking at him for the first time.

'Too dangerous for the Group, he means! To be left without a leader. But I'm working on him and one of these mornings I'll be up there with the rest of the boys. Now suppose – just suppose – that I fly that mission and don't come back. How will you feel then about not sharing this evening with me?' He took another sip of his vodka and smiled hopefully. 'Just one evening together?'

'That is the worst – most blatant – most unforgivable blackmail!'

'You're right, Helen. The very worst.'

She wondered if it was the vodka that had started to give her that warm and mellow feeling.


It was not the first time that Vi Blair had taken an awkward task off her sister's hands, but that did not make it any easier. She still felt embarrassed when she was shown into the sitting room at Dereham House by Pat. The warm and friendly welcome which she received from Ronnie only made it worse because it increased her guilt at having to bring bad news to him. When invited to sit, Vi perched on the edge of a chair, her shopping bag beside her. Though her voice was trembling, she came straight to the point.

'Major Dereham, sir. Dad wanted you to know about Rosie . . . Fact is, she had to see them down the Labour and she's been directed.'

'Ah.'

'First thing Monday morning, she starts at the parachute factory.'

'Well, nobody's allowed domestic servants these days,' he said, philosophically. 'I'm grateful to you, Vi, for taking the trouble to let me know.'

'Rosie was . . . too upset to tell you herself.'

'Was she?'

'Yes, sir. She feels bad about it. You being . . .'

'I'm no less grateful to Rosie, then. She shows great . . . feeling. Question is,' he said, addressing Pat, 'what are we going to do now?'

'Mummy will have to give up her work and stay at home to—'

'Oh, I don't think we need go to those lengths,' he said, cutting in politely. 'What about Nanny?'

'Nanny?'

'Do you think we could persuade her to up sticks and come all the way down here from Scotland? To look after us?'

'It would be marvellous if we could!' said Pat.

'We can try.'

'She is terribly, terribly old, though,' remembered Pat, beginning to have doubts.

'Don't let Nanny hear you say so,' he warned, then gave an apologetic smile to Vi. 'This is awfully boring for you and I've been terribly remiss . . .'

'Sir?'

'Only because I can't get about as much as I'd like, mind. Still, let me offer you my belated but very best wishes.'

'Oh,' said Vi, rather dully. 'Thank you.'

'His name's Chuck!' added Pat.

'American, eh? Well, I'm sure you'll both be very happy.'

Vi thanked him again, rose to go, then recalled the gift that she had brought. She took out a bottle wrapped in brown paper and handed it to Ronnie. He unwrapped it with interest.

'From Dad,' she explained.

'Malt whisky!' he exclaimed in astonishment.

'He says he's very sorry about Rosie leaving you,' said Vi, fiddling nervously with her shopping bag.

'That's hardly your father's fault . . . and he doesn't have to give me this by way of compensation.'

'Oh, please take it, sir. Please!'

'How can I refuse?'

'Dad says that he knows a few round here would like that bottle but wouldn't appreciate it. And he wouldn't mind betting there's plenty of others in safe jobs'd appreciate it, but don't deserve it. So he'd be obliged if you'd have it.'

Ronnie Dereham was suddenly very moved indeed.


The Bowsprit was a noisy, crowded, uninhibited pub with nautical decor, obliging barmaids with professional cackles, and low windows that overhung the Thames, giving the patrons a view of dark, murky water. It was not the first pub they had been to that evening and Mavis, the big, cheerful, welcoming barmaid, saw at once that they had already drunk a fair amount. Twenty years of pulling pints had given her some insight into the effect of beer on different individuals and she could assess that effect quickly. Red Burwash had become loud and pushy, insisting on paying for the next round. Mario Bottone had become even more animated but there was an edge of desperation to his high spirits. The drink had made Elmer Jones look at life through large, tolerant eyes and there was a permanent grin on his face. Only Chuck Ericson seemed to have been immune to the pleasures of the tankard. After four pints, he was more miserable than ever, thinking how much better off he would have been had he stayed in Market Wetherby with Vi Blair.

The GIs had chosen The Bowsprit because Sid had arranged to meet Mario there. Mavis, who seemed to know everybody, nodded when Sid's name was mentioned and promised to send him across to their table if he arrived. The men now sat and drank and laughed. Chuck continued to brood.

'Aren't you glad you came?' demanded Red, punching his flight engineer playfully on the shoulder.

'I been thinking about that, Skip.'

'You have, huh?'

'And to tell the rock-bottom, honest-to-God truth, I don't know what the hell I'm doing here.'

The others assured him that he was having a wonderful time, but they knew that he would need to be completely drunk before he even started to believe them.

Suddenly, there were six at their table. The two women were young, lively, heavily made-up, gaudily-dressed and ready to giggle at almost anything. Mario blossomed at once. Red bought them drinks. Elmer, at first shy, soon responded to the easy candour of Dolly, the bolder of the two, and he quickly got used to the strong perfume that was cutting through the fug of tobacco smoke like a knife. Chuck had no interest in the pleasant vulgarity of the London tart. His mind remained in Market Wetherby.

An hour or more passed and the atmosphere in The Bowsprit grew thicker and jollier. In one corner, a crowd of British civilians and servicemen were singing 'Roll Out The Barrel' at the top of their voices. In another corner, a French soldier was amusing his companions with crude speculations about the anatomical deficiencies of Adolf Hitler. At the bar, Mavis was coping with the orders of half-a-dozen customers at once while still managing to keep a watchful eye on what was going on around the room.

Elmer now had his arm around Dolly and this had brought him to the notice of three beefy US seamen, who began to make jokes at his expense. Dolly told him to ignore them. Mario was still giving Win, the other woman, a sharp-featured Cockney with snaggly teeth, the benefit of his advice on how to make money. Red Burwash urged the gloomy Chuck to drink yet another glass of beer.

Sid Davis came into the bar and Mario spotted him at once. He excused himself from Win and pushed his way towards the counter where Sid was now standing. Before he could speak to his business partner, however, two dark-faced men with broad shoulders beneath their snazzy jackets appeared. Sid recognized them.

'Soapy! Mal! Where's Benny?'

The newcomers took an arm apiece and virtually lifted Sid from the ground. He was rushed out of the bar before he could even protest and Mario was left dumbfounded. When he tried to go after Sid, he found that he was held by Red Burwash.

'Leggo, Skip. You see what those lunk-heads did?'

'I saw.'

'Listen, sonny,' explained Mavis, leaning across the counter. 'The two gentlemen with Sid – they're Benny's friends.'

'I know all about Benny,' said Mario.

'Did you know that Sid's been messing about with his girl?'

'Uh?'

'Benny don't like it. So, if you're a friend of Sid's, don't go advertising it round The Bowsprit. Okay? I don't want trouble. Understand?'

'Yeah, sure. I understand.'

Mario shrugged and went back to the table. The US

seamen had decided to have some fun now and were openly baiting Elmer. Wanting to impress Dolly, he was replying to the men with all kinds of threats that he could never fulfil. Eventually, the biggest of the seamen nudged Elmer deliberately so that he spilled some of his beer over Dolly. Her screech was ear-splitting.

'Owwww! My dress!'

'Hey, knucklehead! Look what you done!' yelled Elmer.

The seaman grabbed hold of Elmer's jacket and hauled him to his feet. Aided by his two friends, he began to push the airman around and a ring of people soon formed to enjoy the entertainment. Red Burwash needed to exchange only a glance with Chuck before the two of them sprang into action. The biggest of the seamen was just about to fell the hapless Elmer with a punch when he himself was lifted bodily, carried over to the open window and, Mario now supporting his legs, hurled through it with amazing ease. The splash brought water well past the level of the window and gurgled cries of alarm started to rise out of the Thames.

Chuck looked around at the two remaining seamen.

'Okay, Sinbad. You're next.'

The men did not stop to argue. Deprived of their leader and not wishing to share the same fate, they took to their heels and ran out. Chuck and Red shook hands then turned to accept the thanks and congratulations of the man they had saved. It stunned them when Elmer instead berated them.

'What you guys go and do a thing like that for?' he asked in aggrieved tones. 'I was gonna flatten him!'

The yells from the water were more desperate now and Mavis suggested that the seaman might not in fact be able to swim, especially after all the beer he had drunk. Chuck immediately grabbed one of the coils of rope that formed part of the decor, and dropped an end through the window.

There was more splashing and gurgling from outside, then the rope went taut. Chuck and Red heaved hard and the man was slowly pulled up to the window, where waiting hands helped him in and lay him down on the floor. He looked white, shaken, sorry for himself and very wet.

'What d'you think, Elmer?' asked Red.

Elmer decided to be magnanimous in victory. 'His turn to pay for the beer,' he said.

They had dined at the Strand Palace and been amused by a menu that included Ballotine de jambon Valentinoise, Assiette froide et salade, Hot Spam and Cold Spam among its offers. What the meal had allowed them to do was to regain their appetite for each other's company. Jim had taken her back to her hotel and gone upstairs with her, but the moment they had stepped into her room, they heard the familiar wail of an air raid warning.

'Hell! Wouldn't you know it!' said Jim.

Helen shut the door and put her arms around him. Outside, feet could be heard running downstairs and a voice advised all guests to get down to the ground floor as soon as possible. Jim suggested that they should go while they could.

'Time enough when we hear the bombers,' she said, crossing to the window. 'Still daylight, so it's almost certainly a false alarm. I saw a bomber once . . . in the searchlights. It looked pathetic.'

'Doesn't it *ever* get dark?'

'When Double British Summer Time ends. You don't mind . . . staying up here, do you?'

'No.'

'If we are bombed . . .'

'What then?'

'They'll find our bodies together.' She went back to him and leaned her head on his chest. 'Poor Ronnie . . .'

They waited and listened for a long time but the tell-tale drone did not come. Jim eventually detached himself and went out of the room. When he came back, he had a bottle of vodka and two glasses. The 'All Clear' sounded as he poured out the drinks.

'Primitive,' he apologized, handing her a glass, 'but c'est la guerre.'

He sipped his drink and waited while she did the same, then he took the glass from her again and put both of them down on the table. He reached for her and pulled her close, his hands feeling for the zip at the back of her dress. She let him start then pushed him gently away, shaking her head.

'I'm sorry, I'm so sorry.'

'It's all right . . .'

'Oh, but it isn't!' she said, angry at herself. 'If I'd had the scruples and the will-power and the commonsense of a mouse, I'd never have let things get this far! I can't even commit adultery properly!'

'Now, let me tell *you* something,' he replied, wiping away her tears with his fingers. 'First day we met, I had you figured.'

'You did?'

'Sure. Where I come from . . . the kind of people I mix with, everybody knows your type.'

'Oh.'

'Classic rich-bitch English aristocrat. Chilly as an iceberg.'

'Me?' she said, surprised.

'You, Helen. Then something happened and I didn't like it. I had to go through the painful business of breaking down my cherished prejudice. And see you as you are. Since that moment . . . my head and my heart haven't stopped spinning.'

She was back in his arms again and he held her tight. It made her both want him and fear him all the more.

'I don't know what to do,' she admitted. 'I know what I ought to do, but I'm not strong enough. Until a few days ago, I thought I could cope. I'm a born coper, you see – ask anyone in the town, in the county! I could cope with the awfulness of things at the hospital. All your young men, shattered, looking to me for hope and strength. I could cope with the war – the endless, miserable, exhausting, bloody war! I could even cope with Ronnie, trying to grin and pretend his life isn't ruined. I thought I could stand like a rock in the middle of the family, and let the war wash round us. But now . . .' She let him take her face between his palms and kiss her tenderly. 'Now, it's destroyed. It isn't the war or anything . . . It's me.'

When Jim Kiley left her room shortly after, he went straight down the stairs and out through the main entrance. He did not see the woman who had been complaining to the barman that her ex-husband had failed to turn up. From where she was sitting, however, with a good view of the reception area, Phyllis Lambourn saw him only too clearly. She glanced up the stairs, came to an instant conclusion and went quickly out of the bar.


Ronnie Dereham had mastered the difficult art of getting in and out of his wheelchair, but he could still not do it at speed. When the telephone rang while he was sitting in an easy chair, therefore, it was some time before he finally wheeled himself into the hall. The instrument continued to ring on as if it knew that it would be answered eventually. Fearing that only an emergency would make someone call that late in the evening, Ronnie picked up the receiver and gave his number. A woman's voice, roughened so that he wouldn't recognize it, and further distorted by the crackle on the line, told him that his wife was at a hotel in London, sharing a room with a Major Kiley. There was a momentary pause and then Ronnie spoke with his customary politeness.

'I'm sorry. I can't hear a thing you're saying. This line really is hopeless.'

It was only when he put down the receiver again that he was hit by the full force of the blow.

\*

It was long past closing time but Chuck, Mario and Elmer, all three pleasantly and harmlessly intoxicated, were still at The Bowsprit, lying back in their chairs with their feet on the tables, singing 'The Rose Of Tralee' with maudlin dedication and coming at the notes from all directions. As they neared the end of the second verse, Elmer felt his pockets and stopped singing.

'Hey, you guys – I been robbed!' He was annoyed when they carried on singing and turned out the linings to show them. 'It was that Dolly! Said I was cuddly and kept putting her arms around me. Now I know why! She was like an octopus, that girl. *She's* got my dough.' He took a deep breath and yelled. 'Red!'

'Knock it off, stupid!' warned Mario.

'Captain Burwash is otherwise engaged,' added Chuck.

'*Red!*' called Elmer even louder.

'We ain't supposed to be here!' hissed Mario.

Mavis came out from the room at the back of the bar and Red followed soon after, his clothes in some disarray and his manner furtive. Mavis, on the other hand, looked complacent and fulfilled.

'*Re-e-e-d!*' bawled Elmer for the third time, not seeing that his captain had returned.

'Naughty boy!' scolded Mavis. 'It's after time. Do you want me to lose my licence?'

'Dolly – she lifted all my dough!'

'Oh, never mind, dearie. It's only money.'

'*Only?*'

'What ya beefing about?' asked Mario. 'Enjoyed yourself, didn't you?'

'Some things are more important than money,' said Mavis, nudging the embarrassed Red.

'Mavis . . . I guess it's kinda late.'

'Ah!' she sighed.

'And we've got to get back to the Base.'

'Oh, well . . . needs must when the devil drives . . . Far to go?'

'No. Suffolk. Market Wetherby.'

'*Where* did you say, Red?' she gaped. '*This* time of night? You just can't!'

'We'll grab a taxi,' he said, nonchalantly.

'But it'll cost a fortune.'

'Sure. But as you said, it's only money . . . Okay, fellers.'

With some reluctance, Mario and Chuck opened their wallets and took out a bundle of notes each. Elmer was now glad of his poverty. Red added his own generous contribution to the pile of money, then scooped it all up and put it into his cap. Mavis crossed to the door and unbolted it carefully, then she told them to keep quiet while she opened the door and took a peep outside.

'All clear,' she whispered. 'Not a sound now, boys.'

'Night, Mavis,' muttered Elmer.

'Don't worry, dearie,' she said, planting a kiss on his cheek. 'I'll kill Dolly when I see her.'

'Oh, thanks,' he mumbled and went out.

Mario came next and he, too, claimed a kiss from Mavis. He had a final request for her. 'When you see Sid . . . kill him, too,' he asked, then disappeared into the darkness.

Chuck was now standing at the door and Mavis knew that she could not be quite so affectionate with him. He had spent most of the evening talking about a certain person and Mavis respected the prior claims that the girl obviously had.

'Well, Chuck. Give my love to the lucky lady. Vi, innit?'

'Yes. Thanks, Mavis. I'll do that,' he said and left.

Red Burwash was still there and it was him that she had singled out for special privileges in her back room. She now closed her eyes and pursed her lips, waiting for him to take his leave with a final, passionate kiss. But his embarrassment was too great now.

'Mavis, you're one helluva fine lady,' he said, then he shook her hand and walked out quickly.

She sighed with disappointment and closed the door.

Elmer was burbling about his lost money, Chuck was thinking about that first meeting with Vi, Mario was hoping that his stomach would stop revolving like a propeller, and Red was grinning. As they struggled up some steps from the embankment and crossed to the street opposite, none of them was aware that, barely fifty yards away, Sid Davis was lying unconscious in a dark alley.

It took a long time to find a taxi and an even longer time to convince the driver that he should leave the city limits and drive all the way to East Anglia, but they succeeded eventually. The journey was not without its traumas and stops were fairly regular. Dawn was rising as the long-suffering taxi driver unloaded them at the main gate of the Air Base and collected his handsome reward. A different kind of reward awaited the airmen.

They languished behind bars in the guard-house and began to take a more jaundiced view of the trip to London. Elmer could not forget that he had been robbed by a woman.

'All the skipper's fault,' he complained, when Red was taken off to give an account of what had happened. 'I shoulda stayed right here. Had a drink at The Plough with my Rosie.'

'*Your* Rosie?' challenged Mario.

'Well, she sure ain't *your* Rosie!'

'My Rosie, Hymie's Rosie, any-guy-on-the-Base's Rosie! Anything but your Rosie!'

'Watch what you say about Rosie and me!'

'Okay, okay!' said the tired Chuck. 'Wait till the morning, huh? Then beat each other's brains out.'

Elmer took out his harmonica and began to play 'Blues In The Night'. The voice of an unseen man in another cell sang the words. When Chuck had been lulled asleep and Mario had sagged with fatigue, Elmer put his harmonica away and spoke with quiet triumph.

'*My* Rosie!'


It was still early when Helen Dereham arrived back home next morning. She let herself into the house, went into the sitting room and drew the curtains with a flourish. When she turned around, she saw Ronnie asleep in a chair he had obviously occupied all night. Beside him, on the low table, was the framed photograph with its shattered glass.

# CHAPTER FOURTEEN

Time was running out for Letty Mundy. Each day that passed made her more conscious of the baby that she was carrying, and each night began with an anxious hour in front of the bedroom mirror. She had started to put on weight and had learned to stand differently in order to disguise the fact. Peter's departure from the house to work at The Plough had been a double blow for her. Not only had it robbed her of the sympathy of the one person who knew the truth, but it had enraged her father to the point where he swore that his daughter would never walk out on him in that way, and his vigilance had become even more oppressive. It was only a question of time before he would see for himself what she was taking such pains to hide.

Fearing his reaction, Letty had been forced into confiding in her mother. It had been a traumatic experience for both of them but they had come out of it much closer. Vera Mundy had been shocked by the news but she had adjusted to it, putting her concern for Letty before any pointless recriminations. She had been so calm, practical and supportive that Letty had almost suspected that her mother was no stranger to the situation.

'I don't know where to begin, Letty . . .'

'Oh, Mum!'

'Well, if I can't, I can't.'

'Shhhh! Dad'll hear us!'

Letty was at the table, finishing off the last of the bubble and squeak for supper. Because her usherette's uniform was too tight for her daughter, Vera was trying to let it out. They had had to wait until Albert had gone to bed before they could even begin.

'There's only one thing for it, Letty . . .'

'What?'

'You can't keep it from Dad any longer. You'll have to tell him.'

'No, I couldn't!'

Vera sighed and took up the uniform again. Her skill with needle and cotton was limited and she was daunted by this particular task. She fiddled with the waistline of the skirt, wondering how and where to gain the extra inches that were needed. Letty finished her supper and was gazing straight ahead of her.

'Sometimes, I forget what he looked like . . .'

'Who?' asked her mother.

'Harvey.'

'Oh.'

'I keep getting him mixed up in my mind . . . with Mario.' There was a pause, then she spoke with sudden desperation. 'Why doesn't Mario come round to see me.'

'I expect he's busy.'

'He only ever seemed to come when Uncle Sid was here. And now that *he's* gone . . .'

'Sid'll be back, never fear. I know my brother.'

'But where is he?'

'I haven't a clue, Letty. I just know he'll be back. He'd never go off for good, leaving all his stuff upstairs.'

'Blow Uncle Sid! Blow Mario!' shouted Letty.

'Oy!' yelled an aggrieved Albert from upstairs. 'You two!'

'Just coming up!' Vera called.

'Going to be nattering all night or what?' he asked.

The women waited until they were sure that he was not coming down. Vera had hidden the uniform under her chair and Letty had altered her sitting position to conceal her slight bulge.

'He loved me, Mum . . . Harvey really loved me. First day we met . . . it was love at first sight.'

'Harvey was a nice boy,' said her mother, carefully.

'He was wonderful.'

'Yes, I know. But you've got to forget about him. It's the

only way, Letty. You've got to set your sights on the future.'

'I'm *trying* to . . .'

Letty shifted her position on the chair and loosened the belt of her dressing gown to make herself more comfortable. Vera watched her and then came to a decision.

'If you won't tell your father, I'll have to.'

'No.'

'Are you going to wait until he can see for himself?'

Letty walked across to her and retrieved the uniform from its hiding place, thrusting it back on to her mother's lap.

'I can't tell him yet. Not till Mario's proposed to me!'

A new anxiety began to clutch at Vera Mundy.


McGraw had dozed off in the chair beside the fireplace. Blitz Week had left him and his men with a mammoth task of repairing damaged planes and the long hours had exhausted him. Sally had finished the washing up and was putting the crockery away. The chink of the lid being replaced on the teapot woke McGraw up. As his eyes opened, he found he was looking at the black-edged photograph of Stan Bilton.

'You two would've got on all right together,' Sally said.

'Uh?'

'Both as tough as old boots.'

As she studied the face herself, there was resignation rather than anguish in her expression. She had not cried herself to sleep for some weeks now.

'Time to go,' said McGraw, standing and stretching.

'Don't have to. Unless you want.'

'I don't want. But I got work to do and some of my young fly-boys are sassy enough without me giving 'em cause.' He picked up his jacket and slipped it on. 'One of 'em don't know no better'n to be going getting himself married.'

'Oh?'

'Girl at the pub. The tall one.'

'Vi's a decent girl.'

'Decent?'

'Well, your fly-boy . . . .'

'Master Sergeant Chuck Ericson.'

'I shouldn't think he's having to make an honest woman of her.' They exchanged a long, direct look. As he was about to speak, she put a finger to his lips. 'I was happy with Stan,' she said. 'The time I had him. But my marriage is over. There's no going back. I'm glad you're here. And grateful. I don't ask anything else, Joe.'

The disappearance of Sid Davis had caused concern among a number of people. Mario Bottone, who had boasted freely to the other GIs about the London girls he was going to lay on for them, now found himself under constant pressure from straight questions. Letty Mundy, who had realized that Mario only seemed to come to the house when her uncle was there, longed for his return. Vera, knowing her brother better than anyone, feared that he had got into some kind of trouble again. Elsie, the waitress at the Empire Cafe, was already missing her daily chuckle with the flamboyant character who always came in for morning coffee. And Albert Mundy, whose business had prospered since he had entered an arrangement with his brother-in-law, now began to shudder at the prospect that Sid might not come back.

Then, early one morning, the prodigal returned. Albert was sitting over a cup of tea and cursing the noise of the B-17s overhead, when there was an insistent knock at the back door. He went to open it and gasped. Sid was almost unrecognizable. His suit had lost its impeccable vulgarity, and was now torn, filthy, and stained on one lapel with blood. His shoes were dirty, his tie was ripped and his hat was battered and muddy. A black eye and a still swollen lip completed the disguise.

'Stone me!' exclaimed Albert.

'Just in time for a cuppa,' said Sid, chirpily, strolling in as if there was nothing amiss.

'Look at the state of you, man! Have you been in a fight?'

'And while we're at it, a couple of bangers and some fried bread'd go down a treat.'

'No letter, no phone call, not even a measly post card to let us know where you were. Now you march in as if butter wouldn't melt in your mouth, and start ordering breakfast!'

'Brewed up, haven't you?' said the other, sinking into Albert's chair and stretching out his legs.

'Enough for one. Me.' He sat opposite Sid. 'You look horrible.'

'Ah – there's a story behind that.'

'I bet!'

'Monday night's raids – no, I tell a lie – Sunday.'

'Nothing on the wireless about any air raids.'

'Silvertown way . . . dockland. Landmine. Just as I was coming out of the pub. Well, I had to lend a hand. Just like you would have done, Albert. Eh?'

'Well . . .'

'Whole block of flats – demolished! Caaah! You never saw anything like it. Fallen masonry, timbers, dead bodies all over the shop.' Seeing that he had now got his listener's attention, Sid went and got himself a cup, poured milk into it then added tea from the pot. 'But you're right, Albert. As always. I am in a state. Even now. Crawling about on my hands and knees under what's left of these flats. Chunks of brick just waiting to fall on my head. More dust up the old hooter than in the Sahara. And what happens?'

'I don't know,' said Albert, now hooked. 'What did happen?'

'Just when I couldn't stand it any longer, I hear this faint cry. Very faint, it was.'

'A faint cry?'

'Well, I can't give up now, can I? Not till I've got 'em both out of the rubble.'

'Got who out?'

'This sweet old lady and her pussy cat. Naturally, the old suit came in for a bit of a dirtying up, and my clock took a pasting as well from all those jagged bricks.'

'Albert!' called Vera from the shop.

'Business still on the up and up?' asked Sid.

'You know it is.'

'My pal, Mario, been round recently?'

'Albert!' The call was louder this time.

'Yes, Mario's been round. And rung every day as well. He doesn't seem any too pleased with you, Sid. I got a strong impression that you'd let him down!'

'Albert!'

Grabbing his overall, Albert answered the call this time and went out, leaving Sid with the problem of concocting a story to placate his partner.

Albert, meanwhile, had gone into the shop to find a queue of customers waiting for him at the counter. Vera, serving her own queue at the Post Office section, indicated the person whom her husband had to deal with first. Albert recognized Sir Arthur Maylie and at once assumed his most unctuous manner.

'Good morning, Sir Arthur!'

' 'Morning, Mundy.'

'The tide is turning now, Sir Arthur. Don't you agree?'

'Tide?'

'Beating the Jerries at Tunis. Then the invasion of Sicily earlier this month. And now old Mussolini's been deposed.'

'I didn't come here to discuss the war, man!'

'Oh, no. Of course not . . .'

Seeing that Sir Arthur wanted a private word with him, Albert moved a few paces further along the counter. His distinguished customer followed him then stretched over to speak in a whisper. Albert nodded, asked him to wait, then went off into the back room. He reappeared with a small box and started to wrap it in brown paper, smiling at Sir Arthur while at the same time trying to listen in on a conversation that two people were having across from him. Vi Blair, in her Land Army uniform, was talking to Sally Bilton.

'We're publishing the banns.'

'Don't be afraid, that's all, Vi.'

'Afraid?'

'Do what *you* want. Other people, what they say . . . it's nothing to do with them. Nothing at all.'

Vi could see that Sally was referring to her own situation as well. Since Ruby Bilton had been evicted from her daughter-in-law's house, she had told everybody in town about the visits of McGraw and what, in her view, lay behind them. Vi Blair knew Ruby too well to take much notice of her scandal-mongering but she realized that it must have gained Sally a lot of strange looks and disapproving comments.

'We were sorry – all of us at The Plough – about Mr Bilton.'

'Thank you,' replied Sally, appreciating the thought but not wishing to talk about Stan. 'Now, what about your wedding dress?'

'Have to make do, whatever I can.'

'Next time you're passing, look in, Vi.'

'Why?'

'I've still got my wedding dress. Try it for size.'

'Oh, I don't think—'

'Nothing lost by trying, is there?'

'No, I suppose not. Thanks. Thanks very much.'

'Next please!' called Vera, and Vi stepped up to the counter.

Albert had now finished wrapping the package. He took some notes from Sir Arthur, got the change from the till, then passed both money and parcel across to him. Sir Arthur was brusquely grateful.

'Much obliged to you, Mundy.'

'My pleasure, Sir Arthur . . .'

'Beats me how the dickens you manage to get hold of them.'

Albert thought about Sid and the self-satisfied grin vanished from his face. He served the next customer.

Rosie Blair continued to dominate the fantasies of more than one man at the Air Base. As the members of the 'Ginger Rogers' crew lounged about in their quarters at the end of their day, they had a visit from Hymie Stutz who arrived in time to hear some disparaging remarks being made about himself by Elmer Jones.

'Watch it, Fatso!' he warned.

'You know this guy?' Elmer asked Mario.

'Not me,' replied the other, staring at Hymie as if for the first time in his life.

'Me neither,' decided Elmer.

'I don't mix with bums,' explained Mario. 'It ain't good for my social status.'

'Who's speaking to you, Bottone?' snarled Hymie. 'Listen, Jones. I'm going to the pub tonight and I don't want no fat sons of bitches muscling in on my girl. Okay?'

'*Your* girl?'

'*My* girl!'

'Elmer,' said Mario. 'I can hear this noise. Like someone chewing the end off a fifty-calibre Browning.'

'You hear me, Fatso!'

'Hymie, will you stop calling me Fatso!'

'Something ya oughta know. Rosie don't like ya no more. She don't like the way ya been two-timing her!'

'When? When did I do that?' demanded Elmer.

'When you went up to London and spent all your dough on them fancy Piccadilly women.'

'Huh?'

'Likewise, Rosie especially don't like the noise ya make with that tin toothpick ya keep stuck in your fat mouth sometimes. Okay, Fatso?'

'Hymie, you call me Fatso just once more and I'll . . .'

'You'll what, Fatso?'

Driven beyond endurance, Elmer put out a tentative fist that sailed harmlessly past Hymie's ear.

'He hit me!' cried the little sergeant with righteous indignation. 'Did you see that? He hit me!'

Elmer swung at him again and this time Hymie stepped back to avoid the blow. He put up his own fists now and danced around on his toes, beckoning his adversary to come and get him. Just as the two men were about to close with each other, Chuck Ericson came out of the washroom and stood between them.

'What gives?' he asked.

'It's the big fight,' said Mario. 'Madison Square Gardens. On my right, Primo Carnera. On my left, Jack Sharkey. Coming up for the sixth and final round.'

'What are they fighting about this time?'

'What else – Rosie?'

'It ain't just Rosie,' said Elmer. 'Hymie keeps calling me Fatso.'

'Why not?' retorted Hymie. 'Everybody else does.'

'Everybody else don't say it the way *you* say it!'

'Elmer,' suggested Chuck, 'take some exercise, lay off the hamburgers and hot dogs, and in a coupla months nobody's gonna call you Fatso.'

'That don't settle who's taking Rosie out tonight.'

'Well, who is, Elmer?'

'I am.'

'No, he ain't!' yelled Hymie.

'Okay, I'll tell you what to do,' said Chuck as the men squared up to each other again. 'You're both going to the pub together tonight.'

'With *Fatso*!'

'With *him*?' asked Elmer, equally appalled.

'You go up to the bar together, and you ask Rosie which one she wants to see after the bar closes. Then, whichever one she chooses, that's it. For tonight, for every night, and always. No more fights, no more arguments. No tricks, no nothing. And that way the rest of us'll get some peace and quiet.'

'Great idea, Chuck!' applauded Mario. He looked at the two men who clearly did not like the notion. 'Okay, fellers?'

'Yeah, okay,' conceded Hymie.

'Elmer?' There was a threat in Mario's voice.

'Okay,' Elmer said at last.

'Blessed are the peacemakers,' said Chuck, then went quickly to his locker and started to dress.

'You still got nearly two hours before they open the golden gates to let us out, Chuck,' Mario pointed out.

'No. I got two minutes. Then I'm gonna be late.'

'What for?' asked Elmer.

'The Colonel. I gotta get his permission for the wedding.'

The others fell silent. They all wished Chuck well but they had reservations. It was banking on a future that might just not exist.

Indirectly, Albert Mundy had been responsible. If he had not sold a box of cigars in his shop that morning, the notion of a bridge four might never have occurred. As it was, Sir Arthur Maylie had been generous enough to want to share his good fortune and he had invited three guests to sit at his card table and sample a quality Havana. Ronnie Dereham, one of those invited, had had doubts about going at first and had suggested to his wife that Phyllis Lambourn might go in his place. Helen had pointed out that since the visit to London, Phyllis had not been seen in Market Wetherby. Mention of London brought memories back to both husband and wife and they were both glad to move away from the subject. Helen herself was not able to go along to the Maylie residence because she had to stay at Dereham House to welcome Nanny, now on her way south from Perth.

Sir Arthur had realized that Ronnie would need a chauffeur and so he had arranged for another of the guests to pick him up. Ronnie was therefore waiting for Jim Kiley to arrive.

'Extraordinary!'

'What's that?' asked Helen, trying to fix a target card to the wall of the sitting room.

'Kiley, fetching me in his jeep like this. The Americans don't seem to have heard of petrol rationing.' He pondered. 'I didn't know the Major was one of Arthur's bridge brigade.'

'Arthur seems to think he's championship class.'

'Very likely.'

'They met here, while you were overseas. I did tell you . . . After a sticky start, they got on very well together.'

Helen had finished putting the target up and stepped back so that Ronnie could look along the barrel of the air rifle that he was holding. He was satisfied with the positioning. Helen excused herself to go and lie down for an hour. It had been an exceptionally tiring day at the hospital and she felt that she had to gather her strength ready for the appearance of Nanny. Because there was a hint that she wished to be out of the way when Jim showed up, Ronnie encouraged her to go. He then reached for a packet of slugs, loaded the rifle and took aim.

He was still firing slugs at the target twenty minutes later when Jim arrived. Pat showed him in and they found themselves staring down the barrel of the air rifle. Jim stood aside so that Ronnie could put yet another slug into the bull's-eye. He himself had a couple of shots but was nowhere near as good a marksman. Ronnie offered him a glass of whisky from the bottle which Vi had kindly brought him, but Jim declined. He felt that it was perhaps time that they made a move. He explained that he had brought a driver with him so that there would be two pairs of hands to help Ronnie in and out of his wheelchair.

Though ready to leave, Jim was all the time hoping that Helen would put in an appearance. Ronnie seemed to read his thoughts.

'By the way, Helen's had rather a heavy day at work. Gone to lie down. You'll forgive her not being here to say hello.'

Before Jim could answer, Ronnie propelled himself

towards the hall in his wheelchair. Jim followed and walked past Pat on the way. She was tense, watchful, unsmiling and he could see the suppressed hostility in her eyes. He could also hear the unspoken accusations.

Nanny was an alert, wiry Scotswoman in her mid-sixties with her own firm opinions and a healthy disrespect for those of other people. When she left her home in Inverness the previous day, it took her six hours to reach Perth and she spent the night there with her married sister. The train which she caught early next morning seemed even less anxious about getting to its destination and she came to believe that the journey would never end. It was well into the evening before the train was far enough south for her to bother to read the names of the stations. As her carriage pulled up alongside yet another platform, therefore, she glanced out hopefully, only to be disappointed yet again. She closed her eyes with a sigh and drifted straight off to sleep, unaware that a man in the uniform of the British Army had just come into her compartment. He put his kitbag up on the rack then slumped gratefully into his seat. Corporal Stan Bilton had had an even longer journey.

# CHAPTER FIFTEEN

It was going to be an unusual evening. The first indication he had of this was when his wife, the compliant Vera, perhaps for the only time in their marriage, told him to shut up. He had been helping her with the washing-up at the sink while Mario and Sid were playing a game of ludo with the excitable Letty. When Albert had asked his wife in a whisper what the American was doing there, she had replied in a way that had knocked the breath out of him. It was a hint of open rebellion where he had feared it most.

'Something you and me got to talk over,' she warned.

'What?'

'Later.'

'Er . . . Albert,' called his brother-in-law.

'But like it or lump it, you're going to hear it,' she said.

Torn for a moment between the twin calls on his attention, Albert eventually put business first and walked into the shop with Sid at his heels. Letty protested that her uncle was leaving in the middle of the game, then saw a chance to impress Mario with her helpfulness. Playing the dutiful daughter, she went across to the sink, picked up a tea towel and started to dry the dishes. It gave her the chance to have a quiet word with her mother.

'I've dropped the hint,' said Vera.

'*Not Dad!*'

'Yes.'

'You haven't told him? Oh, Mum!'

'Not yet. But I'm going to. I'm not asking you to, Letty. *I'll* do it. Can't be left any longer.'

'But what if Dad—?'

'Don't you worry about him,' interrupted her mother. 'Only one thing for you to worry about. Keeping that lad's interest.'

They looked across at Mario who was straining his ears to listen in on the conversation next door. Evidently, Sid was driving a hard bargain with Albert and relishing the ascendancy he now had over his brother-in-law. Before Mario could hear any more, he became aware that he was being watched. His face brightened and he gave Letty a large, confident, artificial smile. She giggled.

There was a purposeful knock at the back door and Letty went off to see who it was. Vera became the considerate mother-in-law.

'I'm sure you could do with a cup of cocoa, Mario.'

'Well . . .'

'Go on. You've got time. It means so much having you here – not only to Letty either. I'll put the kettle on.'

'Thanks, Mrs Mundy.'

Letty came back in. 'Some bloke for Uncle Sid,' she announced.

'Who?' asked Vera.

'I don't know. Some bloke.'

'Well, don't leave him on the doorstep, girl. Ask him in.'

Letty pouted and went out again, annoyed that she had had no chance at all to be alone with Mario. A visitor was the last thing she wanted. Vera called through to Sid and her brother suspended his sales talk long enough to reply that he would be through in a second. Letty returned, this time with a watchful, boot-faced man of middle years, who wore a raincoat and carried a trilby. Mario sensed trouble and tensed.

'Come in, Mr . . . er . . .' began Vera.

'Thank you.'

'Sid's in the shop with Albert . . . my hubby. He'll be through directly.'

'Good.'

'Here, sit down,' she offered, pulling out one of the chairs from the table and flicking some crumbs off it with her tea towel.

'I'll stand if you don't mind . . .'

Sid came walking breezily into the room but stopped

when he saw the newcomer. A sixth sense told him that he could now be in a very awkward situation.

'Friend of yours, Sid,' explained his sister.

'Sidney Percival Davis?'

'Who wants to know?' asked Sid.

'Formerly of Coldbath Street, Hackney?'

'Formerly. I was bombed out.'

Albert wandered in and stared at the newcomer. Sid's gaze flicked around the room, measuring the distance to the back door and assessing the best route. The man took a step nearer to him.

'Bombed out, you say?'

'Landmine. You should have seen it – something chronic. Fallen masonry. Timbers. Dead bodies all over the shop.'

'Sidney Percival Davis, I—'

The man got no further. A well-aimed punch from Sid hit him in the solar plexus and doubled him up. Letty screamed, Mario got to his feet, Albert asked what was going on, and Sid charged out through the back door, knocking over a chair on the way.

'Stop him!' yelled the man and hurtled after him.

'Police!' exclaimed Albert, now terrified on his own account.

'Albert!' cried his wife, alarmed without quite knowing why.

He grabbed her by the wrist and pulled her into the shop. Then he went to his various hiding places under the counter and hauled out all the tins and cartons that had been delivered to him from the Air Base. Vera, who had been kept ignorant of the details of the business arrangement with Sid, watched with utter astonishment as salmon, cigars, cigarettes, chocolate and other luxury items appeared. Albert trembled with fear.

'Right – as much as you can carry!'

'Why?'

'Dump it in the pond!'

'The pond?'

'Do as you're told, woman!'

The force of this order and the obvious seriousness of the situation made Vera start to gather up what cartons she could. Albert himself found a large cardboard box, filled it to overflowing, then stuffed the remaining tins into his pockets. He unlocked the front door, peered cautiously out, then gave her the signal to follow.

A clear night made the long walk to the pond an agony for both of them, Vera because her arms were aching so much, and Albert because he expected a tap on the shoulder at any moment from the boot-faced Detective-Sergeant. Perspiring freely, they finally reached their destination and dropped their cargoes to the floor. Albert was heart-broken at the thought of having to throw it all into the water but there was no alternative. Unless he was caught with the goods in the shop, he could not be shown to be in league with Sid. Working on this rather desperate theory, he took hold of the first few boxes of cigars and flung them out into the water. Many other sad splashes followed. Albert Mundy was a tragic figure as he led the way back to the shop.

When her uncle had fled through one door and her parents had dashed through another, Letty had been totally bewildered. Mario gave her no time to work out the connection between the arrival of the policeman and the sudden departures. Realizing the danger of his own position, he sat down again and decided to use her as his alibi for being at the Mundy household.

'Sit down, Letty.'

'What's going on?'

'Playing checkers, ain't we?'

'Eh?'

'Ludo, then. Whatever you call it.'

'But—'

'It ain't nothing to do with you, baby. Or me.' He took her hand as she came over and pulled her on to his knees. 'All we do is wait. We sit here and wait.'

She was more bewildered than ever now but at least she

was alone with Mario. His arm slipped round her waist and she began to forget all about what had happened. As they came up for air from the first long, guzzling kiss, Mario jerked his head in the direction of the back door.

'I knew that guy Sid'd let me down in the end.'

'I don't care about him,' she purred.

'Shoulda known better than to trust that—'

'Kiss me again, Mario. For real.'

Mario obliged and a couple of minutes passed by. Neither of them even heard the front door of the shop opening.

Back from the race to the pond and still panting from the effort, Albert slotted home the bolts on the door, then turned to the exhausted Vera, who was on the point of collapse.

'If that copper comes back, you don't know anything.'

'I don't . . .'

'Anything!' he snarled. 'Now, come on.'

He crossed to the doorway at the back and was about to go through when he noticed that she had not moved. Still shaking enough to need the support of the counter, Vera was recovering quickly and becoming resentful of the way that things had been kept from her.

'Vera!' he snapped.

'No.'

'Can't you see the mess I'm in?'

'I'm beginning to.'

'Well, then?' he demanded.

'Letty's in a far worse mess,' she said, the words finally jerking out of her.

'Letty? Letty?'

'She's pregnant.'

'Uh?' Albert might have walked straight into a brick wall.

'And she needs your help.'

She took him by the elbow and guided him into the room at the back. Letty was still sitting on Mario's knee and she was determined to stay there, in spite of the murder she could see dancing in her father's eye.

'Letty . . .' he hissed.

'What?'

'You . . . and . . . *him*?'

Detective-Sergeant Roberts came in on this, breathing heavily after his chase. Vera immediately cut across the dialogue between father and daughter.

'Where's Sid?'

'One of my lads'll catch up with him. You can bet on that, Mrs Mundy.'

'If you folks'll excuse me,' said Mario, easing Letty off his lap so that he could stand up, 'I gotta go.'

'Already?' she complained.

'And who might you be, sir?' asked Roberts.

'Sergeant Mario Bottone, 525th Bomb Group, United States 8th Air Force, Market Wetherby.'

'My boyfriend,' added Letty, completing the liturgy.

Albert was about to object to this but a sharp nudge from Vera made him keep quiet. Letty was now glowing at what she took to be official recognition of her relationship with Mario. Roberts looked steadily at the American.

'I won't detain you, sir.'

'Come on, Letty.'

She needed no second invitation. After grabbing a coat, she went out with Mario, calling that she would be back later. Albert watched them sourly then brought his mind back to his brother-in-law.

'I never wanted him here in the first place.'

'Sir?'

'Sid. Only put him up out of charity,' he explained, not seeing the look of contempt from Vera that this remark earned him. 'Take a look around. We've nothing to hide.'

'That won't be necessary, Mr Mundy.'

'He's my brother,' said Vera. 'I want to know what he's supposed to have done.'

'It's what we know he's done. In a nutshell, your

brother's evaded military service by deception with regard to his physical condition.'

'What?' Albert's jaw sagged.

'I'm afraid there's no doubt about it, sir. Mr Davis paid another man to stand in for him at his "medical". Fact is, he's as fit as you or me. Look at the way he sprinted off! But he just won't do his bit. Rather see fellers like our brave American friend, Mr Bottone, defend his country for him.'

'And if he . . . er . . . turns up again?'

'Let us know, Mr Mundy. Wouldn't do any good trying to conceal his whereabouts. Him, or you, sir.' He headed for the door. 'Goodnight,' he called and went out.

Albert sank into a chair as if he were bearing the worries of the world on his shoulders. His head was spinning.

'Vera, I thought . . .'

'I *know* what you thought.'

'Sid. The black market. All that stuff . . . at the bottom of the pond . . . cost me a small fortune.'

'Good riddance! Letty. She's the one to worry about now.'

'That bloody Eyetie!' he yelled. 'I'll kill him!'

'No. It wasn't Mario.'

'Then . . .'

'And you can't kill a dead man, Albert. That poor boy . . . the one she cried over. Harvey. Her young Lieutenant.'

'*Him?*' Disbelief scored his features.

'Such a nice boy.'

Albert put his head in his hands and groaned. 'What's happening to us?' he asked.

'Mario's fond of Letty,' she said, simply. 'We must hope for the best.'

'Principles. Stick to your principles. I told them. Hammered it in. Letty and Peter. Hammered.'

'Yes, Albert.'

'Now, I'm betrayed by my own son who's gone to live with my worst enemy . . . And all because of that brother of yours, I've lost a fortune . . . Now, there's Letty . . . my little Letty!'

The accumulated miseries of the evening were too much for Albert. He crumpled, gave way to his feelings and was racked with sobs. Vera, who had never seen him cry before, could not help putting her arm gingerly around his shoulders.


Jack Blair could sense that Peter was anxious to speak to him and he waited for a lull. As soon as he began to talk to the boy, however, the door swung open and in rushed Elmer Jones and Hymie Stutz, both in their smartest uniforms and both talking at once. Chuck Ericson followed them in, warned them to follow his suggestion and then crossed to enjoy a welcoming peck from Vi Blair. Elmer and Hymie now pushed up to Jack and demanded, in unison, to see Rosie. Elmer insisted that she was going to go out with him while Hymie stuck to his arrogant claim that she preferred him. Rosie had to make a choice between them there and then. Could Jack please get her?

The landlord of The Plough first pulled them a half-pint of beer each before he broke the bad news. Since she had started work at the parachute factory, Rosie had been coming home fatigued. She had been so weary that evening that she had retired to her bed and was not available either for choosing ceremonies or for being taken out by the man whom she favoured. Elmer was stunned.

'She's in bed?'

'Bed,' confirmed Jack. 'And you're not going up there after her. Either of you.'

Robbed of their reason to fight and deflated by circumstance, the two men stared at each other, united by their joint failure. They were soon passing harsh remarks about the legendary unreliability of women. Jack smiled understandingly and moved away.

Chuck Ericson, meanwhile, had been telling Vi about his interview with Colonel Krasnowici. After some token resistance to the idea, the Commanding Officer had told Chuck that he believed marriage was a wonderful institution – and he knew it from personal experience that stretched over twenty-eight years – then granted permission for the wedding to go ahead. Vi was delighted. She decided that they would call their first child 'Rufus'.

'If it's a boy,' she added.

Caught up in their own happiness, the young couple did not observe the intense conversation that was now going on further down the bar between Peter Mundy and Jack. Peter, after explaining how his father's attitudes had made him leave home, was now thinking about going back. He was guilty about having deserted Letty at a time when she most needed sympathy.

Jack Blair scratched his chin and suggested that Peter might try to see things from his father's point of view.

'I've tried. So's Letty. But sometimes . . . it's as if he hates us.'

'No, son.'

'Like he hates you, Mr Blair.'

Jack decided that Peter was old enough to know the truth about the enmity between him and Albert Mundy. It went back twenty years or more. Jack's eyes glistened as he recalled it.

'Lally, my wife – you never knew her – she died when Rosie was born. Reckon I miss her as much now as the day she died. Well, I'd always had a soft spot for Vera and I suppose she liked me. Then, when she came to me for advice, that's when I did the wrong thing. I'd had it at the back of my mind that maybe we'd get married – after a bit.'

'You and Mum?' asked Peter, very surprised.

'It was all a long time ago. But I think she had the same idea. I think Lally would have been pleased, too, as well – I dunno, Peter. Anyhow, when she got pregnant and came to me to ask me what she ought to do, I told her she'd never be happy with your father. I tried my best to put her off him.'

Peter was too shocked to speak.

'It don't reflect any credit on me, Peter, but that's how it was. 'Course, she did marry him, in the end. Your father must've had an idea I'd done my best to turn her against him, so I can hardly blame him for how he feels about me. As to you and Letty . . . you can see now why he's always been so strict, can't you?'

'Yes . . .'

'I can't say it'll make things easier when you go back, lad. But at least you know the truth.'

Its implications were taking some time to sink in, but Peter was glad that his friend had spoken out. It helped him to appreciate a lot of things.

Nanny finally arrived at Dereham House later that evening and she was given a cordial and affectionate welcome by Pat and Helen. They were so grateful to her for having come to their aid. Helen sent Pat off to the kitchen to get coffee and cake for their guest, then took advantage of her daughter's absence to tell Nanny that Pat had recently had some news which had upset her deeply. Determined to do something towards the war effort, she had applied to join the Women's Auxiliary Air Force but she had failed to pass the medical examination. Doctors had detected a spot on her lung which, though not serious, debarred her from joining up. Helen said that her daughter would have to undergo further tests in six months. Nanny listened to it all with sympathy but her shrewd eyes stayed on Helen.

'You're a different woman from when I saw you last.'

'Oh, well . . . it is three years.'

'Seems to me as if the burden's fallen heavy on your shoulders. You must take care of yourself, Helen. Or it won't only be the Major and Miss Patricia who'll need looking after.'

Helen thanked her for her concern. The refreshments arrived and the three women chatted happily about old times. Pat, trying to be bright and cheerful, was clearly depressed by the news she had received. It was almost as if she felt trapped at being in the house, and had looked upon joining up as a way out.

At length a jeep was heard on the gravel outside and Nanny leaped to her feet. Even in her sixties, she had a turn of speed and she was the first out into the hall to greet Ronnie as he was lifted into his wheelchair. Ronnie was thrilled to see her and their playful banter suggested an old and tried friendship. Having been introduced to Jim, she now took charge and went off to make tea for everyone. Helen addressed her husband, avoiding Jim's gaze.

'How did you get on?'

'Haven't enjoyed a game of bridge so much for years,' Jim said.

'Me, neither,' agreed Ronnie. 'Had a splendid time. Made a disastrous tactical error, though. I partnered Arthur. Lost nearly two quid to the Major and old Riggs-Danby.'

Ronnie was in high spirits and asked if Colonel Krasnowici played bridge. When Jim replied that he thought it unlikely, Ronnie insisted that he and his Commanding Officer should come to dinner one evening. Urging Helen to make the necessary arrangements, he wheeled himself off to the kitchen to prevent Nanny from making her notorious weak tea.

Jim noted that Ronnie had been in that mood all evening and Helen told him that he was often quirky and unpredictable. Their eyes met at last and they held the look. Each could see how terribly they had missed the other. Helen's resolve to be strong and to put her duty to her family first had clearly faltered.

'All I want is your arms about me,' she said, simply.

In the silence that followed, they knew there was no going back.


The house was in darkness when he arrived, except for a chink of light showing through the blackout curtains in the bedroom. He knocked hard several times. At last he heard footsteps.

'Come on, Sal! Let us in!'

Sally Bilton was doing up her dressing gown when she realized who it was. Her mind began to swim, she had to steady herself on a wall and then she let out a series of anguished cries. McGraw came down the stairs at once, wearing trousers and pulling on a shirt. She was waving a hand at the door as if expecting some monster to come bursting through it.

'Are you there, Sal! Open up! It's me!'

With a supreme effort, she slid back the bolt and opened the door.

'What is this – the Bank of England?' asked Stan Bilton, as he stepped into his own home again. He threw his kit bag to the floor, reached for Sally and tried to hug away the memory of three long years. 'Oh, Sal . . . Sal!'

His joy was disturbed by the sight of McGraw, standing at the foot of the stairs with his shirt still unbuttoned. Stan could feel how stiff his wife was in his arms and he brought his head back to look her full in the face.

'I thought you were dead, Stan . . .'

'*I* thought I was dead.'

'They told me . . . you were dead.'

Still trying to work out who McGraw was and why he was there, Stan launched into an explanation of what had happened. 'Doctors, nurses . . . they all thought I'd had it,' he said. 'Flat on my back for weeks on end. No sense, no feeling. But you can't keep a good man down. I mean, if a dirty great Jerry eighty-eight millimetre couldn't kill me, I must be fire-proof.' He nodded towards McGraw. 'What's he doing here?'

'Why didn't you write, Stan? Let me know?'

' 'Course I bloody wrote!'

'Well, I didn't get anything.'

'Wrote enough to fill a book.' He indicated McGraw again. 'Cat got his tongue?'

'Missing! They said missing! Feared dead!'

Stan was taken aback to see his photograph on the mantelpiece, edged with black for mourning. He looked at Sally, at McGraw, at the photograph once more, then back at his wife.

'It's you and him, isn't it?'

'I didn't *know*,' she pleaded.

'All that time out there . . . and I come back to *this*!' he said with disgust, pushing Sally to one side and confronting McGraw.

'I guess there's just one thing—'

'Shut your face!'

'You gotta understand—'

'Ha! I might have known. A Yank! A bloody Yank!'

'Honest, Stan, we didn't know . . .'

'Didn't *want* to know.'

When he shoved his wife away this time it was with much more force and she hurt herself falling across the table. McGraw moved forward protectively and Stan called him closer with a finger. Sally tried to get between them to stop the fight but McGraw, calm and quiet, told her to go upstairs. Unable to cope with the situation, and responding to McGraw's advice, she went off upstairs.

'That's right, Sal,' sneered her husband, 'with a bit of luck you'll find the bed still warm.'

McGraw was preparing to defend himself, keeping Stan at long range by holding both arms out in front of him. He appealed to Stan to accept that Sally did not know, but the latter's anger had left no room for reason and restraint. With a quick feint, Stan dived, grabbed McGraw's shoulders and fell to the floor with him. They grappled violently, McGraw not wishing to hurt his man but having to defend himself from a very determined attack. Stan got him on his back and put his hands to McGraw's throat. An upward jerk of a knee sent the enraged husband sailing through the air, to land with a thud by the fireplace. He clambered quickly to his feet and turned to see that McGraw had done the same.

Another feint, another dive, but this time it was parried

with a few punches. Stan swung his fists as well and connected with a cheek-bone. A left hook made his ears ring and gave him more respect for his opponent. Next he tried to butt McGraw in the pit of the stomach but the American danced aside and Stan went crashing to the floor, knocking over an easy chair in the process. He saw the poker in the fireplace but McGraw was too fast for him. As Stan's fingers closed around the weapon, a large boot came down on his wrist and the poker was wrenched from him and hurled to the far side of the room.

And so it went on. Punches, kicks, grabs, dives, feints, butts, even bites. Blood flowed and the furniture took as much punishment. McGraw had the advantage of height and reach, but Stan had the more aggressive approach, throwing himself fearlessly at the other. McGraw was trying to contain and subdue him without hurting him too much but this was proving difficult. When he himself began to take a real battering, the American replied in kind.

Two men who were practised in the art of unarmed combat. They were well-matched and the fight was long. McGraw eventually got the upper hand and tried, literally, to knock sense into Stan. When Sally tried to stop them, her husband made a lurch for her and she retreated back up the stairs once again. McGraw slowed him with a punch under the heart, then took one near the eye himself. After another ten minutes, they had fought themselves to a standstill. McGraw was on the floor, leaning against a wall, while Stan was spread-eagled across a table.

'Want some more, Yank?' asked Stan, groggily.

'Do you?' Upstairs, a child cried. 'Billy boy,' explained McGraw.

'I've never seen him.'

'I'll make a deal with you, Stan—'

'I don't make deals with Yanks!'

'I'll go now and never come back. But first . . . you gotta make me a promise.'

'*You?* Make *you* a promise?'

'Yeah. Promise me you won't hurt Sally. If you don't . . .'

'What? Tell me, Yank!'

'Then I guess we gotta go through all this again,' said McGraw, hauling himself to his feet. 'And when we done busting each other in two, I still ain't gonna quit till we gotta deal.'

'Bloody Yank!' called Stan, but he was thinking about the terms of the deal.

'Okay. Bloody Yank. Do I get your promise?'

After a long, bleary-eyed pause, Stan Bilton nodded.

'Stan,' said McGraw, crossing to him. 'You never gave me a chance to say it. I'm sorry.'

McGraw staggered to the front door, picked up his jacket and hat on the way, and went out into the night. Stan heard a sound behind him. Sally was holding William in her arms and both of them were watching him with some apprehension. She came close enough for him to put out his hand to touch William's face.

'My son.'

'Nobody else's, Stan Bilton. Let's get you cleaned up. You look as if you've been hit by a bus.'

She led him to the kitchen and sat him down near the sink.

# CHAPTER SIXTEEN

Inside the Parish Church of St Stephen a small but attentive congregation gathered to witness the ceremony. Vi Blair, deciding against a wedding dress, had opted for a cream suit with a wide-brimmed, matching hat. She looked serene and happy as she stood beside Chuck Ericson at the foot of the altar steps. He was wearing his best uniform and had got the air force barber to trim his hair for the occasion. Jack Blair stood proudly beside them, his only regret being that his wife was not alive to share in the joy of the marriage. Rosie, with best dress and coyest smile, was in attendance as bridesmaid. Elmer Jones, taking his duties as best man very seriously, completed the group.

Friends, relatives and a few nosey local people, mostly women, filled four or five rows on the left of the nave. Vera Mundy was amongst them. To the right, on the bride-groom's side, were Mario Bottone, Red Burwash and the rest of the crew of the 'Ginger Rogers'. The other flyers who had come along included Herman Krotnik and Hymie Stutz, whose eyes were fixed on the bridesmaid throughout.

The Vicar asked Chuck to take Vi's hand in his and to repeat the words of the service after him.

'I, Charles . . .'

'I, Charles . . .'

'Take thee, Violet . . .'

'Take thee, Violet . . .'

'To my wedded wife,' continued the Vicar, with Chuck repeating each phrase after him in a strong, clear voice. 'To have and to hold from this day forward, for better for worse, for richer for poorer, in sickness and in health, to love and to cherish, till death us do part, according to

God's holy ordinance; and thereto I plight thee my troth . . .'

When it was Vi's turn to take her vows, she did so with a nervous dignity. The Vicar then indicated that the ring should be produced and Elmer stepped forward.

'With this ring, I thee wed . . .' prompted the Vicar.

'With this ring, I thee wed. With my body I thee worship, and with all my worldly goods I thee endow; in the name of the Father and of the Son, and of the Holy Ghost. Amen.'

As husband and wife knelt together, the handkerchiefs were already out to the left of the aisle and more than one sniff was heard. The Vicar began to intone the prayer.

'O Eternal God, creator and preserver of all mankind, giver of all spiritual grace, the author of everlasting life . . .'

When the service was over, Master Sergeant Chuck Ericson and Mrs Ericson walked down the aisle between the well-wishers. Peter Mundy played the Wedding March on the organ and the couple passed through the arched doorway into the porch outside. Church bells had been silenced since the start of the war and so there was no peal of welcome for the newly-weds, but they did not seem to mind at all. They were happier than they had believed possible as they moved down the path that led from the church.

Some other local people had turned out to see them leave and joined the congregation. Vera Mundy ran after the couple to throw a packet of confetti over them. A woman standing nearby was surprised.

'Where'd you find it, Mrs Mundy?'

'Old stock. From before the war. Just two packets. I've kept one in case my Letty . . .'

'Oh, yes,' said the woman, knowingly.

Vera walked on down the path until she was aware of a man at her elbow. Jack Blair was delighted to see her.

'Thank you, Vera.'

'I had to come. Vi looks so lovely.'

'She does that.'

'And he's a good boy. Not like some of them.'

'You'll come back and have a drink, Vera. Just a few friends.'

'Well . . .'

'Would've sent you an invitation. Didn't think you'd get away.'

'No,' she sighed.

'I'd like it if you came back,' he said, smiling affectionately.

'Just for half an hour, then. Thank you, Jack.'

There were no photographs and the wedding party was making its way straight back to The Plough for the reception. Red Burwash was sceptical about the marriage, believing that it was a mistake for any airman to take such a serious step when he was flying regularly on bombing missions. Mario, thinking only of the pleasures of the marital couch, envied Chuck immensely. Elmer was trying to escort Rosie back, arguing that it fell within the duties of the best man. He was mortified when she told him that she had asked Hymie to accompany her.

'Hymie? Is *he* coming?'

'Oh, yes. Dad's invited everybody.'

Elmer was crestfallen and his spirits were not revived by the single flower that she plucked from her bouquet to give to him. Rosie had chosen Hymie. That said it all.

The wedding reception was held in the Lounge Bar which had been closed to the general public for that morning. A table had been set out in the middle of the room and covered with the large, white linen tablecloth that was kept for special functions. Light refreshments had been arranged carefully to show off the central feature of the table, which was a small but endearing wedding cake with white icing, silver decorations, and the names of the newly-weds piped on the top. Another table sported a huge enamel teapot and some cups, with what looked like a month's ration of sugar in a bowl. Everyone was soon eating, drinking, chatting, enjoying themselves or wondering where the icing sugar for the cake had come from.

Chuck and Vi spent most of the time thanking people for coming and for the presents they had been given. They also listened to advice, some of it sage, some of it obscene, all of it unsought, about what they should try to get out of their marriage. When they did finally get a moment to speak to each other, it was a fleeting one.

'Hi, darling. Know what I'd like to do? Put you in a jeep and drive you some place where we could be away from all of this. Just the two of us, Vi.'

'I'd love that, too,' she said, then saw the vicar bearing down on them.

'Oh, hello, Father,' welcomed Chuck.

'It isn't necessary to call me "Father",' replied the Vicar with his usual heartiness. 'You know, I'm sorry more of your chaps don't come to church to join us in our worship. There's plenty of room.'

'We have our own chapel at the Base, Father.'

'Yes, of course. But I hope that now you've become one of us, so to speak, we shall see something of you on Sundays.'

'I'll surely try, Father – sorry, it slipped out again. I guess I used to call the priest at home "Father". It's a kind of habit.'

'You're not a Catholic?' asked the Vicar, suddenly worried that he might have overlooked an important detail.

'No, sir. Episcopalian.'

'That's all right, then. They count as Anglicans.'

'Have some more sandwiches,' Vi suggested, easing the vicar back to the table and getting a smile of gratitude from her husband.

Whatever else Chuck Ericson wanted to do it was not to trade small talk with the parish priest. He looked around the room at some of the people he was now related to, and began to have doubts. They were so very different from the family he had left behind in America some three thousand miles away, and he felt almost like an alien as he stood there with a cup of tea, a jam tart and the voices of maiden aunts in his ears. Then he saw Vi again in her cream suit and she swept aside all doubts.

Mario Bottone, who had been offering whisky to selected friends, now sidled up to Red Burwash and poured him a tot into a glass.

'Where the hell did you get it, Mario?'

'Don't ask!'

'Nobody told me it was going to be teetee.'

'The old man's going to open a bottle of champagne later on.'

'He'll need to,' noted Red, grimacing. 'I've seen livelier funerals. God! What a country! They don't even know how to have a party.' He sampled his drink and burped gently. 'That's better. And you reckon Chuck's serious about her?'

'He's married her. That's serious, ain't it?'

'Doesn't have to be. I tell you there's going to be one helluva lot of divorces in this man's army when the war's over.'

'You think Chuck is crazy?'

'You bet I do. Can't even take her away on honeymoon, and the way things are just now, she stands a good chance of being a widow by the end of the week.'

'You married, Skip?' asked Mario.

'I was.'

'Divorced?'

'That's right. Best thing I ever did. Say, gimme some more of that, will you?' He took the bottle and helped himself to a generous measure. 'Thanks.'

While Red and Mario were discussing marriage, two of their colleagues were having another round in their running debate about which of them was to take out Rosie Blair. Elmer Jones put his case first while Hymie Stutz plied her with sandwiches. Hymie then tried his charms on her, handicapped by the glowering presence of his rival. Eventually, having drawn all kinds of promises out of both of them, Rosie plunged them further into misery by announcing that she had to work at The Plough that evening and could not go out at all.

'How about tomorrow night?' they asked in harmony.

'I don't know,' she said, evasively.

Elmer and Hymie repaired to the refreshments for consolation.

Jack Blair, meanwhile, had managed another brief chat with Vera Mundy. Memories long dormant had been awakened for them both by the emotional impact of the wedding service, and they both knew that, but for a decision taken twenty years earlier and regretted ever since, they might well have been attending the reception after the marriage of their own daughter.

'Why didn't you bring Letty?' he said. 'You could have brought Letty. Vi would have liked her to be here.'

'I would have, Jack . . . but she's been poorly.'

'Poorly?' His expression altered as he realized. 'Yes, Peter told me about that. In confidence . . . You can't hide her away like that, Vera. It'll cause just as much talk.'

'I know. But Albert won't have it. She's to stay in till the child's born. It's cruel, Jack.'

'Stubborn old fool! I'd like to tell him a thing or two.'

'He wouldn't listen. Least of all to you.' Conscience pricked her. 'I shouldn't be talking like this about him.'

'Thanks for coming, anyway,' he said, squeezing her hand.

'Time for me to go.'

'Not before the champagne.'

He went behind the bar and lifted a tray of glasses on to the counter. A second tray was covered with bottles of champagne. Cheers went up and there was no shortage of volunteers to help to open the bottles, fill the glasses and pass them round. Vi made sure that she kept the first cork that was popped as a souvenir. Suddenly Chuck began to panic.

'I don't have to make a speech, do I?'

'It's customary for the bridegroom to propose the health of the bridesmaids,' she told him.

'We only had Rosie.'

'Then propose a toast to her.'

'But, Vi – I mean, what will I *say*?'

'Ladies and gentlemen,' began Jack Blair. 'You've all got glasses, haven't you?'

'No,' said Elmer, unaccountably left out, but the omission was soon remedied. 'Carry on, sir.'

'Now, I'm a man of few words, as some of you know,' Jack continued. 'I'll say two things then shut up. First, I'd like to welcome you all to The Plough on this happy occasion. And second, I want you all to raise your glasses and drink a toast with me to my daughter and her husband; to wish them a long and happy life together, and may they soon be able to enjoy that life without any interference from Mr Hitler. Ladies and gentlemen, I give you Chuck and Vi. God bless you both!'

'Chuck and Vi!' The response was immediate and enthusiastic.

The couple smiled around at their guests and then looked long and hard at each other, unafraid to show their love and now convinced that their decision to marry so soon had been the right one.


Other opinions of the marriage were expressed at Dereham House that evening where Colonel Rufus Krasnowici and Major Jim Kiley were the guests. Over an inferior blend of coffee, talk turned to the still noticeable friction between the Air Base and the local population. Helen suggested that the wedding that day would help to foster good relations between the two sides but, while Rufus thought there was some truth in this, he said that he hoped the example of Chuck Ericson would not be followed by too many of his men. He emphasized the danger of hasty marriages, made because the Americans were homesick and in a high pressure situation that craved some relief. Rufus shuddered at the prospect of a spate of divorces. That really would create bad feeling all round.

Jim pointed out that there was a risk of some sort in every marriage, however well thought out, and he was perceptive enough to see the shadow of anger pass across Pat's face. Ronnie feared that his guests were putting all the blame on their own men and argued that he had the impression that some of the local girls had almost thrown themselves at the American servicemen.

'Well, that may be the case,' admitted Rufus, not without a hint of pride. 'I guess some of our boys look pretty glamorous to your women.'

'Oh, I think it's only the uniform,' said Pat, spikily.

'But surely it's not like that with Chuck and Vi,' countered her mother.

'I've no idea.'

Helen asked her why she had not gone to the wedding as she had originally planned, and as Vi had wanted. Pat replied that she had had too many other things to do. She then excused herself on the grounds that she had a headache and rose to go. Her parting remark was addressed to Rufus but aimed, as he well knew, at Jim.

'I shouldn't worry too much about British girls. We're a pretty sensible lot on the whole.'

Pat kissed her father on the cheek, said goodnight and left. Rather disconcerted by her manner, Rufus apologized if he had upset her. Ronnie brushed the topic aside by saying that his daughter was tired, as well as nursing her disappointment at being rejected by the WAAF. The offer of more coffee prompted the Americans to decide it was time to leave. They thanked their hosts for an excellent meal and for the kind of civilized company that they did not get at the Base. Jim had to be content with one long look into Helen's eyes but what he saw there made the whole evening worthwhile. Ronnie saw his guests to the door then wheeled himself back into the sitting room.

'Funny fellow, that Major Kiley.'

'Why?' she asked.

'Doesn't say much.'

Jim, meanwhile, was driving the jeep towards the Base and listening to Rufus's complaints about the evening, delivered in the raw, crisp language he had kept in check while with the Derehams. His moans began with the coldness of the house – 'enough to freeze the ass off you' – and ended with the undrinkable coffee. Somewhere in the middle of his diatribe was the protest that being with people like Ronnie and Helen Dereham made him feel as if he was at school again, on his best behaviour.

'They're so goddam superior, Jim!'

'I don't think they mean to be.'

'Your lady doctor was pretty quiet.'

'End of a hard day.'

'She's a fine-looking woman.'

'Yeah.'

'Pretty tough on her, with a husband in a wheelchair. Pretty tough on him, too.' A pause failed to yield the reply he was seeking. 'Do you ever wonder how a guy like that . . .? I mean, if he's paralysed from the waist down . . . I knew a lawyer once in Baltimore—'

'Rufus,' Jim interrupted, 'shut up, will you?'

'Okay,' said the other, amiably. 'Sorry.'

They drove on for a bit then Jim took advantage of his companion's mellow mood to ask when Rufus would let him lead a mission again. Rufus told him that he was needed on the ground and would never fly on a combat mission again. The news hit Jim like a thunderbolt. When they reached the Base, he could not bear to look out at the serried ranks of B-17s on their hard-stands. Desperate to fly yet condemned to stay on the ground. He began to understand how Ronnie Dereham must feel, trapped in a wheelchair.


'I bumped into that woman again on the landing,' said Chuck, coming back into the bedroom. 'She gave me a real funny look.'

'She probably doesn't believe we're married. I expect they get lots of Americans bringing their girlfriends here. She probably thinks I'm your bit of stuff.'

'My what?'

'It's an expression Dad uses. Sort of tart.'

'That's crazy, Vi!' he said, angrily. 'Nobody could possibly think that about you.'

'Couldn't they just. You'd be surprised what suspicious minds some people have. Especially where Yanks are concerned.'

'Yeah, I guess it's our own fault, too,' he sighed.

'Not altogether. Anyway, I don't care what they think.'

'Nor me.'

Their honeymoon was to consist of one night at a quaint Olde English Hostelrie in a quiet corner of the county. Dark oak beams, whitewashed walls and a faintly musty smell gave their bedroom the charm of antiquity and its main feature, a four poster bed with elegant hangings, revived memories of a more tranquil age when sleep could not be disturbed by the drone of heavy bombers.

Chuck had hung up his jacket before going to the bathroom and was now in trousers and open-necked shirt. He put down his toothbrush and moved across to take her in his arms.

'Hello, wife.'

'Hello, husband.'

The first kiss was cut short by her impatience. She jumped into bed and urged him to hurry, telling him how comfortable the mattress was. He asked her not to pull the curtains so that he could watch her, lying there in her nightdress, while he took his things off. When he was naked, he was suddenly shy and climbed in quickly beside her. They embraced again and the shyness disappeared with her nightdress very soon indeed. Vi then became worried that the door was not locked and someone might come in.

'Let 'em,' he said. 'They'll soon realize their mistake.'

They began to make love with the desperation of two people who knew that they would be separated in the morning.

*

The film was 'Sun Valley Serenade' and long before the Glenn Miller Band had glided melodiously through its last number, Letty Mundy was awash with tears, John Payne always had that effect on her. Mario Bottone, seated alongside her, had been more interested in the music, the wisecracks of Milton Berle and the appealing, if chunky, figure of Sonja Henie as the war refugee. He could not understand Letty's tears, especially when she kept saying how much she had enjoyed the film.

It had been her first visit to The Roxy since she had given up her job there as usherette and returned the uniform that no longer fitted her. It had also been her first evening out since her father had become acquainted with the fact of her pregnancy and put her more or less under house arrest.

When they came out into the night air, she was still dabbing away with her handkerchief, ignoring Mario's argument that it was supposed to have been a happy ending. They strolled along in the gathering gloom and then she grabbed his hand and asked him if he loved her. Only half-listening, he assured her that he did, then came to the real reason he had taken her out. He wanted to hear the news about her uncle. Learning that Sid was now in prison, and still fearing the consequences of his own involvement in the illegal disposal of USAAF supplies, Mario pressed for details. Letty had none.

Instead, she asked him about the wedding the previous day. The fact that she had already heard her mother's account more than once did not deter her from wanting to know everything that Mario could remember. He was offhand in his answers, even more so when she began to drop clumsy hints about her own readiness to marry a handsome American airman. Mario's thoughts were clearly on something very different, and when they reached her house, he gave her no more than a perfunctory kiss on the cheek before setting off.

Albert and Vera were in the middle of a row about their daughter when Letty walked in. He talked about shame and humiliation while she reminded him that Letty was not the only girl from Market Wetherby who had got into trouble out of wedlock. Before Albert could answer this reference to their own situation all those years ago, Letty came in, humming 'It Happened In Sun Valley' which had been her favourite number from the musical.

Her mother guessed where she had been and asked if she had had a nice evening, but as soon as Albert heard that Mario had taken her out, he ordered her to bed. Letty went without protest, her mind filled with a fantasy amalgam of John Payne and Mario Bottone, her hopes buoyed up by the fact that she had been taken out at last.

She paused at the door. 'You know, Mum, I really think it's serious this time,' she said, dreamily.

As she went out, Albert Mundy looked at his wife in despair.


Four o'clock next morning, as sleep was providing a pleasant escape from the gruesome realities of strategic bombing, the crew of the 'Ginger Rogers' were aroused by the call of a burly sergeant, who marched unceremoniously into their quarters, switched on the light, and yelled in a way that dragged even those most heavily asleep back to the rigours of another day.

'Okay! Up! Briefing at 0500. Get your chow first!'

He had gone out and banged the door behind him before the first groans were heard. One by one the men adjusted to the light and the unwelcome call to duty. Mario, the first out of his bunk, crossed over to the still torpid Elmer.

'Come on, Fatso. Time to go bomb some Germans!'

'Eh? What? Oh God!'

'I feel just the same, Elmer,' said Chuck, sympathetically.

'We all do,' added Mario, 'but we gotta get up.'

Grabbing the blankets under which Elmer was now hiding, he tugged them right off, leaving his colleague cold, unprotected and vengeful. Eventually, Elmer coaxed his body out of bed and into the washroom.

After breakfast and briefing the men took their jeep out to the 'Ginger Rogers' which looked as tired and unwilling as they did in the first light of dawn. Red Burwash stood beside the plane to supervise his crew as they climbed aboard, having a joke or a word of encouragement with each man as he always did. Chuck Ericson came up.

'I guess we'll have to take special care today,' observed Red with a grin. 'We got a bridegroom aboard. Bet you never thought you'd be going to Stuttgart for your honeymoon?'

'I'd prefer Miami.'

'Hey, Skip,' pleaded Elmer. 'Take it easy this trip, will you?'

'What's the matter? You sick or something?'

'He's okay,' explained Mario. 'He thought this one'd be scrubbed because of the weather.'

'No such luck. Climb aboard, Elmer.'

As Mario started to give the waist gunner a leg up, the jeep carrying Herman Krotnik and his crew went past and the usual friendly abuse was heard. Mario was reminded of something he had forgotten to tell Elmer.

'Hymie says he's got a date with Rosie tonight.'

'*I* got a date with Rosie tonight.'

'Have you really?' asked Chuck.

'No,' admitted Elmer, 'but if *he* has, then *I* have . . .'

He pulled himself up into the plane and his rubber-soled flying boots made dull clumping sounds as he walked on the aluminium surface. Elmer had another mission to face and another possible rejection by Rosie. Superstition got the better of him and he began to fear that it was going to be a terrible day in every way.

Chuck was the next to climb into the 'Ginger Rogers'. As Mario was about to follow him, a sergeant came running up with a message for him, shouting it into his ear as the whirring propellers all around them made normal conversation impossible. Mario blanched.

'God dammit, that's all I need! Skip,' he implored, catching hold of Red's arm, 'get this crate moving. I gotta get out of here fast.'

Through the window of his office, Jim Kiley, still smarting at the news that he was effectively banned from further combat missions, watched the B-17s taking off from the concrete runway at regular intervals. When he turned back to the two MPs who stood in front of his desk, he was not in the best of tempers. The information that they had brought caught him on a raw spot. Behind the two men was Detective-Sergeant Roberts, wearing the smug look of the policeman who believes he has a watertight case. On the far side of the room, Rufus was watching proceedings with interest. Jim addressed one of the military policemen.

'Let's go over this once more. You're telling me that one of my radio operators has been passing PX stores to this guy, Davis, who sells them on the black market in London?'

'That's right, Major.'

'How the hell did Bottone get hold of the stuff in the first place?'

'We don't know, sir. Detective-Sergeant Roberts would like to ask him a few questions.'

'We caught Davis last month,' explained Roberts, 'and he is now in custody at one of His Majesty's prisons. We learned about his activities on the black market when he was being questioned about another matter.'

'And he says Bottone was in it with him?'

'Yes, Major.'

'I guess you can prove that?' asked Rufus, casually.

'We would like to question Sergeant Bottone, sir.'

'Sure you would,' retorted Jim, 'but how do I know this isn't all based on some guy with a grudge shooting his mouth off?'

'The two men were often seen together,' argued Roberts. 'I believe that Sergeant Bottone was a frequent visitor to the house where Davis was staying.'

'Is there a girl inside that house?' questioned Rufus.

'I believe so, sir.'

'So maybe he was visiting her,' suggested the older man.

'I have a list of items,' persisted Roberts, not going to be deflected. He handed a piece of paper to Jim. 'Here, Major . . .'

Jim glanced at the first item on the list, which was four dozen tins of peaches. He whistled in surprise as he saw how many other items there were. Rufus came over and took the list from him.

'Looks bad, Jim.'

'As you can see,' said Roberts, 'it's more than just a case of petty pilfering. Now, if I might have a word with Sergeant Bottone . . .'

'Are you a patient man?' asked Jim.

'I like to think so.'

'Well, you'll need to be, Sergeant. The guy you want is at present 20,000 feet over the English Channel. He'll be back here this afternoon – God willing – any time after five, six o'clock, possibly much later. So if you'd like to wait some place, I'll arrange for you to see him then. Okay?'

The MPs decided at once that they were not going to wait. They saluted and left. Roberts thought it over for some time and then decided that he would go as well. He thanked Jim and took his leave.

'Goddammit! Bottone's one of my best radio operators!'

'Looks like he has other talents as well,' sighed Rufus, handing Jim back the list of stolen items.


They were well on their way to the target area before they had any serious problems. Tucked away in their cramped compartments, wearing bomber jackets, flying helmets, flak vests, Mae Wests and oxygen masks, the members of the crew of the 'Ginger Rogers' looked virtually indistinguishable from each other. Beneath their heavy flying gear, however, were ten very different individuals, each with his

226

own special functions to perform in the plane, and each with his own particular fears to combat. Red Burwash was thinking about his beloved B-17, fearing that it might be damaged more extensively this time around. Elmer Jones was afraid that Hymie Stutz really did have a date with Rosie and was convinced that it was a bad omen. Chuck Ericson was thinking about the fears that his wife must be experiencing while he was on the mission, and he sustained himself with remembered sequences from a wedding night in a four poster.

Mario Bottone, flicking switches with gloved hands, was dreading the return to the airfield where the police would be waiting for him, and part of his mind was already rehearsing his alibis.

Elmer Jones peered into the sky and all at once forgot Rosie Blair.

'Hey, Skip! We got company!'

'How many?'

'Six, I think. Here they come!'

'There's more,' warned Chuck in the top turret. 'Another six. Ten o'clock high.'

'Okay, you guys. Let 'em have it!' ordered Red.

Elmer, Chuck and the other gunners gave the FWs a searing welcome. Mario, determined not to be left out, moved up to the machine gun at the top of his compartment and began to manoeuvre it on its swivel. His field of fire was limited but he was able to fire short, sharp bursts at the attackers. The dog fight escalated as the dozen enemy fighters harried the formation, and the first victim that dropped out of the sky was a B-17, engulfed in flame. Chuck recognized it.

'Jeez. That was Herman, wasn't it?'

'Yeah,' said the white-faced Elmer. 'And Hymie, too.'

'I got one, I got one!' yelled Mario, as his shells ripped into a fuel tank and sent a fighter spiralling down. 'I got one!'

'Great,' said his captain, 'now get another one!'

But Mario had no chance to do so. The FWs suddenly

peeled off and disappeared into the clouds. Chuck yelled out that they had gone, but Red knew they would be back. He addressed the navigator in the nose compartment.

'Give me a position, will you, Dave?'

'We're coming up to the IP at 25,000. Six minutes to target.'

'Don't like that cloud. Might have to make another run.'

'Roger. Do we have enough gas, Skip?' asked Lieutenant Dave Conners.

'Just about. Okay, you guys. We're going in.'

The gunner sergeants still kept their eyes on the sky around them but they were able to relax a little. It was the bombardier's turn to demonstrate his skill. Chuck Ericson thought once again about Vi Blair. Elmer Jones realized just how much he had liked Hymie Stutz. Mario Bottone, exhilarated at the thought that he had shot down his first enemy fighter, burst out laughing. He had the feeling that he was going to enjoy the day after all.

# CHAPTER SEVENTEEN

Stan Bilton wondered how much more of it he could take. As he stood at the counter and stared into his glass of beer, he reviewed his situation and found it quite hopeless. It would have been far better for everyone, himself especially, if he had been killed in that tank battle in Tunisia. He had come home to find that his wife had out-lived him in every sense.

Jack Blair, who had been clearing away empty glasses, told Vi to go off to lunch. He strolled over to the last customer in the Lounge Bar in the hope of cheering him up.

'Well, Stan, how's the world treating you?'

'Bloody terrible!'

'I see. Like that, is it?'

'You knew all about it, I suppose?' challenged Stan.

'About what?'

'Sally and that – Yank.'

'She thought you were dead,' explained Jack, quietly. 'We all did.'

'Oh, yes. Didn't waste much time, did she?'

'Don't be too hard on her, lad. It hasn't been easy for Sally. Two young children to look after.'

'Other women manage,' came the bitter retort. Stan's tone softened a little. 'She's changed, Jack. She's not the girl I married.'

'How's the hand?' asked the other, trying to change the subject, and indicating the fist that was still bandaged.

'Half the time, it's like I wasn't there. William, my son. He doesn't know who I am.'

'He's only a baby.'

'And Betty's no different. Treats me like I didn't belong

229

in the house. It's sickening. You know, it'd have been easier all round if that shell had actually—'

'Don't talk so daft,' said Jack, cutting in. 'Look, lad, you walked in, what was it – a week ago, two? – like a ghost, a man who'd come back from the dead. Now, I'm not saying we weren't pleased to see you – oh, no – but it takes some getting used to. You've got to give us time.'

'And why did she have to go and sling my mother out of the house? That was his idea as well, I dare say!'

'Time, Stan. Give us time.'

There was a hurt silence during which Stan emptied the glass and then examined it as he turned it in his hands. He had gone well beyond the point of consolation now.

'I hate them, Jack,' said the soldier. 'Oh, not just that McGraw. All of them. With their fancy uniforms and their money and their smooth talk. I wish to God they'd never come!'

'Take it easy, Stan . . .'

'I know, I know, your daughter's married to one of them. Well, good luck to her, that's all I can say!' He put the glass down with a bang and leaned across towards Jack. 'You know, when I was on my way here on the train, all the time I kept thinking about Sally; how she'd look when we met; what she'd say. I had it all worked out in my head. And then, when she wasn't at the station, I thought – well, maybe she's delayed or something. All the time I had this picture of her running into my arms – so excited and happy – and I'd pick her up and hold her and kiss her.' He laughed. 'What a joke, eh? She didn't even know I was coming. And when she saw me . . . well!'

Before Stan could enlarge on what had happened, he was checked by the arrival of a group of Americans from the Base. They were members of the ground crew, off duty until the B-17s started returning from their mission later that afternoon. They were affably noisy and Vi came out at once to serve them.

'Look at 'em!' snorted Stan. 'So bloody full of themselves, you'd think they owned the place!'

'Cheer up, for God's sake!' urged Jack. 'They're entitled to come in here and they're not doing you any harm.'

'No? Well, I'm off. Always been particular about who I drink with.'

'Goodbye, Stan.'

'Poor Mr Bilton,' sighed Vi.

'He's a sight too sorry for himself, that's his trouble.'

'It's funny, hearing him talk about his wife like that.'

'Well, you can't blame the man there.'

'I can't imagine Chuck speaking about me like that,' she said.

'You'd never give him cause, Vi.'

'No, Dad.' She became thoughtful. 'They'll be coming back now. They'll be on their way home.'

Still thinking about Chuck, she carried on pulling pints for her customers, getting pleasure out of simply looking at their uniforms. In only four or five hours, her husband would be ringing her to say that he was safely back from Germany.


From their position on the control tower they had been able to count the planes as they came in and make cursory estimates about the extent of the damage that some had suffered. Even with their experience, they could still be surprised at the resilience of the B-17, at its ability to take massive punishment yet still remain in the air. One of the returning aircraft had lost a propellor, some of its tail section, even part of a wing and yet it had somehow limped home to make an inelegant but safe landing.

'I make that five missing,' said Jim Kiley.

'With two badly damaged,' noted Rufus.

'3289, 5898, 3564 . . .' began the Controller, listing the numbers of the planes that had not returned.

'Give me the pilots' names, will you?' asked Jim.

'Bailey, Krotnik, Johnson, Kovacs, and Burwash.'

'Oh, Jesus . . .'

'Wait a minute. There's one more,' said Rufus.

231

The distant rumble that Rufus had heard became a harsh roar and the 'Ginger Rogers' came out of the low cloud and began its approach to the runway. Red flares were dropped by way of a warning signal and the men on the control tower reacted at once.

'That's Burwash!' identified Jim.

'Looks like he's got some trouble with his undercarriage . . .'

'And wounded aboard.' Jim went into the control room. 'I want a couple of meat wagons and a fire truck.'

The 'Ginger Rogers' was now low enough for the holes in its fuselage to be clearly visible. It was rocking violently and its undercarriage was not opening at all. As it hit the hard surface of the runway, it skidded along for fifty yards or more, metal screaming against the concrete. Then it burst into flame.

'Oh my God!' Rufus said.

'Make that every meat wagon you can get!' ordered Jim. 'And every fire truck as well!'

Men ran or drove towards the blaze from all directions. An ominous crackling filled the air and almost drowned out the cry of the sirens and the squawk of the klaxons. The 'Ginger Rogers', one of the veteran B-17s, was now a bonfire on the runway. Red Burwash and his co-pilot managed to climb out and run to safety. Dave Conners, the navigator, and Tim Parkes, the bombardier, also clambered out of the wreckage, though their flying gear was smoking and they had to be doused with water. That made four out of the ten-man crew. The heat was too intense for the rescuers to get close to the plane and the hoses that were playing on the flames were having no immediate success in controlling the blaze. Just as the watchers were giving up all hope of any more survivors, Elmer Jones came struggling through the black smoke, falling into the arms of one of the rescuers, Sergeant Berkowitz.

'Any more back there, Elmer?' shouted Berkowitz.

'No.'

'Jeez! What happened? Where's Mario?'

'He's dead. So's Bob. The others baled out.'

Elmer looked down at his hand which was streaming blood and giving him so much pain that he felt he was in danger of passing out. Berkowitz called the medics and another patient was soon helped to the waiting ambulance.

Red Burwash watched the blaze with tears in his eyes. The death of the 'Ginger Rogers' meant almost as much to him as the loss of members of his crew. He had to be led away. Later, in Jim Kiley's office, he underwent an informal debriefing. His hands were shaking as he recounted what had happened and Jim had to calm him down more than once. Rufus listened grimly to the account.

'Then what, Red?' asked Jim.

'We were under attack for about ten minutes. I couldn't see too much because they were coming from behind. That was when Krotnik got it. I saw him losing height – and he just exploded. Poor bastards didn't even have time to bale out. We hit one or two. Mario reckoned he'd got one. He was shouting out – then they disappeared.'

'That was before you reached the target,' said Jim.

'Yeah. It all happened on the way back. We dumped our load. Had to make a couple of runs. The cloud was pretty bad. We got a break over the target but it didn't last. Then we headed home and wham! There must have been thirty FWs. We all thought we'd had it. That was when Mario was hit . . . and Bob Stevens. There was a lot of flak, too. A shell burst underneath the bomb bay, wrecked the undercarriage, started a fire. I didn't think we'd make it back so I told the guys to bale out. Chuck went out, and a couple of the gunners. Then Elmer and Dave somehow got the fire under control. I figured to try and bring her back.' A smile darted across his lips. 'We almost made it.'

'Only the radio operator and the tail gunner were hit, then?' said Rufus. 'The rest of the men baled out.'

'Yes. Apart from Elmer. I think he got stuck in the hatch.' There was a long pause. 'Sorry.'

'Don't be a damn fool, Red,' replied Jim. 'It was a miracle you got back at all.'

'I thought I could sort of belly flop her down. The fuel tanks must've exploded. Thank God we were damn near out of gas. If those tanks'd been full, you'd have been sweeping up my cinders now.' Red shook his head ruefully. 'Twenty-two missions. What a goddamn way to go!'

Before Jim could reply, there was a knock at the door. He barked a welcome and the door opened to reveal Detective-Sergeant Roberts with the two MPs who had accompanied him earlier.

'Oh, no!' Jim did not bother to conceal his disgust.

'Sorry to trouble you, Colonel,' said Roberts, looking across at Rufus. 'I believe your flying crews have returned. Is that correct?'

'Yes. That's right.'

'I wondered if I might have a word with Sergeant Bottone?'

'What the hell . . . ?' began Red, bewildered.

'Take it easy,' advised Jim, a hand on Red's shoulder. He faced Roberts. 'No, I'm afraid you can't have a word with Sergeant Bottone. Sergeant Bottone is dead. Killed by some German gunner while doing *his* best to defend *your* country . . . *Okay?* Sorry it turned out to be a wasted journey for you, but would you kindly get the hell out of here? We're pretty busy just at this moment.'

'I'm afraid we lost a few planes today,' explained Rufus.

'Yes, sir,' said Roberts, mustering some dignity. 'I'm very sorry, sir. Goodbye.'

He went out and closed the door. Red Burwash got up and looked after him, wondering what the visit was all about. He turned to Jim for clarification.

'Mario was involved in some kind of black market deal with a guy in the town.'

'Well . . .' Red answered, considering the idea, 'it figures. Look, I'd better get down to that pub. Someone's got to tell Chuck's wife.'

'No. You get some rest. We'll call in there on our way to Division.'

'But Vi knows me, sir.'

'Get some goddamn rest, Red. That's an order.'

'Okay, sir.'

Red went slowly out, utterly fatigued by what he had been through. Jim and Rufus grabbed their coats from the hooks. Rufus was trying to fit a face to a name.

'Bottone? Dark guy – from the Bronx?'

'That's him. Best damn radio operator in the whole Group.'

Jim Kiley led the way to the waiting jeep.


Jack Blair had braced himself for bad news long before the Air Executive walked into his pub. He had heard the squadrons overhead as they returned to the airfield and he had waited with Vi for the telephone call from Chuck. It had not come. Vi's excitement had turned to anxiety and this in turn had given way to a deep, inner dread. She had kept searching for possible explanations as to why her husband had not yet made contact. Jack was as reassuring as he could be in the circumstances but, in his heart, he already suspected the worst. The news that Jim Kiley brought, therefore, gave him a hint of relief. It was a terrible blow but there was still some hope.

Rosie Blair came through from the Public Bar and saw Jim there. When she heard about the fate of the 'Ginger Rogers', her first thought was for Elmer Jones and she let out a sigh of gratitude when she heard that he had come back and was at the hospital receiving attention to his wounded arm. Then Vi Blair came running in, desperate to know what had happened, sensing at once that all was not well. As gently as he could, Jim explained that Chuck had baled out over Germany and that there was a good chance that he was still alive. The shock of it all was too much for Vi and she slumped to the floor in a faint. Jim picked her up and carried her out into the back room. Vi had been married for only two days. It was too soon to be a widow.

The news did not reach the Mundy household until the next day. Albert was serving in the shop, Vera was preparing the lunch, and Letty, bored and restless, was fidgeting with a magazine. Peter came in through the back door and saw at once that his sister had not yet been told. He cleared his throat and felt unequal to the task that now fell to him.

'I thought you'd have heard by now. Yesterday's raid. I stopped at The Plough as I came past. Jack told me.'

'What's happened?' asked Vera, alarmed.

'Well, it's pretty bad, Mum. I'm sorry, I thought you'd have . . .' He looked at Letty. 'That chap you've been going out with – Mario – he's been killed.'

Letty said nothing but she seemed to collapse inside. She sat there staring ahead, a puzzled frown darkening her features.

'Poor boy!' said Vera.

'I'm sorry, Letty,' offered Peter, sitting beside her and putting an arm around her.

'Are you sure?' she asked, dully.

'It's what Jack told me. Apparently, Mario and the tail gunner both got it during an air battle on the way home.'

'I knew they'd lost some of them,' she murmured, then turned to look up at her brother with real intensity. 'What did Mr Blair say? Was he *certain* about Mario?'

'Sort of. He seemed to know all about it.'

'Well, I don't believe it,' said Letty, getting up and crossing to take down her coat from a peg. 'I don't believe he's dead.'

'Where are you going, dear?' asked her mother.

'Down to the Base.'

'But they won't let you in,' argued Peter.

'I'll make them let me in. I'm going to find out about Mario. He can't be dead. He *mustn't* be dead!'

236

Before they could stop her, Letty ran through the archway and into the shop. Albert was stacking some tins on a shelf as she dashed past.

'Hey! You're not allowed to go out!' he yelled, but she had already opened the shop door and left. Albert went angrily to his wife. 'Now what's the matter with her?' he demanded. 'I thought I told you—'

'It's that boy she was going out with, Albert. The Italian one. He's been killed. Peter heard about it.'

'On the raid. Yesterday.'

'I see,' said Albert, chastened. 'But where's she going?'

'She doesn't believe it. She's gone to the Base.'

'Get after her, Peter,' said Albert, gently.

'Okay, Dad,' Peter needed no second bidding.

'She thought he was going to marry her,' sighed Vera, sinking into a chair.

'There was never a chance of it, Vera. It was all in her head.'

'Yes. I suppose it was.'

She looked up at him, surprised by the hint of tenderness and understanding that there had been in his voice.

Letty, meanwhile, was running, walking, stumbling towards the Air Base, telling herself that it was all a mistake, that Mario was still alive, that it could not possibly happen to her a second time. When she finally arrived at the main gate she was white and distraught. The MP was considerate but could not give her the information she demanded. As she insisted that she should be allowed to speak to someone in authority, a jeep approached from inside the Base. Jim Kiley was at the wheel and he wanted to know what was going on. As soon as he was told, he got out and crossed over to Letty.

'Is it true that Mario Bottone's been killed?' she gasped.

'Yes,' he confirmed, quietly. 'Yes, I'm afraid it is.'

'Oh . . .'

'Was he a friend of yours?'

'Yes,' she said with the utmost difficulty.

'I'm very sorry . . .' Jim watched as she first twitched,

237

then quivered, then burst into tears. 'Look, would you like me to take you back to the town?' he asked.

'No, thank you,' she said through her sobbing. 'I'll be all right.'

'Would you like to sit down for a while?'

'Letty!'

They both turned to see Peter Mundy coming towards them on his bicycle. He jumped off it and ran over to his sister. She had stopped crying now and was simply numbed with grief.

'Oh, Peter. He's dead. It's true.'

'Come on, Letty,' he said. 'I'll take you home.'

Wheeling his bicycle with one hand and helping his sister with the other, Peter went off slowly down the lane. Harvey Wallis and now Mario Bottone. It was too much for anyone to bear alone.


Rosie Blair hung around in the corridor for a long time in the hope of being allowed into the ward to see Elmer Jones. She bumped into Helen Dereham who explained that the injuries were painful but not serious. Elmer had first-degree burns to the hand, arm and shoulder and would be kept in the hospital for a while yet. Rosie thanked Helen and waited on.

What had distressed her as much as the news about Chuck had been the information that Herman Krotnik's plane had been shot out of the air and that the entire crew had been killed. Hymie Stutz had been part of that crew. It was only now, as Rosie thought about it, that she realized how unkind she had been both to Hymie and Elmer, teasing them both along, enjoying their rivalry for her favours, playing with them. Hymie's death made her wish that she had been nicer to him.

'Hi, Rosie!'

'Elmer!'

He was walking towards her down the corridor in his dressing gown, arm and shoulder bandaged. Though pleased that she had come, he was still very shaken by the ordeal of the Stuttgart mission, by the loss of close friends. Elmer tried to make light of his own injuries and asked how Vi had taken the news about her husband. Rosie explained that her sister had taken to her room and would not come out of it. She then grabbed Elmer's arm and told him that she had always liked him better than Hymie.

'Is that a fact?' he said, his voice flat.

'Yes, and I'm not just saying that because . . . because . . .'

Rosie Blair's eyes began to bulge with astonishment. Coming down the corridor in a wheelchair, his leg in plaster, was Hymie Stutz. She did not know whether to laugh or cry and so did both at the same time. Neither Elmer nor Hymie could understand it.


Red Burwash was inconsolable. He sat over his beer in the Lounge Bar and ignored the attempts of his navigator and bombardier to cheer him up. When they tried to point out that no other pilot in the Group would have managed to fly a plane home in that condition, Red replied that he had crashed the 'Ginger Rogers'. It was his fault that the aircraft was now a charred wreck. What kind of flyer could not get his plane down? He had to take the blame.

Before he left, Red had a brief word with Jack Blair and heard how totally stunned Vi still was. With a shrug of his shoulders, Red noted that he had warned Chuck against marriage for just that reason.

'You know what the odds are against any of us getting through, Jacko. It's not fair on the girls.'

'I don't think Vi would agree with you, Captain,' replied Jack, firmly. 'And I'm damn sure I don't.'

Red shrugged again and walked out of the pub. Half an hour later he was back at the Air Base, walking around the shell of the 'Ginger Rogers', which was silhouetted against the moonlight. The nose had been badly burned but the logo had miraculously survived. Red stared up at the name that had meant so much to him, at the famous legs, at the proud reminder of the twenty-two missions that he and his crew had come through together. Anger replaced his sentimentality and he picked up some stones to hurl at the metal. Finally, he leaned his head against what was left of the fuselage and muttered to himself.

'Stupid bloody machine! What did you have to go and do a damn fool thing like that for? I figured you'd bring us through.' He kicked his boot against it once and then glanced over at the line of bombs on the nose again. 'Twenty-two missions . . . No, I guess it wasn't your fault.'

Red turned around and, with his back against the fuselage, he slid to the ground. He sat there for a long time. Very softly, he began to sing a song to himself. It was 'I Got A Girl In Kalamazoo'.

While her daughter and husband were waiting for her to return to Dereham House, Helen was being driven at speed through the Suffolk countryside on a balmy evening. She had met Jim earlier that day when he came to visit some of his men at the hospital, and the moment she saw him, all her new resolutions about duty and fidelity crumbled away. She still loved Ronnie and she still valued her reputation, but she also knew that she could only be truly happy when she was with Jim Kiley.

'Am I going too fast?' he asked.

'No, I like it.'

'It's not far now.'

'Where are we going?'

'Don't remember the name,' said Jim. 'The pub's a cute little place with a thatched roof. I guess you'll know it.'

'It doesn't matter.'

'Seemed like a good idea to get right away from Market Wetherby.'

'Perhaps.' She was smiling to herself.

'Thanks for coming, Helen. It means a lot to me.'

'I wanted to come,' she said.

Steering the jeep with one hand, he used the other to hold her. Neither of them really cared where they were going now, as long as they went there together.

# CHAPTER EIGHTEEN

None of the books had been able to hold her attention for long. She had tried Henry James, Virginia Woolf, Aldous Huxley and P. G. Wodehouse without success. Even Dickens had let her down. She had finally settled for J. B. Priestley but had been on the same page of 'The Good Companions' for over twenty minutes. When she heard the front door open, she snapped the book shut and put it down on the table beside the empty coffee cups and the remains of a light supper. Her pulse was racing by the time her mother came into the sitting room.

'Oh, darling, I am sorry,' said Helen, flushed and rather excited. 'I never thought I'd be this late. You shouldn't have stayed up.'

'Where have you been?' accused Pat.

'Has Ronnie gone to bed?'

'Ages ago.'

'You had supper?'

'We waited till half-past nine then gave you up for lost,' said her daughter, coldly. 'Have you eaten?'

'Yes, thank you,' replied Helen, going back into the hall to hang up her coat. 'I got something at the hospital.' She came back in and glanced at the side table. 'Is there any coffee left in that pot?'

'I shouldn't think so. It'll be ice cold by now, anyway. Would you like me to make some more?'

'No, no. It doesn't matter.' Pat's anger and disapproval made her nervous. 'I . . . met Major Kiley as I was leaving work. We had a drink together.'

'Yes,' said Pat, levelly.

'What's that supposed to mean?'

'How is *Major* Kiley?'

'He's very well.' She met her daughter's stare. 'Am I to take it that you object?'

'It's nothing to do with me.'

'No, it isn't,' said Helen, gently.

'I just hope you weren't seen by anyone around here.'

'Why on earth – ?'

'The squire's wife drinking with the handsome American Major. The gossips would have a field day.'

'Don't be ridiculous!'

'Just warning you, that's all.' She got to her feet. 'Well, I might as well go to bed. Now that you're back, at last.'

'Pat, there's something the matter. What is it?'

'There's nothing the matter,' replied the other, but her whole manner belied her statement. 'I was disappointed for Daddy, that's all. He kept delaying the meal, putting it off a little longer and a little longer in case you came back. Very touching.'

'Yes, well, I must speak to him about that.'

'I should,' advised Pat, reining in her anger. 'Tell him you met Jim Kiley and simply *had* to have a drink with him.'

'Pat!'

'Well, it's the truth, isn't it?'

Helen checked herself and looked at her daughter for a moment, weighing her answer. 'No. It isn't.'

'I'm sure Daddy will understand,' retorted Pat. 'After all, it's pretty common around here these days. Most of the girls in Market Wetherby have American boyfriends.' She picked up the tray and moved towards the door. 'Are you on call early tomorrow, or shall we see you for breakfast?'

'Sit down, Pat,' invited Helen, calmly. 'I want to talk to you.'

'Do you mind if we make it some other time? I'm rather tired. Goodnight, mother. Sleep well.'

She left the room before Helen could say anything to stop her. Pat's attitude had annoyed her mother intensely, but it had also sharpened her guilt. She had had a wonderful evening with Jim and they had both laughed when his jeep had broken down and delayed their return. She was now paying for that laughter. Her duties as a wife and mother had been brought home to her again. While they were at the pub, Jim had told her that he loved her and wanted to take her away for a few days. At the time it had seemed so right, so easy. Now, however, it looked impossible. She would have to tell him so the next time they spoke.

Helen switched off the lights in the sitting room and went to see if Ronnie was still awake.

Sergeant Billy Colvero was a young, good-humoured, eager flyer with a boyish face, tousled hair and a confident grin. He had found an empty locker, thrown his gear down on the bunk beside it and started to unpack, whistling happily as if he was perfectly at home. He was still putting things away in the locker when Elmer Jones came back to his quarters for the first time since the Stuttgart raid. Elmer had been discharged from Hospital but his hand was still lightly bandaged. He glanced sharply at Billy as he walked past him to his own bunk. Billy replied with a broad grin.

'Hi. I'm Billy Colvero. They told me to find a bed in this hut.'

'Elmer Jones,' conceded the other man, guardedly.

'I'm in Captain Burwash's crew. Maybe we'll be together.' He put out a hand and Elmer shook it perfunctorily. 'What happened to your – ?'

'I burnt it.'

'Gee, that's tough.' Billy's grin faded. 'You're . . . you're not new here, then?'

'Nope.'

'I trained as a tail gunner, see. I'm sure as hell glad I got to this Group.'

'You are?'

'Yeah,' said Billy, as he continued to put things into the

locker. 'It's one of the best. I heard about that Major Kiley back in the States. He sounds like he's really something.'

'He's okay,' agreed Elmer. 'You know, Sergeant, I wouldn't take that bed, if I was you.'

'Why? Something wrong with it? The locker was empty so I figured that it'd be—'

'The man who had that bed . . . well, he might come back just about any time.'

'I don't get it.'

'He baled out,' explained Elmer. 'Over Belgium some place, on the last trip. Chuck Ericson. He was quite a guy. Got married the day before. Anyways, I reckon he'll be back so—'

'Yeah. Okay. Sure.' Billy was suddenly uneasy, gathering up the items on the bed quickly and looking around the room. 'Could you tell me which bunk I could have?'

'Well, there's one down at the end . . . or I guess you could have this one right here.'

Billy moved towards the second option. 'Who had this bed, then?'

'Guy by the name of Mario Bottone.'

'Uhuh. What happened to him?'

'He's dead.'

Billy paused as he was about to drop some of his gear on to the bunk. He looked nervously across at Elmer, then relaxed, feeling that he had got the other man's measure. He spread his things over the bunk and went to get another load. Red Burwash came in.

'Sergeant Colvero!' he barked.

'Sir!' Billy jumped to attention, saluting.

Elmer had done the same. 'Relax, Elmer,' said his Captain. 'How's the hand?'

'Not too bad, sir.'

'Can you fire a gun?'

'I guess so.'

'Hallelujah! You're going to help me get a new crew together, Elmer. Okay.'

'Sir.'

Red turned to appraise the newcomer. 'They tell me you're a tail gunner, Colvero.'

'Yes, sir.'

'Training?'

'Three months at Casper, Wyoming, sir.'

'An old hand,' observed Red with irony. 'Okay, Colvero, now hear this. My name's Burwash and it just so happens that I get to have the best damn crew in the Group. I don't know why it is, but I've kind of got used to it, and I like it that way. So if you're going to fly with me, you gotta be good, and I mean good. Now, I suppose you know the tail gun is just about the most important defence position in the whole damn plane. It's also the most dangerous. If you foul up once, I might just manage to forget about it, then again, I might not. If you foul up twice, you're probably dead! Got it?'

'Sir!'

'Oh, and don't let Elmer here fool you. He may look sleepy, but he's the greatest little waist gunner you'll ever know.'

'Sir.'

'Okay, Colvero. See you later.'

Red Burwash turned on his heel and strode out. Billy stared after him in admiration.

'Do you think he liked me?' he asked.

'I shouldn't bank on it,' Elmer said.


Ronnie Dereham was not a man to sit around and feel sorry for himself. When he had come back to England as a cripple, he had thrown himself heart and soul into the kind of work he was still able to do, in order to stave off the long periods of brooding that he had succumbed to while still in the military hospital. The running of his estate kept him at his desk most days. He was leafing through some papers when his daughter brought him in a cup of tea. Pat was dressed in her working clothes – riding breeches and a shirt — and her unkempt hair suggested that she had been busy.

'I've brought you some elevenses, Daddy.'

'Ah thanks,' said Ronnie, looking up from his desk. 'All well?'

'They've started lifting the sugar beet.'

'Good. Slow going, I expect.'

'Yes. The girls actually do it more quickly, but they get tired sooner. A problem of stamina.'

'Of course.'

He took the cup from her and put it down beside him. He could see that she was slightly on edge and waited patiently till she was ready to take the plunge.

'I want to talk to you,' she said at last.

'Talk away, my dear,' he encouraged, but instead she started to pace the room. 'What is it, Pat?'

'You'll hate me for telling you.'

'I doubt it,' he replied, easily.

'It's mother. She's seeing Major Kiley.' Surprised that his expression had not altered in the slightest, she became more explicit. 'She's having an affair with him.'

'I know,' he said with studied calm.

'You *know*? But – have you spoken to her about it?'

'No. Nor do I intend to.'

'You mean . . . ?' She was quite perplexed.

'Darling, I don't want to hurt you,' he said, the words not coming at all easily now, 'but this is something between your mother and me. It isn't really any of your business.'

'You're not going to do anything about it,' she said, horrified by his apparent complaisance.

'I don't want to discuss it.'

'You're going to let this man—'

'That's enough!' he interrupted. The mask had started to slip and she was able to see now her father's deep emotional hurt. 'I'm sorry, darling, but I love her very much and I believe that she loves me . . . I know that she wouldn't willingly do anything to hurt us . . . And if she is going through a difficult time at the moment, then we must

247

try to understand and be patient.' There was a long silence then he spoke with deliberation. 'It may be that Major Kiley can give her something that . . .'

He was unable to finish the sentence and stared at the floor instead. She was embarrassed, and ashamed for him.

'Oh, Dad,' she whispered.

'I want you to promise me,' he began, pulling himself together, 'that you will say nothing of this to your mother.'

'I don't see why not.'

'I want you to *promise* me,' he insisted, then a note of desperation came into his voice. 'Oh, my darling, don't you see? It's the only way if we're ever to get her back.'

His eyes were almost pleading with her now. Pat felt deeply sorry for him but found herself beginning to despise him. For someone who had looked up to her father so much and for so long, it was a shock to find such a fundamental difference of outlook on something so important. Pat had to bite back the answer she really wanted to give him.

'Very well,' she agreed. 'If that's what you want.'

'That's what I want.'

'Well, I suppose I'd better get back to work,' she said, making no attempt to hide her reservations.

'Pat . . .'

'Yes?'

'I think – I hope – that one day when you're married, you'll understand.'

'No!' she retorted, unable to contain her disapproval any longer. 'I shall never understand. I thought you were strong, but this . . . this is giving in! Letting her do as she pleases, walk all over you. And I hate it!'

'Pat, please . . .'

'Oh, don't worry. I won't say anything. We'll all go on just as usual, pretending that nothing's happening. That *is* what you want?'

'Yes,' he replied, firmly. 'I'm sorry, my dear.'

'I'll see you later. Don't let your tea get cold.'

As soon as she went out, he heaved a sigh then turned

back to his farm papers, not daring to dwell further on their conversation.

The days since the raid on Stuttgart had been long and difficult ones for Jack Blair. As well as coping with his own sorrow at the news about Chuck, he had to try and buoy up those around him. Rosie had been persuaded to take a more optimistic view now but Jack could not convince his other daughter that there was any hope at all. Vi was virtually entombed in her bedroom. She wanted no visitors and little food. She had refused even to think about resuming her job on the Dereham estate. Jack had tried again and again to coax her out of her despair, but the very mention of her husband's name only seemed to intensify it.

Almost as a last resort, Jack telephoned Helen Dereham at the hospital to ask her advice. She took the trouble to call at The Plough herself and speak to Vi, but even she, with her practical suggestions and her argument that the girl was needed at the farm, failed to pull Vi out of her depression. When she had a private word with Jack afterwards, Helen confirmed that there was nothing physically wrong with his daughter. She was still in a state of shock and they would simply have to be very patient.

When Helen left, Jack looked across the bar to see that he had another problem on his hands. Stan Bilton, moody, embittered, lonely, was sitting on his own and staring into his glass again. Jack knew the danger signal all too well. Each time that Stan came into the pub, he would sit apart and brood, occasionally sounding off to the landlord. Jack had heard all about the continuing awkwardness between him and his wife, about his sense of being made to feel a stranger in his own house, and about his rage whenever his daughter talked fondly about 'Uncle Joe'. It was only a matter of time before Stan Bilton and 'Uncle Joe' met again because McGraw came to The Plough quite often.

Vi Blair locked herself away in a bedroom with her grief:

Stan Bilton nourished his with beer. What Jack found hard was the fact that he had to suffer the consequences of both.

'Two half-pints of bitter, please, Rosie.'

'Coming up.'

The moment that Jack had been fearing had come at last. His daughter was serving Red Burwash and McGraw. Out of the corner of his eye, Jack could see Stan sit up, react and stare in the direction of the two Americans.

'Do you think Chuck's all right?' Rosie was asking.

'I reckon so,' said McGraw. 'Maybe he's on his way back right now.'

'Unless the Germans got him,' Red pointed out.

'The truth is we don't know, Rosie,' added McGraw. 'Anything might have happened.'

Rosie was keen to ask about Elmer, rather peeved that he had been discharged from the hospital without bothering to tell her. Before she could learn anything, however, her father interrupted to send her off for her supper. Jack wanted to be close to McGraw himself if there was going to be any trouble. Rosie did as she was told and McGraw noted how obedient she was.

'They're both good girls,' said Jack.

'Still think you were right to let Vi get married?' asked Red.

'I do.'

'Okay. So what if Rosie comes to you next week and says she wants to marry Elmer – or even Hymie. Would you let her? After what happened to Chuck? Would you?'

'Lay off, Red,' McGraw said.

'I want to know, Mac. If it's okay for one daughter, then it's okay for another. Why should Rosie miss out on her share of the suffering?'

Jack felt hurt and defensive but had no time to explain his position. Stan Bilton had walked over to the bar and was confronting the two Americans.

'Evening, gentlemen,' said Stan.

'Let's go, Red,' McGraw said.

'I haven't touched my beer yet.'

'Don't run away, Sergeant.'

'Now, watch it,' warned Jack. 'I don't want any bother.'

'There'll be no bother, I promise you. I just want to buy these gentlemen a drink. Finish what you've got and have the same again.'

Red looked at McGraw in surprise, wondering what was going on, quite aware of the situation that existed between his colleague and Stan Bilton. 'I think this guy's on the level, Mac.'

'You reckon?'

'I'm on the level all right,' urged Stan. 'You see, I want a word in private with Sergeant McGraw. We got things to discuss. So if it's not too much trouble, Jack . . . the next round is on me. And have one yourself while you're at it.'

Jack Blair was so relieved that he did just that.


A cluster of B-17s came out of the low cloud and began the long descent towards the airfield. The leading plane was piloted by Red Burwash. It had the name 'Ginger II' painted on its nose, along with the inevitable picture of the lady herself. Of the crew that had been on the Stuttgart raid, only Elmer Jones and Dave Conners, the navigator, were still flying with Red. Most of the other crew members were raw and inexperienced, which increased the burden of responsibility on their Captain. It also increased the risks.

Red dipped the nose of the plane, lowered the undercarriage and came into land. When the 'Ginger II' had taxied to its hard-stand and halted, one of the first to alight was Billy Colvero. It had been his maiden combat mission and his brash self-confidence was not noticeably shaken. Elmer joined him.

'Still glad you're a tail gunner, Billy boy?'

'Yep!'

'You're lucky. That was just about the easiest trip we've had. They won't all be like that.'

'I hope not, Elmer. I want to see some action.'

'Stick around, kid. There'll be plenty.'

'Sergeant Colvero!'

There was an authority in Red's voice that made Billy stop and turn quickly around. Red was standing beside the plane with Dave Conners and he looked angry. Billy tried a winning smile.

'Sir?'

'Get your ass over here – fast!' When the young gunner ran over, Red looked him up and down. 'How did you like your first mission, Sergeant Colvero?'

'I liked it just fine, thank you, sir.'

'Sorry we didn't run into any of their fighters. I'll try and do better for you next time.'

'That's okay, Captain.' Billy was starting to sound cocky again.

'What you got in your hand?' asked Red, casually.

'It's . . . it's my flak jacket, sir.'

'You just took it off, did you?'

'Well, I . . . yeah, I guess so.'

'You were wearing it during the mission, weren't you?'

Something in his Captain's manner warned Billy that he would not get out of the situation by lying. He swallowed hard. 'I guess not, sir.'

'You goddam little fool!' yelled Red. 'What in hell d'you think you're doing? That was no high school picnic you were just on. If we'd met up with a bunch of FWs . . .' He lowered his voice. 'You want to stay in this crew, Colvero?'

'Yes, sir.'

'Well, get this: you wear that jacket at all times, and I mean all times, during a mission. And just to help you remember, if I so much as hear you've taken it off in the next two days, I'll have you transferred out of the Group so fast you won't know what's happened to you. Am I making myself clear?'

'Yes, sir. Thank you, sir.' A thought occurred. 'Even in bed, sir?'

'In bed. In the john. And make that a week, Sergeant Colvero!'

'Yes, sir.'

'That's all!'

Red walked off with Dave Connors and Billy was left to reflect upon his punishment. He looked down at the flak jacket, then quickly put it on. Elmer had been waiting.

'He's a nice guy when you get to know him, Billy.'

'I may not be around that long.'


Sally Bilton sat opposite her husband and watched him as he ate his way through a bowl of pudding and custard. She had been washing all evening and the kitchen looked like part of a laundry. At her own insistence, she had kept on taking the fatigues from the Air Base and washing them each week even though it had led to more friction with Stan. The laundry was her last link with the Americans, a reminder of the other world she had inhabited so briefly, but happily, until her husband arrived home. Though Sally had made every effort to adjust to the situation, she still found herself missing McGraw. What was worse, in her eyes, was the fact that she was still resenting the man she had married for coming back to his own house. As she reflected on this now, it made her guilt stir again. She suggested that she and Stan might go out together for a drink.

'No, we'll stop in tonight,' he said.

'But you're always complaining I never go out with you.'

'We'll stop in.'

Sally asked him if he was afraid that The Plough would be full of Americans but, for once, Stan did not want an argument on that particular subject. He simply finished his meal, pushed his bowl away and poured himself a cup of tea. When there was a knock on the door, he did not seem at all surprised and went off to answer it. Sally was both confused and embarrassed when he came back into the room with Master Sergeant Joe McGraw.

'Hi, Sally!'

'Mac!'

Stan Bilton was almost amiable as he invited McGraw to sit down and then poured his visitor a cup of tea. When the men exchanged a few jocular remarks about the Air Base, Sally could not believe her ears. She remembered all too well the last time they had met under that roof, and her husband had continued to punch away, verbally, ever since. Dazed, she sat at the table with them. Stan cleared his throat.

'I asked Sergeant McGraw to come round here tonight because what I'm going to say concerns you both. When I arrived home – sort of unexpected – some six weeks ago, I behaved like a damn fool. And I've been going round like a bear with a sore head ever since. Right, Sally?'

'Well, yes . . .'

'Now I like to think I'm a sensible, practical fellow who can face facts. And although it's taken a long time to penetrate, the simple fact that's been staring me in the face is that my wife, Sally, is a damn sight happier with a certain Sergeant McGraw than she ever was with me.'

'Stan!' protested Sally, colouring.

'No, no, let me say my piece. I went up for a medical board last week and they told me that I'd be fit for active service by the end of this month. That means Italy – and I reckon I'll be gone a long time. So what I'm proposing is this. I'll go and stay with Ruby the last two weeks before I'm due to report. And after that . . . well, after that I'll be out of your way for good and all, I shouldn't wonder.' He turned to McGraw who was as astounded by what was being said. 'You can move back in here, Mac. Take up where you left off. I won't raise any objections . . . Well, that's it. That's it and all about it.'

'Have you finished?' asked Sally, quietly.

'Yes.'

'Did you know about this, Mac?'

'No.'

'I'd rather know the truth,' she said.

'Cross my heart. He met me in the pub. Insisted on

buying drinks and then invited me round here. That's all. I promise.'

'I see.'

Sally looked white and tight-lipped, clearly not believing what McGraw had told her. Stan tried to sound chirpy.

'Well, Sally, what do you say? I think it's pretty fair, all things considered.'

'Oh, you do, do you?' she asked, her anger building.

'Yes.'

'Well, I'll tell you what I think. You do what you like, Stan Bilton, but you can leave me out of it. If you think I'm having my life settled for me by two men – over a drink in a pub – you're very much mistaken!' She glowered at McGraw. 'I'm surprised at you, Mac. I thought you'd have had more sense.'

'Look, Sal—' he protested.

'But I thought—' began Stan at the same time.

'No. I don't want to hear another word from either of you,' she said with dignity, stopping them before they had finished. 'There's been enough foolishness for one night. I'm going to bed. Don't forget to turn out all the lights when you're through. And don't make too much noise or you'll wake the children.' She sailed towards the doorway. 'Goodnight!'

The two men sat there, chastened. They also realized why they both loved her.

# CHAPTER NINETEEN

Vi Ericson lay on her bed without moving and gazed up at the ceiling. Her mind was still dominated by the image of a solitary airman, baling out of a burning plane and floating down into nothingness. Rosie's mind was dominated by her new silk blouse. She had put it on and was admiring it in the bedroom mirror.

'What do you think, Vi? I bought it at Footnan and Pretty in Ipswich. Fifty-four and eleven.'

'How many coupons?' asked her sister, looking across at her.

'Four.'

'It's very nice. Suits you.'

'I couldn't resist it. Don't tell Dad.' She regarded herself in the mirror for another minute or so and then walked over to Vi. 'Are you going to come down later?'

'I don't think I'll bother. You can manage without me, can't you?'

'Oh, yes. I just thought . . .' Rosie sat on the end of the bed and spoke softly. 'You'll have to face people one day.'

'I know.'

'Everyone's asking after you.'

'Are they?' Vi did not seem interested.

'I saw Letty in the shop. You know that Italian-looking one she was going out with?'

'Mario?'

'He was killed in the same raid as—'

'Yes,' interrupted Vi. 'Is Letty all right?'

'She's still serving at the shop, so I suppose she must be . . . Oh, Vi, I wish there was something I could do! It's awful without you. Honest.'

'I just want to be on my own, Rosie.'

There was a tap on the door and Jack Blair appeared.

He told Vi that she had a visitor and then stepped aside to let that visitor come into the room.

'Hello, Vi . . . Rosie.'

'Captain Burwash!' Vi was as surprised as her sister.

'Can you give me a hand downstairs, Rosie?' said Jack, anxious to leave the others alone. 'It's getting busy.'

'Yes, Dad.'

'Like your blouse,' observed Red. 'Is it new?'

'No . . . yes,' stuttered Rosie, afraid of her father's reaction. 'Well, almost.'

Jack Blair had hardly noticed the blouse. 'Come along, Rosie.'

She gave Red a dazzling grin and then went out after her father, closing the door behind her as she did so. Vi was sitting up now. She managed a pale smile for her visitor.

'It's very nice of you to come and see me, Captain Burwash, but I'm not sure that—'

'You know something, Vi?' he said, cutting in. 'I didn't want to come and see you. I didn't want to come and see you one bit. The way you're behaving now . . . well, it just proves that all I've said about our guys marrying English girls is the goddamn truth! I'm sorry.'

'Oh . . .' Vi was quite bewildered.

'You see, I've always been against it. Go out with them. Do what the hell you like with them. But don't fall in love with them and don't marry them. That's the way I look at it.'

'Yes?'

'Don't get involved. That's a kind of motto with me.'

Vi's anger was stirring now. 'In that case, I'm afraid I don't see what—'

'What the hell I'm doing here?' he continued. 'Well, I'm coming to that. When your Dad told me a couple of nights back that since you heard about Chuck, you've been hiding yourself away in your room, do you know what I said? I said – you see, what did I tell you? That's what happens if you get involved. And I went back to the Base feeling

257

pretty pleased. Then I got to thinking how Chuck always said it was maybe true with most girls, but that you were different. You were special. Whatever happened to him, you'd never give up . . . And you know, for some kind of reason, I kind of wanted that to be true.' Red paused but got no reply out of her. 'How about that? Must be getting real sentimental in my old age.' He came right over to her. 'So you know what I'm going to do now? I'm going downstairs to the bar and I'm going to ask your father to set up a couple of drinks, one for me and one for you. And I'm going to wait there in that bar for you to come down if it takes me all night.' He grinned for the first time since he had come in. 'You wouldn't stand *me* up, would you, Vi?'

He sauntered back to the door and went out, leaving it wide open. Vi listened until the sound of his footsteps on the stairs died away and then she rushed over to close the door and lean with her back against it. She was breathing heavily now and was conscious of a deep pain somewhere inside her. She felt hurt and indignant, as if her private grief had been shattered by a stranger. But then she thought instead about Chuck, what his expectations of her would be. She remembered what Red had said and saw his offer as a kind of challenge, a way to prove to him that he was wrong about at least one English girl. Vi crossed to the mirror and reached for a hairbrush.

When she got down to the Lounge Bar, she saw that Red was talking to her father. Jack welcomed her casually, as if all the business of her staying up in her room had never happened, then he turned away to serve a customer. Red indicated the glass of brandy that was standing on the counter beside his own tankard of beer.

'Looks like there's a drink right here for you.'

'Thank you, Captain Burwash.'

Vi picked up the glass, sipped at its contents, then smiled at the man who had made her come downstairs. Within an hour, she was helping behind the bar again.

*

Helen Dereham was in an agony of indecision all day as she weighed the conflicting claims upon her. Either way, she stood to lose something of vital importance to her. If she went off with Jim Kiley for the weekend, she would be betraying Ronnie and all that their marriage had stood for; if she refused the invitation, she knew . . . More to the point, she might never get the opportunity again. Her alibi was a medical conference in Norwich, and she had indeed booked to go. Ronnie had been extremely keen that she should honour her commitment as a doctor, and he told her that a few days away from Market Wetherby would do her nothing but good. Helen had been conscience-stricken when he said this and decided that she would ring the Air Base and cancel the arrangement with Jim. But when she lifted the telephone, her other hand refused to dial the number. She loved Jim, she needed him, she wanted to be with him for one snatched weekend, whatever the consequences. More doubts crowded in upon her when she was packing her suitcase and choosing her prettiest nightie, but once again she fought them off by thinking of what lay ahead.

There was another consideration. While her husband had, apparently, not been suspicious about her weekend away, her daughter had been nothing else. Helen was annoyed by Pat's attitude, which veered between watchful resentment and sullen indifference, and she kept asking herself what right the girl had to sit in judgement on her. At the same time, however, she was aware that Pat, despite everything, cared deeply about Jim Kiley and was motivated partly by jealousy. It was all too complicated and Helen could not begin to sort it out in her mind.

In the end she relied on instinct. As a result she found herself walking along a deserted beach with Jim Kiley and watching the waves roll leisurely in.

'Reminds me of home,' he said. 'We've got a summer place on Cape Cod. On the Atlantic coast of Massachusetts. Beaches and sand. Just like this.'

'Do you ever get homesick?'

'Sometimes. Places more than people. I don't miss the life I had. Playing about. Sometimes I thank God for the war. Brought me to my senses. I'd have gone on fooling around for ever if I hadn't enlisted.'

'I doubt it.'

'You didn't know me then, Helen. I guess you wouldn't have liked me if you had . . . Ever read "The Great Gatsby"?'

'Scott Fitzgerald.'

'Yes.'

'I always thought Gatsby rather a glamorous figure.'

'Not in real life,' he promised her. 'Getting cold. Let's walk back now.'

'All right.'

He stooped to pick up a flat stone and sent it skimming over the water, counting five separate little bounces before it finally disappeared with a faint plop. When he turned back to look at her, her cheeks seemed to be glowing and the wind was disturbing the soft wisps of hair that were peeping out from under her headscarf.

'God! You're beautiful,' he murmured.

'I used to do that with my brother when I was a child,' she said. 'Make stones skim over the water.'

'When I look into your eyes, I feel that everything makes sense. I feel as if I've stopped running around in circles, looking for something that I wasn't even sure existed. Does that sound crazy?'

'No.'

'I love you, Helen,' he said.

'I love you.'

He pulled her to him and they kissed as if nothing else in the world mattered. Only when the sea began lapping at their ankles did they realize that the tide was coming in.

They said nothing on the way back. They just walked along, hand in hand, luxuriating in their happiness. For the first time in weeks, Jim was not having to give orders or brief combat crews or watch the skies for returning aircraft or endure the frustration of being effectively grounded. By the same token, Helen was able to forget all about a demanding job at the hospital and a conference she was supposed to be attending and a daughter who was becoming an increasing problem and a husband confined to a wheelchair. They were alone together, relaxed, easy, unhurried, totally absorbed.

When they got back to their hotel, they went straight to their bedroom where the blackout curtains had already been drawn by the chambermaid. Helen went to switch on the main light but Jim's hand stopped her. He crossed instead to put on the bedside lamp which cast a soft circle of light on the bed itself. Then he came back to her, looked deep into her eyes and undressed her slowly, dropping her clothes gently to the floor. Helen did the same for him and they stood there naked, not touching but close enough to feel the warmth of each other's bodies.

At length he took her by the hand and led her over to the bed. They lay down beside each other and then looked at each other properly for the first time. All the love and desire that they had had to suppress for so long came rushing to the surface and they were in each other's arms. They made love and murmured to each other until they fell asleep in the drowsiness of their joy.


'Forget it, Billy boy,' advised Elmer Jones. 'The skipper'll grow to love you – just like we all do.'

Billy Colvero, sitting there in his flak jacket, was not reassured by this. While two of the other sergeants were sprucing themselves up for a night out, and while Elmer had started to play his harmonica again, he was left in the humiliating position of being the butt of endless jokes. Sergeant Charlie Berkowitz, who had dropped into the hut for a chat, asked why Billy had not worn his flak jacket during the mission.

'I was going to put it on as soon as we got to the IP, but when we didn't see any German fighters, I guess I forgot.'

'How much longer you got to wear it?' asked Berkowitz.

'He said a week. That's four more days!'

'Shoot. I'd take it off when you're in here. We won't tell.'

'I don't dare. If he was to find out, I'd be out of the crew.'

'You coming into town tonight?' asked Berkowitz, trying to cheer him up.

'In *this* thing?'

'Oh, yeah. Too bad.'

Elmer stopped playing his harmonica and slipped it back into his pocket. He studied the tail gunner more closely.

'Where you from, Billy?'

'New York City.'

'Yeah? The guy that had that bed, Mario, he was from New York. The Bronx. What do you do?'

'Models flak jackets!' said one of the sergeants.

'Knock it off, fellers!' called Elmer over the laughter. 'Ignore these bums, Billy. What do you do?'

'Oh . . . you know . . . lots of things.'

'Like what?'

'Well, I had a few jobs. Worked in a soda fountain for a while.'

'A soda jerk! Hey I did that, too!' Elmer said.

'Yeah.'

'That was one helluva job. I thought it would be easy but they had me rushing round that place like – Where'd you say it was?'

'What?'

'The soda fountain. Where you worked.'

'Oh, on the corner of Seventh Avenue and Fifty-fourth Street,' replied Billy.

'Think I know that one,' said Elmer. 'Mine was up town a ways.'

'Hey, Colvero!'

Another sergeant had come into the room and his yell shot Billy to his feet. The newcomer ran an amused eye over the flak jacket.

'Yeah?' asked Billy.

'Burwash wants to see you. He's in the debriefing room. He says to make it fast.'

'Okay, okay, I'm coming.' Billy grabbed his cap and ran out past the messenger.

'What's that about?' asked Berkowitz.

'The skipper'll tell him he can take off that flak jacket.'

'You reckon, Elmer?'

'Yeah. Red's made his point. The kid won't forget it.' He paused. 'Know something?'

'What?'

'He's a pretty funny guy, Colvero.'

'I like him,' confessed Berkowitz.

'Me, too. Only he couldn't have worked in a soda fountain on the corner of Seventh Avenue and Fifty-fourth Street.'

'Why not?'

'Because there ain't no soda fountain there. That's why not.'

'Maybe he got the streets wrong.'

'Maybe he didn't.' He dismissed all thought of Billy Colvero and slapped his thigh. 'Say, you coming into town, Berkowitz?'

'Yeah. Sure. Why not?'

They were soon heading towards the main gate where the trucks were waiting to take them into Market Wetherby.


Ronnie Dereham was delighted to hear that Vi was ready to come back to work for him. As he wheeled himself into the sitting room, she followed and apologized for letting him down and for being so stupid. He assured her that no apology was necessary and he was so caring that her nervousness began to disappear. She still had no definite news about Chuck but she suspected that he might have been taken prisoner. If that were the case, Ronnie told her, she would hear something in a few weeks.

'Chuck seemed a fine chap. I'm sure he'll pull through.'

'Thank you, Major Dereham.'

When Vi offered to start work again that afternoon, he was so pleased that he invited her to join them for a light lunch. Pat then walked into the room. Like Vi, she was in her working clothes. Her jaw was tight and her manner abrupt, and she did not even seem to notice that they had a visitor.

'That dreadful man from the Agricultural Committee was here earlier. Did he find you, Daddy?' She became aware of Vi. 'Oh, hello.'

'Yes, he found me, darling. Seems to think we should plough the seven acre.'

'Officious little toad!'

'That field's been a paddock for as long as I can remember,' said Ronnie, defensively. 'Still, it's not all gloom. Vi's starting back this afternoon.'

'Oh, good,' said his daughter, abstracted. 'Is lunch in the kitchen? I'm starving.' She walked to the door, then stopped. 'What did you tell him?'

'The man from the Committee? I said we'd think about it. I want to talk to your mother about it before I make up my mind.'

'I shouldn't think she cares one way or the other,' snapped Pat, involuntarily. 'She hasn't been near the farm in months.'

She went out leaving both of them shocked. Ronnie tried to smooth over the embarrassment by saying that Pat had been working very hard lately and was suffering from strain. Inwardly, he was deeply ashamed that family tensions had got to such a pitch that his daughter could reveal them in public. He made a mental note to speak sternly to her when he had the opportunity. Meanwhile, he tried to put a little enthusiasm into his voice.

'Yes, it's wonderful to have you back again. Come on. Let's go and see what Nanny's managed to find for lunch.'

Vi went out after him.

*

Sally Bilton was tidying things in the kitchen, keeping her hands occupied as she talked because that somehow made it easier. McGraw was at the table, impassive but attentive.

'The note just said he was going to stay with Ruby in Ipswich for the rest of his leave, and that he'd keep out of our way.'

'Just like he said the last time I was here.'

'Yes.'

'Have you tried ringing?'

'He wouldn't speak to me and Ruby – well, she was awful. Called me the most dreadful names. You know the tongue she's got on her when she's roused.' She looked over at him and shrugged in despair. 'Oh, Mac. I don't know what to do. When he said all that about me being happier with you and so on, I thought he was drunk. I thought you both were.'

'Yeah. I remember,' said McGraw, ruefully.

'But now, well . . . it looks as if he meant it. What can I do?' She brought the pot across to the table and poured tea into his cup. 'There. Drink it while it's hot.'

'The British answer to everything . . .'

'What?'

'Leave that alone and sit down,' he said as she started fiddling with some crockery in the sink. He waited till she took the chair opposite him. 'Now, the way I see it, Stan's been hurt pretty bad by what happened. Oh, I know it's nobody's fault, but it'll take a good long while for him to get over it. You've got to be patient. Give the guy time to sort it all out.'

'I didn't mean to hurt him, Mac.'

'Of course, you didn't. You thought he was dead and then, well, I came along. Maybe I should've kept away, but hell, Sal, you're a beautiful lady and there didn't seem any reason . . .'

'I don't blame you,' she said.

'I know, I know. But with Stan not being dead like we thought . . . well, it sort of changes things a bit.'

'Oh, yes,' she sighed. 'It does.'

'Okay, he's gone away again, but I want you to understand that don't make no difference. I respect you, Sal, and I won't be around here making demands on you. I give you my solemn word.'

'Mac, you are a fool!'

'What d'you mean? See, I figure I don't have the right any more.'

'But I want you to come here,' she said, seriously. 'I don't want to stop seeing you.'

For once it was McGraw who was nonplussed. 'Well, that's nice . . . But I guess we have to get our relationship on a different—'

'Yeah, I guess we do,' she replied, unable to resist the temptation to mimic him. They both laughed.

'Uncle Joe!' Betty had come running into the room in her nightie.

'Hey, what is all this?' he asked, lifting her on to his knee and cuddling her affectionately. 'My best girl! Wherever did you come from? I thought you were in bed asleep.'

'She ought to be,' said Sally.

'Watch out!' he chuckled as the girl clung tightly to his neck. 'You don't want to strangle me.'

'Welcome home, Uncle Joe!' she cried, planting kiss after kiss on his cheek.

'Betty!'

'Well,' observed McGraw, 'at least one member of the family loves me.'

Sally Bilton could not help smiling, but her heart was still heavy.


When Ronnie tried to pacify her by saying that Helen was working late at the hospital, she felt that she could take no more. It was the third evening in a row that they had postponed supper in order to wait for Helen. Pat rounded on her father and told him that his wife was probably out with Major Kiley somewhere. Ronnie was hurt and refused even to discuss it which only made her more annoyed than ever. Her concern was for him, she argued, and she was not going to stand by and see him made a fool of in this way. Before he could even ask where she was going, she raced out of the room and left by the back door of the house.

After finding her bicycle in the shed, Pat cycled as fast as she could towards the Air Base, determined to prove something to herself. It was almost dark by the time that she arrived and the guards were surprised to see her speeding towards them out of the gloom. A message was taken to Jim Kiley and he agreed to see her. When Pat was ushered into his office, it was her turn to be surprised because she was certain that he would not be there. She quickly recovered.

'I expect you know what I've come about.'

'No, I don't,' he said, firmly.

'You're having an affair with my mother, aren't you?'

'Now, wait a minute—'

'Oh, please don't bother to deny it. I've spoken to her.'

'Does Helen know you're here?' he asked, after a pause.

'No, but we've talked about it.' She was trying to sound calm but her voice was trembling. 'I want you to stop seeing her. It isn't fair on my father. Oh, I know he—'

'Pat—'

'He behaves as if nothing is happening, but—'

'Pat!' he interrupted for the second time. 'Just hang on, will you?'

'Please, I beg you. I've no right to ask, I know, but—'

'Will you listen to me for a minute?' he asked. 'The first thing you have to understand is that I love your mother. I'm not just fooling around.'

'I didn't think you were,' replied Pat with bitterness.

'There's something else which is just as important. I believe that your mother loves me.'

'*No.*' She refused to believe it.

'I'm sorry. It isn't something that either of us wanted to happen, but since it has, there's no point in pretending. It won't just go away, even if we wanted it to. Pat, I'm . . . That's the way it is.'

'Not you – and my *mother*!'

'You've got to be grown up about it and try to understand. I *can't* promise to stop seeing Helen. I don't think I could keep my promise if I did.'

'Don't treat me like a child,' she pleaded, on the verge of tears.

'I didn't mean to.'

'Oh, Jim, why? Why? It's so *unfair*!' She said it with such passion that she seemed to be thinking more about herself than her father. She took a deep breath. 'I'd better go.'

'I'll come with you.'

'No, I'm all right. It was stupid of me to come. You must think I'm a real – what do you call it? – pain in the ass.' She was perilously close to breaking down and it needed only a gesture of sympathy from him to make her cry. As he put a hand on her shoulder, the tears flowed uncontrollably. 'Oh, Jim. I'm sorry. I'm sorry. But I can't help it. I'm so unhappy!'

She had taken his hand from her shoulder and was clinging to it as if for dear life. With his other hand, he stroked her head.

'Come on, kid. I'll take you home.'

He put her bicycle in the back of his jeep then drove her back to Dereham House. She was still devastated when they arrived and he had to help her out, but he was anxious not to hang around. The vehicle had been heard from inside the house, however, and Nanny came out to investigate. When she saw Jim lifting a bicycle out of a jeep, she told Ronnie who it was and he told her to invite Jim in. Reluctantly, the American followed Pat into the house.

When he had asked Nanny to take care of Pat, Ronnie called Jim into the sitting room and thanked him for bringing her home in the jeep. He then offered his visitor a whisky and Jim was only too glad to accept. He sipped the drink as soon as it was handed to him. Ronnie, too, was clearly finding the situation awkward.

'I'm afraid Helen's gone to bed. She's on early call tomorrow.'

'Oh. Yes.'

'I suppose my daughter tried to see you at the Base.'

'That's right.'

'I'm sorry about that,' said Ronnie, briskly. 'She got rather upset earlier on, but she should not have involved you.'

'I guess I'm involved anyway, Major.'

'I daresay.' There was a long pause and they both drank more of their whisky. Ronnie then blurted out the next question. 'Do you think it would do any good to talk about that?'

'I think we have to talk about it,' suggested Jim. 'You see . . . I love your wife.'

'I know.'

'You *know*?'

'Oh, yes. I've known it for some time.'

'But I thought—'

'Not from Helen. It might have been better if she and I could have talked. But I find that sort of thing rather difficult. I was waiting for her to come to me.'

Jim stood to attention and sounded formal. 'Major Dereham, I want you to know—'

'Please. Don't say anything for a moment, old chap,' Ronnie asked. 'I won't pretend I'm happy about all this but the important thing is that Helen should be happy, don't you see? What I'm trying to say is that . . . I won't stand in your way.'

Jim Kiley was dumbstruck.

'I'll give Helen her freedom, if that's what she wants.' There was another pause and then he slapped the arms of his wheelchair. 'So! I don't know there's very much more to say, is there? Doubtless you'll talk to her.'

The full impact of what he had said had only just hit Ronnie himself. Suddenly he could not even look at the other man. He simply stared ahead as if in some kind of trance. Jim watched him and felt the remorse taking over.

'Godammit,' he muttered to himself. 'Okay, Major, you win. I won't see her again. I'll get the hell out. Transfer to another base.' He glanced up towards the bedroom then took a step closer to Ronnie. 'Do me a favour. Don't tell her we talked like this.'

'No, of course not . . .'

'I'll write to her. Make up some excuse.' He looked into Ronnie's face for a moment then spoke quietly. 'Your wife's a fine woman . . . but I guess you don't need me to tell you that. Goodnight, Major.'

Only after Jim Kiley had gone did Ronnie reply. 'Goodnight.'

He remained motionless in his wheelchair. Outside in the dark, the sound of an engine starting up could be heard. Then the jeep roared away down the drive as if it could not get away fast enough.

# CHAPTER TWENTY

'Letty's fine, thank you, Mrs Jenkins. She doesn't help in the shop any more, that's all. But she's fine in herself. Goodbye.'

'Oh. Goodbye, Mr Mundy.'

Mrs Jenkins found herself ushered politely towards the exit. Albert opened the door for her and then closed it after her, sighing with relief. It had been the same for weeks now. He had been fending off questions about Letty and using all sorts of excuses to try to explain away her virtual disappearance. Inquisitive but well-meaning old ladies like Mrs Jenkins were bad enough, but Albert preferred them to the knowing gossips who had long since fastened on to the truth about his daughter and whose eyes held a mocking look.

'Your tea's ready, Albert,' said Vera, coming in. 'I'll take over here. Have a break while it's quiet.'

'Right.'

He left his wife in the shop and went through into the living room. Peter Mundy was hunched up in a chair, reading a newspaper, and he gave his father no more than a glance. Albert took the mug from the table and sipped it a few times before speaking.

'You going to sit there reading all day? When I was your age, I'd been three years working with your grandfather in this very shop.'

'I've offered to help.'

'It's time you got yourself a proper job, my lad. Mooning around all the time. How long is it since you left school?'

'Only two months.'

'Two *months*! And what have you done since then? Waste all your time with that blooming band of yours!'

'It's not a waste of time,' said his son. 'I want to play professionally one day.'

'A pianist!' Albert was scornful. 'What sort of a job is that? You'd do better to get yourself apprenticed, learn a trade.'

'Oh, Dad.' Peter had heard it all before so many times.

'Oh, I know, you think I'm old-fashioned, but you've had it too easy – your generation. I was nineteen when the first war started. I served in the trenches for my country and . . .' He stopped as a thought alarmed him. 'Where's Letty?'

'I dunno. Upstairs, I think.'

'She's not gone out?'

'No.' He saw his father relax and muttered: 'I wouldn't blame her if she had.'

'What's that?'

'Nothing.'

'I heard what you said. You take her side, don't you? Just like her mother.'

'It's not a question of sides, Dad.'

'That girl's brought shame to this house,' said Albert, bitterly. 'Almost everyone knows. They come into the shop, look at me with their stupid, ignorant faces. I know what they're saying. Only yesterday, that Mrs Bilton from Bridge Cottage, do you know what she said? I heard her telling your mother just how sorry she was to hear about Letty!'

'Where's the harm in that?'

'*She* can talk! Living openly with one of them and her husband not gone back more than a fortnight. It's disgusting!'

'Jack Blair says it's not like people think,' defended Peter.

'Oh yes? And what does he know about it?'

'He says . . . he says . . .' Peter gave up. 'Never mind.'

'No, no. Go on. I'd like to hear what Mr Know-it-all Jack Blair has got to say about it. Trust him to have an opinion!'

Peter was now wishing that he had not mentioned Jack's name. The fact that he now understood the cause of the hostility between his father and the landlord of The Plough did not make the situation any less awkward. Unwilling to speak, he could see that Albert was determined to have an answer.

'Apparently, Stan arranged it all before he left,' he mumbled.

'Arranged it all! That's a likely story, isn't it? I don't know what we're coming to in this country. I don't, really!'

Vera appeared in the doorway to say that the shop was suddenly full of customers. Albert dismissed her with a nod then gulped some more tea down. He crossed the room to Peter.

'I tell you one thing. I shan't be sorry when you're old enough to fight. A bit of army discipline'd do you a power of good. Yes, and you won't have Jack Blair to run to when things get tough.'

'I may not go in the Army, Dad,' said Peter, quietly.

'Yes, I've heard that sort of talk before. But you'll go, my lad. You'll get no choice in the matter!'

Albert Mundy went off into the shop and left his son to reflect upon what he had said. Slowly drawn towards the idea of becoming a conscientious objector, Peter still had many reservations. He decided to talk the whole matter over with Jack Blair.

Unaware that his advice would once again be sought, Jack Blair served the customers in the Lounge Bar that evening with his usual good humour. He had been heartened by Vi's return to work and by the new, more positive attitude about her husband. Although there was still no definite news about Chuck Ericson, his wife was keeping herself going with a guarded optimism and fighting off the temptation to give up all hope. Jack supported Vi as much as he could and he now seemed much more able to get through to her. But as one daughter ceased to be such a problem, the other was taking her place. Rosie Blair was turning into an inveterate flirt. After the shock of the Stuttgart raid, when she heard that Elmer was injured and thought that Hymie had been killed, Rosie had resolved to be less of a tease with the servicemen. But she was now worse than ever, and only had to see an American uniform to offer up her fetching smile, her enticing roll of the eyes, and her provocative remarks.

When a group of GIs came in through the door, Jack did not even bother to try to serve them. Rosie was greeting them as warmly as if each one were her closest friend. The problem was that at least two of the newcomers wanted to be just that. Jack Blair watched.

Rosie complained that she had not seen the men for such a long time. Elmer Jones explained that they had been particularly busy and Hymie Stutz, his leg now out of plaster, told her that he was now a member of Red Burwash's crew. Though both men were trying to sound cool with the barmaid, it was clear that they were as interested in her as ever. Charlie Berkowitz was more interested in getting a drink but the fourth member of the group, Billy Colvero, was quite dazzled by Rosie. He had heard a great deal about her from Elmer and Hymie, both of whom had claimed to be her guy. Now that he was finally with her, Billy decided that his colleagues had misled him. She was far more attractive than either had said. When he was introduced to her, he beamed gratefully and did not mind at all when he found himself paying for the drinks.

Rosie took the pound note and went off to the till, followed every inch of the way by the goggling eyes of Billy Colvero. Elmer Jones, a more assertive member of the crew since Mario's death, warned the young sergeant that she was already spoken for, and Hymie Stutz reinforced the warning. An accident with a jeep on the morning of the Stuttgart raid had put Hymie's leg into plaster and saved his life. The loss of Herman Krotnik and his fellow crew members had been a great blow to him, but it had somehow brought him closer to Elmer. Though they were still rivals for Rosie's favour, they found themselves joining forces amicably to keep Billy away.

Berkowitz saw an empty table and the four men walked towards it. Rosie's voice stopped Billy in his tracks. He had forgotten his change. As he went back to retrieve it, Rosie bestowed her most charming smile upon him, pressing the money back into his hand and letting her fingers run tantalizingly across his. Elmer stiffened, Hymie bristled and Billy himself simply gaped in wonder.

Jack Blair sighed and wondered what he could say that would stop Rosie doing things like that.


The letter was waiting on her desk when Helen arrived at the hospital. She recognized the writing at once and tore open the envelope eagerly. As she read Jim's letter, she tried hard to catch the tone of it. The words, if spoken, could be said in so many different ways.

> 'My darling,
>     We've got a few problems here that look like they're going to keep me busy, so I guess I won't be able to see you for a while. I hope you'll understand. Nothing's changed. It's just that this damn war seems to take up more and more of my time. Take care of yourself. I think of you so much.
>
> Jim.'

Acting on her first impulse, Helen grabbed the telephone, dialled the number of the Air Base. When she was told that Jim was not available, she was utterly deflated, assuming at once that he was trying to avoid her. She put the telephone down, leaned against the edge of the desk, and read the letter through a few more times. Her eye kept halting at one sentence – 'Nothing's changed.'

Two nights earlier, Jim Kiley had brought her daughter back home and come into Dereham House for a chat with Ronnie. As a result of it all, Pat had gone off to stay with an aunt, not even bothering to say goodbye to her mother, but leaving the message that she would probably go on to London and would not be back for some time. Unable to get any details of what had happened that night from her husband, Helen had given up trying. But there was something about Ronnie's manner that had unsettled her. And now she had had the letter from Jim. Whether its tone was evasive, dismissive, affectionate or contrite, the message it contained was clear. He did not want to see her.

*Everything* had changed.


'She told me she works in a parachute factory during the day, but she helps her father in the pub in the evenings.'

'I know,' said Elmer.

'We *all* know,' added Hymie.

An early morning call had got the men out of their bunks in readiness for another mission. Billy Colvero was still talking obsessively about Rosie Blair.

'You mind if I ask you guys something?'

'What?' asked Hymie, checking the strapping that he still had to wear as a support for his leg.

'Is either of you serious about her? I mean, going steady?'

'Going steady?' repeated Elmer.

'How the hell can you go steady with a girl in this job?' demanded Hymie.

'See, I don't want to bust in, fellers, but the way she was looking at me, I figure I've got a real chance there.'

'You do?'

'Yeah,' replied Billy, airily. 'I had quite a bit of experience with girls back home, and I reckon one of them only looks at you like that if . . . if . . . Well, jeez, she sure as hell wasn't giving me the brush off!'

'No,' said Elmer.

'No,' echoed Hymie.

'I think she *really* liked me.'

'Could be. What do you say, Hymie?'

'Could be.'

'You mean, neither of you minds? Heck, you've been real good to me, Elmer. You, too, Hymie. I wouldn't want to take your girl.'

'Thanks, Billy, that's very big of you,' said Elmer, winking at Hymie.

'On the other hand, if you two ain't getting anywhere . . .'

'Let me tell you something, son,' said Hymie. '*Nobody* gets anywhere with Rosie Blair. She's not that kind of girl. Oh, she looks as if she was ready to give it away, but when it comes to it – well, let's just say that you won't be the first who's tried.'

'You mean—'

'Hymie means she's a tease, Billy boy. Know what that is?'

'Sure,' said Billy, sounding experienced. 'I guess she just hasn't met the right guy yet.'

Elmer and Hymie exchanged a glance. The same thought had come into both their minds and it made them smile.

'Come on, lover boy,' said Hymie, easing him towards the door. 'You don't want to be late for briefing.'

It was Elmer who put the idea to him. 'I tell you what. I bet you thirty bucks you can't make it with Rosie. Okay?'

'I'll take you!' shouted Billy. 'Thirty bucks. Oh boy!'

'I got another thirty says she'll freeze you out,' announced Hymie, wanting his share of the betting.

'You're on!' Billy was jubilant as he shook hands with them.

After a light breakfast in the canteen, they made their way to the briefing hut and Billy suddenly asked what day it was.

'Thursday,' supplied Elmer.

'No, I mean the day of the month.'

'October fourteenth,' said Hymie.

'Hell, it's my birthday tomorrow.'

277

'How old are you?' asked Elmer.

'Twenty.'

'Twenty, huh? We'll have a party when we get back.' Elmer's tone was lugubrious. 'If we get back.'

'No doubt about that!' boasted Billy.

But there was considerable doubt and it was more evident when the flyers assembled in the briefing hut were told what the target area was. The name of Schweinfurt brought a tremor to the most experienced of them. Two months earlier there had been a daylight raid on Schweinfurt and its ball-bearing factories, and it had developed into one of the most savage air battles of the war so far. Of the two hundred and thirty American planes that had been sent off in huge armadas across the North Sea, thirty-six planes had been destroyed by German fighters and well over a hundred of those that returned had been damaged, some so badly that they never flew again.

Schweinfurt, a peaceful, beautiful, historic town, had been left in ruins but the cost of the raid to the USAAF had been enormous.

Major Jim Kiley was the briefing officer and he read out a message that was being heard by many other aircrews at many other American bases. The squadrons from Market Wetherby were only a small part of a massive operation that would put over four hundred planes into the sky in a concerted attack on the most dangerous target in Europe. Jim read out the words of General Anderson at Bomber Command.

'The air operation today is the most important air operation yet conducted in this war. The target must be destroyed. It is of vital importance to the enemy. Your friends and comrades that have been lost and that will be lost today are depending on you. Their sacrifice must not be in vain. Good luck, good shooting and good bombing.'

Jim went on to underline the importance of Schweinfurt to the Nazi war machine. He assured the men that flak would be light over the route, except over the Ruhr and over Schweinfurt itself, where the Germans had mounted three hundred 88 millimetre guns in the wake of the August raid. The target area, though not impregnable, was extremely well-defended.

A short film was shown of the town, its factories and certain key landmarks. The Group navigator then took over and explained the route that would be flown, making Jim even more frustrated that he would not be going on the mission. A weather expert gave his forecast. It was a cold morning in East Anglia with thick fog that cut down visibility to a quarter of a mile. He told them it should improve to a mile by the time of take-off. At two thousand feet they could expect to break out of the overcast and when they reached the Continent, they should find the skies quite clear.

'Does that mean no enemy aircraft?' someone asked.

The laughter was distinctly muted.

Jim Kiley resumed his briefing and promised the crews that the formations would have fighter cover from fifty P-47s. Red Burwash observed in an undertone to his neighbour that they would have fighter cover all the way.

'Our P-47s take us as far as Aachen. Then Messerschmitts and Focke-Wulfs take us to the target and back. Then the P-47s pick us up when we reach the Channel again.'

Winding up his speech, Jim gave his usual advice to keep the formations tight, fill a hole quickly if any plane dropped out, conserve ammunition, and keep all guns loaded until landing. He wished them the best of luck and sent them off.

The crew of the 'Ginger II' were silent as they drove out to their B-17. A few of them had actually flown on the first Schweinfurt raid and those who had not had heard all the legends. When the jeep pulled to a halt, it was Billy Colvero who broke the silence.

'Hey, Elmer, I'd like to tell you something,' he said.

'Yeah? What?'

'I wanted to tell you before but—'

'Well?'

279

'Come on, you guys. Get aboard!' ordered Red Burwash, and they obeyed him at once.

'So? You were going to tell me something, Billy boy.'

'Was I?'

'What was it?'

But the moment had passed and Billy could not bring himself to confide in Elmer now. 'It don't matter. Maybe tell you later.'

'Supposing we ain't got a later?'

Billy shrugged and made his way to his compartment in the tail. Elmer was soon at his waist gun position, checking the great loops of shells, trying to forget the traumas of the earlier visit to Schweinfurt, wondering what it was that the tail gunner had been on the point of saying.

Ten minutes later 'Ginger II' was rising into the fog on its way to join the most hazardous mission it had yet flown.


Letty Mundy heard the planes passing overhead not long after ten o'clock that morning but visibility was too poor for her to be able to see them. She spent the whole day thinking about the mission and tried all sorts of things to take her mind off it. Towards the end of the afternoon, she was seeking refuge in a magazine that Mario had given her. The advertisements could still make her gape.

'They have lovely clothes in America. Look at this, Ma.'

'Where?' Vera was putting things on the table and came across to look over her shoulder. 'Bit skimpy!'

'That's the fashion.'

'Not one that I'd care for, Letty.'

'Nor me – at the moment,' said her daughter, sadly, glancing down at her very evident pregnancy.

Vera went back to her job and Letty leafed idly through the rest of the magazine, sighing with a mixture of resignation and envy.

'I wish I could go to America.'

'Perhaps you will one day,' encouraged Vera. She saw

the forlorn look on Letty's face. 'You never know, love. There's plenty of time.'

'Is there?'

At that moment the first of the returning aircraft passed overhead in formation, their combined noise making both women look upwards. When Vera glanced across at her daughter again, she saw the tears coursing down Letty's cheeks. She went over to comfort her immediately.

'Now, now, love. Don't take on.'

'I can't help it. I keep thinking of Harvey . . . and Mario.'

'I know.'

'What am I going to do?' asked Letty in desperation. 'What am I going to do?'

She clung to her mother and Vera patted her head soothingly. 'You're going to be all right.'

'I'm frightened!'

'There's nothing to be frightened of. Now, stop crying.'

'I wish they'd never come here!' howled Letty with an anguish that made her whole body shudder.

Vera did not know what to say. She waited until her daughter had stopped sniffling, then detached herself gently. Letty had reached a new level of hopelessness. She had never regretted the arrival of the Americans before and Vera was shocked.

'You know, I was like you when I was a girl,' she said.

'You?' Letty was surprised.

'Oh, yes. Hard to believe now, isn't it? But I liked the men, too. Couldn't wait to find myself a young man. You ask your father.'

'What'll happen to me?' asked Letty, softly.

'There wasn't a boy in the area I didn't go out with at one time or another. Proper little flirt, I was.'

A few more B-17s flew over the town but neither of the women heard them. Each was too absorbed in her own thoughts.

'No one will want me if I've got a baby.'

'I remember one lad—'

'What man would even look at me—?'

'It was in the summer. Those woods near—'

'I might as well be dead!'

'What's that?' Vera was wrenched away from her own memories. 'Now that's silly talk. You'll have your baby and I daresay that, in a year or two, you'll meet a boy who won't mind a bit. There's lots of men who aren't bothered by that kind of thing.'

Albert Mundy, having locked up the shop for the night, now came in. He saw at once the state that Letty was in.

'What's the matter with her?'

'She's all right,' said Vera, not wishing to involve him.

'Aren't you going to help your mother, young lady?' challenged Albert as his wife continued to lay the table.

A picture of dumb insolence, Letty got up and began to set out the cutlery. More planes rumbled overhead and this time both women stopped to listen.

'That's the third lot,' noted Albert.

'They're late today,' murmured Letty, who had heard so many B-17s returning from so many missions in the past few months.

'Where's Peter?' her father asked her.

'Over at The Plough, helping Mr Blair,' she retorted, deliberately hurting him with the information.

'He'll be back soon,' promised Vera, trying to mollify.

'At The Plough!' Albert was seething as he headed for the door.

'Where are you going?' asked his wife.

'Never you mind!'

'Albert! I'll be dishing up directly!'

'I told the lad I wouldn't have him hanging about that place any more. I should've put my foot down that time he moved in there. Peter's not eighteen yet. Jack Blair's no right to encourage him. It's against the law.'

He grabbed his coat and his cap, then stormed out. Vera looked accusingly at her daughter.

'Now look what you've done, my girl!'

'Shall I lay spoons?' Letty seemed unconcerned.

'No. We had pudding last night.'

They carried on at their work without speaking.

The anger that had arisen inside his house had carried Albert Mundy all the way to the door of The Plough. He pushed it open and strode up to the bar where Jack was chatting with Rosie. Concealing his surprise, the landlord welcomed Albert as pleasantly as he could.

'Good evening.'

'Where is he, then?'

'Can I get you a drink, Albert?'

'No, thank you. I've not come to pass the time of day. Where's my son?'

'What makes you think he's here?' asked the other, defensively.

'Now, don't get clever with me. He's here all right. He's always here. You've seen to that.'

Jack admitted that Peter was on the premises, doing a job for him in the cellar. He sent Rosie off to get him then tried to get his visitor to relax a bit. 'While you're waiting, what can I get you?'

'You've turned my son against me, Jack Blair.'

'That's ridiculous!'

'Ridiculous, is it!'

'You don't have to shout—'

'Can you deny he spends more time here than in his own home?'

'Peter does jobs for me. You know that. Bit of pocket money.'

'And who asked him to come and work in a pub? He could just as easily make a bob or two in the shop.'

'You don't pay him for his help.'

'He shouldn't want paying,' replied Albert, stung. 'Not when he's helping his family. It's his duty. But that's not good enough for Peter. Oh, no! You've filled his head with all sorts of fancy ideas.'

'That's not true, Albert.'

'Then what's all this nonsense about going to be a

283

conscientious objector? About refusing to fight for his country? He never used to think like that.'

'Look,' argued Jack, exasperated, 'your son's an intelligent boy. And if he asks questions, it's only natural in a lad of his age. All right, I've talked to him about the call-up . . .'

'There! You see? You admit it.'

'I admit nothing,' said Jack with real anger. 'If your son comes to me for advice, it's because you're too busy or stupid to talk to him yourself!'

'Don't you talk to me like that!'

'You're a fool, Albert!'

'I'll have the law on you. The boy is under age.'

Peter Mundy walked in on the row and was amazed to see his father. Albert ordered him to get his coat and come home.

'What's the matter?'

'I won't have you working in this place. It's not right!'

Peter waited for a cue from Jack. The landlord suggested that he should go home with his father. Rosie offered to get his coat but his voice stopped her before she had reached the door.

'No!' he said, firmly. 'I haven't finished yet. I told mother I'd be back about eight. I'll see you then, Dad.'

His defiance was all the more crushing for being couched in such polite terms. Summoning up all his bitterness, Albert faced his enemy.

'You see what you've done? Turned my own son against me! God damn you, Jack Blair!'

As Albert stumped off towards the exit, the door opened and five weary and jaded Americans came in, causing him to stand aside. Elmer Jones looked exhausted and not even Billy Colvero could raise a grin for Rosie. None of the newcomers noticed Albert slinking out behind them as they crossed to a table and slumped into some chairs. The men seemed to be completely devastated.

Sergeant Charlie Berkowitz ordered the beer for them.

'What happened?' Rosie asked.

'It's bad, Rosie. The worst so far. We lost fifteen planes. Only five crews got back intact.'


Listening to the news on the wireless was a ritual at Dereham House as in so many homes across the nation. At nine o'clock on a cold October evening, Ronnie and Helen were in the sitting room to hear about the latest advances made by the Allies in Italy. When the news was over, Helen switched the wireless off. Ronnie picked up a letter and read through it again.

'Pat sounds cheerful,' he commented.

'Yes.'

'Only gone a few days and already she's got herself a job in a canteen. Shouldn't have thought it was quite her style.'

'It's temporary, surely,' observed his wife, her mind still elsewhere. 'She'll find something better.'

There was a long pause and they both began to feel the weight of the tension between them. Ronnie tried to ease it, speaking slowly and with some difficulty.

'Helen, I'm more or less tied to this place the way things are . . .'

'Yes?'

'I hope, my dear, that if at any time you felt you wanted to leave . . .'

'Leave?' She was astonished.

'Yes. You have your work, after all. And I should hate to think that you only remain here for . . . for . . .' He cleared his throat and started again. 'I'm told there comes a time in every marriage when . . .'

'Ronnie.'

'My dear?'

'Do you want me to go?'

'Good God, no! I just thought that—'

'Then let's not talk about it any more.'

'I say, old girl, are you sure?' he asked, delighted.

'Perfectly. I'm not leaving.'

'You can't know how wonderful it is to hear that!' He was beaming at her now with unconcealed gratitude.

'I've been behaving rather stupidly,' she confessed. 'I'm sorry.'

'No. You had too much to do and I've not had enough.'

'That wasn't what I meant, Ronnie.'

'I suppose it's something we shall both have to get used to.'

Helen looked across at him and wondered how much he knew and how much more he wanted to know. Something told her that he was happy with the situation as it was and would prefer to leave certain things unsaid. It suited her as well.

'Yes,' she answered, and the conversation came to an end.

He picked up his newspaper and she took out some medical forms that had to be checked. They were both absorbed in what they were doing, but they felt closer than they had done for a very long time.

# CHAPTER TWENTY-ONE

Vera Mundy had endured it as long as she could. When it continued with unabated fury throughout breakfast the next morning, she could take no more. She waited until her children left the table and went out, then she turned on her husband and spoke with an anger that really shook him.

'Stop going on about it, Albert Mundy! It serves you right for charging over to The Plough the way you did. Making a fool of yourself in front of everybody.'

'No one there except a few Yanks,' he muttered.

'Jack Blair's been a good friend to this family,' she argued.

'Jack Blair!'

'Only you're too stupid to see it. If it hadn't been for Jack Blair—'

'Jack Blair! Jack Blair!' he interrupted, scornfully. 'Will you shut up about him, woman, for God's sake!'

'I'm surprised Peter came back at all last night,' she continued, not deflected by him. 'That was probably Jack's doing, I shouldn't wonder.'

'He's turned the boy against me, Vera.'

'Oh, no, he hasn't. If your son spends more time there than he does here, then it's because you've driven him to it – with your old-fashioned ways and your endless talk about discipline and duty!'

'That's not fair,' he said, feebly.

'You've been too hard on those children, Albert, and look where it's got you. Your son's a stranger in his own home, and your daughter falls into the arms of the first American who looks at her.'

'It's my fault she's pregnant, is that it?'

'If you hadn't made such a song and dance about the Yanks, I daresay she'd have behaved more sensibly.'

'All right,' he countered. 'And what about all this talk from Peter about refusing his call-up? Are you saying that he got those ideas from me?'

'No.'

'No. You're damn right. I'll tell you where that pacifist talk comes from. Your wonderful Jack Blair!'

'Jack's no pacifist,' she replied, calmly. 'If Peter's worried about going into the Army, it's only natural. And if he talks to Jack about it, well, are you surprised? It'd be no good talking to you, would it? You'd just tell him that the discipline would do him good, or some such nonsense.'

'It's not nonsense!' said her husband with passion. 'That's what he needs. Make a man of him.'

'Oh God, I hate that phrase! Peter's not eighteen yet, he's still a *boy*. He'll become a man in his own way and in his own time – if he's given the chance.'

'You agree with this pacifist rubbish, then?'

'No.'

'Because I tell you it makes me sick. To think that a son of—'

'You're a fool, Albert Mundy!' she said with feeling. 'A fool!'

She cleared away the things from the table while he sat there and glowered at her. Eventually he got up, went for his hat and coat, then crossed to the back door.

'Open up for me, if I'm not back.'

'Where are you going?' she asked.

'I shan't be long,' he said and went out quickly.

Vera clicked her tongue irritably and then saw that her daughter had just come into the room. Still in her nightie and dressing gown, Letty crossed to the table and took the last piece of toast almost absent-mindedly from the rack. She nibbled it and watched her mother clear away the things from the table.

'Did you always feel hungry, Ma?'

'I'll make you some more toast,' Vera offered.

'Where's Dad gone?'

'He didn't say.'

'It's awful being pregnant, isn't it?' complained Letty, slumping into a chair.

'I think I enjoyed it, dear,' her mother said.

'Did you? I hate it. It's so . . . boring. And I'm sure I look awful.' Vera had started to wash the dishes now. Letty finished the toast before she spoke again. 'Do you think the war's going to be over soon?'

'What, dear? I shouldn't think so.'

'I just wondered how much longer the Yanks'll be here.'

Vera Mundy was too busy at the sink to see the expression on Letty's face, at once bitter and wistful.


Colonel Rufus Krasnowici had been as shocked as anyone by the appalling cost of the Schweinfurt raid. Nearly twenty per cent of the total number of B-17s committed to the raid had been shot down over Germany and many of those that had returned to their respective bases had been severely damaged. The losses that Market Wetherby had sustained were shattering and Rufus had not been reassured in any way by the information that the October raid on Schweinfurt had been much more 'successful' than the August mission. Bombing had been more accurate and all five target factories had been pulverized. What Rufus could not forget was the debriefing session at which grim-faced pilots had talked about the huge swarms of ME 109s, FW-190s, ME 110s, ME 210s and JU 88s that had buzzed around them as soon as their own fighter cover had petered out after Aachen. The Luftwaffe had even thrown Stuka dive bombers into the attack on the Flying Fortresses and the result was an aerial battle of terrifying ferocity.

Spurred on by Jim Kiley, and in common with the Commanding Officer of every other Bomb Group involved, Rufus had pressed hard for replacement B-17s and crews, large supplies of drop tanks that could be fitted to the P-47s to extend their range, and more fighters, especially the long-range P-38 and the Mustang. In the meantime, he had his repair crews working around the clock. He himself was kept busy informing the families of dead airmen of the fate of their sons, and he also had to make regular calls at the hospital to see some of those who had only just survived the raid.

One of these visits took him past Helen Dereham's office at the very moment that she was coming out. He saluted politely to her and was surprised when she seemed a trifle flustered. Rufus asked if he could have a word with her and she invited him into the office, now at her most efficient and businesslike. It was his turn to feel slightly embarrassed. He coughed.

'Well, I guess it's none of my business, but . . . you're a friend of Jim Kiley's . . .'

'He's all right, isn't he?' she asked, suddenly anxious.

'Sure, but . . . well, he's been kind of difficult to live with recently, and that's not like him one bit.'

'No,' she murmured.

'I wondered if you could throw any light on it.'

'He's not ill?'

'No. But something seems to be bothering him. Now, he's too good an officer to let whatever it is affect his work, but . . . the guy's got something on his mind. I thought you might be able to help.'

'Me?' Helen played for time.

'Yeah. Oh, I realize you're pretty busy and that . . .'

'Did Major Kiley ask you to come and see me?' she said, carefully.

'Good God – no! He doesn't know anything about it.'

'I see.'

There was a long pause then it looked as if Helen was on the point of confiding in him. Rufus tried to encourage her.

'He's such a great guy, Doctor. I hate to see him down.'

'Well, I'm sorry, Colonel, but there's nothing I can do,' she replied, retreating behind her brisk manner again.

'Ah. I was afraid you'd say that.'

'I mean, unless he's actually ill . . .'

'No, no, it's not a physical thing.'

Rufus looked into her eyes and she could see that he knew what had happened. Equally clearly, he could see that she was not prepared to discuss it. He shrugged, thanked her for her help, apologized for bothering her, and went out of the office. Rufus knew that Jim Kiley would continue to be moody and irascible for some time yet.

The humiliation he had suffered in The Plough, and the subsequent row with his wife, had done more than upset Albert Mundy. It had fired him with a purpose and sent him rushing out of the house to the chemist's at the far end of the High Street. When he returned, he first checked that Vera was coping in the shop, then went upstairs to the bathroom and locked the door behind him. Stripping down to his vest, Albert took out a bottle, read the instructions carefully and, peering into the mirror, started to streak his grey hair with the liquid. It was a long and painstaking process, because he wanted the results to look as natural as possible.

Satisfied that he had taken years off his age, Albert went back downstairs and told Vera that he would be going out again. The fact that neither she nor Letty noticed any dramatic change in his appearance reassured him of the subtlety of the dyeing, and made him even more anxious to be on his way. His wife simply could not understand why he was going into Ipswich all of a sudden and she was even more amazed when, at her suggestion that she might not be able to manage on her own, Albert had simply announced that she should close the shop.

'Close the shop!'

'There's more important things in life than a bloody grocer's, Vera! You'll see.'

Giving her a peck on the cheek, Albert strolled out boldly without looking back.

He caught a bus to Ipswich and soon found what he was

after. The Army Recruiting Centre was part of a converted house set back from the road. Posters filled the windows. Albert went into the waiting room which was large, covered in a cheap linoleum and filled with rows of upright chairs. More posters shouted from the walls. The other four in the room were thirty years younger than Albert but he tried to ignore it.

He sat, he chatted, he studied the posters, he thought ruefully about his son's pacifist leanings, he waited. At length a uniformed sergeant conducted him into the interview room, where a thin, shrewd man of middle years was sitting at a table that was hidden beneath a mound of forms. In a voice that sounded weary but educated, the official invited Albert to sit in the seat opposite him. He himself continued to fill in a form.

When he looked up at his latest would-be recruit, the official frowned slightly. The hair dye had been quite discreetly applied both to hair and moustache, and it had softened Albert's appearance. But there were certain things that hair dye could never do.

'Can I see your Identity Card, please?'

'Yes. Here.' Albert handed it over and watched anxiously as the man scrutinized it.

'How old are you, Mr Mundy?'

'Forty-two. Like it says there.'

'You're a brave man,' sighed the official, 'I'll say that for you. Now go back home.'

'But I want to serve my country.'

'I'm sure you do but I'm afraid we can't take you, so don't waste my time, there's a good chap.'

'You . . . you couldn't make an exception?' pleaded Albert, giving up the pretence that he was still in his early forties.

'No. Nice try, Mr Mundy. Sorry we couldn't help you.' As Albert got up and walked towards the door, the official called him back. 'One moment. In case you didn't know, it's an offence to alter an Identity Card like this.'

'Oh.' Albert took the card back, fearing the worst.

'Goodbye, sir.'

There was a wealth of pardon and understanding in the man's smile. Albert nodded gratefully and scurried out.

He stayed in Ipswich for several hours and brooded on the irony of it all. Peter, eligible for call-up, was unwilling to go: he, willing to go, had been rejected. In his eyes, both father and son had let the family down. Then there was Letty.

When he got back home later that night, he was on the maudlin side of drunk. Vera had to help him into the house and listen to his moans about being turned down at the Recruiting Centre. Peter Mundy came into the room and was shocked when he saw the crumpled figure of his father, the hair dye more noticeable and ridiculous in the harsh light of a bulb, the face sagging, the spirit gone from him.

Billy Colvero did not even bother to notice the name of the movie. When Rosie Blair agreed to go the The Roxy with him, all that he could see on the screen was the money he was expecting to win from Elmer and Hymie. As its hero and heroine came together in a clinch, Rosie let out an involuntary sigh of pleasure. It was signal enough. Slipping an arm around her rather clumsily, he put the other on her thigh and began to stroke it. Though he had boasted to his colleagues about his experience in such situations, he was less than expert and his nervousness was making his hands tremble.

'Stop it, Billy,' she said.

'Come on, Rosie.'

'Watch the picture.'

The love scene in front of them was becoming more torrid and it prompted Billy to try again. He leaned over and whispered:

'I think you're prettier than any movie star.'

'Don't be silly!' she giggled.

'I mean it. You're the prettiest girl I ever saw.'

She giggled again and he tried to put his arms around

her. She conceded one brief and innocent kiss then insisted on watching the screen. While the kiss had meant nothing to her, it had had a profound effect on Billy. He was on fire.

When they left the cinema, they walked back towards The Plough holding hands and chatting. It was when they came to the alley at the side of the pub that Billy made his move. Grabbing Rosie in an awkward embrace, he tried to kiss her.

'Stop it! What are you doing?'

'Don't I get to say goodnight?'

'Of course, but—'

'Oh, Rosie! You're beautiful.'

She let him kiss her a few times before trying to push him away, but it was too late. Billy Colvero had been aroused in a way that had never happened before and there was an element of desperation about him now. He pulled her close to him, covered her face with kisses, then started to fondle her breasts. Ignoring her protests, he slobbered over her until Rosie could take no more. She swung her hand and smacked him hard on the cheek. He jumped back and let go of her.

'Goodnight, Billy,' she said and disappeared into the pub.

'Gee, Rosie,' he murmured, rubbing his cheek.

On the way back to the Air Base he tried to shore up his self-esteem by telling himself that she liked him really. As soon as Billy walked into his quarters, Elmer looked up enquiringly.

'How did you get on at the movies, Billy boy?'

'Great. Just great,' said the other, vaguely.

'You mean, she *let* you?' Elmer was aghast.

'Well, no. I didn't want to rush things . . . but she was begging for it, I could tell.'

'Yeah?'

'She's crazy about me. Honest injun! You're gonna be handing over any day now.'

'You gotta go all the way or no deal.'

294

'Get your dough ready, pal. I can't fail.'

Billy Colvero had almost persuaded himself that it was true.


They met in a corridor at the hospital and people were walking past all the time. Jim Kiley had come to visit some of his men and Helen had been making her ward rounds. They were almost afraid to look at each other.

'You okay?' he asked.

'I'm all right.'

'Look . . . I'm sorry. About my letter.'

'I understand.'

'I miss you like hell.' He was finding it difficult to go.

'I miss you.'

When they parted, she went straight to her office and closed the door behind her so that nobody could see the tears when they came. Helen loved him as much as ever and the pain had become unbearable.


In the fading sunshine of an autumn evening, Albert and Peter Mundy strolled across the fields near Market Wetherby, going nowhere in particular but trying to talk to each other properly for the first time in years. Albert's hair was still streaked with dye and he was wearing a cap to hide the worst of it. Peter, hands in pockets, kept thinking about the humiliation his father must have suffered. They came to a fence and paused to lean on it.

'Damn fool thing to do!' admitted Albert. 'Your mother was right as usual.'

'Oh, I don't know. You might have got away with it, Dad.'

'Not a chance. I'm lucky they didn't nab me for changing my Identity Card . . . By the way, don't mention that to your mother. She doesn't know.'

'I won't.' Peter grinned.

They walked on again and Albert searched for words of

apology that were very difficult to find. 'You know, son . . . I've been a bit hard on you, but I meant it for your own good.'

'I know.'

'Your mother thinks it's my fault that Letty's . . . well, the way she is. And she blames me for the fact that you're down at the pub all the time. I'm not sure it's all my fault.'

'No.'

'I just wanted the best for you.' He said it with such touching candour that Peter was moved. 'It doesn't seem to have worked out, does it?'

Peter took a hand out of a pocket and scratched his head. He was finding the conversation as awkward as his father, but knew that they had to go on. The resentment on both sides was still there, however muted.

'Letty'll be all right, Dad. When the baby's born—'

'Don't talk about that!'

'But we've got to.'

'If I could get my hands on that Yank!' Albert lapsed for a moment.

'He's dead,' Peter reminded him.

'Oh, God.'

'She believed that Harvey would have married her.'

Seeing that his father was now more morose, Peter abandoned the subject and walked on for a few minutes without saying anything. He began to turn over an idea which had occupied his mind a great deal. It was time to confide in his father.

'Dad?'

'Yes?'

'I've been . . . thinking about things,' he began.

'If you're going to tell me that . . .' Albert made an effort to control himself. 'No. No, go on. You've a right to your own opinions. What were you going to say?'

'I'll be eighteen next month. I . . . I thought I might enlist right away.' He could see the delight in Albert's eyes. 'They'll take me, I'm sure of it. By the time I've had my medical—'

'You've decided to go and fight!'

'If they'll have me.'

'Oh, that's wonderful, Peter. I thought you were going to start all that pacifist nonsense again.'

'No.'

'This is marvellous news!' Albert clapped his son on the back. 'At least one member of the Mundy family will be serving his country, eh? Eh?'

'I suppose so, Dad.'

'Come on, lad. Let's get back home.' Albert was really excited. 'We must tell your mother.'

'All right.'

They turned and walked back across the fields, neither of them realizing that they had been within a dozen yards of the boundary fence of the Air Base. Behind them, on the other side of a row of trees, was the enormous bulk of a B-17, looming up out of the English countryside like a great avenging monster.

# CHAPTER TWENTY-TWO

It had been a bumpy, uncomfortable flight but Sergeant Billy Colvero was still able to walk towards the debriefing hut with a spring in his step. His alertness and accuracy with his twin machine guns had been responsible for two FWs spiralling to the ground in flames, and the other members of the crew were full of praise. Even Elmer Jones, who still had nagging doubts about the tail gunner, was keen to congratulate. Billy was delighted. What he wanted more than anything else was to be accepted.

By the time that debriefing was over and the men had returned to their quarters, however, even Billy's high spirits had waned. The mood was now one of despondency as the flyers recognized that their mission had in fact been a failure. Billy took off his jacket, untied the laces of his boots, then sat on the edge of his bunk, feeling as exhausted and disappointed as any of them. Elmer shook his head.

'Do you ever get the feeling you're not doing as good as you thought you were?'

'I dunno,' said Billy. 'Seems like whenever the weather's okay here, it's bad over the target area.'

'It ain't the first time we've had to drop short of the target.'

'The chief seemed pretty sick about it all.'

'Look, kid, they're short of planes, they can't get replacements, and there's not enough crews. What d'you expect?' Elmer gave a tired smile. 'But you showed 'em, Billy boy. They can't take that away from you.'

'No . . . Er, you going into town tonight?'

'Maybe. How about you?'

'Yeah. I guess so.'

'Got a date?'

'I promised Rosie,' said Billy, casually.

'All the way, remember!'

'Yeah, well, I might just want to forget about that bet, Elmer.'

'What's the matter? You scared or something?'

'No!'

'I thought you said it was going to be a piece of cake.'

'Oh sure but . . . well, I kind of like Rosie, see. I like her a lot.' He thought it over for a moment. 'I guess I love her.'

'You *love* her!'

'Well, I don't rightly know,' said the other, embarrassed. 'But when I'm with her, I sure feel something pretty good.'

'You do?'

'Yep!'

'Oh boy! Oh boy! Oh boy! You love her!'

'Don't yell about it like that.'

'When did it start?' Elmer used a stage whisper.

'I dunno. I was thinking about her when we were in that fight back there. And when I got those two FWs, I was kind of glad because I'd have something to tell Rosie.' He shrugged. 'Sounds crazy, I guess, but . . . well, I figure you and Hymie should keep your money.'

'Yeah, yeah, the bet's off.'

'If that's okay with you.'

'Fine,' said the other, slapping him on the thigh. 'Now get changed or you'll miss the liberty wagon. Little ole Rosie is out there waiting for you, Billy boy.'

Billy was at once excited and relieved, glad that he had extricated himself from a bet that he might not be able to win yet warmed by the thought that perhaps he did love Rosie Blair after all. Since that night at the cinema, she had never been out of his thoughts for long. As he took his boots off, he mused fondly about other times they had spent together chatting in the Lounge Bar. Hymie strutted in.

'Hey, Billy,' he called. 'You've got to get over to HQ. The Major wants to see you.'

'Me?'

299

'Unless there's two guys on the station called Colvero. You better get going, kid. The man said right away.'

Billy nodded and pulled his boots on again. He was suddenly quiet and not a little apprehensive. Elmer tried to cheer him up.

'I guess Kiley's heard about those two fighters.'

'Yeah,' murmured Billy.

'Don't look so worried about it,' advised Hymie. 'Maybe you got a promotion or something.'

'Maybe.' Billy did not sound as if he thought this was at all likely. 'Look, Elmer . . . if I don't come back, would you tell Rosie that I'm real sorry?'

'What d'you mean? You'll be back. Major Kiley just wants to tell you that you done real good.'

'I sure hope so.'

Billy finished tying his shoelaces and got up. Hymie urged him to be on his way and Elmer helped him with a friendly push. At the door, Billy took a last forlorn look around and then went out.

As soon as he entered the office, his worst fears were realized. Jim was behind the desk, holding a letter. Rufus was seated. Both men had grim expressions that left no room for a welcome.

'It says here that you are at present sixteen years of age, and that you were fifteen when you enlisted.' Jim waited long enough to be sure that there was going to be no reply. 'Is that true, Sergeant Colvero?'

'Yes, sir.' There was a long pause, during which both men studied him carefully, a hint of admiration mixed with their disapproval. Billy cleared his throat and spoke up. 'Sorry, sir.'

'I should damn well think you are!' exploded Jim. 'What in hell did you think you were doing?'

'Dunno, sir. I wanted to fly, I guess.'

'So you lied about your age. Well, it's not the first time it's happened, Colvero, but it's still a very serious offence.'

'Yes, sir.'

'Don't you realize you could have been a liability to the other members of your crew?'

'Yes, sir. I was afraid of that, sir. But . . . well, I had to try.'

'So you took the United States Army Air Force for a bunch of suckers who couldn't figure the difference between a kid of sixteen and a grown man, is that right?'

'I didn't think of it that way, sir.'

'You didn't think at all, Colvero!' Jim yelled. 'And it's about time you started.'

Unable to answer, Billy stood there and looked at the ground. Rufus got up, rubbed a hand across his chin and strolled over to the tail gunner.

'Where you from, son?' he asked, quietly.

'Wyoming, Colonel, sir.'

'Your parents know what you did?'

'I don't have any parents, sir.'

'I'm sorry to hear that.'

'I lived with my grandfather,' explained Billy. 'We were dirt poor. He was glad to see the back of me, I guess.'

'You mean you ran away from your grandfather's house and enlisted? Just like that?'

'That's right, Colonel, sir. I was crazy to fly, see. In fact—'

'Yes, you told me,' interrupted Jim. 'Well, you're finished with flying for a while, Colvero.'

'You're gonna . . . *ground* me?'

'That's exactly what I'm going to do,' said Jim, firmly. 'You'll be grounded immediately and you should consider yourself technically under arrest until we can get you back to the States. What they'll do with you there . . . well, it's anybody's guess.'

Billy was stunned. There was a moment when it looked as if he was about to cry. He fought back the tears and turned to Jim.

'They'll let me fly again one day . . . won't they, sir?'

'I doubt it. You tried to take the Air Force for a ride, Colvero. They won't like that.'

There was another agonizing pause and the tears were even closer this time. Rufus came to Billy's rescue.

'Red Burwash tells me you're a pretty good gunner. Shot down two German fighters today.'

'Yes, sir.'

'I guess maybe we should mention that when we report on you. What do you think, Major Kiley?'

'I shouldn't think it'll make much difference,' replied Jim, 'but everything gets written down.' He stared at Billy. 'You're a damn fool, Colvero, but you've got guts, I'll say that for you!'

'Thank you, sir . . .'

'Okay. Get going! And you'll be flying back home just as soon as we can fix it. Now, move!'

'Sir!' Billy came to attention, saluted, then headed for the door.

'Oh,' added Jim, 'and you're confined to the Base until you go. Understand?'

'But I have to say goodbye to someone in the town,' said Billy, almost pleading.

'No! Now get out before I decide to lock you up!'

Bill Colvero stepped out into the corridor and closed the door behind him. The thought that he might never see Rosie Blair again was unbearable. He decided to go back to his quarters and confide in Elmer at once.


Albert Mundy paced up and down outside the Army Recruiting Office in Ipswich and wondered what was keeping his son. He was afraid that Peter, too, would be rejected and that his family would have to suffer a double indignity. Taking out his pocket watch, he checked the time, thought about going into the office to see where his son was, feared that he might be recognized, and continued his pacing. A young man walked towards him, took a last drag on his cigarette, then dropped it to the pavement and put his heel on it before going in through the door of the building. Albert started after him, unable to contain his impatience any longer, eager to know what was happening.

'Hello, Dad.' Peter came out as his father reached the door.

'Well? How did it go? Did they take you?'

'Yes. They took me. I'm in.'

'What did they say?' asked Albert, suddenly breathless.

'I told them I wasn't eighteen till next month, but they said I'd be old enough by the time I'd had my medical.'

'Good lad, good lad!' said his father, delighted. 'I'd have come in with you but—'

'Yes, I know. That's all right, Dad.'

'Where are they sending you?' pressed Albert, wanting to know every detail. 'Did they say? You'll be in the Suffolk Regiment, I shouldn't wonder. It's a fine thing for a man, the Army. Especially when there's a war to fight. Of course, this one's not quite the same as the last, but you'll do well if you keep your wits about you.'

'We ought to go or we'll miss the bus,' said Peter, embarrassed by his father's enthusiasm.

'Just wait till I tell them in the shop about this!'

'Don't tell people yet, Dad. I mean, I haven't even got a uniform. I'd rather keep it in the family just for now.'

'Anything you say, son. We'll keep it a secret, then you can surprise them when the time comes. That's the ticket. Eh, you'll have to have your haircut, you know, before the medical.' They were walking towards the bus stop now. 'I expect they'll send you out to Burma. There's a battalion of the Suffolks been out there since '41.'

Peter Mundy could still not believe that it had been so easy to join the Army. He had simply answered a number of questions and then watched while a form was filled in with all his particulars on it. There had been something rather unreal and impersonal about the whole thing and he was not able to respond to it in the way that Albert was. Throughout the journey home, his father kept up a running commentary that consisted of memoirs of his own wartime service, speculations about his son's future in a khaki

303

uniform and theories about how best the enemy could be subdued. Peter was relieved when they reached Market Wetherby again.

They entered the shop to find Vera Mundy handing some ration books back to Rosie Blair. In his excitement, Albert forgot all about his earlier promise.

'Here we are, then!' he announced, waving a hand in the air. 'Hello, Rosie . . . We did it, Vera. He's in the Army now. They'll call him for a medical in the next few weeks and by the end of the year—'

'Dad!'

'What?'

'We were going to keep it a secret, remember?'

'Oh yes but . . . well, Rosie's almost like family, aren't you, dear?' he said, overlooking his dislike of the girl. 'What do you think of him, eh? He'll make a good soldier, won't he? Wait till you ladies see him in his uniform!'

'Please, Dad,' Peter begged.

'The Suffolk Regiment has a fine record. The 12th Foot they were. Fought at Ypres and on the Somme.' He inflated his chest proudly and leaned over towards Rosie. 'I was with them in the first show.'

'Will you take over here while I get the tea, Albert?' Vera said.

'What? Yes, fine, just get my coat off.'

Rosie now gathered up her purchases, wished Peter good luck and quickly left the shop. Peter, whose embarrassment had largely been due to the fondness he had developed towards Rosie, gazed after her wistfully with his lips slightly parted. His mother blighted the fantasy romance at a single stroke.

'It's no good standing there like a love-sick ninny.'

'Eh?'

'Rosie's going to marry one of them from the Base. A rich fellow, she says. Two houses and a yacht back in America.'

'Did she tell you that, Mum?'

'Just now.'

'No, she won't,' said Peter, almost sagely. 'There's all sorts of them at the Base after her. Rosie strings them along and changes them round. She never goes out with any of them for long. I'll bet you anything she doesn't marry a Yank. Take my word for it.'

Albert was rather subdued by this shift to the uneasy topic of local girls and Americans. He grunted to himself as he thought about Letty and went off into the back room to get his overall. Peter could see that his confidence had really surprised her. He grinned and went out as well.

They returned from their walk happy, McGraw still carrying William and Betty still imploring 'Uncle Joe' to tell her a story. He promised that he would do so later but suggested that her first task should be to put the flowers that she had picked into some water. Betty ran over to the sink. Sally Bilton took the boy from McGraw's arms and put him into his cot, bestowing a kiss on his forehead as she sat him down. McGraw himself, completely at home in the cottage, went to the fire which had been banked up and searched for the flames with a poker. Sally asked if there was a mission the following day but he explained that fewer were being flown because of the shortage of planes and crew. Betty came running with a piece of paper that she had found tucked under the door. Recognizing the handwriting at once, her mother suggested she take her flowers up to her bedroom in a jam jar of water. McGraw knew.

'Your mother-in-law?'

'She's mad,' sighed Sally, reading the spidery scrawl.

'What does she say?'

'What you'd expect. "I waited more than half an hour. All the way from Ipswich and no one to let me in. Thought you was supposed to be doing the laundry for those Yanks. If it's any satisfaction to you, Sally Bilton, you've ruined a good man. Driving my Stan out like that. And that Sergeant McGraw turning the children away from their right father. May you both rot in hell for what you've done. I never want to see you again." ' Sally looked up and sighed once more. 'She's signed it "Ruby Bilton, Mrs". Oh, and there's a PS. "You'll never be happy with that Yank. I know his sort. Only after one thing – just like all men." If it wasn't so sad, it would be funny.'

'She's crazy.'

'Yes.' But Sally was clearly upset.

'Hey, come on!'

'I know she's a terrible woman, she always was . . . but so much *hate*.'

'Forget it. If Ruby's got a screw loose, it ain't your fault.'

'No.' Sally was not convinced. 'Oh, Mac, we'll never get away from it, will we? She'll always be there!'

'No, she won't. I got other plans.'

He went quickly to the cot and started to play with William, bouncing him up and down and talking to him in a mock confidential way. Sally was soon laughing again as the little boy gurgled with delight. McGraw had managed to dispel the clouds yet again. But the problem remained.


Elmer Jones was not looking forward to the job in hand but he had to fulfil his promise. The Lounge Bar of The Plough was crowded when he arrived and he had to jostle and wave and shout before he finally got Rosie's attention. There was another wait while she served some customers, then Elmer finally had a few minutes alone with her. She was clearly disappointed that Billy Colvero had not been near the place for days and asked where he was. Elmer took his cue.

'He's been confined to Base.'

'Why? What did he do?'

'Oh, well, nothing really . . .' Billy had made him swear to say nothing about being under age. 'He's in a bit of trouble back home, see. They're going to send him back to the States.'

'Billy!' She was hurt.

'He doesn't want to go. He's crazy to stay here and keep flying. But that's it. An order from up top.'

'That's awful! Will he be able to stay in the Air Force?'

'Dunno. Look, Rosie, he wants to say goodbye to you – special. And he can't get out.' Elmer licked his lips as he came to the difficult part of the promise that had been wrested from him. 'So I got to get you in.'

'In?'

'To the Base. It's real simple. Here's what you do . . .'

'I'm not doing anything, Elmer Jones,' she retorted, wondering if the whole thing was not some kind of practical joke. 'If Billy wants to say goodbye to me, he can come and say it here!'

She had gone off to serve another customer before Elmer could explain. Jack Blair came up and Elmer bought his own drink. Sensing the importance of what he had seen take place between Elmer and his younger daughter, Jack worked his way down the bar to relieve her. When Rosie returned she was beginning to suspect that Elmer had told the truth.

'What I don't understand is this. If Billy's family's so rich, why don't they do something to make him stay over here?'

'*Rich?*'

'Couldn't they fix it up with the people in charge?'

'Rosie, he ain't got no family. There's some old guy – his grandfather, I guess – lives in a shack in the Big Horn Mountains, but that's all the family he's got.'

'Are you sure?' she asked, as the cold hand of disillusion began to touch her. 'He told me his father had this bank in New York. He said they were very rich. Two houses and a yacht.'

Elmer was about to laugh but the look in her eye warned him against it. He remembered his mission. 'You *must* come, Rosie. Please!'

'We'll see,' she said, thinking it over. 'Where are the Big Horn Mountains, anyway?'

'Right in the middle of America. And a hell of a long way from New York.'

Rosie Blair was beginning to wish that she had not hinted to Vera Mundy that she might one day be marrying a wealthy young American. The odd thing was that she still wanted to see Billy Colvero again.


Ronnie Dereham was working at his desk when he heard the knock on French windows. He invited Vi in and gave her the warmest of welcomes, saying how much better the farm was running now that she was taking a more active part in it. Vi was pleased though tired after a day in the fields, she looked healthier and more cheerful than she had done in weeks. Ronnie commented on this too and she seemed to be on the point of confiding something. At the last moment, however, she changed her mind and asked instead how Pat was getting on. He smiled rather sadly and told her that Pat was still working in a Forces' Canteen. While he himself had reservations about her job, he supposed that it was necessary work and he accepted that his daughter was determined to do something towards the war effort. A thought came into his mind.

'Any word yet?'

'No,' she replied, her face clouding.

Ronnie quickly talked about something else and regretted that he had asked about Chuck Ericson. It was evident from Vi's general manner that she had not heard anything distressing about her husband, and she would hardly have kept good news to herself. By way of apology, Ronnie was now complimenting her again on the way that she had helped him in the actual administration of the farm. With a kind of old world gallantry, he told her that she had inspired him and he lifted her hand to kiss it with his lips. Vi was a little taken aback by the gesture. Ronnie tried to put her at her ease, and then surprised her even more by suggesting that she might stay and have dinner with them one evening instead of always rushing off.

The front door opened and closed in the distance and Helen came into the room. She was pleased to see Vi and asked after her father and her sister. Vi took her leave and had a private word with Helen in the hall before she left.

'I was suggesting she had dinner with us one night,' explained Ronnie when his wife came back into the room.

'Do you really think she'd enjoy it?' wondered Helen.

'Why shouldn't she, darling?'

Helen pointed out that her sister had been their house-maid, but Ronnie swept this aside as irrelevant, arguing that Vi was very different and was virtually running the farm for them now.

'She won't be able to do that much longer, if she's right about herself.'

'What do you mean?' he asked.

'Vi thinks she's pregnant. Came to see me about it yesterday. She was asking me in the hall just now when the results would be through. Didn't she tell you, Ronnie?'

'No,' he admitted, a trifle hurt at the realization. 'She didn't say a word. Well, that's . . . wonderful, for her, isn't it? At least she'll have the poor chap's child. I expect that's why she's looked so happy recently. Blooming, in fact.'

'Yes. I'm afraid she may be in for a disappointment, though.'

'A false alarm?'

'I can't be certain at this stage, of course, but my guess is yes, she's imagined the whole thing. I don't think Vi is pregnant at all.'

Helen went back into the hall to take off her coat and Ronnie was left to consider what had been said. If his wife was right in her diagnosis, Vi was in for a serious let-down. Ronnie Dereham was mildly astonished to find that he felt so protective towards the girl and he even began to think of ways to shield her from the blow. What puzzled him most was that another part of him was rather glad that she might not be pregnant after all.

# CHAPTER TWENTY-THREE

It was late in the evening but Sally Bilton was still working, crouched over the sink as she washed yet another pair of fatigues, her sleeves rolled up and her forearms glistening with soapy water. The wireless was turned on but the volume was so low that she could hardly hear the dance music that was being played by Joe Loss and his band. Her mind in any case was on other things, on the children, on herself, on the letter she had received from Ruby, on the letter she had still not had from Stan even though it was now a month since he had gone back into the Army. A shuffling noise outside the back door caused her to stop but she soon carried on with her task when she realized who it was. As McGraw entered and walked up to her she caught the faint whiff of beer on his breath.

'Sorry, honey,' he said.

'Where've you been?'

'I had some business to do at The Plough.'

'Oh.'

'Kids in bed?'

'Of course they're in bed. D'you know what time it is?'

'Time?' McGraw glanced at his watch and then became even more apologetic. 'I guess we talked longer than I thought.'

'Do you want any supper?'

'No thanks.' She was still bent over the washboard, working the soap into the material. He put a hand on her shoulder. 'Don't be mad at me, Sal.'

'I'm not mad,' she said, still not turning.

'That guy took a lot of persuading.'

'What guy?'

'One of the pilots,' he said.

Sally forgot all about the washing now. Drying her

hands on a towel, she swung round to confront him. 'Go on.'

'We had a couple of beers and I guess I didn't notice the time.'

'This pilot . . . what were you trying to persuade him to do?'

'Nothing,' he lied, moving away.

'Mac . . .'

'Well, I figured maybe—'

'You're going with them, aren't you?' she asked, cutting in. 'You're going to fly on the next mission with them.'

'No point in trying to keep it from you,' he confessed.

'Oh Mac, *please*. I'd much rather you didn't. Stay on the ground. After all, that's your job.'

'I'm sorry, Sal, but it's been driving me crazy, watching the boys going up week after week and never once going with them.'

'But so many of them never come back,' she urged.

'That's a chance I gotta take.'

'No, Mac. What you do is just as important, you know that. If it wasn't for you and your—'

'Don't worry,' he said, stopping her with a raised palm. 'I'll be fine. Red's just about the most experienced flier in the Group?'

'I don't want you go to,' she pleaded. 'You've done your share.'

'Might still be of some use up there. At least I know how things work if we get trouble.'

'*Please*!' She put her hands around his neck. 'For my sake.'

'I'm going,' he said, then put a finger gently to her lips, stifling her protest. 'Don't, Sal. I love you, you know that, but I'm going. Don't make it difficult on me, huh?'

She looked up at him and then buried her face in his chest to hide her anguish. McGraw put his arms around her and held her tight, making soothing noises as he did so. Then he cupped her chin in his hand and lifted it until her lips met his. The kiss was long and intense and it left both of them breathless. McGraw eased her towards the stairs.

'I haven't finished the washing.'

'Who cares about the washing?'

'We'll have to be quiet. I don't want Betty to wake up.'

'She never has before,' he said with a grin.

Sally tidied up the room, switched off the wireless, attended to the fire then went slowly upstairs with him. They needed reassurance from each other more than ever.


When Vi Ericson had got hold of the notion that she might be pregnant, she had been so thrilled that she wanted to tell everyone. Her natural sense of caution, however, made her decide to find out for certain before she spread the news, so she confided only in her sister. Rosie was shaken at first and had foreseen only the problems, but Vi convinced her how important the baby was to her and how the child would be a reminder of the brief happiness that she and Chuck had shared. She swore Rosie to secrecy and made an appointment to see Helen Dereham at the cottage hospital. Helen sensed just how much the pregnancy would mean to her and was quietly supportive. Vi was told to return in a few days when she would be given the medical verdict.

By the time she went into Helen's office for the second appointment, Vi had persuaded herself that she was without doubt going to have a child. She had even begun to make plans for bringing it up and firmly decided in her own mind that, if the child were a boy, it would be named after its father. Though she had not given up all hope of ever seeing Chuck again, she was coming to accept that the chances of his returning to her were slender indeed. Confirmation of pregnancy, therefore, would be a way of telling her that part of her husband was still alive.

Helen motioned her to a seat and then broke the news to her as gently as she could. The results of the tests had been negative. Vi was not going to have a baby. Helen went on to suggest that it might be better if she put all thought of Chuck out of her mind. She had clearly willed the pregnancy and come to believe in it because it was so important to her. She ought to be easier on herself by trying to forget about her husband.

Vi was too shattered even to hear the advice properly. What had really stunned her was the realization that she would never have Chuck's child now. It was too late. She had nothing but a few memories. Vi asked Helen how reliable the tests were and was told that there was no room for error. Having entered the room actually *feeling* pregnant, Vi now felt empty, wasted, abandoned.

She thanked Helen for seeing her, knowing that if she had gone to her own doctor her father would have found out at once. The one consolation was that she had not announced her news to anyone but her sister. Helen was kind and sympathetic and did her best to cheer Vi up, but the girl still left in deep depression. It seemed as if she had no husband, no child, no future.


Long before she saw the high perimeter fence, Rosie Blair was beginning to have second thoughts about the whole enterprise. Why should she go to such lengths to see someone who had lied so freely to her about himself? What was she doing out there on a cold and cheerless evening, picking her way over marshy ground and talking in whispers to Hymie Stutz?

There was a loud squelch as her shoe sank into water.

'Hymie! Help!'

'Keep it quiet!' he hissed. 'We're almost there.'

'I've lost my shoe. It just came off. I can't see a thing in this dark.'

'Yes, you can. Look – there's the fence just up ahead there.'

'I'm not going over that!' she protested. 'And what about my shoe? Help me find it.'

The pair of them groped about for the missing shoe. On

the other side of the fence, a figure appeared from behind a hut and came towards them. It was Billy Colvero.

'Hymie! Is that you?' he whispered.

'Yeah. Where are you, kid?'

'Over here.'

'We're just looking for Rosie's shoe.'

'Found it,' she said, and lifted it from the ground with a low slurping sound. 'It's soaking wet.'

'Are you okay, Rosie?' asked Billy, full of concern.

'No, I'm not okay. We've been walking in circles for the last half an hour because Hymie didn't know the way. Elmer was supposed to bring me, not him.' She silenced Hymie's protest by leaning on him while she put her shoe back on. 'That's better.'

She limped towards the fence and got within a few feet of Billy. For once he seemed quite bashful.

'Hi, Rosie.'

'Hello. You wanted to say goodbye.'

'Yeah. It's great of you to come!'

'I'm sorry you're in trouble. What did you do?'

'Nothing really. Sort of misunderstanding. I made some mistakes when I signed the enlistment papers.'

'Is that all?'

'Sure.'

'And they're locking you up just for that?'

'Rules, Rosie. That's the rules.' He wondered how she would react if she knew the truth of the situation and decided not to find out. 'Gee, you look terrific, Rosie.'

'I look a mess. Hymie brought me through the middle of the wood. I've got scratches everywhere.'

'Would you two kids like me to take a powder?' offered Hymie, not wishing to interrupt a tender scene. 'I could come back in half an hour.'

'Stay right there,' ordered Rosie. 'You're taking me home.'

'Whatever you say, Rosie.'

Hymie moved away a few paces to give them the illusion of privacy. Billy now slipped a hand through the fence and

314

took her fingers in his, disappointed when she did not return his squeeze.

'I can't stay long, Billy. I'm supposed to be working.'

'I know. I'm real glad you came. Sorry about the shoe.'

'That's all right.'

'I'd have come to the pub but they won't let me out of here.'

'Do they watch you all the time?' she asked, ghoulishly.

'Yeah. Kind of,' he sighed and his play for sympathy worked.

'Why did you tell me all those lies?' she whispered. 'About being rich and that.'

'I dunno,' he said, ashamed. 'I wanted to impress you, I guess.'

'Elmer said you lived with your grandfather on some mountain or other.'

'Yeah. That's about right.' Anxiety made him press himself against the fence. 'Did Elmer tell you anything else?'

'He said you were really very poor.'

'Anything *else*?'

'No, I don't think so. Why?'

'Nothing.' Relief made him grin for the first time. 'Can I kiss you, Rosie? Just once.'

'I suppose so.'

Because he was not trying to impress her, Billy was arousing a much warmer response. She felt desperately sorry for him. The fence reduced the embrace to a rather inexpert grope but their lips finally touched for a moment.

'Hate to break up the party,' said Hymie, emerging from the shadows, 'but I think I hear someone coming.'

'I better go,' announced Billy.

'Me, too,' she said.

'Goodbye, Rosie.' He kissed her again. 'I'll write you.'

'Goodbye, Billy.'

'I'm real glad you came.'

'Yes, well . . . goodbye.'

'And thanks.'

She left him standing at the fence and moved away. Hymie offered his hand to lead her back to the road but she refused it, remembering the traumas of the journey there.

'No thanks,' she said. 'I can manage better on my own.'

Rosie stumbled off into the darkness and soon found herself in water up to her ankles, but she was no longer angry. For all the hazards of the journey, she was quite pleased that she had made the effort to see Billy Colvero.


Major Jim Kiley was getting increasingly restless and annoyed at the Base. The second Schweinfurt mission had decimated his planes and crews and full replacements had still not arrived. It seemed to him that the USAAF was on the point of losing the battle for strategic daylight bombing, and he was deeply frustrated that he could not get more directly involved himself. When Rufus Krasnowici informed him once again that he would not go on a combat mission, Jim decided that it was time to disobey the orders of his Commanding Officer. As the B-17s began to take off early one morning, therefore, a figure in flying gear came jogging across the concrete towards 'Ginger II'. Red Burwash, who had already taken a risk by letting McGraw join his crew for the flight, was put in an even more difficult position by the arrival of Jim. He was quite certain that the Air Executive was not flying with Rufus's approval and he knew that there would be trouble for Jim and himself when they returned to England. But Jim was insistent and so the B-17 set off with two passengers aboard.

Simply to be in the air again was a tonic for Jim and he felt that many of his problems had been left behind as the plane gathered height then joined the formation. He was even managing to put Helen Dereham completely from his thoughts.

Shortly after they had flown over the French coast, the first enemy fighters came out of the clouds, guns blazing.

Before Jim really knew what was happening, a string of bullets pierced the fuselage beside him and he felt a searing pain in his leg. Red Burwash was told at once of the casualty and his first instinct was to turn back but Jim ordered him to fly on to the target area. First aid gave him minimal relief but the loss of blood continued. It was an enormous relief to him, therefore, when 'Ginger II' dropped its bomb load directly over its target and then began the homeward journey.

By the time that the plane was over England once more, Jim was very weak indeed and fighting to retain consciousness.

A red flare was dropped as 'Ginger II' came in to land and an ambulance was with it seconds after it had taxied to its hard-stand. Rufus Krasnowici, who had rehearsed some caustic speeches for the benefit of Air Executive, now found himself offering words of sympathy instead as Jim was helped out of the plane and on to a waiting stretcher. In no time at all he was being driven off towards the hospital.

Helen Dereham was waiting for him when they brought him in. He just had enough strength to speak to her.

'Don't be mad at me, Helen . . . I couldn't help it.'

'You're going to be all right, Major Kiley,' she assured him when the wound was inspected. 'You're going to be all right.'

Her tearful smile was the last thing he saw before he lapsed into unconsciousness. Jim was taken to a side ward and prepared for the operating theatre. Half an hour later, he was being wheeled off to a bed, the bullets having been removed from his leg without too much difficulty and a blood transfusion having restored the loss.

Jim awoke next morning to find himself in a small, neat room that smelled of disinfectant. Helen Dereham was watching him.

'Hello,' she said. 'How did you sleep?'

'Just fine, thank you, Doctor. I think they gave me something.'

'You needed a long rest.'

'What are they going to do with me?'

'You'll be transferred to your own hospital in Bury tomorrow,' she explained, still using her professional voice. 'Then it's just a question of waiting for the wound to heal.'

'Bury? Do I have to go there? I mean, why can't I stay here?'

'I think you're a little too important for us.'

'That's nonsense. I'll get Rufe to talk to them.' He smiled and extended his hand lazily. She took it in hers. 'It's good to see you, Helen.' He read the question in her eyes. 'I don't know why it worked out like it did. When I saw your husband that night . . . he told me he'd give you a divorce.'

'I know.'

'He's a great guy, Helen. I like him too much to—'

'I can't leave him,' she said, firmly. 'Not ever.'

'No.'

Without releasing his hand, she sat beside the bed. All trace of her formal manner had now disappeared. 'I'd like to see you again, Jim.'

'You mean that?'

'It's silly to go on – as we have been – punishing ourselves.'

'You know that it won't be enough,' he warned. 'Just seeing.'

'Yes, I appreciate that.'

'It's why I wrote you. I knew if I saw you and . . .' He grinned as she lifted his hand and kissed it very gently.

'I'm much nicer to Ronnie when I can see you,' she admitted. 'I've been beastly to him these last few weeks. And he doesn't have Pat around for moral support.'

'Pat?'

'She ran off to do her bit towards the war effort – and to escape from her shameful mother! She's working in some dreadful Forces' Canteen. Might do her good.'

'It might at that,' he agreed.

'Have you missed me?'

318

'Like hell! I don't think I've been too pleasant to live with either.'

'I know. Rufus came to see me.'

'You're kidding!'

'No, he was here visiting one of your officers. He sort of dropped in to tell me that you were being difficult and to ask if I could do anything about it.'

'What did you say?' Jim was amused at the idea.

'I said I couldn't.'

'Well, maybe you can, after all.'

They sat there holding hands for a very long time. Despite the wound, Jim Kiley was very glad that he had flown on the last combat mission.


Although he had lost the chance of collecting thirty dollars in a bet, Elmer Jones believed that he might have won himself something worth much more. At the first available opportunity, he went into Market Wetherby for the evening and made straight for The Plough. Jack Blair gave him the usual smile of welcome but Rosie ignored him deliberately. He waited till she came to his end of the bar and leaned over towards her.

'Rosie, *please*!'

'What can I do for you, then?' she asked, frostily.

'I just wanted to say that I'm sorry. About the other night. When I was supposed to meet you and bring you to the camp. It wasn't my fault.'

'No?'

'I couldn't get off the Base.'

'So you sent Hymie instead.'

'I told him where to meet you and gave him all the details.'

'Well, he led me on a proper wild goose chase, I can tell you! All but ruined a good pair of shoes.' She pouted at him and then relaxed a little. 'Has Billy gone?'

'Yep. Flew back to the States yesterday. There was a

flight came over with replacement crews. Billy went back on it.'

'Will he be all right? What'll they do to him?'

'Nothing much,' said Elmer, without thinking. 'It ain't his fault he's only sixteen. I mean he shouldn't have lied about it but I guess they won't . . .' He realized what he had done. 'Shoot! I wasn't supposed to tell you that.'

'Sixteen?' Rosie found it amusing. 'Billy was only sixteen? He seemed much older than that!'

'Yeah, well . . .'

'Sixteen! Well, I never!'

She thought about Billy Colvero and about the arrogant charm that had belonged to someone so much older. Elmer, thinking to profit by the absence of a rival, now moved in to take advantage.

'Look, Rosie . . . now that Billy's gone and you've seen through that bum, Hymie . . . how's about me and you, when you have a free evening, that is . . . what I'm trying to say is . . .'

'You want to take me out again.'

'Yeah. I sure would love to.'

'That might be very nice, Elmer. I'll have to see.'

Before he could commit her to a definite date, however, she had moved away to serve the three American servicemen who had just come in. The young man who ordered three beers was tall, lazily confident and gifted with the sort of classic good looks that Rosie found quite irresistible. She flashed her famous smile at him.

'You're new around here, aren't you?'

'That's right. We got in yesterday.' He and Rosie appraised each other and both liked what they saw. 'What's your name?'

'Rose Blair.'

'Hello, Rose,' he said, shaking her hand. 'I'm Walter Leroy.'

Elmer saw the handshake and the look on their faces and he cursed inwardly. Then he saw the stripes on Walter Leroy's arm and realized that he was now in competition

320

with a Lieutenant. It was simply not fair. Rosie seemed as far from his grasp as ever.

While Sally Bilton was at her usual place at the sink washing fatigues, McGraw was doing some hard bargaining. Only by promising to read Betty another story on the next day did he manage to persuade her to go up to bed. The child kissed him on the cheek.

'Goodnight, Uncle Joe.'

'Goodnight, princess.'

'Goodnight, Mummy.' Another kiss.

'Goodnight.'

Sally saw her daughter to the bottom of the stairs, wiping her hands dry in her apron. When Betty had gone on up, she came back and sat down at the table opposite McGraw.

'You look tired, Sal.'

'I'm all right. Make some supper soon.'

'I wish I could take you out for a meal,' he said. 'Have someone wait on you for a change.'

'I don't mind, Mac. I'm just so glad you're back . . . How's Major Kiley?'

'They reckon he'll be okay.'

'Don't ever do that again, will you?' she said.

'Couldn't get anyone to take me. Not for a while.' He reached across and stroked her arm. 'You were really worried there for a bit, weren't you?'

'I love you, remember?'

A rattling of the handle of the back door caused them both to sit up. Loud knocking soon followed and McGraw went to see who it was. When he had unbolted the door and opened it, Ruby Bilton thrust her way in.

'Oh, *you're* here, are you?' she said, scornfully. 'I might have known. And what did you have to go and bolt that door for, Sally?'

'We always do that at night, Ma.'

'Well, you've done it now!' exclaimed the old woman. 'You've done it and I hope you're both satisfied.'

'What do you mean?' asked Sally, bewildered.

'You've killed him. You've killed my Stan between the two of you. Can you hear what I'm saying? He's dead. My Stan. Killed out in Italy and it's your fault.'

'What are you talking about?' McGraw was getting angry.

'I had a letter from one of them in his company. He said it was like Stan wanted to die. Ever since he came back the last time. Like he didn't care about anything else. Nothing to live for.'

'I'm sorry.'

'Sorry? Don't come that with me, my girl. You hoped this would happen. You wanted this to happen so that you could marry your fancy man here.'

'Don't talk to Sally that way,' warned McGraw, quietly.

'You never loved him, Sally Bilton, not from the start. And the moment something better came along—'

'Stop that,' said McGraw.

'You were off, leaving that poor man—'

'*I said stop it*!'

'And you're no better than she is,' she sneered, rounding on him, 'with your smart talk and your free fags, buying your way in here . . .'

'Please, Ruby,' Sally asked. 'You'll wake Betty.'

'Let 'er wake. It's time she knew her mother's no better than a common whore.' McGraw stepped towards her as if about to strike but Ruby was not afraid. 'That's right. Hit me. Go on. You would, too. I know your sort.' When McGraw relaxed a little, she turned back to Sally. 'You see? He can't do it because he knows it's wrong, what you've been doing together. Well, I'm going to make you pay for this. You're responsible for this! You're responsible for Stan's death as sure as I'm standing here!'

All three suddenly became aware of the figure of Betty, standing in the doorway with a doll under her arm.

'What's the matter, Mummy? Why is Gran angry?'

'It's all right, darling,' said Sally, going to her. 'Nothing's the matter. I'll come and tuck you in, shall I?'

'Is Gran going to stay with us now?' asked the girl.

'I expect so. Now let's get you to bed.'

With a glance of reproof at her mother-in-law, Sally took her daughter back upstairs to soothe her and put her to bed. McGraw watched them go then thought hard about something. When he turned to Ruby Bilton, her face was as bitter and accusing as ever. He took his jacket from the back of the chair, slipped it on and then let himself out of the cottage. Ruby came to the table and sat down. She gazed slowly around. And behind her bitterness there was now a hint of triumph.

# CHAPTER TWENTY-FOUR

Ronnie Dereham sat at the main window and gazed out at the drive. He was waiting for Helen to come home from the Hospital and the waiting was beginning to prey on him. She said that she wanted to remain his wife and he had been delighted, but since that time she had been moody and preoccupied. He had felt more excluded than ever. Then there was Pat, who had given up her studies at Cambridge in order to help the war effort but who was now toiling away in a menial job in a Forces' Canteen. The longer he waited the more his anxieties weighed in upon him. In the end he made a conscious effort to escape from his brooding, swinging his wheelchair around and propelling himself across the room. The newspaper would be his refuge.

When he reached down to pick it up from the occasional table, however, he nudged it on to the floor. Grunting in irritation, he took out a pair of tongs that he kept in a side-pocket of his wheelchair and tried to retrieve the paper with them. It was to no avail. Each time he thought that he had a firm grip on the paper, it slipped from the tongs. Ronnie became so annoyed and frustrated that he eventually hurled the tongs to the floor in disgust. He could have called for Nanny to help him, but something stopped him doing so and made him want to cope on his own. It was ludicrous that he should be defeated by a bloody newspaper.

Manoeuvring his chair around, he tried to lean over the side to pick up the paper with the tips of his fingers but it was marginally beyond his grasp. He tried to lever himself up so that his reach was lengthened but this only made it difficult for him to retain his balance. With a supreme effort, he lifted himself up and grabbed with his hand but his balance went completely and he was pitched out of the chair and on to the floor.

At that moment, Nanny walked into the room and stopped in astonishment when she saw him lying there.

'What on earth are you doing, Major?'

'Trying to finish the crossword, woman.' His sarcasm was lost on her.

'I'm sure you'd be more comfortable in your chair,' she told him. 'Anyway, you have a visitor – a Captain Anderson.'

A tall, well-built man in his thirties came through the door. He was in uniform and had an unmistakably English quality about him.

'Hello, sir,' he said, looking down at Ronnie.

'Ken!' The absurdity of his situation made him burst into laughter and it verged on hysteria before he stopped himself and apologized. 'Come in, come in. What a marvellous surprise! How about some tea or coffee or something, Nanny?'

'Which?' she asked the visitor.

'Whatever you have.'

'Do you take sugar, young man?'

'Not necessarily . . .'

'Tea, then,' she decided, going out. 'No sugar.'

'Who was that?' wondered Ken Anderson, amused.

'Nanny. She looks after us. I'm afraid she tends to forget that there are some people over the age of seven.'

Ken offered to help him up and though he would have preferred to have got back into the wheelchair alone, he accepted the aid. He smiled his thanks to the newcomer.

'How are you keeping, sir?'

'Oh, I'm a bit of an old crock.'

'You're dashed lucky to be here at all. When we got you out of that tank, we all thought you were a goner.'

'I dare say.'

'It's good to see you again.' Ken had been Ronnie's second-in-command and the two men had the greatest respect for each other.

325

'Nice to see *you*, Ken. Are you on leave?'

'Three weeks. Managed to scrounge a flight home on an RAF transport. I thought I'd look in and see how you were. A lot of the chaps keep asking after you.'

'That's decent of them,' said Ronnie, touched. 'I admit, I miss the whole sweaty bunch. Who's in command now?'

'Lomax. He's doing a good job, but . . . well, you took us right across North Africa.'

Ronnie was embarrassed by the strength of the younger man's admiration. He remained silent, not wanting to get drawn into a discussion of his combat experiences. Ken asked after Helen and was told about her job at the hospital. Ronnie then invited his visitor to stay to lunch when he would have a chance of seeing Helen. The sound of heavy bombers approaching interrupted the conversation. Ken moved to the window.

'They don't sound like ours.'

'Flying Fortresses.' He stopped for a moment. 'They're back early. Something must have gone wrong.'

'Yanks?'

'We have a Bomb Group just down the road.'

'That must've shaken things up round here!'

'You could say that.'

He smiled at his guest and waved him to a seat, then glanced up as the full noise of the bombers was heard above their heads. He waited until the thunder had started to fade then: 'Yes, it's wonderful to see you again. What do you intend to do with your leave? Have you made any plans . . . ?'

Sitting up in his bed at the cottage hospital, Jim Kiley had heard the returning planes as well. He knew at once that another mission had aborted. Bad weather over the Continent had already caused three missions to be abandoned that month and it had badly bruised morale. This last failure would have the same result. It would also send Rufus Krasnowici into one of his controlled rages. Jim

326

wished that he could be at the Base to hear the full details of the raid and to lend what help he could, but his wounded leg was going to put him out of action for a couple of weeks at least.

Helen Dereham popped into his room to tell him that he was being moved to another hospital that morning. They had the chance of a quiet moment together, then a nurse opened the door to find them holding hands. Helen's manner changed at once and she wished Jim a polite goodbye before going out. The nurse, understanding the situation, went out after her. Jim Kiley lay back in the bed and smiled. Then he noticed how much he was perspiring.


Installed in her favourite seat by the fire, Ruby Bilton inhaled her cigarette and glanced at the paper. A burning smell drifted into her nostrils and she was on her feet at once, rushing to the stove where a saucepan was steaming away. She snatched the lid off and yelped as her fingers were burned. Grabbing a cloth, she lifted the saucepan off the gas ring and stirred the stew with a wooden spoon to detach it from the enamel. When she heard someone coming, she turned the gas down low, set the saucepan back on it and continued stirring.

'It's all right, Sally. I was watching it all the time.' Her expression hardened when she saw that it was McGraw. 'Oh, it's you. Walking in here without so much as a by your leave.'

'It's Sally I came to see.'

'Yes, well maybe she doesn't want to see *you*.'

'I'll wait till she tells me that. Where is she?'

'Gone to fetch Betty from school.'

'School?' McGraw was surprised.

'Started in the Infants Class yesterday.'

'Sally didn't tell me.'

'Why should she? It's none of your business!' Ruby was almost crowing over him. 'Hasn't it sunk in yet? You're not wanted. My son's wife – or should I say, his widow –

doesn't want you. Only she doesn't know how to tell you. She's come to her senses at last, see. While you were smarming your way in here, her hubby – my boy, Stan – was out there fighting for Sally and the children, dying for them. So now the very thought of you disgusts her!'

'If I believed that . . .' he began.

'Oh, you can believe it, Sergeant. These are her words. She wants to keep her head up in this town – not have people sneering and sniggering at her all the time on account of you.' McGraw had heard enough. 'You're nothing compared to my boy! Do you think you could ever take the place of a real man like him?'

The door closed behind him and she smiled, hurling her cigarette into the fire and finding another from the packet in her cardigan. She saw that the American had absent-mindedly put his own cigarettes and lighter down on the table and forgotten them. Picking up the lighter, she lit up, inhaled deeply, then tossed it carelessly down again. A minute later, Sally came in the front way with the children. Sally smelled the burning and dashed to the stove. She switched off the gas and stared into the saucepan angrily.

'It only caught a bit in the bottom.'

'It's burnt, Ma! That was going to do us for two days! You promised me you'd keep an eye on it!'

'I turned my back for a second, that's all,' said the old lady.

'Where's Uncle Joe?' asked Betty.

'At the camp, love,' explained her mother, holding the saucepan under the tap and running water into it.

'No, he's here!' insisted the girl.

'What are you talking about?' snapped her grandmother.

'He's here, he's here, I know it.'

'Don't shout, Betty,' said her mother. Then she saw the cigarette lighter that her daughter was holding up and she came to the same conclusion. 'He's been here, hasn't he, Ma?'

'He . . . just looked in.'

328

'I've only been gone twenty minutes. Why didn't he stay?'

'He couldn't . . . He was in a hurry.'

Sally could see that her mother-in-law was lying but she did not want another argument in front of the children. She told Betty to take her brother to the bathroom, ignored the child's protests and ushered her out. Then she turned to confront Ruby.

'What's been going on?'

'Don't know what you mean.'

'Come off it. I want the truth. Why didn't Joe wait? Or leave a message at least?'

'He just came in and . . . went out.'

'Have you been getting at him?'

'I just told him the truth!'

'And what's that?'

'He's not wanted here!' snarled Ruby. 'I told him you want to live decent and not have the whole town pointing at you and the children because of him.'

'You said that?' Sally's temper was rising.

'It's no more than you said yourself last night, my girl. I had to tell him 'cos you don't know how to do it yourself. I'm here to look after you, that's what I said. Then I suggested that he took himself off and never came back. That's what you want, isn't it?'

Sally-Bilton's heart was pounding. She hardly dared speak. She crossed quickly to the back door, opened it and stepped out. But there was no sign of McGraw.

Letty Mundy was not enjoying her pregnancy. Apart from the steady increase in weight, there were bouts of sickness, swollen ankles and a general malaise to cope with, and it was all too much for her. She seemed to have forgotten how to smile and complained unendingly. Vera, the chief recipient of the complaints, always gave her as much reassurance as she could, already resigned to the idea of the baby and determined to make the most of the situation.

As she stood at the stove cooking lunch, Vera became aware once again of her daughter's unhappiness. Letty had brought her own atmosphere into the room with her.

'Can I help, Mum?' offered the girl, gloomily.

'No, no, you sit down, Letty. Have to rest, you know.'

'The doctor said I was to take exercise.' She lowered herself into her chair beside the table. 'Except that I hate going out. Everyone stares at me.'

Peter, who was also seated at the table, asked how long the lunch would be because he had to go into Ipswich early that afternoon for his medical. His mother told him that it was more or less ready and they were simply waiting for Albert to come in from the shop. On cue, her husband came striding in through the archway and took his place at the table. Vera began to serve the rissoles that she had been frying. Albert glared at his plate.

'Rissoles again, is it?'

'They're Vienna Steaks.'

'Mario used to call them meatballs,' Letty said.

Peter cut himself a slice and popped it into his mouth. The others took it in turns to help themselves to the boiled potatoes that stood in the tureen. Albert ate his way through two before jabbing a fork in the direction of Peter's head and telling him that he should have had a haircut before his medical. When his son argued that a haircut was not important, Albert insisted that it was. An applicant who was smart and well turned out, for whatever job it might be, always caught the eye.

'Same with the Army. They notice, lad. If you went in there all spruced up, they might even write you down as Potential Officer Material.'

'I don't want to be an officer.'

'You never know what you want,' Albert said.

'I just want him to be happy,' said Vera. 'And to come back safe.'

The family munched away noisily, then Albert had another mild upsurge of patriotism.

'He's not afraid of sacrifice, I'll say that for him. Ready to fight for King and country. I'm proud of him.'

'I don't want Peter to go,' said Letty, quietly.

'Let's not have any of that kind of talk, my girl.'

'I was thinking of Harvey and—'

'We all have to do our duty,' her father told her. 'I thank God that Peter is ready to do his and uphold the good name of the family.' He speared a rissole with his fork then remembered something. 'That Mrs Bilton was in the shop this morning.'

'Sally?'

'No. Old Mrs Bilton. Stan's mother. She wanted some fags. Well, I let her have some, of course. Least I could do under the circumstances, wasn't it?'

'Yes,' agreed Vera. 'How's she taken it? Stan's death?'

'Very well, considering. An inspiration to all of us. That's what I mean about doing our duty, see? Not like that daughter-in-law of hers. Carrying on with a Yank from the . . .' He saw the warning look that Vera was flashing him. 'Yes, well, least said about that the better, I suppose.'

But he had already said too much. Her mind was full of Harvey and Mario again and the tears welled up in her eyes. Albert thrust the rissole into his mouth and chewed it with distaste. Letty's pregnancy was something that he had still not yet got used to and he seemed able to say the wrong thing without even trying.

When Helen got back to Dereham House she was delighted to see Captain Ken Anderson chatting to her husband. She pressed him to stay to lunch but Ronnie explained that that had already been arranged, adding that he had also tried to persuade their guest to stay the night. Seeing how much her husband wanted this, Helen renewed the invitation as warmly as she could and Ken accepted. She then went to pour three glasses of sherry from their one remaining bottle. Ronnie suddenly had an idea.

331

'Why don't we ask Vi to join us for dinner?'

'Vi?' The idea would not have occurred to her.

'We said we'd ask her some time and it would be someone else for Ken to talk to. Might be more fun for both of them.'

'Well, if you think so,' agreed Helen, not convinced.

'Who is this Vi?' Ken asked.

'Oh, a marvellous girl!' said Ronnie, enthusiastically. 'She's our . . . well, I suppose you'd call her our Head Land Girl. Virtually run the estate since I've been laid up.'

'Fine with me,' said Ken, then he took the sherry that was handed to him. 'Thanks.'

'I'll ask Vi, then,' decided Helen, passing another glass to her husband. 'She's working down in Far Meadow. I shall have to go that way to get back to the hospital.'

'I thought you'd finished for the day?' Ronnie said.

'No, we had some casualties in this morning. I want to check on them.' She could see from his reaction what he believed. After sipping her sherry, she tried to relieve him of that anxiety. 'Oh by the way, Jim Kiley sent you his regards.'

'Really?'

'Yes, he left today for the American hospital at Bury. He'll be going on to one of their convalescent homes from there.'

'Oh. I see.'

Ronnie Dereham enjoyed his sherry much more than he had expected. Helen spent her time trying to conceal her disappointment over Jim's transfer.


Master Sergeant Joe McGraw had left Bridge Cottage with the feeling that he would never return. If Sally did not want him there – and he believed Ruby on this point – then he would stay well clear. He walked aimlessly through the woods for a time and had then drifted towards the town, vaguely hoping that he might find some consolation at The Plough. Jack Blair welcomed him by reaching for a half-pint tankard but McGraw told him to make it a pint for a change. Charlie, the British sergeant from the Ack-Ack Unit, offered to pay for the drink and came over to chat. Seeing how depressed McGraw was, both Jack and Charlie suggested to him that he needed some leave, but he seemed hardly to hear what they were saying. Then he had surprised Charlie by asking him about Stan Bilton. He had wanted to know as much about the man as possible, feeling now that he had never really understood him or known him properly.

Charlie had talked well of Stan and his listener had been able to see why Sally had been so attracted to her husband. By the same token, he could appreciate what attraction he had had for her in contrast. He finished the whole of his pint by the time that Charlie's description had come to an end, but he was not able to buy his friend a drink in return. Ruby Bilton came into the pub, saw McGraw and started to sound off about what he had done to her son and his wife, widening the scope of her attack to include everyone at the Market Wetherby Air Base. Rather than get involved in a row, McGraw promised to buy Charlie a drink another time and slipped out quietly, missing the moment when Jack Blair called Ruby over and warned her to keep her opinions to herself if she wished to be allowed into his Lounge Bar.

Once outside, McGraw reached into his pocket for his cigarettes and lighter, was unable to find them and realized where they were. Knowing that Ruby Bilton was no longer at Bridge Cottage, he decided to return at once to collect what he had left. Sally and the children were in the middle of their lunch. He mumbled his apologies and reached for his things but Sally stopped him. She told him that her mother-in-law would not be coming to the cottage again after what had been said to her. Put in the position of having to make a choice between McGraw and Ruby, she had not found that choice difficult to make. Even as she said this, McGraw could not quite take it in and she

333

mistook his lack of reaction for indifference. But he soon came to see what a big step it was for her to admit such a thing to herself, and he took her hand and kissed it.

The afternoon passed leisurely and happily. Betty went back to school, Sally carried on with her washing, McGraw played with William, chatted and generally settled back into the role that he had learned to love so much. He then went to fetch Betty when the afternoon session at school finished and told her some stories when they got back. Evening found him still firmly established as a central figure in the family.

Sally was ironing. She looked up as McGraw crossed to the black-ribboned photograph of Stan Bilton.

'What are you thinking?' she asked.

'That you're soft-hearted and Ruby knows it and she'll play on it for ever, if you let her.'

'She won't stay here again, I promise you.'

Seeing that he had run out of cigarettes, he announced that he would walk to the pub to get some more. Sally said that she would finish the ironing by the time he came back.

'You will come back, won't you, Mac?'

'Just try and stop me.'

Now that the children were in bed, he was able to kiss her properly.


'They said they weren't going to let me leave until they'd found the cause of the fever. I could have told them what it was, Helen.'

'What?'

'Being so near to you for a couple of days. It's the longest we've ever had together.'

Helen Dereham smiled. She had arrived back at the hospital to be greeted with the news that Jim Kiley had a high temperature and could not be moved. He dozed most of the afternoon and it was not until the evening that she was able to speak to him.

'What are we going to do with you?' she asked, mockingly.

'What are we going to do with *us*?'

'I'd rather not think about that, Jim.'

'Don't we have to?'

'Yes, I suppose we do. But every decision we've made so far has been the wrong one. I'm afraid that . . . once we really *think* about what we should do, it will be the end of everything. I couldn't bear that.'

'Helen,' he said, caught by the strength of his feelings, 'I wanted to tell you that . . . I love you . . . but . . .'

She took his hands in hers and they said nothing for a few moments, but their commitment to each other was renewed.

'I must go soon,' she said.

'Do you have to?'

'We've got people coming to dinner.'

'Well, at least I'll see you when you bring in my boiled egg in the morning.'

'I do have other patients, you know.'

Before she could bend over to kiss him, Red Burwash and McGraw came into the room. They apologized for interrupting but she told them she was about to leave in any case. She took her leave and closed the door behind her. McGraw, who had met Red at the pub and been invited to join him for the visit, let a knowing smile spread over his face.

'Wipe that grin off, McGraw!'

'Yes, sir. Er, we couldn't find a bunch of grapes so . . . we brought you this instead.' He held out a flagon of beer.

'It's from Jack Blair at The Plough.' Red produced two more flagons from behind his back. He took the top off one of them and gave the beer to Jim. 'Here, Major.'

'It's going to put my temperature right up again,' warned Jim, 'but who cares? Cheers!'

They all drank. Then he asked about the mission that had been scheduled for that morning.

'Another abort, Major,' Red said. 'Then the Krauts hit

335

us on the way back. Two ships crippled, two lost, twenty-eight men . . .'

Jim Kiley needed another beer.

'The Colonel was real upset,' McGraw said. 'He's gone off to Divisional HQ for some big pow-wow.'

'So what happened today, Red?'

'The Krauts caught us with our pants down. They've stopped attacking us from below.'

'Our firepower's too heavy for them.'

'Yeah. Well, they got this new technique. They stand off out of range, but high. They've been fitted with longer-range, bigger-calibre shells, and when they've blasted our formation apart, they dive down through it. When our guys start shooting back, we end up hitting our own ships.'

'Jesus. It's no way to fight a war.'

They sat swigging their beer for some time before taking their leave.

# CHAPTER TWENTY-FIVE

After dinner they adjourned to the sitting room for coffee. The blackout curtains were drawn, the standard lamp created a warm circle of light, the fire glowed in the grate and a record played quietly in the background. As Vi Ericson looked around, she still felt a little uneasy. Although she had enjoyed the dinner party, the civilized comfort of Dereham House was very different to anything she had known before. But there was another reason for her unease. Ken Anderson had clearly taken an interest in her and paid her a number of compliments throughout the evening. While she might have been able to enjoy this on its own, Vi was surprised and somewhat confused when Ronnie Dereham, too, started to make flattering remarks. It was almost as if the two men were rivals for her attention.

Helen, wearing a smart, calf-length dress, poured the coffee and handed the cups around.

'You're very quiet, Vi.'

'A paragon among women!' Ken said with a laugh.

'She is. She really is,' Ronnie said seriously.

'Now, now, you two. Don't embarrass her. I must say, though, you're looking well tonight, Vi. That's a very pretty dress.'

'It was . . . my going away dress.'

'I didn't know you were married.' Ken was taken aback.

'Didn't I say?' Ronnie was flustered. 'Yes. Vi married a chap from the US Air Force.'

'Where is he now?' Vi's silence and downward glance gave him his answer. 'I'm terribly sorry. I'd no idea.'

'He was shot down months ago,' said Vi. 'I'm over it now.'

'How did it happen? Do you know?'

'We're very lucky to have Vi here,' said Helen, steering

the conversation away from the subject of Chuck. 'She more or less runs the farm.'

'More or less?' Ronnie repeated. 'I'd say totally. I couldn't get by without her. In fact, I'm thinking of asking her, when this war's over, of staying on to manage the whole estate.'

'What a marvellous idea, Ronnie!'

'I'm not sure I could cope.'

'You're the only one who can,' Ronnie argued.

'What about Pat?'

'I'm afraid my daughter's heart is not in it, Vi. It needs someone who knows it from the mud up.'

'I certainly know all about the mud, Major Dereham!'

Their laughter was interrupted by the sound of the doorbell. Nanny was heard answering the door.

'There's that Mrs Lambourn here, and an American gentleman. Will I show them in?'

Phyllis Lambourn did not wait for a proper invitation. She swept past Nanny, told her how sweet she was and then greeted Helen. Captain Lester Carson followed her in and stood by the door.

'Phyllis – what a surprise!' said Helen.

'I'm so sorry to burst in on you like this, my dears, when you have company, too. But this dear man brought me a divine present and I simply had to share it with someone.' She tore the paper off the bottle she was carrying. 'There – gin! Now isn't that a sight for sore eyes!'

Helen gave her a welcome and nodded to Nanny, who went out. Introductions were made and Lester Carson and Phyllis were invited to sit down. Helen had not seen her friend since the night they had stayed at the hotel.

'Where on earth have you been all this time, Phyllis?'

'Oh, that's a long story, darling!'

'Last time we spoke,' observed Ronnie, drily, 'it was on the telephone, I believe.'

'Was it, really?' Phyllis covered her discomfort with a laugh. 'I don't remember. Such a long time ago. Look, we're not interrupting anything, are we?'

338

'Hate to be in the way,' said Lester, who had not anticipated this kind of evening when he had called at Phyllis's house with the bottle of gin. 'Kick us out if we are.'

'You're both very welcome, Captain Carson,' Helen assured him. 'So is your bottle of gin. Why don't you see to some drinks and then Phyllis can tell me this long story?'

Drinks were poured and passed round. Lester started to talk to Ken Anderson about the problems at the Air Base and Vi listened in patiently. Ronnie, though seated next to the men, was trying to keep an ear open to catch what Helen and Phyllis were saying. For her part, Phyllis had already made her own mind up about why Vi Ericson had been invited along for the evening.

'Ronnie seems very fond of little Vi.'

'We both are,' said Helen.

'Of course, darling. Anyway, to me and my story. That night at the hotel. I thought I'd stay in my old flat in London for a while. Even air raids seemed preferable to the boredom of being marooned out here.'

'Did you see Dickie?' There was a short pause and Helen saw her friend tense slightly. 'Well, did you?'

'Yes, my dear ex-husband eventually showed up. He stood me up a couple of times, of course, just to run true to form. Then one day he breezed in to spend a week's leave. Some girlfriend or other had let him down.'

'How was it?'

'Divine! Virtually a second honeymoon. At the end of it, he went back to sea and – naturally – not a word since.' Phyllis was hurt by the memory and tried to hide behind a forced brightness. 'Don't imagine I was upset by it. Just what I expected. Oh, by the way, I ran into Pat when I was in town. She was with a nice little Free French boy.'

'Really?'

'Pity she gave up Cambridge. Still, she did seem ever so fond of that sweet little Frog.' Phyllis was peeved that Helen did not react. 'Well, that's about it. I came home two weeks ago.'

'Then why haven't you been in touch?'

'Oh, I just flopped out, my dear. I did my tiny best to raise the morale of the troops myself after Dickie had disappeared. The most recent was a Polish colonel – and what a jealous creature he turned out to be. I didn't leave London. I fled. He was literally brandishing a revolver.'

'Now I see why you've been hiding yourself away.'

'Today I decided I'd had enough of looking at the same four walls. Went to a meeting of the Goodwill Committee in the hope of seeing you there.'

'We had Ken staying.'

'Ah . . .'

Phyllis glanced across at Ken who was telling Vi something and making no attempt to hide his admiration for her. Ronnie and even Lester Carson were now watching Vi with interest and when she said something, all three laughed appreciatively.

'I think we're going to have to break that up,' said Phyllis bitchily. 'Come on.' She crossed to the others as Lester was about to top up Vi's drink. 'There's no point in plying her with drink. It won't get you anywhere.'

Even though it was couched in a laugh, the remark upset Vi. She immediately retreated into herself and refused the drink. Ronnie tried to smooth over the awkwardness by praising Vi's work on the farm but she was now too unsettled to want to stay. Having to cope with the attentions of the men was problem enough without any comments from Phyllis Lambourn, whose tone was so condescending. Vi announced that it was time for her to go. Ronnie pressed her to stay but she told him that she wanted to make an early start in the morning.

'It looks like being a fine day,' she explained, 'and it'll give us a chance to finish the far field.'

'So conscientious!' Phyllis said.

'May I see you home, Vi?' offered Ken.

'Thanks, but I came on my bicycle.'

Lester Carson decided that it was time for Phyllis and himself to leave as well and they were soon moving towards the door. Ken and Vi went out into the hall first, but Lester paused as he remembered something. He turned back to Helen.

'Pity about Jim Kiley having to stay on at the hospital here.'

'Yes.'

'We were hoping he'd be shipped off today. I mean, the sooner we have him on duty, the better.'

'It's only a slight fever,' said Helen. 'Nothing serious.'

Phyllis latched on to the mention of Jim's name at once. 'You've got Major Kiley down at the hospital, have you?' she asked. 'Poor dear man . . . whatever happened to him?'

They all moved into the hall and left Ronnie alone in the sitting room. The casual remark had left him feeling utterly betrayed.


McGraw walked into his first real row with Sally Bilton when he got back to the cottage. She had been waiting for two hours for him and was not at all appeased when he told her where he had been. Annoyed at the thought that she was being taken for granted, Sally was even more angry when he produced two bottles of beer and she asked him why he had not stayed at the pub to drink it if he was having such an enjoyable time there. McGraw abandoned his attempts to conciliate and retorted that he was free to do what he wanted. He warned her not to behave as if they were married. The jibe stung her and she went off to bed, telling him to put the lights off before he went. McGraw sat at the table and started to drink. Remorse soon set in and he wished that he had not upset her. When he had finished both beers, he went to the bottom of the stairs, wondering if he should go up. In the event, he decided against it and switched off the lights. The walk back to the Air Base was a lonely one.


Vera Mundy also arrived home that night to a frosty

welcome. Albert, wearing his black ARP uniform, had been wondering where she was for an hour or more and his temper was not improved when he opened a packet of tea and accidentally spilled the contents over the draining board and the floor. Vera chose this moment to return.

'Where've you been?' he demanded.

'You know where. The meeting.'

'Till this time?'

'Look at the mess you've made,' she said. 'Oh, Albert, get out of the way. That's nearly two weeks' ration.'

'I've got my Blackout round to make,' he muttered, as she grabbed a spoon and tried to save what she could of the tea. 'I wanted a cuppa before I went out . . . Why are you so late?'

'We had to discuss something special. Letty in bed?'

'Went up hours ago.'

'Peter back?'

'Just after you left.'

'How did he get on at the medical?'

'Passed A1. 'Course, he'll have to wait till he gets official notification.'

'Well, that's nice . . .'

She put what she could of the tea back into the caddy and brushed up the remainder with her hands. Albert could see that she was excited about something and not really interested in talking about their son at all. Immediately, he became suspicious.

'What was this meeting about, Vera?'

'Oh – just an idea of the Goodwill Committee.'

'Like what?'

She got up and smiled at him. 'For us to adopt a GI.'

'For us to *what*?'

'Only in a manner of speaking, Albert. You see, so many of them are lonely, got nowhere to go. We've been asked to open our doors to one of them, so he can drop in when he likes, feel like one of the family.'

'We've had enough trouble from that lot already!' wailed

her husband. 'There's no more of them dropping in here, I can tell you.'

'It's too late. I've put our name in the box.'

'Box?'

'In the Church Hall. You put your name and address on a piece of paper. Any one of them that wants to, he just puts his hand in and takes one. Calls round.'

'You can't even *choose* which one you get?' asked Albert, frankly appalled.

'It's more natural that way, the Vicar says. After all, you don't choose your family, do you?'

'If one of them turns up here, he won't come back in a hurry.'

'I want none of your funny business, Albert Mundy. If one turns up, you be particularly nice to him – be warned! We must do our bit.'

'And what about Letty? The state she's in. Have you thought about that, woman?'

'It's Letty I was thinking about when I put our name forward. A nice American boy, like her young man was. Be company for her.'

Albert stared at her in disbelief.


Colonel Rufus Krasnowici sat beside Jim's bed, pain and bitterness on his face. He was coming to believe that the Luftwaffe might win the war in the air after all.

'Have you any idea how many ships Bomber Command's lost in the past year, Jim?'

'Two – three hundred.'

'That's what we lost in the last month alone. In one raid the whole 100th Bomb Group was wiped out. We can't go on like that!'

'We're giving up daylight precision bombing?'

'Nope. Though some would argue we should.'

'So what's happening, Rufe?'

'We need a pause. A breathing space to lick our wounds.

We can't absorb the kind of losses we've been having and still function.'

'How long would this breathing space be?'

'That depends. Aircraft frames and spare parts have been held up by strikes back in the States.'

'Strikes!' Jim was incredulous.

'Yeah. Hard to believe, isn't it? But in a couple of weeks, things should start to flow again. And by then, we're due for another intake of replacement crews. They should both come at the right time.'

'For *what*? The German Air Force will be doing victory rolls all over Europe.'

'Let them,' said Rufus, getting up and pacing to and fro. 'Let them think they've chased Uncle Sam out of the skies. Let them get a little cocky. Because in three or four weeks, we're going to hit them with the biggest air armada ever put together – and knock Marshal of the Air Force Hermann Goering's front teeth out through the back seat of his long johns. We can do it, Jim!'

'Sure – given time. But the RAF still flies by night and us by day. Our guys'll be behind the same old eight ball. We need bigger bomb loads and long-range fighter support. Without that, we're just setting them up as sitting ducks.'

'We'll have those things sooner or later,' Rufus said. 'Until then, it's up to us to make sure most of those ducks reach the target, hit it with maximum impact and get back again. That's why I need you, Jim. And by Golliver, if I didn't, I'd throw the book at you for going on that crazy mission! You know that, don't you?'

'Yeah.'

'Okay, we'll say no more about it. But from now on, you don't go up in anything, not even a training flight, without my permission. Understood?'

'Understood.'

'Right. You got two weeks, three at most, then I want your butt back on that chair, at that desk – even if you're on crutches!'

'I'll be there.'

Rufus was about to reinforce his warning when the door opened and Helen came in. She looked a little crestfallen when she saw her patient had a visitor.

'Oh – good morning, Colonel.'

'Dr Dereham – good to see you!' he said, beaming. 'I wanted to thank you for everything you've done for this boy here.'

'Yes, he's made an excellent recovery,' she said.

'This fever of his – what was it exactly?'

'It's quite common after gunshot wounds. It can subside quickly, though. The danger is of it turning into pneumonia, and we couldn't risk his being moved until we were quite satisfied.'

'But now he's fit to travel, eh?'

'Yes. There's an ambulance coming for you this afternoon, Major.'

Jim was visibly put out by the news. Helen, too, was disappointed but did not show it. Having had to explain to Ronnie that she had not in fact lied about Jim's departure, she now felt that it might be better when he did actually go. In the meantime, she wanted a moment alone with him.

'Moved today!' Rufus was delighted. 'That's just dandy!'

'I have to examine him now, Colonel. If you don't mind . . .'

'Go right ahead. I haven't finished with him myself, yet, but I've no objection to waiting. You go ahead, doctor.'

Rufus sat down heavily in the chair at the end of the bed, clearly intent on staying in the room. Helen put her clipboard down on the bed and reached over to feel the pulse in Jim's wrist. She angled herself in such a way that her body shielded him from Rufus, and she was able to gaze down into his eyes. Unable to speak, they were nevertheless able to communicate all that they needed to know.

*

345

Rosie Blair was almost the only visitor that Letty Mundy had these days and her conversation, inevitably, was about American servicemen. As they sat facing each other by the fire, Letty had to listen to her friend's description of her latest favourite, Walter Leroy.

'A real officer and gentleman. Opens doors for me, things like that. And he's so tall and handsome. A bit like Don Ameche.'

'Does he have a moustache?'

'Without the moustache.'

Rosie continue to talk in wonderment about Walter and to insist that he was the man for her at last. Letty remembered all the others about whom Rosie had said this, not least Billy Colvero, but she did not remind her. Peter arrived to interrupt the chat and Rosie was rather offhand with him. He was quite philosophical, having long got used to the fact that he liked her much more than she liked him. When Rosie announced that she had to go, Peter offered to stroll back with her but she refused the offer. At that moment, Vera Mundy came marching in with a rather serious-looking GI of medium height. He introduced himself to them all.

'Private, First Class, John Wyatt.'

Seeing that Rosie took an immediate interest in the guest, Vera shepherded her out, determined to give Letty a chance to get to know John quietly on her own. The young man was polite with none of the assertiveness that so many of the new arrivals seemed to show. He sat down with Peter and Letty and talked easily about himself. Because of an astigmatism in the eye, he had not been able to train as a flyer and he had had to take a job on the ground instead. At present he was working in the Control Tower. Though he had neither Harvey Wallis's charm nor Mario Bottone's thrusting personality, John Wyatt was making a deep impression on Letty. At the same time, Peter was warming to his straightforward honesty.

Vera came back in and was pleased to see how well they

seemed to be getting on. She was glad that John had chosen their name out of the box at the Church Hall.

'You said you came from California,' she prompted.

'Santa Barbara.'

'Is that near Hollywood?' asked Letty, excited.

'About as near as you are to London. One or two movie stars live around Santa Barbara – Ronald Colman, Bing Crosby . . .'

'Really!'

'Of course, they keep pretty much to themselves. I never had much occasion to mix with them.'

Peter liked the humour behind the remark.

'Where is everybody?'

Albert came bustling in from the shop to complain that he needed help. His irascibility was not helped by the sight of Pfc John Wyatt, who stood up to meet him and extended his hand as Vera performed the introductions.

'It's a genuine privilege to be allowed to come here, Mr Mundy. I guess it's proof of that fine old English hospitality that good folks like you should invite a complete stranger like me into their home.'

'Say something, Albert,' urged his wife.

Albert gave a strangled cough and got close to a smile.


Ronnie Dereham was more than delighted when Vi called in at the end of her morning's stint in the fields. There was something soothing about her presence that he could not quite understand, but he enjoyed her company immensely and it was a source of great consolation. When Vi told him that she had finished the job that morning, he was mildly amazed at the speed with which she and the other Land Girls had worked. It gave him an excuse to praise her yet again. Vi had wanted to thank him for inviting her to the dinner party, but he assured her that he ought to thank her for brightening up the evening the way she had. He told her of her impact on Ken Anderson and brought a shy smile to her lips. Then he asked if she would care to join him for lunch as he was on his own. Vi thanked him but explained that she had to go across to Bridge Cottage to look after Sally Bilton's children. Ronnie waved her off before he let the disappointment show.

McGraw stood at the window and watched the children playing in the garden. Then he turned to face Sally. The row which they had had the previous night had left them both jangled and confused. He led off with an apology for what he had said.

'I didn't really mean it, Sal.'

'You told me we didn't have any claim on each other—'

'Look—'

'You said I wasn't to behave like a wife.' She bit her lip. 'You know I love you, Mac, but I never thought of myself as your wife.'

'Sure.'

'You've never given me the chance.'

'I thought that was how we both wanted it,' he said, thrown back on the defensive.

'It's how *you* want it that matters. I was happy enough just to be with you. But lately . . . well, you've started acting as though you're trapped.'

'It's not that, Sal.' He was finding it difficult to tell her the truth. 'The more I've felt at home here, the more I've never wanted to leave.' He shrugged and looked at her rather helplessly. 'Can't we just go on as we were?'

'How can we, Mac? Once, I could have drifted on, accepted it. But how can I do that now – knowing you feel trapped but not knowing why. I've never made demands on you.'

'Dammit!' exploded McGraw, unable to hold it back. 'I'm in another man's house, with another man's wife! Another man's kids! Everything I touch is his. Everywhere I look. Sometimes you talk like you expect me to settle down and run a garage after the war, same way that you

348

wanted Stan to. I'm not even allowed my own future!' She was staring at him, deeply hurt, but he had to go on. 'I keep coming back here like it's a drug. And each time it gets harder to leave. This place, it's taken me over, Sal! I got no other life. I'm not me any more!'

There was a long, tense pause. She avoided his eyes and took a deep breath before speaking. Her hands were trembling.

'If you feel that way . . . you'd better go now. And forget us. And don't come back.'

'Sal—'

'Don't say any more,' she begged. 'Just go. Please.'

McGraw picked up his hat, looked towards the back door, realized that that route would take him past the children and so went off smartly into the hall. Involuntarily, Sally took a few steps after him but she was checked by the sound of a door opening behind her. Vi Ericson came in with William in her arms and Betty beside her.

'Hello, Sal. Not late, am I?' She saw the other woman's drawn face. 'Is something wrong?'

'I . . . a headache . . . I'll just get an aspirin.'

Sally went out quickly into the hall and left Vi bewildered. Betty looked around the room.

'Where's Uncle Joe?' she asked.


Immediately before Jim Kiley was due to leave, Helen Dereham managed to contrive a few minutes alone with him. Before they could do much more than exchange a few pleasantries, however, Helen was called away to take an urgent call. It was her daughter and she was crying at the other end of the line. Helen tried to calm her, to get her to explain, but all that Pat would say was that she wanted to come home as soon as possible. It was the first time that they had spoken since before Pat had left Market Wetherby and it made conversation even more uneasy. As Helen was urging her daughter to come whenever she wished, the telephone was suddenly put down at the other end and she was left to wonder what had happened. Remembering Jim, she put down her own receiver and went back into the corridor that led to his room. The first thing she saw was his empty wheelchair being brought back in. Major Jim Kiley had gone.

# CHAPTER TWENTY-SIX

Eighteen candles decorated the top of the little chocolate
birthday cake and it took all the breath that Peter and
Letty Mundy could muster to blow them out. Their parents
applauded and John Wyatt laughed his encouragement,
then all three joined in the traditional song:

'Happy birthday to you!
Happy birthday to you!
Happy birthday, dear Letty and Peter,
Happy birthday to you!'

The twins were at once pleased and embarrassed. Earlier
that day, each of them had had private reservations about
reaching their eighteenth year. For Letty, it was a reminder
of how young and unready she was for her impending
motherhood; for Peter, it was the seal on an army service
about which he had more than a few doubts and fears. In
the general excitement of the party, however, the worries
were stilled. John was saying how much he was enjoying
himself, Albert was boasting about how he had managed
to get hold of some icing sugar for the cake, and Vera was
urging that someone should cut it. Letty cleared away
some of the candles then picked up the knife.

'And make a wish,' reminded John. 'You have to make
a wish.'

Letty smiled at him gratefully, made a wish that involved
him, and then cut the first large slice. It was given to John
because he was the guest and he tasted it at once,
announcing that it was delicious. Letty served everyone
else to a slice and then sampled the cake herself, surprised
at how rich it was. John Wyatt sat up and reached into his
pockets.

'Hey, I nearly forgot. I brought you both a little something.' He gave one little package to Letty and one to Peter. 'Many happy returns!'

'Thank you,' said Peter.

'You shouldn't have,' said Letty, delighted that he had.

'It's not much, I'm afraid.'

'It's the thought, John,' observed Vera. 'Isn't it, Albert?'

'What? Oh yes . . .'

Letty undid her package and took out a small metal brooch in the shape of a pair of wings, with the letters USAAF under it. She was thrilled and she thanked John shyly.

'A guy at the Base makes them. I thought it'd be a kind of . . . memento.'

Vera was touched on her daughter's behalf and tried to get her husband to admire the brooch as well, but as Albert saw the bright metal against the dark of Letty's maternity dress, he was shaken. His daughter already had a memento of the American fliers.

Peter took his present out of its wrapping. It was a pocket compass. John explained that he thought it might come in handy when Peter was in the Army.

'My Dad gave it to me when I joined the Scouts.'

'You have Scouts where you come from?' asked Albert.

'Boy Scouts of America. I spent some of the best times of my life with them.'

'Did you now?'

'I missed it when I went to College.'

'What were you studying?' wondered Peter.

'I'd only just started. I was planning on becoming a teacher.'

'But you were called up?'

'Yes, Mr Mundy. I could've gotten an exemption, I guess – but I reckoned it was more important to do my duty.'

Albert was impressed. Until that point in the evening, he had been sceptical about the whole idea of 'adopting' an American serviceman. The other members of the family might have welcomed their guest but he was still very much on trial as far as Albert was concerned. Now, however, Albert was having second thoughts about Pfc John Wyatt.

'So you decided to join the Air Force, did you?'

'Strictly speaking, Mr Mundy, I'd have preferred to have been in the Infantry. Like my old man was in 1917–18.'

'Your father was in the first show?'

'Wounded at Belleau Wood. He was in the First Volunteer Unit to get over here.'

Albert was moved. Vera, aware how important it was for her husband to like the young American if anything was to come of the latter's relationship with Letty, filled in the pause.

'Fancy that, Albert!'

'I was wounded, too. On the Somme.' He looked shrewdly at John and put the deciding question to him. 'And what do you think of England so far?'

'Well, sir, that's a sore point.'

'Oh?' His tone made the others tense.

'You see, my great grandpa and grandma came from England, somewhere over the West Country. I keep trying to wangle a few days off, so I can go over there and look up the little place they lived in. You know, to see where we all began.'

'Is that a fact?' asked Albert, spellbound.

'So your family's *English*?' Letty was fascinated as well.

'Once upon a time – on my Dad's side.'

'You'll stay and have supper with us, won't you?' invited Vera, taking advantage of a rare moment when her husband was exuding goodwill.

'I don't think I can, ma'am.'

'Why ever not?' Letty was disappointed.

'Well, I just don't think it would be right. I mean, I feel I was butting in on the birthday party as it is. And with things being tough on you folks with food and that, well, it wouldn't be fair.'

353

'I insist,' said Albert, firmly. 'You're welcome to eat with us and to drop in any time you're free – eh – John. May I call you John?'

'My pleasure, sir.'

Vera, Letty and Peter watched in amazement as Albert actually smiled. John Wyatt had succeeded where Harvey Wallis, Mario Bottone and every other American service-man had failed. The party continued and the chat was happier than ever. Albert was so won over that he did no more than pull a face when the latter suggested that the men should step across to The Plough to buy some drink to celebrate the birthdays in style. In the event, it was Peter and John who went over to the pub, stared after from the shop window by the wistful Letty who would have loved to have been able to go with them.

The Lounge Bar was fairly quiet when they entered. Red Burwash was at one end with his navigator, Dave Conners. McGraw was perched on a bar stool sinking a pint and ignoring the advice of Charlie, the British sergeant from the Ack-Ack Unit. Jack Blair and Vi were chatting behind the counter and Rosie was welcoming Elmer Jones and Hymie Stutz, both of whom were in a teasing mood. It was Elmer who first noticed the newcomers.

'Hi, Peter,' he said.

'What are you doing here?' asked Rosie.

'I brought him over for a drink,' said John.

'I was eighteen today,' announced Peter, a little self-conscious about it, 'so I can come in the front door.'

'And nobody more welcome!' Jack Blair had overheard them. 'Many happy returns, Peter!'

'Thanks,' he replied, shaking Jack's hand.

'Oh!' exclaimed Rosie, realizing that it was someone else's birthday as well. 'Will you tell Letty I'll look in tomorrow? I just forgot. Say I'm sorry.'

'Yeah, happy birthday, kid,' Hymie said.

'Many happies,' grinned Elmer.

'Thanks.'

'So what'll it be?' offered Jack. 'This is on the house. Will four beers suit you gentlemen?'

'Just fine!' said John.

'Hey, they must think a lot of you around here, Peter,' noted Hymie, struck by the landlord's gesture.

Peter smiled at Rosie. 'I'm an old friend of the family.'

'We've known him since he was in his cradle,' she said, rather tartly, and moved off to join her sister.

'Rosie's got it in for you, Pete,' John said.

'What did you do to her?' asked Elmer.

'Nothing.'

'Maybe that's the trouble,' chimed in Hymie.

The door opened and a group of GIs came in. Among them was Lieutenant Walter Leroy, as confident and debonair as ever. Rosie immediately perked up and asked her father if she could leave. Walter was evidently going to take her out.

Peter Mundy watched with a faraway look. It was not difficult for John to guess the reason.

'Did you used to have a thing going with Rosie?'

'Well . . . I went out with her once or twice.'

'But you didn't get anywhere?' Elmer was blunt.

'No.'

Hymie Stutz lifted one of the pints of beer that were now standing on the counter and handed it over. 'Here, kid. Join the club.'


It had been a long time since they had last sat and listened to a musical concert on the wireless and they had found it oddly comforting. As the pianist came to the last few bars of the concerto, Ronnie started to wheel himself slowly towards the set, arriving in time to turn off the applause which greeted the end of the piece.

'That was lovely!' Helen said.

'Yes. Funny, really. Chopin wrote it at a time of war and invasion, when his country was occupied. How little times change!'

'They do change, though. Things must be better after the war, Ronnie. They must be.'

'It's nice having you home for an evening, Helen.'

'You make it sound as if I'm never here!'

'Well, I mean, for this last week or so, I've seen more of you than I have for some while.'

'I haven't been needed at the hospital so much,' she explained, 'with the Base stood down.'

'Yes, they've lost a lot of aircraft. One wonders if things are going more badly than they admit . . . Er, any news of . . . ?'

'Jim Kiley? He's in a convalescent home somewhere. He should be back any day now.'

'Ah.'

'Ronnie—'

'I'm sorry, my dear. I know I promised not to talk about it. It's just that . . .' He sighed and shrugged. 'It's pointless, really. There's nothing more either of us can say.'

'No. You've been very understanding.'

There was a long and awkward pause during which the gulf widened between them. They were rescued from having to continue the conversation by the sound of the front door opening and shutting. No callers were expected and they both looked up in surprise. Then the door of the sitting room opened and Nanny led the way in, impassive and drily humorous.

'The return of the prodigal,' she said.

'Pat!' Helen was out of her seat at once to welcome her daughter.

'Hello, Mummy.' She seemed subdued but somehow mellowed. She crossed to give her father a token kiss. 'Daddy . . .'

'Hello, my dear,' he said, hugging her. 'It's been too long.'

'We expected you days ago,' Helen said.

'I had some things to clear up before I left London.'

'You've left? Do you mean for good?'

'I think so, Daddy.'

356

'What about your job?' asked Helen.

'There's hundreds of people wanting to work in the Forces' Canteens. They won't miss me.'

'She came by train,' Nanny said. 'Silly girl walked all the way from the station – with a suitcase. No wonder she looks tired.'

'Why didn't you ring, Pat?' asked Helen. 'I'd have fetched you.'

'I'd forgotten how far it was. I was too exhausted to think straight. The train kept stopping. It was so crowded I had to stand.' She sank to the arm of a chair. 'I could do with a drink.'

'I'll get you some hot milk at once,' decided Nanny.

'I don't think milk was quite what Pat had in mind,' Helen said.

'Best thing for her.'

'I don't want any, thank you, Nanny.'

'You'll drink it if I make it for you, my girl. And I'll stay with you until you finish it.'

Nanny strode off to the kitchen and the others smiled.

'Now I know I'm really home.'

They sat and chatted but Helen became increasingly uneasy. Not only was Pat evasive about her time in London and her real reason for returning home, a sadness hung about her, a world-weariness that seemed to put years on her. The milk duly arrived and Pat, under the eagle eye of Nanny, consented to drink it. They talked some more and Pat caught up on the local gossip, although only half-listening most of the time. Eventually, she announced that she wanted an early night and went off to bed.

Next morning after breakfast Ronnie took the opportunity to have a quiet word with Helen. She was packing some things into her briefcase when he wheeled himself in.

'Have you seen her this morning, Helen?'

'She's not up yet. She was very tired last night.'

'Do you think that's all it was?'

'She looked as if she'd been under a bit of strain. Why?'

357

'She seemed . . . different somehow. I can't put my finger on it . . .'

'She did seem a little more grown-up. Not before time, perhaps.'

'When she telephoned you at the hospital that day, did she give you any indication of what was wrong? Why she was coming back?'

'No. I assumed she was feeling lonely. Homesick. If there is something else, no doubt Pat will tell us when she's ready.'

There was a knock on the door and Vi Ericson entered in response to Helen's call. They exchanged greetings and Helen set off to work, saying that she expected to be back for lunch. Vi gave Ronnie some forms to sign and he wheeled himself across to the desk, apologizing for still being in his pyjamas and dressing gown. He mentioned that Pat was back.

'Oh, is she here?' Vi was pleased.

'Arrived last night.'

'How long for?'

'For good, she says. Though just what that means, we're not sure.'

'Where is she now?'

'She's having a long lie in. She looked as if she could do with it, quite frankly.'

'If she's home, I expect she'll be taking over the paperwork.'

'Oh no,' he insisted, 'I want you to carry on, Vi.'

'But Pat would probably like to do it again, if she doesn't have anything else to do.'

'That doesn't come into it,' he said, almost brusquely. 'In farming continuity is all-important. As I've told you, I hope you'll think of this job as something that could go on – not just during the war, but afterwards as well.'

Vi was grateful but she could see that much was due to his quiet but growing fondness for her. And she was not sure how to cope.

'I wouldn't like Pat to think that I was taking her place,' she said, carefully.

'There's no fear of that, Vi. She knows you're very much part of the team now. And I had to face the fact some time ago that I don't honestly know where her future lies. But not here, I suspect, not in farming.'

He signed the forms and handed them to her. Vi thanked him and moved towards the door. Ronnie suggested that she came back in an hour or so for a chat. She stopped for a moment.

'Oh, I had a letter this morning. From Captain Anderson.'

'Ken? What about?'

'He just said how nice it was to be here, and asked if he could look me up on his next leave.'

'Just like that?'

'It was a surprise, I must admit.'

'He has a nerve!' said Ronnie, almost angry. 'What will you tell him?'

'That I liked meeting him, too, and that I hope he'll be safe. It sounds as if the fighting in Italy's really fierce.'

'Yes. Will you . . . invite him to come and see you?'

'There'd be no point. I liked him but I can't think of anyone in that way. Not now.'

'No.' Ronnie was relieved.

'I mean – Chuck was shot down. We'd only been married for a day. I couldn't believe it. It seemed so unfair. It took me months to accept it – that he wasn't coming back. But because I've accepted it, that there's nothing to hope for, people think I've forgotten.'

'It'll get easier in time, Vi.'

'I'll never forget. Dad says that I'll get over it. He thinks that one day I'll meet someone else. He doesn't understand. There can't be anyone else, not ever.' She was starting to get upset. 'I'm sorry. It's not something I ever talk about.'

Vi went out and left him to absorb what she had said. Deeply moved, Ronnie could see that she was trying to tell him something about their own relationship, in her gentle, confused way. Ronnie sighed and decided that it was perhaps just as well that Pat had come home again.

Lunch at the Mundy household was usually a routine affair and Albert was therefore a little surprised when he found his wife putting a clean cloth on the table and setting out the best china. He asked where Letty was and she told him that John had taken their daughter for a walk. When Albert protested that she ought not to go about in public in her condition, Vera argued that the girl could not be kept prisoner and that people took a much more tolerant attitude about unmarried mothers these days. Then she asked him if he had any regrets about marrying her when she was pregnant. Embarrassed, he told her that he had none, but preferred not to talk about it.

When Vera started to polish the cutlery with special care, he finally put two and two together. Realization made him gasp and stare at her incredulously.

'Him and our Letty?'

'It might not even happen, Albert. But if it was going to, I thought I might just help it along.'

His first instinct was to unload some of his general resentment against the Americans. Then he remembered his daughter's plight and recalled how pleasant and untypical John Wyatt was. Admiration came into his voice.

'I've got to hand it to you, Vera. It wouldn't half settle a few problems. I mean, his parents – John's, that is – they run that store selling agricultural machinery. They're shopkeepers, the same as us. It would be sort of appropriate.'

A few minutes later Letty and John returned from a walk that they had both enjoyed enormously. Letty talked excitedly about some of the stories John had told her about Bing Crosby. Vera clucked over her guest like a mother hen and told him that he must call more often now that Peter had gone off to the Army. He was, in a sense, taking their son's place. Albert quickly reinforced the invitation, offering to get some bottles of cider from the shop for John and himself. Letty was amazed at the sudden concern her father was showing towards her friend. It seemed so completely out of character.

McGraw had started his sixth pint before Jack Blair spoke to him. As gently as possible, the landlord suggested that the line chief might be overdoing it a bit for a lunchtime. The response was morose and surly.

'You telling me to clear out?'

'Of course not, Mac. Just seems to me there must be better ways to deal with what's bothering you than drinking beer.'

'Name two.'

'Well, for a start, you could talk it over with someone.'

'I'm fed up with people sticking their noses in, Jack – even you. It only concerns Sally and me. Anyway, nobody could understand.'

'Maybe not.' Jack wiped the bar top with a cloth. 'Though from what I hear, she doesn't really understand either.'

'Well, she ought to. I spelled it out.'

'But you were made for each other. The couple of times I saw you together, it stuck out a mile. And there's the children. You were more of a father to them than their own had been.'

'Yeah, that was the trouble.' There was a long pause as McGraw thought it all out. 'I slotted in too easily. I didn't want anything else. I couldn't think of anything else. And I don't like being dependent on anything.' He gulped down some more beer and stared ahead of him. 'I didn't want it to happen again.'

'Again?'

'To go wrong. Like with my ex-wife.'

'You've been married?' Jack was surprised. 'When?'

'Ten years ago, when I was stationed in Hawaii.'

'What happened?'

'She was really something! I could never believe she'd chosen a big lunk like me. I was crazy about her. Then I got promoted and transferred to Gower Field. She came along, didn't like it. I did everything I could to make her happy, then I got transferred again. And she headed back for Hawaii.' He drained his drink. 'I had a letter from her, just one. She said she should have realized I was married already – to the Air Corps.'

'Were you divorced?'

'Yeah.'

'And because of her – your first wife – you won't give Sally a chance?'

'I guess so. I mean, I know how it would turn out. Sooner or later, whatever she said or did, I'd start to back off.'

'So as not to be hurt again?'

'Yeah.'

'But your relationship with Sally is totally different,' argued Jack, feeling that it was time to speak out. 'You can't compare the two. Listen, Mac—'

'No, you listen,' interrupted McGraw. 'Nobody else knows a word of this. I told you because I thought I owed you, and because I can trust you. But that's the end of it. If you mention it again, or anyone else tries to butt in, I'm going to walk out of this pub for good. Understand?'

Jack Blair understood all too well. He sighed and went off to collect some of the empty glasses from the tables.


Colonel Rufus Krasnowici was delighted when Jim Kiley came into his office, albeit with a limp. He had not been expecting his Air Executive back on duty for a few days yet. Jim explained that he had more or less bullied the medics at the convalescent home to send him back. He was anxious to be on duty as soon as he could. Rufus told Jim that he had arrived back just in time for the start of the new bomber offensive. Things had changed quite a bit in the fortnight or so that he had been away. Replacement B-17s and crews had arrived, some of the men fresh from combat indoctrination in Ireland.

'So we're not starting from scratch with hundred per cent greenhorns, Jim.'

'That's something, anyway.'

'There's more. A lot of the new ships have modifications to the armour plating that makes them thirty per cent more secure. And best of all, the days of unescorted missions are over. The P-38s come into service, giving us an escort range of well over five hundred miles from Base.'

Rufus told him that he would have to work the new men hard to familiarize them with procedures but that he must not overdo it. By the same token, he was not to push himself too hard either. Jim agreed but he was not even listening. Pleased at the news of the improvements that had taken place in his absence, he was eager to get back to work as soon as was humanly possible.


Vi Ericson had had as little success as her father in healing the rift between Sally Bilton and Joe McGraw. When Vi arrived at Bridge Cottage to look after the children while Sally went out, she took the opportunity to suggest that Sally might wander down to The Plough some time. Day after day she had seen McGraw sitting there alone and drinking heavily. Only Sally could bring him out of the heavy depression in which he seemed to be trapped. Vi even offered to pass on a message to McGraw that he would be welcome at Bridge Cottage if he cared to call – and she was sure he would. But Sally did not wish to discuss the matter. She could not bear the thought that she had made a man feel imprisoned. Her children might ask about him all the time and she might miss him, but she was not going to get involved with McGraw again.

Sally collected the books which she intended to change at the Market Wetherby library and set off for the town. Vi began to play with the children who were as chirpy and excitable as ever. Half an hour had passed before the game was interrupted. As the back door was heard opening, Betty jumped up and ran to it, hoping that it might be 'Uncle Joe'. William, too, clearly wanted to see the American again.

But it was Ruby Bilton who walked in, watchful and guileful, a half-smile on her lips. Vi was surprised to see her and taken in by the old woman's apologetic manner. Ruby produced chocolate for the children who were grateful but wary. Their grandmother had not been in the habit of giving them gifts before. When Vi told her where her daughter-in-law had gone, Ruby nodded and stood in silence for a few moments as she worked something out.

'I'd hate to have come all this way to miss Sally,' she said, eventually. If she's gone to the library, maybe I'll wander over and meet her on the way back.' She bent over her granddaughter. 'Would you like that, Betty, love? Come for a walk with your Grandma?'

The child was too innocent to recognize the sly look in Ruby's eyes.

# CHAPTER TWENTY-SEVEN

When Helen Dereham walked into her office at the end of the morning, she saw something which made her halt in her tracks. Jim Kiley was standing by the window on the other side of the room. His smile of welcome turned her surprise into delight.

'I can't believe it!' She closed the door. 'When did you—?'

'I got back a couple of hours ago.'

'Your letter only came this morning. It said nothing at all about your coming out so soon.'

'I was lucky. I heard they were short of space at the convalescent hospital, so I volunteered to go back on duty.'

'Are you sure you're all right?' the doctor in her asked. 'It's not too soon?'

'I'm fine,' he assured her. 'And all the better for seeing you.'

He held out his hands and she crossed to him instinctively. Drawing her to him, he kissed her gently on the lips. She held him for a moment then stepped back and glanced guiltily towards the door, conscious that she was still on duty and that someone might come in.

'I've missed you,' he said.

'I've missed you, too.' He took a few paces towards her. 'You're limping.'

'The muscles in my leg are still a little weak. It'll fix itself in time, they say.'

'Not if you overstrain them.'

'Yes, sir, ma'am,' he said, perching on the edge of her desk and looking down at her. 'You're the most beautiful doctor I've ever seen!'

'Well, whether that's true or not, you're certainly one of the worst patients. I'm not surprised they threw you out of that Flak House, or whatever you call it. But I'd have said it was far too early for you to start work again.'

'Rufus agrees with you. He won't let me do anything, except read the mail, for the next forty-eight hours.'

'Good for him!'

'Which brings me to the object of my visit.'

'Oh, it has an object, does it?'

'One of them's been achieved,' he said, leaning across the desk to take one of her hands in his. 'I can't begin to tell you the ways in which I've missed you, Helen.'

'Try.'

'Sitting there, surrounded by guys, half of them griping because they hadn't been wounded badly enough to be sent home, the others scared of what was waiting for them or just staring into space . . . The only thing that stopped me going crazy was thinking about you, remembering the times we've had together. Trying to remember your face, your smile, the sound of your voice.'

'Do you think I haven't done the same, Jim?'

They looked at each other, startled again by the depth of their feelings. Jim's letter, which had arrived that morning, asked Helen to find time to have a long talk with him. She was about to accept his invitation to lunch when she recalled a promise that she had made. Her face fell.

'So what's the trouble?'

'I'd love to come, but Ronnie rang not long ago to make sure I'd be back. Pat arrived last night.'

'Oh.' He masked his disappointment with a rueful smile.

'I'll make it up to you, I promise.'

'When?'

'Tomorrow. I won't let anything interfere. Will you be free?'

'I'll make darn sure I am!'

A knock on the door brought their conversation to an end, but they were both looking pleased with themselves when Sister Dickson came into the room.

*

Elmer Jones and Hymie Stutz sat together at a table and watched every move that Rosie Blair made. They did not hear her father speaking to her, they did not see McGraw crouched over his beer, they did not notice any patrons who came or went. Rosie occupied their attention completely. Hymie eventually found some words.

'Say, Elmer, you ever get the feeling that we're missing out?'

'How?'

'Other guys do all right. They've got cute little chicks who keep their motors running for them. And what do we end up with?'

'Rosie is kinda special,' Elmer reminded him.

'Yeah – and permanently out of bounds! You know, we've flown seventeen of our twenty-five missions. According to the statistics, we're lucky to be alive.'

'Don't be morbid.'

They sat up in unison as Rosie moved away from her father and went down to the other end of the bar. Before she had wiped up the spilled beer with her cloth, the Americans were facing her across the counter. They grinned hopefully.

'Hi, Rosie,' said Hymie.

'Hello.'

'What's up?' he asked.

'Dad. I wanted to have my hair done. If he won't let me go before closing time, it'll be too late.'

'But your hair's pretty just the way it is,' said Elmer.

'Thank you.' He had coaxed a wan smile out of her.

'It's beautiful,' added Hymie. 'It don't need doing, Rosie.'

The smile switched to Hymie and then evaporated as someone came in through the main door. Both Americans looked around to see Lieutenant Walter Leroy and conceded defeat once more. As they were about to move away from the bar, Rosie told them to stay.

'Aren't you gonna give us the gate?' said Hymie.

'I don't know what you're talking about,' she retorted,

primly. 'But if you mean, do I wish to see Lieutenant Leroy, I do not!'

'He's out?' Elmer was amazed.

'Loverboy out, Rosie? What happened?'

'It's not something I care to talk about.'

'Come on, Rosie,' urged Hymie.

'Yeah, you can tell us.'

'All I'll say is that he's not the gentleman I thought he was.'

'You mean he tried to . . . ?' Hymie was outraged on her behalf and reddened from the neck upwards. 'The bum!'

'He didn't ought to be allowed to get away with it,' said Elmer, equally roused, glaring over at Walter.

'He didn't, Elmer. And he said some very unkind things. You never thought I was . . . that sort of girl, did you, Elmer?'

'Gee, no, Rosie!'

'You always behaved with respect. And you, Hymie.'

'Well, gee, of course, we would,' insisted Elmer. 'So you won't be going to the dance with the Lieutenant tonight?'

'Certainly not!'

'We'll be there. Hymie and me.'

'That'll be nice,' she said.

'Hey, Elmer, we left our drinks on the table.' Hymie seized the initiative.

'Oh yeah. I'll get 'em.' He wandered off.

'If the Lieutenant ain't gonna take you, Rosie, how about coming with me?' Hymie said, one eye on his friend.

'What about Elmer?'

'I don't wanna kid you. I love him like a brother. We been through a lot together. But just for once, I'd appreciate spending a coupla hours with you on my own. Okay?'

'It doesn't seem fair on him. What'll you say?'

'Leave that to me. Is it a deal, Rosie?'

'Well . . . maybe.'

When Elmer came back with the drinks, he saw Hymie's face bathed in a grin of satisfaction. Rosie retired a discreet distance so that the men could talk together and her attention was soon diverted away from them.

Her sister, Vi, came bustling in through the door, looked around the bar, saw McGraw, and dashed across to him. She seemed relieved to see him.

'You'll have to do something!' she pleaded, breathless.

'What's up? Is it Sal?'

'The children.'

'What's happened?' he asked, swaying slightly from the drink.

'It's all my fault! All my fault!'

Vi was on the verge of tears and it brought her father over. Elmer and Hymie drifted across to listen in and the sergeant from the Ack-Ack Unit, Charlie, also joined the group. McGraw, though not visibly drunk, had to force himself to concentrate.

'You're not making much sense, Vi,' her father said. 'Pull yourself together.'

'Have the kids been hurt?' asked McGraw.

'No. It's their grandmother. She's taken them away from Sally.'

'Old Ruby?' Charlie knew her well.

'What's she done?' Jack wanted to know.

'Taken them away?' McGraw was trying to absorb the news.

'I was babysitting for Sal, you see,' explained Vi, controlling herself a little. 'Old Mrs Bilton arrived and I let her take the children for a walk. I didn't see any harm in it. Then Sal came back and saw this note from her mother-in-law. It said that she'd taken the children away because Sal wasn't fit to look after them any more.'

'Poor Sal!' Jack said. 'She must be going frantic.'

'She is, Dad. We searched everywhere, but there was no sign of the children. Or Mrs Bilton.'

'But they were here not more than half an hour ago,' volunteered Charlie.

'Where?' demanded Vi.

'In the square. Standing by the bus stop to Ipswich.'

McGraw leaned against the bar, shaking his head in an attempt to clear it. He heard Jack say that a bus had left about twenty minutes ago and then reached for the jug of cold water on the counter. He poured the water over his head, causing the others to stand back in surprise.

'Did you say the bus was going to Ipswich?' he asked.


Nervously pleased with what she had done, Ruby Bilton sat in the single decker bus as it rolled steadily along the country road. William was on her knee and Betty was beside her, staring out through the window and fidgeting. There were only a few other passengers and none of them was close to Ruby. She was able to smile to herself in triumph. She had beaten Sally at last and, as she saw it, claimed her right to look after her own grandchildren. Stan, she felt, would have been proud of her.

The bus slowed and then came to a halt, its engine still running. Knowing the route well and aware that there was no scheduled stop at this stage of the journey, Ruby asked what was going on. She soon got her answer. Through the front window of the vehicle, she saw two British soldiers standing in the middle of the road, rifles in their hands. One of them, a sergeant from the Ack-Ack Unit, told the driver that they were engaged in an Army Exercise and that all passengers had to alight so that there could be a routine search of the bus. Complaining bitterly, Ruby allowed herself to be brought out on to the road. The soldiers went into the bus and Charlie, grateful that his dash had got him to the bus before it reached Ipswich, pretended to carry out the search.

As Ruby watched them, the children strolled off. McGraw appeared out of nowhere. Within seconds, he was driving them off in a USAAF jeep, ignoring the yells of an old woman to bring her grandchildren back. Both William and Betty were thrilled to be playing another of Uncle Joe's games. A game Ruby Bilton had finally lost.

McGraw drove swiftly but carefully back to Bridge

Cottage, comforting the children as he went along and making them laugh with silly remarks. When they arrived, they found Sally in the living room, her eyes still red from crying, her body sagging. She looked up with disbelief as the children ran in and embraced her.

'Joe! You found them?'

'With a little help. It's okay, Sal. They're back for good. So am I – if you'll have me. We're all back.'

She lost herself in his arms, sobbing afresh.

The following afternoon Helen Dereham had an unexpected visitor at her office door. She invited Pat in, showed her to a seat.

'You don't look as washed out as when you arrived home.'

'I was very tired then.'

'Nanny thought it might be more than just tiredness.'

'You know Nanny,' said Pat, and then tried to mimic the old woman's voice. ' "Irregular bowel movement is the root of all evil." '

'Is that your trouble?' said Helen, laughing.

'No.' There was an uneasy pause. 'I thought I might sit with you for a while, then drive home with you.'

'That would be lovely,' said her mother, evasively, 'but I may have to stay on a little later tonight.'

'I don't mind waiting.' Pat could see from Helen's expression that it was not medical business that was detaining her. 'Is it Jim Kiley?'

'Pat—'

'You don't have to worry about it,' said her daughter, quickly. 'Once, not so long ago, I was very childish about that. I was so sure of my judgements – by the standards of the Sunday School. That was really all I had to go by.'

'It's easy to condemn something you don't understand.'

'I know. At least, I should say, I know that now.'

'How do you mean?'

'Let's just say that I've grown up in the last few months.'

371

Pat shrugged and tossed her hair. 'Oh, you don't want to hear all about my juvenile neurosis!'

'I think I want to very much,' said her mother, gently.

'You must know that, when I took off for London, all I could think about was getting as far as possible away from you and Daddy and Jim and . . . the whole business.'

'Yes.'

'It was tearing me to pieces. And I knew there was nothing I could do to help any of you. It wasn't only that, though. I wanted so much to contribute, to do my bit, as they say. Finding out that I had a weak lung and that no one would take a risk with me, well, it knocked the bottom out of my world.'

'I should have taken it more seriously. Helped you to adjust. We all should have.'

'It was something I had to come to terms with myself, Mummy. Anyway, I went up to London and got the job with the Forces' Canteen. I thought I'd found myself.'

'How?'

'Everyone – all the boys who came – they were so *alive*. Today, tonight, they kept saying, that's all we have. To hell with tomorrow. It seemed the only sensible attitude with the air raids, the bombs falling. Where would any of us be tomorrow?'

'You . . . had an affair?'

'I wish I could say it was only one. Everything had turned upside down and nothing mattered.'

'Phyllis said something about a Free French boy . . .'

'Yes, we met her once. That was Gilles. He was the last, the reason I rang you that night. Do you remember?'

'Very clearly.'

'Gilles was older than he looked. I found out that he had a wife and two children back in France – but I didn't care. He told me it could never come to anything between us. As long as . . .' Pat was finding it difficult to talk about the more intimate details. 'As long as we could be together when we could, I said I . . . didn't mind.'

'Go on,' whispered her mother.

'Suddenly I knew what it felt like to need to be with someone so much that nothing else exists. I'd never felt like that. Then one day, I told him I was pregnant.' She saw her mother tense. 'He was very good about it, said he'd take care of me. But the next morning he'd gone. Just vanished.'

'My poor darling!' Helen was stricken. 'And what about the baby?'

'It was a false alarm. Like so much of my life has been.'

Helen got up from her seat and crossed to her but Pat waved her back, afraid that she might break down if her mother put her arms around her. She insisted that it was all over, that she had grown up.

'Thank you for confiding in me, Pat.'

'I just wanted you to know that . . . I'm not the same. I understand so much more now. And I'm sorry I ever dared to criticize you.'


Because the real world had been so harsh and unkind to her, Letty Mundy had retreated more and more into her private fantasies. It was only when Pfc John Wyatt called at the house that evening and found her alone, that she realized how central a place he had come to occupy in those dreams. She welcomed him warmly, convinced that his feelings for her were as deep as hers for him. But reality intruded once more with cruel effect. Learning that Albert was not at home, John apologized for calling and took his leave. He had come to see her father and was palpably uneasy at the thought of spending time alone with Letty. She felt utterly shattered.

When her mother came in, she saw the despair in Letty's face and put it down to Peter's departure. She soon discovered that it was the idea of having the baby which was tormenting her daughter. Vera tried all she could to lift her spirits, telling her how pleased she herself was about the baby, and how much she was looking forward to being a grandmother. But Letty was beyond comfort.

Albert arrived back in his ARP uniform, saying that the skies had just opened and the rain was torrential. He went out to remove his wet coat, muttering that a Nazi invasion that night would have to be in submarines or barges. There would be no air raids in such weather. Left alone with Letty again, her mother taxed her about her attitude towards motherhood but only deepened the girl's despair. Letty saw the baby as a complete hindrance to everything she wanted to do.

Vera argued that someone would come along who would be glad to take care of Letty and her baby. When she mentioned John and pointed out how fond of Letty he was, her daughter saw for the first time their efforts to contrive a romance. What had been a warm devotion to her was nothing but a manipulative exercise to Vera and, by extension, to Albert. Her own parents were encouraging him to call in order that he could be drawn into some sort of trap.

Letty was horrified. Before Vera could stop her, she rushed out through the archway and into the shop. Albert came in a minute later and asked why the front door had just slammed. Then they realized that Letty had run out in the pouring rain. They rushed to the front door, but there was no sign of her.

Elmer Jones came bursting into the Lounge Bar of The Plough and headed straight for Hymie Stutz. The little sergeant, who had been making Rosie laugh, now swallowed hard. Elmer knew.

'You were supposed to be playing pool tonight!'

'So I changed my mind, Elmer.'

'Like you changed it last night?'

'I'm not with you, buddy boy.'

'No? I met Hank Muller and he told me you weren't with him last night, like you said. You were at the dance with Rosie.'

'Yeah, I guess I was. You were busy at the crap game, so I thought I'd mosey down to the old hop.'

'You fixed up for me to go to that crap game!' Elmer accused. 'You took advantage. You stabbed me in the back, you goddamn Fifth Columnist!'

'What you call me?' said Hymie, bridling.

'You heard!'

'If I was you, I'd button my lip – Fatso!'

'Say that again!' challenged Elmer, squaring up to him.

'Fatso!'

Both men put up their fists and glared. Old grudges were rekindled as they moved towards each other. Jack Blair stopped them in the nick of time.

'All right, boys – that's enough! Cool it now.'

'Did you hear what he called me, Mr Blair?' bleated Elmer.

'It doesn't matter. I won't have trouble in here. If you don't settle down, you'll have to leave – both of you.' He turned to Rosie, who was giggling. 'As for you, young lady, you ought to be ashamed of yourself, laughing at grown men behaving like that.'

'They're so funny, Dad.'

'It wouldn't be funny if they started fighting.' He looked from one man to the other. 'Now sit down quietly or out you go.'

Jack had made his point. Both men looked deflated, particularly when Rosie continued to find them so comical.

'You haven't changed a bit, have you?' she said, grinning. 'It's all just like it used to be.'

Elmer Jones and Hymie Stutz exchanged a rueful look. In all the time they had been at Market Wetherby Air Base, they had made no real progress with Rosie. They were right back where they had started.

It was mid-evening before Jim Kiley finally showed up at the hospital. His coat was spattered with rain and he was full of apologies.

'Another half hour and I'd have had to go,' she said.

'I'm glad you didn't, Helen. We must talk.'

'I think I know what you're going to tell me, Jim.'

'You do?'

'I can't be the one to say it.' She felt the tension rising inside her.

'I hadn't meant it to be like this. I was going to lead up to it. But come tomorrow, or the day after, I'm not going to have time for anything.' He turned away. 'Oh, God, I had it all straight in my head. But seeing you there . . .'

'You were going to say that last time we decided not to go on seeing each other, it was for the wrong reasons. And it didn't work.' Helen took a deep breath, then looked at him levelly. 'Now we have to decide to give each other up for the right reasons.'

'That's about it,' he sighed. 'We're neither of us the type to play the two-timing game with any conviction. I know it hurts you, that in many ways you still care more about Ronnie and hate having to lie to him.'

'Yes,' she murmured.

'But you have to. And sooner or later, it would come between us. Left to myself, I'd say to hell with it and just take you away – but I can't. Until the end of this lousy war, there's nothing I can do.'

The sense of hopelessness consumed them both and they were in each other's arms. She fought back tears and he tried to find a ray of hope.

'Couple of days ago, when all I could think about was you, I booked a room. It's still there, Helen. Over at Norton.'

'Jim, I can't.'

'Why not?'

'I can't just stay away from home for a night. Ronnie's changed. He checks up on me now. Rings the hospital every day just before I'm due to leave. I have to account for every minute of my time.'

'I didn't know,' he said. 'Can't you even manage a couple of hours, Helen? Two hours – it might have to last

376

us for years. Until the war's over and I can come to you and say I want to be with you always. I want you to be my wife.'

Helen needed to look into his eyes for only a few seconds, then she crossed to the telephone. She explained that there was an emergency at the hospital and that she would be late back. When she put down the receiver, her guilt was stirring yet again but his smile subdued it. She grabbed her coat and led the way to the car.

The night was dark and the rain heavier than ever. Helen thought she knew a short-cut to the village where the room had been booked, and so she drove down a narrow, twisting road, peering through the windscreen. Something appeared in her headlights and she put her foot down hard on the brake. Jim had seen the figure in a dress as she had raced across the road, and he cursed. But Helen thought that she had recognized the girl. She switched off the engine and got out of the car.

'Letty! Letty! Is that you?' she called.

'Can't see a goddam thing in this weather!'

'Letty! Letty! . . . We'll have to split up and search.'

They left the road and began to look about in the bushes. When Helen eventually found her, Letty was lying on the sodden earth, clutching her stomach and moaning. She had gone into premature labour.

'Jim! Jim! Over here!' she shouted.

'What's up?' he asked, rushing towards the sound of her voice.

'Let's hope we're in time. Get back to the car with her.'

The journey to the hospital was panic stricken. Letty was suffering unbearably as the pains intensified. Helen and Jim forgot all about themselves and thought only of helping the girl, even at the sacrifice of their last few precious hours together. When they reached the hospital, Letty was rushed to a delivery room and Helen told Jim that she would have to go and get ready. He knew what he had to do. He collected his jeep from the car park and drove towards the Mundy household. Five minutes later he was bringing the anxious parents back to begin their long vigil in the waiting room.

It was in the early hours of the next morning that mother and baby were ready to receive their first visitors. Vera and Albert went into the room where Letty lay exhausted beneath the sheets, her daughter wrapped in a warm blanket beside her. Her mother was delighted, her father was clearly disappointed that it was not a boy, and Letty herself was withdrawn and hurt. She felt none of the pleasure that her mother had told her about. She simply felt a distant gratitude that it was all over.

Helen had a final word with Letty and then went home. At breakfast that morning, Ronnie was watchful and suspicious. He had obviously not believed her telephone call about an emergency.

'Letty Mundy had her baby, six weeks premature. It was touch and go, Ronnie. For a time, it looked as if we'd lose one or the other of them. But in the end, we were lucky.'

'I see.' His relief was evident. 'Fortunate you were there.'

'Yes. Yes, it was . . .'

Suddenly, she felt intensely lonely.


There was peak activity at the Base that morning as the news spread that the bombing offensive was to be resumed. Berlin was the target for the first massive attack and Red Burwash passed on the information to the crew of 'Ginger II'. He and Elmer Jones then reported to Jim Kiley's office, only to find a surprise awaiting them. Seated in front of the desk and wearing civilian clothes, was a figure whom they knew at once.

'Chuck!' yelled Red. 'Chuck Ericson!'

'Is it really you?'

'Hi, Skip. Hi, Elmer.' Chuck got up.

The three men hugged each other with delight, watched

by Jim and Rufus. Red and Elmer wanted to know all the details of Chuck's return. The latter glanced over at Rufus.

'Go ahead,' said the Colonel, patiently.

'Thank you, sir . . . When I baled out, I landed in a wood so the Krauts missed me. I lay low and travelled by night, heading south. I didn't want to wind up in a POW camp. It took me a couple of months to get across France to Spain. I still had to keep out of sight, because I didn't want to be interned. Another month and I made it to Portugal. I hitched a ride on an RAF transport, and they dropped me last night at Biggin Hill.'

'You make it sound so easy,' said Red, admiringly. 'And all the time we thought you were up there, looking after us.'

'Okay, men,' interrupted Rufus, pleasantly, 'the reunion's over.'

'Thought you'd like to see him before you took off,' explained Jim. 'That's why I sent for you.'

Red and Elmer were deeply grateful. As they went off to the briefing session, Rufus became more businesslike.

'Okay, son. We're glad you're back. Get yourself some chow and a new uniform. The Debriefing Officer will check your story, then Major Kiley will arrange for you to be driven up to Command Headquarters.'

'This morning, sir?' Chuck was aghast. 'Have a heart, sir. I've got a wife out there. Don't I even get to see her?'

Rufus looked across at Jim and came to a decision.

Vi Ericson was working in the field as the first bombers roared overhead. She leaned on her hoe and looked up. Memories came back to her and she tried to banish them by starting work again, jabbing the hoe into the hard soil. Suddenly, she saw a figure in the distance, climbing over a fence and waving to her. She stared in disbelief, then dropped the hoe, then opened her mouth to scream something that did not come, then ran madly across the field. Chuck Ericson took his wife in his arms and tried to kiss away the agonies of their time apart.

Everyone in Market Wetherby was aware that strategic bombing had been resumed in earnest. The squadrons thundered overhead on their way to Germany and the local people watched or listened or sighed. Albert Mundy, who had had breakfast alone with his wife, looked upwards and shuddered. Ronnie Dereham, doing the crossword, gazed out through the window of the sitting room then glanced across at Pat, who was curled up on the sofa, and smiled gently. Letty Mundy, lying in bed with her baby beside her in a perspex crib, heard the sound that had tormented her so often and bit her lip. Jack Blair stepped out through the front door of The Plough and waved an encouraging hand to the flyers whom he had come to know and respect so well. Rosie, on her way to work, thought about Elmer and Hymie and realized just how much they both meant to her. Sally Bilton, about to wipe Betty's face with a wet flannel, looked up and felt sad. Helen Dereham, driving to the hospital, stopped the car and got out, her eyes searching the sky, her mind wondering if Jim was up there, her heart in turmoil.

Major Jim Kiley was on the control tower, watching the last of his planes take off, envying Rufus the mission. Master Sergeant Joe McGraw came and stood beside him.

'The enemy doesn't know what's going to hit them, Mac.'

'That they don't, sir.'

'We've still a long way to go, but it's like Winston Churchill said. It's not the end, nor the beginning of the end. But it's the end of the beginning.'

They stood there gazing up into the sky until the last few B-17s had disappeared from sight.

**AIRLINE**

An exciting new television drama series from Yorkshire television, AIRLINE is the story of Ruskin-Air, brainchild of the stop-at-nothing entrepreneur Jack Ruskin.

In 1946 the airline business is up for grabs — for men with enough nerve to stay the course. Jack Ruskin, newly demobbed from the RAF, is one of them. He buys his first Dakota, ruthlessly fights the competition and the bureaucrats and sees Ruskin-Air take off — while his long-suffering wife and family pay the cost.

AIRLINE is a Yorkshire Television production starring Roy Marsden with Richard Heffer, Polly Hemingway and Terence Rigby.

FUTURA PUBLICATIONS
FICTION/FILM TIE-IN
0 7088 2141 3

# THE BORGIAS

Set against the rich background of Renaissance Italy, the story of the most notorious family in history: the Borgia Pope, Alexander VI, and his bastard children, beautiful, brilliant and dangerous.

For over a decade Rodrigo and his ruthless son, Cesare shocked the world by the singlemindedness of their dynastic ambitions. Using the power of the Papacy as their weapon they overturned states, played off Kings against each other and disposed of their enemies with poison, the sword and the garrotte.

The scandal of their age — murder and incest were to stain the family name — the Borgias were as proud, ruthless and amoral as the turbulent times they lived in.

FUTURA PUBLICATIONS
FICTION/TV TIE-IN
0 7088 2019 0

# EYE OF THE NEEDLE

## Ken Follett

First published in the UK as STORM ISLAND

'An absolutely terrific thriller, so pulse pounding, so ingenious in its plotting and so frighteningly realistic that you simply cannot stop reading'
*Barbara Bannon, Publishers Weekly*

His weapon is the stiletto, his codename: THE NEEDLE. He is Henry Faber, coldly professional, a killer, Germany's most feared deep-cover agent in Britain. His task: to get the true facts about the Allies' invasion plans to Germany. His master: The Führer – in person.

EYE OF THE NEEDLE: a dazzling and totally gripping adventure thriller of World War II, that ranks with THE EAGLE HAS LANDED.

'Top notch thriller, as gripping and persuasive as THE DAY OF THE JACKAL'
*Ira Levin, author of THE BOYS FROM BRAZIL*

'A tense, marvellously detailed suspense thriller built on a solid foundation of fact'
*Sunday Times*

FICTION/FILM TIE-IN
0 7088 1470 0

All Futura Books are available at your bookshop or newsagent, or can be ordered from the following address:
Futura Books, Cash Sales Department,
P.O. Box 11, Falmouth, Cornwall.

Please send cheque or postal order (no currency), and allow 40p for postage and packing for the first book plus 18p for the second book and 13p for each additional book ordered up to a maximum charge of £1.49 in U.K.

Customers in Eire and B.F.P.O. please allow 40p for the first book, 18p for the second book plus 13p per copy for the next 7 books, thereafter 7p per book.

Overseas customers please allow 60p for postage and packing for the first book and 18p per copy for each additional book.